THE CROSSROADS OF LIGHT & BLOOD

Book Four

Between Worlds Series

TRACEE FORD

Edited by
Crystal Bland

Copyright OZWIND PUBLISHING LLC (USA)
Piketon, Ohio 45661 USA

This is a work of fiction. Names, characters, places and incidents are products of the author's imagination or are used fictitiously and are not to be construed as real. Any resemblance to actual events, locations, organizations, or persons, living or dead, is entirely coincidental.

THE CROSSROADS OF LIGHT & BLOOD
BETWEEN WORLDS SERIES
BOOK 4

CoverArt: Select-O-Graphics

ISBN: 979-8-218-93342-5

DEDICATION

The book is dedicated to the hopeful mystic and to my son.
He is my inspiration and my north star.

Table of Contents

ACKNOWLEDGMENTS

To Jayme for his Wiccan teachings.

To Crystal Bland, my brave editor.

To Kelly D. Abell my cover designer for sharing her talent once more.

Prologue

Eighteen-year-old David Gregory stormed into Pikeview Manor, anger swelling up inside of him. He felt like a volcano on the verge of erupting. This was the last time she'd humiliated him. This kind of nonsense had been going on his entire life, and he was finished with it. The goofy, paranormal garbage he'd been raised around was taking over his life. Enough was enough.

He grabbed the screen door handle tightly, nearly pulling it off the hinges. His mother, Robin, stood at the island in the kitchen slicing an apple. David saw the startled look on her face, and although she tried to get his attention, he rushed past her and bolted toward the stairs.

His feet hit the hardwood of the second floor, the boards sounding as if they might crack beneath him. He just couldn't believe he'd fallen for another one of her tricks. He wasn't going to hold his tongue anymore either. She may be the baby of the family, but he was done with her hijinks.

He didn't even knock. David pushed the door open with all of the anger he could muster. The doorstop managed to keep the knob from putting a hole in the wall.

Hope looked up at him as she sat on the bed typing on her laptop.
"David, what the hell?" she shrieked. "I could have been naked!"

"Let me ask you the same question. What the hell, Hope? What the hell were you thinking? She is a freak! I am never, ever going to let you set me up with any of your friends again! They're all nuts! I should have known better!" he shouted as he nervously ran his fingers through his thick, dark hair. The frustration coiled around him like a serpent.

Hope looked at him obliviously. “What are you even talking about?”

“The girl you set me up with! Don’t you even remember?”

“Oh, yeah! I thought you’d like her.”

David crossed his arms. “Do you mind telling me what a psychic vampire is? It sounds pretty freakin’ scary to me. That was the first thing she told me. That she was a psychic vampire.”

He paced with his arms still crossed and continued on. “You know what? Don’t even tell me what it is. I don’t want to know. I don’t think you understand, Hope. I don’t want any part of this voodoo bullshit! I don’t believe in any of it!”

The commotion quickly drew the attention of their dad, Matthew. He stood in the doorway leaning against the facing, his hands in his pockets. A calm, yet perplexed expression covered his face.
“So, anyone want to tell me what’s going on, and why we’re all yelling?” he asked as he met David’s gaze.

“She set me up with another one of her crazy-ass friends,” he answered as he pointed at her.

“Jessie?” Matthew asked casually.

“Yes!” David exclaimed.

Robin now stood behind Matthew.

“What is going on?” she asked quietly, looking up at Matt.

“I’m still trying to figure it out,” he answered. “I don’t think his date went well.”

“Everything was fine,” David continued. “I took her to the restaurant you told me about, Dad. We were talking about the movie we just saw and how she sings with Hope in choir and how much she loves the violin. There was a spark! I could tell! She is intelligent and pretty, and then out of nowhere, BAM! She tells me that she is a psychic vampire!" He turned his attention back to Hope. "What are you trying to do to me? Are you trying to make me think I'm insane?"

"David, Jess isn't a psychic vampire in the way that you think."

"I don't even know what it is, Hope! I told you, I don't want to know. All of this 'spiritual' stuff you guys do. I don't want any part of it. Hope, you touch people and something happens. Mom dreams about stuff and then it happens. Olivia sees dead people. Dad and I just go along for the ride. Well, I can't do this anymore! This isn't who I am! None of this is real! You've all probably got some sort of mental disorder!"

"That's enough," Matt scolded. "Your mother and your sisters can do things that none of us understand. You and Hope have no clue what we've been through in this house. Long before you two were born, things happened here, and it took years for me to process everything. I saw things and experienced things I can't even begin to explain. I would have lost my mind if it hadn't been for Olivia and your mom. So, I'm not going to stand here and let you accuse your sisters or your mom of being crazy. We may not understand what they can do, but I'm sure as hell not going to question anything after what I've lived through in this house. After what I've seen, I'd be a fool to do that."

"I'm sorry, Dad. I just can't keep acting like any of this is okay. It's just not something I buy into. I never could say anything because I knew how much it would hurt everybody, but I just can't be quiet anymore. I can't keep pretending! I don't believe in any of the things you guys believe in! None of it!"

"That's because you didn't live through what happened in this house," Robin added.

Finally composed, Hope put her laptop on the bed. “David,” she began, “Jess is a great person. You are judging her based on something you don’t understand. You are afraid because you don’t understand. You should try again. She is really a wonderful person. You said it yourself. There was a spark.”

“Oh, no! I am done! You are not setting me up anymore. I cannot wait until fall. I can get the hell out of this freak show!”

“David!” Matt shouted disapprovingly.

Robin didn’t say anything. A heaviness washed over her. Tears welled in her eyes. David watched as the disappointment forced her out of the situation and down the stairs.

“Go to hell, David!” Hope yelled as she sprang to her feet.

Angrily, David walked to his room and slammed the door, leaving Matt in the hallway wondering where things went wrong.

Later that night, as David sat in his room typing in his journal, guilt clouded his thoughts. Hurting his mother was more than he bargained for. He had an incredible bond with Robin. He had always been able to talk to her about anything. She didn’t meddle or pry. She was simply there when he needed her, and he needed her more and more as he grew older. She had always made him feel safe. He knew he needed to apologize to her.

As for Hope, he wasn’t sorry at all for anything he had said to her. She was always touching people to figure out what they were thinking. He was sure that she was faking it. Sometimes she wasn’t even right.

His half-sister, Olivia, had abilities, too, but those didn’t bother him as much. She was significantly older than him, and she was busy with her husband, children, and career. She visited on holidays and sometimes throughout the year, but she didn’t really talk about what she could do. After her involvement with the Tic-Tac-Toe Killer case and her daughter’s abduction, Olivia seemed to put all of the paranormal phenomena behind her. She was much more discreet about it, at least.

David stood up and looked at his watch. It was late, but he knew his mom would be up, and he knew exactly where to find her. It was the same place she always went at the end of every day.

He walked downstairs and walked to the porch. When he pushed the screen door open, Robin's gaze met his. The full moon lit up the night. The blue glow made Robin look like an angel.

"Hey Bubby," she said as she returned her focus to the field.

"Hey," he said as he walked to the swing and sat beside her.

He cleared his throat and looked out at the field, too. "Um, Mom," he began, "I'm really sorry I hurt your feelings."

Robin sat quietly. She just nodded.

"I know that you don't understand my point of view," he continued, "but I don't think I can explain it to you any more than you can explain your point of view to me. That still doesn't give me the right to hurt you or Dad."

"Or your sister," Robin added.

"Hope drives me crazy."

"She's your sister. She's supposed to drive you crazy."

"I don't know why she just can't mind her own business."

"Because she's your sister, and she wants what's best for you. Most of all, she loves you and looks up to you."

"She makes me so angry," he admitted.

"David, you have no idea what your dad and I have been through. You love this house, right?"

"Yes, I do."

"Well, this place was a nightmare when we first moved in. If it weren't for your dad and Olivia, I know I wouldn't be here. I wouldn't have even survived. The things we've experienced in this house changed all of us. We will never be the same. That isn't something we chose. It was something that happened, and it was completely out of our control."

"I just don't understand."

"You couldn't. You weren't born yet. You've always known this place as something bright and beautiful. It's always been home, a safe haven. It wasn't always like that."

The silence held sway for a moment.

"I'm going to miss you when I go to college, Mom."

"I am going to be lost for a little while, I think. You have been such a blessing to me, David. You've been my world. I didn't think I could love anyone more than I love your dad, but you and your sisters have made my life complete."

He smiled.

"David, I think the reason why I'm so close to you is because I lost a child before I had you."

"Really?"

"Yes, Bryan was his name. It was because of this house that I miscarried."

"I'm sorry. I didn't know that."

She sighed while tears brimmed in her eyes. "I have never forgotten that dark place, that corner I cowered in. There were times I tried to forget. I felt like it was best that I forget, but it reminds me of where I've been. It reminds me of the hell I had to endure before I could actually see the sunshine again. Being blessed with you didn't take away the pain of losing your brother, but it showed me that there was more to be happy about. There were still so many things to look forward to. That's exactly why your sister's name is Hope."

"I'm sorry, Mom."

"Your dad and I kept Bryan from both of you. Olivia knows because she was here when it happened. She pulled me out of the abyss." She paused for a moment to compose herself.

"I've raised you the best I knew how, David. Now, you're a man. You're graduating in a few weeks and going off to college. You have always been free to believe whatever you want. I have never, nor will I ever, push my beliefs off on you, but what I won't tolerate is you mocking someone else's beliefs. That's judgmental and bigoted, and I didn't raise you like that.

"You owe your sister an apology, too. She can't help the way she is no more than I can help the way I am. We didn't choose these abilities. They chose us."

"I just…"

"I brought you up to be open-minded."

"I know. She just gets on my nerves so much, and these girls she hooks me up with… God!"

Robin laughed. "Well, then don't go out with them. You know what kind of friends Hope has. They're all sensitives and mystics."

David chuckled. "Yeah, I guess I kind of know what I'm getting into when I go out with one of them. Or at least I should."

"Spend time with William this summer. You guys are going to be in the throes of adulthood before you know it. Go see your grandpa. You're going to miss all this, honey. Someday, you'll wish you could go back and either live this life again or do things much differently. Embrace the now."

Without another word, he leaned against her, just like he had when he was small. He rested his head on her shoulder. The reality of growing up was terrifying. Still, knowing his mom would always be there to guide him and help him make sense of things gave him some comfort.

1

Present Day

The ballroom was filled with local celebrities, politicians, judges, other attorneys, and members of the community. The smell of warm bread and gourmet food drifted through the air. It seemed like everyone who lived in the little town was present to see which nominee would receive one of the highest honors of the year.

As the anxiety built, David nervously folded, unfolded, and refolded the linen napkin in his lap. His half-sister, Olivia, and her husband, Danny, sat at the table, both of them finishing their wine. David's niece, Amelia, now a beautiful eighteen-year-old young woman, sat beside Hope. His two nephews, Liam and Brock, sixteen and thirteen respectively, were also present to lend support.

Robin and Matt conversed with David's best friend, William Garmen. David's paralegal, Joan Erickson, and her husband, Scott, were also involved in the conversation.

"It's going to be fine," Hope said as she took a drink from the wine glass.

"You are the only attorney in this rinky-dink town who has ever defended a capital murder case with multiple victims," Will added.

"That alone qualifies you for the award," Joan said as she took a bite of steak.

The room quickly quieted as Judge George Shanks walked to the stage. He cleared his throat and gently placed his hand on the glass podium. The sound of metal utensils against the china plates stopped, and the low hum of conversation slowly ended. Everyone's attention immediately shifted to the front of the room.

"Ladies and gentlemen," he began, "I want to thank you all for being here tonight. It's April, which means it is time to present the John J. Atkins Award.

"This award was established in 1992 to honor John, a dynamic attorney who served as a prosecutor and then moved through the ranks, eventually becoming a judge on the Ohio Supreme Court. From there, his career took him to the State Senate, where he served for many, many years. Not only was John an inspiration to all of us, but he was also a role model.

"To honor his memory as well as his contributions, his family established the award to keep his accomplishments alive and to pass the torch to a deserving member of society, an attorney who reflects John's determination and professionalism.

"If you're not familiar with the nomination process, then let me educate you. If you are familiar with it, just keep drinking," he joked. Polite laughter echoed throughout the room.

"Members of the professional community make up a board of trustees for the award. Attorneys are nominated by community stakeholders. Members of the board vote anonymously. The county treasurer counts the votes, and then we plan this little shindig. The recipient receives this beautiful plaque to hang in his or her office." Shanks held up a shiny piece of wood with a bronze plate mounted on the front. "The winner will also receive a monetary prize of fifty thousand dollars. Additionally, the attorney receives special recognition in the Ohio Supreme Court and the Ohio Bar. So, as you can see, this isn't just a local award.

"I was last year's recipient, so it is my honor to present this year's award."

He nodded toward a table off the stage. A short, middle-aged woman approached. She wore a modestly tailored pantsuit, and her black hair sat atop her head in a bun. With a smile, she walked to the glass podium.

"As most of you know, I couldn't have earned the award without the help of my wife, Cynthia. So, I've asked her to help me with the presentation this evening."

He handed her an envelope, which she quickly opened. Her eyes moved across the words, and she looked back up at the crowded room. "This year's award goes to Attorney David Gregory."

A collective gasp filled the room while David looked over at Robin. She beamed. Matt stood and clapped proudly, which caused the entire table of guests to stand and applaud. In moments, everyone rose to their feet.

David pushed away from the table and stood. He buttoned his tuxedo jacket and then nervously ran his fingers through his hair. With a tight-lipped smile, he nodded and walked toward the stage.

"Most of you here know David," Cynthia continued as he made his way to the front.

George chimed in. "He defended Dean Miller last year in a high-profile murder case, the first of its kind for our small town. Mr. Miller was accused of taking eight lives. David and his professional network figured out who the murderers really were, clearing Mr. Miller's name and ensuring that he didn't pay for a crime he did not commit."

David finally stepped onto the stage.

George continued. "You have a bright future ahead of you, David," he said, turning his attention to him. "I think we can all agree that although he is only twenty-seven, he is wise beyond his years," he said, extending his hand. He pulled him into a friendly embrace, and then his wife handed over the plaque along with the envelope. "Congratulations, David," she concluded with a smile. The two quickly exited stage right.

As the shock seemed to lessen a little, David did his best to compose himself. He thought that his age would have been a detriment during the voting process. However, the Miller case undoubtedly carried some weight.

The adrenaline coursed through his body as he looked down at the plaque. Carefully, he set it on the podium.

"I suppose I need to make a speech now," he joked as he looked out over the crowd.

"You'd think I'd be okay with speeches. I talk in front of people every day. In fact, some could argue that I never shut up," he teased.

The room laughed at his witty introduction.

He took a deep breath and then exhaled quickly. "I would like to thank all of you for this distinguished honor.

"I would also like to congratulate all of the nominees: Richard Resnick, our county prosecutor; Emma Johnson, a very talented domestic relations attorney; and Antony Neilson, a highly esteemed juvenile attorney. You are all wonderful, talented lawyers. I feel privileged to work and serve with you."

He paused thoughtfully and looked down at the plaque. "I just want to do what's right. That's all I've ever wanted, really." He looked back up at the spectators. "That was one of my primary goals when I entered law school. Most of my time is spent in juvenile court, so when I was retained for Mr. Miller, I was shocked and nervous. I also made it my mission to hire the best consultants to work on Mr. Miller's case. If it weren't for the help of my sisters, Hope Gregory and Olivia Knight, and their brilliant colleague, Dr. Lauren Harris-Bennette, I don't think the crime would have been solved so quickly, and I don't think Mr. Miller would have gone free. I trust them, and I saw firsthand what they can do. They did not fail me, and most of all, they didn't fail Mr. Miller.

"In every single facet of my job, whether I'm working with an estate settlement or a divorce, in juvenile, criminal, or domestic court, my highest objective is to ensure that justice is served, that things are done properly and aboveboard. It should be our goal as lawyers to serve honestly, without corruption or influence. That's how the system is supposed to work. I don't want anyone on my watch to feel as if the system failed them. As upholders of the law, we should want to help people. I couldn't do what I do without my talented paralegal, Joan, and my best friend and colleague, Will. This award is just as much theirs as it is mine.

"I would be remiss if I didn't thank my entire family. They have always pushed me to move forward and to believe in myself. When I decided to go to law school, I think my mother almost had a heart attack," he said with a laugh. His eyes met Robin's. She smiled back at him.

"You see, my father is a doctor, and I think she was hoping I would pursue something in the medical field. My mom worked in child welfare for as long as I can remember, and she used to tell me horror stories about the lawyers and judges she had to work with. She talked about corruption and politics and how that all too often drove legal decisions in cases she worked on. It shouldn't have. So, I think that's why I have tried to navigate through my practice with honor, morals, and ethics, to make sure that the system works for everyone. So, in a sense, her experiences inspired me."

He took another deep breath, and his words carried on the exhale. "So, I bet you all are ready to go home, huh? And I just keep talking," he joked. The crowd laughed again. "I guess that is the trademark of an attorney. All we do is blab," he joked again.

"In all seriousness," he continued, "I want to conclude with another heartfelt thank you to all of you for having so much faith in me. It's a debt I'll never be able to repay. The only thing I can do is keep moving forward, keep serving the citizens of this town, and keep doing what's right. Thank you," he said as he held up the plaque and then walked off the stage.

2

Richard and Amy Hillard had been the greatest grandparents in the world. They had been long-time residents of the small community where David now lived. Typical small-town life was just fine with him, too. People were friendly and still kind to one another. Folks helped each other out, and community members rallied around those in need.

Richard had been a pastor for a local church for over twenty-five years. Even though they had lived in town their entire lives, they owned land in the western part of the county. When Richard died, he left the land to his grandchildren, Olivia, David, and Hope.

From the age of five, David and Hope had spent nearly every single summer with Richard and Amy. Richard had always taken David fishing and hiking in the surrounding forests and state parks. Those activities nourished David's deep love of nature. His Uncle Corbin attempted to introduce him to hunting, but David couldn't stomach it.

Olivia decided to give her portion of the land to David and Hope equally. David and Hope decided to parcel off some of the land and sell it to Will. He put a trailer on the land and planned to build a home eventually. Hope built a summer cottage. The parcel with the pond belonged to David.

No one knew how much money Richard and Amy had accumulated over the years. The inheritance was a surprise to the entire family, and the monetary investments were large enough to be shared, setting everyone up comfortably. The information about the wealth, nevertheless, remained a secret to everyone outside of the family.

David built a large cabin on his parcel. Since his paternal uncle, Charlie, had overseen the renovations at Pikeview Manor years ago, David decided to hire him and his construction company for the building project. The results of his handiwork were breathtaking. Finally, David had the solitude in nature he'd craved all of his life.

3

David rolled over onto his left side to avoid the slices of sunlight coming through the curtains. He heard his golden retriever, Cecily, and his black German shepherd, Artemis, panting in unison. They anxiously awaited their breakfast and the morning romp outside.

David flung the covers off and then sat up on the side of the bed with his head in his hands. He looked up at the dogs. They wagged their tails, their tongues still hanging out, as their eyes filled with anticipation.

"Outside?" he asked.

Both of them stood up and danced around. They rushed out of the bedroom and led the way to the mudroom. Groggily, David followed behind them and opened the back door, setting them free. He grabbed their food and poured it into the bowls. He made his way back to the porch and sat them down. He walked back inside for their large water dish, filled it, and then walked back out, placing it between the two food bowls.

He glanced down at his watch. Time was moving fast, and he needed to get going. Otherwise, he would be late for a 9:00 a.m. hearing.

He put on a suit and chose a burgundy tie. He rushed around desperately, trying not to be tardy. It was a thirty-five-minute drive from his cabin to the courthouse. If something didn't change fast, he was going to be about ten minutes late. That would not go well with Judge Quill. He always started promptly, unlike the juvenile judge, who made it his mission to be at least twenty minutes late for hearings.

David didn't make coffee. Instead of making his usual scrambled eggs and ketchup, he grabbed a protein bar. He couldn't believe he'd overslept. Joan would likely be waiting for him, but because she was a paralegal, she couldn't present the case.

As he ran through the mudroom, he stopped at the antique mirror on the wall and took one last look at himself. Straightening his tie, he realized he needed to trim his goatee. He didn't have time. He rushed to the garage, darted to his car, and slung the back door open. He tossed his messenger bag into the backseat and, with a quick flick of his wrist, slammed the door shut. After pulling the driver's side door open, he hopped into his SUV.

The commute allowed him time to breathe and calm down. He hated rushing around, especially in the morning. It messed up his vibe for the entire day. Taking his time, eating breakfast, and calmly preparing for work was much more desirable.

The crisp autumn air flowed in through the slightly cracked windows. With his eyes on the road, David pondered the scheduled divorce and custody hearing. It would be short and sweet. Everyone had already agreed to the terms. Getting the judge to sign off was the last step in the process.

Of greater concern was David's current caseload. He was taking on entirely too much work. Some cases were simple, while others were not so easy to manage. Divorces were typically drawn out and involved a lot of hatred and fighting. Juvenile court cases also dragged on because the judge wouldn't follow the timeline statutes set by the state.

David needed help, and fast. He wanted someone qualified to share some of the burden. His mind raced as he tried to think of candidates, people he knew he could trust.

Although David had some outstanding personal qualities, his lack of patience was one of his more toxic traits. He expected things to be done right—and the faster, the better. That's why juvenile court was such an annoyance. The cases went on for no other reason than the judge's laziness. To add to his level of disdain, the juvenile judge was outrageously corrupt. Steven Meyers was also a fiend, and his personal life almost always spilled over into his professional life.

Steven hated the administrator of the local child welfare agency, and anyone representing the agency was equally hated. This created quite a conundrum for David. He was contracted with the agency to present their cases. Still, the incompetence at the judicial level meant he was stranded with cases that could be closed.

As he drove, the wheels in his head kept turning. He didn't know of anyone looking for an opportunity like that. There were a few young lawyers in town, but not many. Most law school graduates didn't return to the small community. They got jobs with bigger firms in the larger cities.

Unquestionably, David would have to place an ad in the paper and post a "Help Wanted" callout on social media. Surely, some young, ambitious lawyer would take the bait. At least, that's what he hoped.

Of course, there were pros and cons to bringing in someone new. First of all, the person would have to become acclimated to Will. David had been friends with him since high school. They attended college together, too. While David was busy learning the law and how to try cases, Will studied criminal justice and cybersecurity.

David knew early on that he wanted to be an attorney, and Will always had a knack for figuring things out, especially with the assistance of technology. Will's investigative skills had been naturally acquired, which made sense. Both of his parents were retired detectives.

Will's original aspiration was to become a police officer. He quickly realized how lucrative freelance investigative work could be. So, when he graduated from college, that's the path he chose. He contracted with several law firms, the first being the county prosecutor's office. He gained a reputation, and soon after, larger firms in the central and northern part of the state reached out to him.

Will stood five-foot-nine, had wavy, reddish-brown hair, blue eyes, and was built like a tank. Women swooned when they met him. He was incredibly charming, too. He captivated women with mystery, and compliments fell off his tongue easily. He knew how to work the opposite sex to his full advantage. Every single time David and Will went to a bar or to a restaurant, Will left with some poor, unsuspecting female. After his conquest was finished, he didn't call or text, but simply dropped off the face of the earth, never to be seen or heard from again. It was a bit repulsive, but David loved Will like a brother, so he endured his unscrupulous practices.

Joan and Will were cousins, but an outsider would never know it. They were complete opposites. She was wise and responsible in every single aspect of her life. She was used to Will's dark, perverse sense of humor, along with his thirst for conquest. She was also used to hearing about his one-night stands at the break table in the kitchen. Bringing someone new into the office environment might be a little challenging, especially if the attorney was female. Of course, David didn't condone behavior that would offend anyone, but because they had all grown up together, they worked within a different dynamic. That lax behavior would have to change for the sake of a newcomer.

When David turned onto the street leading to the courthouse, he glanced down at the clock radio in his car. The digits read 8:53. He hastily found a parking space in the municipal lot, grabbed his bag from the backseat, and slammed the car door. He ran to the courthouse doors and abruptly stopped. He took a deep, cleansing breath, straightened his tie, and calmly opened the large, wooden doors as if he had no worries at all about being late.

Joan stood on the other side of the security barrier, arms crossed and looking rather disgusted. Her chin was fixed, and her ginger hair looked like it might catch on fire. The anger in her green eyes made David apprehensive. She glanced down at her watch and then back up at him.

Joan was like a mother hen. She was exactly the same age as David and Will, but fussed over them like an old woman. She ran a tight ship, but David was fine with that. He and Will needed someone like her to keep them focused.

After the deputy cleared him through the doors, David walked toward Joan, then sprinted right past her as he headed up the three flights of stairs.

"Take the elevator," she called as he hurried up the marble steps.

"Takes too long," he shouted back.

"You look like a gazelle," she shouted, hoping to wound his pride.

As he arrived at the third floor, he saw his client, Jasmine Mott, pacing anxiously. She looked pretty angry, too. Two angry women first thing in the morning was not a good indicator of how the rest of the day might go.

"I'm so sorry I'm late," he said as he caught his breath and straightened his tie again.

"I was getting worried," Jasmine admitted, wringing her hands.

"I'm here. You don't even need to go in. All I have to do is give the agreement to the judge orally, and then once Justin's lawyer verbally agrees, it's done. Simple as that," David explained.

"Okay. You don't think he'll fight this time?" she asked as she gulped some air.

"No. Your ex-husband knows better. We ripped him apart in the last hearing. The custody fight was just his last grasp for control. I've drawn up an agreement. He's signed it. The worst is behind you," he reassured her.

Joan finally walked out of the elevator, her face still filled with frustration.

"Told you the stairs were faster," David joked with a wink.

She didn't say anything, but instead gave him a squinty, spiteful look.

Brandon Higgins, the opposing attorney, poked his head out of the domestic relations courtroom.

"You coming, man?" he asked impatiently.

"Yes. Sorry," David answered as he walked through the doors.

It was just the two of them for the moment.

"If you would have been late…" Brandon remarked.

"I know. I know. Contempt for sure."

"I don't care what kind of award you've got hanging on your wall. Your ass would've been grass."

"Yeah," David nodded as he put his bag on the table. "Hey, Brandon, do you know of any attorneys looking for work? Anyone looking to combine firms even? I need someone else in my office. I'm swamped," he asked bluntly.

"Mmm…" Brandon said as he thought for a moment. He sat down at the defendant's table. "There's a guy who's interning for municipal right now. I know he will be looking for something. He graduates in December."

"No, man. I need someone, like, yesterday."

"Let me think about it and see if I can come up with any ideas," Brandon promised.

The hearing went off without a hitch. It was done. David could file the entry, collect his last payment from Jasmine, and close the case.

4

After speaking to Jasmine one last time, David walked down the stairs with Brandon. They stood in the parking lot, catching up.

"Hey, you know," Brandon started, "there is a lady working under Richard right now, and I don't think she's happy there."

"How do you know she isn't happy?"

"She's friends with my wife. I guess Rich kind of creeps her out. She's been there for about three months, I think. Fresh out of law school. She interned for him, and he hired her when she graduated."

"What's her name?"

"Alexandra Ritezal."

"Oh my God! Little Alex? She's an attorney?" Memories flooded David's mind.

"Yep. Graduated in June. Do you remember how smart she was when we were growing up? I swear she had a photographic memory. Remember that time we got lost in the woods and all of us panicked? She just stood there, closed her eyes, and like five minutes later she led all of us outta there. We were all freaking out and being stupid, and she was so calm."

David laughed as he reminisced. "She always had a great sense of direction, which is why we always dragged her everywhere."

"Claudia is her stylist," Brandon continued.

"Wow! Who knew! Little Alex. A lawyer."

"I'll have Claudia send her a text."

"That would be great. Give her the office number. I'd love to see her and do some catching up. We used to have a blast in Corbin's pool. Every summer was an adventure for us." David paused sorrowfully. "I remember when her brother died."

"Me, too. Sad," Brandon agreed after a short pause. "Hey, I'll send Claudia a text as soon as I get back to the office."

"That's awesome. Thanks, Brandon. I'm drowning in cases," David admitted.

"That's what happens when you're famous," he joked.

As David drove to his office, exhaustion hit him like a bag of bricks. The adrenaline high from the morning's agenda was over, and now he was crashing. He spent most of his evenings reviewing and writing law textbooks for various publishers, but he hadn't stayed up any later than usual. He suspected that the sudden downward spiral had to be from rushing around all morning and a lack of caffeine.

When he graduated from law school, David purchased a little cottage in town and converted it. Once upon a time, it was a three-bedroom house with a full basement. Now it served as David's office.

The house was built in the fifties. It needed several updates. David was going to use the money from the award to upgrade to a central heating and air system along with new windows. The rest of the prize money was tucked safely away and earmarked for other upgrades.

After parking the car in the back, David followed the walk path to the front. He pushed the door open. The blast of cool air hit him squarely in the face. Will was sitting in his office with a tall glass coffee mug in his hands. He concentrated intently on the computer screen, his black glasses looking like they might fall off his nose at any moment.

"Please tell me that's fresh coffee in your cup," David said as he stood just outside Will's office door.

"Yep. Made it about ten minutes ago."

"Thank Christ!" he said as he loosened his tie.

"Rough morning?" Will asked as David turned the corner into his office.

"It feels like I've been in fast forward since I woke up," he answered.

"Staying up all night banging those chicks'll do that to ya," Will joked.

"I think you have my life mixed up with yours," he replied.

"That's your problem," Will quipped. "You need to get laid."

David rolled his eyes as he threw his bag onto the couch in his office and then peeled off his suit jacket.

"We can run right after work if that's okay with you," Will added.

"Sounds good to me. I need to blow off some steam," he admitted.

"Then maybe we should go to The Tavern instead," Will suggested.

"No," he answered curtly. "Nothing interesting there at all."

"See, that's the problem. You're all wound up," Will reiterated as he stood at David's door. "Laid."

David walked out of his office, passing Will and making his way down the short hallway toward the kitchen. He heard the bell ring as the front door opened and shut. Then he heard Joan's voice.

"It's just me."

The smell of the dark roast woke David up a little. He carefully poured the revitalization tonic into his mug.

"Do you think you could have cut it any closer?" Joan asked pointedly as she walked into the small kitchen.

"I'm sorry," David said as he pivoted to the fridge and grabbed the creamer.

Will was already sitting down at the break table in the middle of the room. He took a sip of his coffee and then set the mug down on the tabletop.

"I need to talk to both of you," David began.

"What's wrong?" Joan asked as she poured a cup of the coffee and sat down at the table, too.

"I am overwhelmed and overloaded with cases."

"It's because of the Miller case and the Atkins Award. That's what all of this is about. Now everyone wants to retain you for every little thing," Joan said.

"She's right," Will agreed. "You're a local celebrity. So, I'm still wondering why you aren't getting laid."

David shook his head disapprovingly and rolled his eyes. Then he continued. "I don't want to be a local celebrity. I just want to go back to wills and estates and custody and juvenile court. That murder case elevated me more than I'm comfortable with. I don't want to turn away business, though. I wanted to give you two raises again in January. The way to accomplish that is to continue to take all of the cases I can. I have the award money, but I'd like to leave it where it is."

"You do not need the money," Will argued. "You literally have fifty thousand dollars to dip into."

"I don't want to do that. I gave both of you a raise out of that fifty thousand dollars the moment it hit my account. You both deserve another raise with all of the hard work you do. At least ten thousand dollars is going toward the HVAC update and the windows. I certainly don't want to dip into my personal savings to pay your salaries, pay the bills here, or make payments on this office. That has to come from profit. That profit comes from clients," David replied angrily. "Which is why I don't turn anyone down. Which, in turn, is why I'm overworked, overwhelmed, and losing my fucking mind."

"Easy, easy. I didn't mean anything by that," Will clarified.

David shook his head and leaned against the counter. "It's fine. I'm saying all of this because I am going to start looking for a partner. Joan, I'm not worried about you," he said as he made eye contact with her. "Will, you're a different story," he added as he shifted his gaze and then took a swig of his coffee.

"Me?" he asked, a look of shock covering his chiseled face.

"You have a tendency to offend sometimes. If I hire a female, I don't want her filing a sexual harassment lawsuit because you don't know when to stop. Or if your advice to her is to get laid so she can deal with her anxiety."

"You do have a problem with boundaries," Joan agreed as she nodded at Will.

"What the hell? Is this 'gang up on Will' day?"

"Come on. We know how you operate, Will. Some of the jokes you tell, they can be offensive to someone who doesn't know how to take them," David said.

"So, do you have anyone in mind?" Joan asked, changing the subject and looking up at David.

"Brandon told me about Alexandra Ritezal."

"Oh yeah," Will exclaimed. "She works in Richard's office. She's the assistant prosecutor. She's not going to give that up, man. The pay over there is phenomenal."

"She might," Joan interjected. "The environment is less than ideal. Every woman who works for him eventually goes to private practice or moves or disappears in some form or fashion. He can't keep people."

"If Alex calls, just put her right through to me," David said, directing his attention toward Joan.

She nodded in agreement.

"I am going to post something on social media tonight about it. See if I can get any leads," he concluded.

5

The day flew by as clients came and went. David had an 11 a.m. and a noon appointment. He took an hour lunch break at noon and looked over the textbook he was composing. Then, from 1 p.m. to 3 p.m., he filed entries at the courthouse, organized other cases, and worked on some juvenile filings. By 4 p.m., things were calming down, and the phones were starting to quiet as well.

David's tie now lay on the vacant sofa with his bag and jacket. He opened his white Oxford shirt to the third button and rolled up his sleeves. He began typing up another entry for another case.

The hum of the window air conditioner distracted him, but more than anything, it made him sleepy. He was counting down the days until the workman arrived for the HVAC upgrade.

Joan walked into David's office, but his eyes didn't move from the computer scree

"Alex is here," she whispered.

"Who?"

"Alexandra Ritezal."

"She's here?" he asked as he continued typing, still not looking up.

"Yes. She's in the reception area."

"I'll be right out," he said as he finished the last sentence and then shut his laptop. David stood up and followed Joan out of the room.

The collective purr of the A/C units made it hard for him to hear, but the smile on Alex's face cut through the noise. She was excited to see him again.

David reciprocated. "Little Alex," he said sweetly.

"David Gregory!" she replied as she walked to him.

He wasn't sure if it was okay to hug her or not, so he waited for her to make the call, and she did. She threw her arms around him, pulling him into a friendly embrace.

"It has been ages since I've seen you," she admitted.

"Where've you been hiding yourself?" he asked.

"Oh, around," she replied as she broke the embrace.

"You've gotten tall," he said, looking her over.

"I know. I know. I got my dad's genes," she remarked with a nonchalant shrug. "And you look fantastic. So grown up."

David quickly recalled that Alex used to be a short little thing with blonde pigtails and skinny, chicken legs. Now, she was only slightly shorter than him. Her hair was grown out past her shoulders and was now a shiny ash-brown color with darker undertones. Her eyes were still a beautiful shade of green, full of life and wonder, just like David remembered. Her high cheekbones offset her delicate features, and her plump lips encased a beautiful, inviting smile.

She wore a very modest black jacket with a matching skirt and heels. Her earrings were simple half-carat diamonds. She seemed quite conservative in her appearance, which David liked.

"Well, come on into my office," he said. "Can I get you something to drink? Water? We have some coffee left."

"Oh, no. I'm fine," she said, following him.

David shut the door and then moved his things off the sofa onto an empty chair in front of his desk. They sat down. Alex still smiled graciously.

"So, what've you been up to, Alex?" he asked as he sat back against the leather cushion, his arm stretched out on the armrest.

"Working for Richard. Trying to figure out what he wants from me," she answered dejectedly.

"What do you mean?"

"David, he is a tyrant. He has no respect for women either. None. I have no idea why he hired me after my internship. All of the ladies in the office are miserable."

He furrowed his brow. "Tell me what's going on."

"Have you ever been around someone and it's not what they say, but the energy they put off? How they look at you? Like you're beneath them?" she asked rhetorically.

David nodded, even though he didn't believe in that 'energy' mumbo jumbo. He did, nonetheless, know what it was like to feel devalued and unwelcome.

"Well, that's what's happening," she continued. "I swear I think there's something wrong with him. Like, really wrong with him. He gives me the heebie-jeebies."

"Have you talked to him? Tried to figure something out? Maybe you're just misreading the situation. Maybe you should just be honest and tell him how you feel."

"There is no talking to him. That's why I'm here. Claudia sent me a text and told me that you are looking for a partner. I am here to beg," she admitted. "Please consider me. I just can't work at the prosecutor's office anymore, but I have to have a steady paycheck. I have student loans to pay and bills, of course. I had scholarships, but I still had to take out loans to finish law school."

"What law school did you graduate from?" he asked curiously.

"Case Western Reserve."

"That's where my sister, Hope, attended. She majored in psychology and minored in anthropology. She's working on her master's right now. She lives near my other sister, Olivia. She's going to Wright State for her graduate degree."

"I was in the same sorority with Hope. It was nice to know someone from home. Spending summers with her when we were kids made it easy to pick right back up. We took some classes together, but mostly we hung out during our downtime."

"What a small world. I had no idea you two had gotten so close."

"It is a small world," she agreed. "So, I graduated summa cum laude," she continued.

"And you graduated in June? So, you've been working with Richard since then?"

"Yes. I wanted to do my internship here in my hometown. I missed my dad. I also knew I could get a job here when I graduated. I was sort of done being up north," she explained.

"I'm really surprised you didn't get hooked up with a large firm in one of the bigger cities."

"I had a lot of offers, but this is where I belong, here with my family and my friends."

David nodded. "What kind of salary are you looking for, Alex?"

"Well, as an assistant prosecutor, I'm making $80,000 a year. Richard makes $130,000 because he doesn't do private practice. If he did, the county would pay him much less."

"And you can try capital cases, yes?" David asked. "I didn't think I'd ever have to ask that question, but after the multiple-murder case, I have to ask."

"Yes, I can, but let's face it, how often do we have murders here, let alone multiple murders?"

David leaned forward, placing his elbows on his knees. He laced his fingers together and looked down at the worn hardwood floor.

"Alex, I have to be honest. I don't know if I can match the $80,000. Our medical insurance isn't going to come close to the county's. Since we're small, our premiums are a little higher. Joan and Will both get a salary. I can't pay them by the hour. I tend to charge what folks can afford. People around here don't have a lot of money, so I make what I make, you know?"

Alex leaned forward, matching David's posture, and tucked her hair behind her ear. "Listen, I just want to get out of there. It's not the place for me. How much can you pay me?"

David thought for a moment as he calculated numbers in his head. He felt terrible about the number that came to his mind.

He shook his head reluctantly. "I can't afford you, Alex."

"Just pitch me a number, David. Please. I have to get out of the prosecutor's office."

He hesitated. "I… I could start you out at $62,000, but it really depends on the influx of cases. If we get more, you get more. Everyone gets more. Alex, that's a pay cut of over $18,000 for you. Are you sure you can do that?"

"My loans take out the biggest chunk of my money, but I can have them recalculated based on my income. The payment amount will drop. How much would come out for insurance?"

"I don't have family plans here, so your husband and children wouldn't be covered."

"Well," she began as her cheeks flushed pink, "I'm not married, and I don't have any kids, so it's just me," she replied.

David explained their insurance plan as well as their retirement options. He wanted to make sure that Alex had all of the information she needed in order to make an educated decision.

"David," Alex said in retort, "you aren't scaring me off." She smiled. "So, do I have the job?"

David shrugged. He couldn't believe she was still entertaining the thought.

"If you want the job, it's yours. We're a little crazy around here, so I hope you can ride the waves."

"I'm good at waves," she said confidently.

"Two weeks then?" David asked.

"Two weeks sounds perfect," Alex concluded.

6

By 6:00 p.m., David and Will were running the track at the park. It was busy with soccer games and other activities. A yoga group gathered on the East Lawn. Others took leisurely walks on the gravel track. A Zumba class was going on near the tennis courts.

The sun was still alive, giving off its warm light, but it wouldn't be long before the days grew shorter and winter made an appearance. Then jogging outdoors would be a memory until spring. Of course, there was the treadmill or the gym, but it wasn't the same as breathing the fresh air and absorbing the vitamin D.

After forty-five minutes, Will and David stood in the parking lot beside the fountain. A refreshing drink of water made everything right with the world. David bent over with his hands just above his knees, trying hard to catch his breath. Will panted as he ran his fingers through his sweat-soaked hair.

"So, Alex is coming on board," Will said breathily.

"Two weeks," David answered as he straightened up.

"She's a good lawyer. I've seen her try cases at County. She'll be great. She is assertive, and she's always been a good person. She's genuine."

"That was a mature assessment, Will," David nodded. "I'm proud of you."

He shrugged. "I can be mature when I need to be. I see how stressed out you are. You need someone to help you."

"Yes, I do."

"She was always a lot of fun when we were kids, too," Will added. David started toward the vehicles.

"Yes, she was," David agreed.

"I remember when her brother Marvin died in that really bad car accident. He was a senior in high school, wasn't he? A few years older than us? Didn't Alex stay with your grandparents that summer?"

"Marvin was twenty when he died. And yes, she stayed with us. I got to know her quite well then. I think she was maybe fourteen or so. Her mom and dad ended up fostering kids after that, didn't they? My grandpa really tried to help her parents get through Marvin's death. I remember when her mom passed. That family has had a lot of loss."

"At least her dad remarried. Maybe he can have a shot at happiness, you know?" Will remarked.

"Yeah," he replied. "Things should be fine at the office," David resolved. "We all have history together. Sometimes that can be a bad thing though. Too much history can cause problems."

"I don't think it will. I think it'll be fine," Will said. "It didn't cause any problems with me and Hope."

"What?" David asked as he turned his head quickly and looked at Will.

"When Hope worked on the Miller case. I've known Hope my entire life, right?"

"Yes, but what does that have to do with any of this?" David asked.

"Well, I helped with the investigation, remember?"

"Yes," David replied wearily.

"So, we were kind of hooking up before then, and we worked together just fine. That's the point I'm trying to make."

"Are you kidding me?" David asked angrily.

"Oh, dude. I thought you knew."

"No, I did not know. How did this happen?"

"You're not going to punch me in the face, are you?" Will asked expectantly, defensively throwing his hands up in front of his face and taking a step back.

"It depends on what you tell me next."

"I practically lived with you, man. I grew up in your house. When she built her house here, it just happened one night. We got a little drunk and, you know, things got a little physical. Every time she comes here, it's like a standing arrangement now."

"Are you fucking serious?" David asked as he looked up at the dimming sky, his hands firmly resting on his hips.

"Don't get all bent out of shape, man."

"I know how you are with girls, Will. I know how you treat them. This is my sister. How can you expect me not to get bent out of shape?"

"It's cool with us, really. She doesn't want a relationship, and neither do I. She's totally okay with it, I promise. We text back and forth all of the time and talk on the phone at least once or twice a week. We never run out of things to discuss, even after all of these years. When she comes home, we hang out and stuff, too. She's not like the other girls. We're really close friends. She likes the stuff I like. You know? It's all good." David looked over at Will, who still anticipated a physical confrontation.

"Oh my God…" he said with a smirk. "You're in love with my sister. I never thought I'd see the day when you, of all people, would be in love. And it's with my sister."

Will shook his head in vehement disagreement. "No, no. I'm not in love with your sister."

David snickered. "Oh yes, you are."

Will shrugged as he paced. "Okay, so I'm a little in love with your sister."

"You can't be a 'little' in love with someone, dumbass. You either are or you aren't. Never thought this day would come. No wonder you didn't tell me. All of that bullshit about 'you just need to get laid.' It was crap. You've been sleeping around because you miss Hope. You're filling a void. Jesus."

"Don't get all psychological on me. You know I don't like that shit." Will shrugged again. "I really dig her. She's awesome, you know?"

David couldn't stop laughing as he walked to the driver's side of his car. "You can't handle the psychological stuff, yet you're involved with someone who specializes in picking someone's brain. Irony. Beautiful, glorious irony!"

Will quickly changed the subject as he peered at David across the hood of the SUV. "But, Alex, she's hot, right?"

David smiled and nodded. "She is very attractive," he admitted.

"Is that going to be a problem for you, Chief?" Will asked.

"Nah. I have some self-control, unlike you. She won't be a friend with benefits. I'll leave the carousing to you," he concluded with an eye roll.

7

He got into his car, started the engine, and headed out of town. David turned down the county road and onto the lane leading to his cabin. Pulling his car into the garage, he sighed. He was so thankful to be home.

He got out of the car as the dogs jumped around the vehicle. He grabbed his bag and his suit out of the backseat. After shutting the car doors, he walked into the mudroom, the dogs following on his heels.

After feeding them, David took a very hot, relaxing shower and then spent the rest of his evening lounging in his enclosed back porch. With his legs propped up on a short, wooden coffee table, he peered out at the woods behind his house. The sound of crickets and frogs would end with the first frost. He would miss the soothing sounds of nature.

Reflecting on the conversation with Will made him smirk. He shook his head, still in disbelief. He couldn't stop himself, and he picked up his phone. He sent Hope a text:

You didn't tell me you were banging Will. WTF? I thought you talked to me about everything.

As he waited for a reply, he turned his focus to his laptop. He had about half of a chapter edited in the textbook. He really needed to get cracking with it because he knew they expected the completed edits by the end of next month. He wouldn't get paid until those were done.

His phone buzzed. He smiled, knowing that Hope replied to his text. He swiped the screen and saw the words:

This is none of your business, big brother!

Reluctantly, he let it go. He needed to concentrate on the task at hand. He reached over and grabbed the beer bottle off of the end table. Putting it to his lips, he took a sip. Then he put it back down, prepared to concentrate on his work, but the outdoors always sidetracked him. He wondered why he even tried to do any editing at all while sitting on the porch.

The moon looked gorgeous above the trees. He was glad he decided to clear off more of the land than his uncle advised. Cutting back some of the trees and selling them to a logging company served a dual purpose. He wouldn't have to worry about storm damage and trees falling onto his house. He was also able to put the money he made in his savings.

The dogs rested on the large rug in front of the sliding door as they enjoyed the cool night air coming through the screens. David put his hand down, which attracted the attention of his golden. She quickly got up and met his hand with a lick. Artemis stood and walked over, jealous of Cyc's attention.

Suddenly, the social media messenger alert popped up on his computer screen. It was from Alex.

He grinned as he read it:

Thank you so much for meeting with me today AND for hiring me on the spot. I owe you big! I didn't know your phone number, but I saw your social media account, so I thought I'd message you. I hope that's okay.

David typed back.

Of course, it's okay. We're partners now... partner.

LOL was her response. Then she attached a picture to the message. When David clicked it open, the photograph brought back a flood of memories. It was a Polaroid of him with Alex. They stood arm in arm in Corbin's backyard. David remembered they'd been swimming all day, which was typical for them. Will and Hope stood behind Alex throwing up bunny ears.

Who are those two skinny-ass kids in the middle? David typed.

I know! Can you believe I still have this? she responded.

He replied, *I still have pictures of all of us somewhere. They are probably in my basement. That was one of the best summers.*

She sent a smiley face emoji and typed, *It sure was. You and Will were going into the eighth grade, I think.*

Nope. Ninth, he replied.

David studied the picture. The emotions rushed back as he closed his eyes for a moment, remembering Alex's smile and the sound of her laughter. Not much had changed. Nevertheless, it was the sound of her crying that brought back the most vivid memories.

During Alex's stay with his grandparents, she grieved her brother's death. David often woke to her cries in the night. His bedroom had been next to the guestroom, and the walls were thin. David had often intervened. He couldn't stand to hear her sobbing. He had walked to her room and knocked. He heard her usher him in, and then he sat on the side of the bed while she cried. He usually rubbed her back until she fell asleep. Sometimes he'd even hold her while the emotions poured out. Eventually, he started sleeping on the floor beside the bed. Many times he would lie on the floor and hold her hand while she lay on the bed. She had told him that she slept better just knowing he was there.

It was so long ago, but the compassion and those strong, protective feelings were resurfacing. When they were younger, he thought of her as a sister, someone he needed to watch over and protect. Things were obviously different now. She was a beautiful woman, capable and strong. He knew that. She didn't need him the way she once did. The bond, nonetheless, was still there for him.

He clicked over to her social media profile and read some of the information. He scanned over her photos, too. Pictures of Brandon and Claudia were a common theme. There was also a guy in some of the pictures, but he didn't look familiar. He even saw photos of Hope and Alex during their college days.

Then the alert box popped back up.

Well, I won't keep you. I just wanted to say thanks and share that pic with you. Have a good night, David.

He concluded with, *Night.*

8

With a new partner coming into the practice, the office cottage needed an overhaul to accommodate a new associate. The space would have to be cleaned up, and what used to be a third bedroom would need to become an office. It was currently stacked from floor to ceiling with boxes of files. Most of the files needed to be shredded. Others needed to go into storage in the basement.

David stayed late the next night. He sat on the floor going through old cases. He lost track of time as he cleared the piles of paperwork. His head started hurting, and he realized he hadn't eaten since around 1:30 that afternoon.

Will had left at 5:30 for a date. Joan left shortly after him. David didn't expect them to stay over. In comparison to theirs, his life was very boring.

Alex drove through town hoping she wouldn't be imposing. She had to tell David what had happened at work today. Besides that, Joan had sent a text saying that David needed help going through files. She was more than happy to lend a hand.

Her heart thumped like a drum as she turned onto the street. She parked in front of the cottage and saw that there were lights on.

David sat in the midst of the cluttered, soon-to-be office and heard a knock on the door. He got up and saw Alex waving through the glass. He smiled and unlocked the deadbolt.

He opened the old, heavy oak door and grinned. "Hey, you," he said.

"Hey, Joan sent me a text and told me you were in the middle of cleaning out one of the rooms so I could have an office. It's only right that I help you," she said.

"You don't have to do that," he protested.

She pointed at him. "I bet you haven't eaten dinner either, have you?"

He shook his head and leaned against the doorfacing. "No, I have not."

"Tell you what. Let me take you to get something to eat. If you still don't want my help, I shall leave you be. If you think you could use an extra set of hands, I'll stick around."

He nodded. "You've convinced me. I'm starving," he replied with a smile.

David checked his jeans for his keys and pulled the door closed behind him. After he locked it, he walked to Alex, who stood patiently on the sidewalk.

"Where do you want to go?" she asked.

"Oh, that's up to you."

"Well, why don't we walk to The Hacienda? It's just a few blocks away. You still like Mexican food?" she inquired.

"Absolutely," he replied.

"Good," she remarked.

As they walked to the restaurant, they talked about her dad, some of her siblings, her stepmom, and her grandparents. The weather also made for a good subject.

When they finally arrived at the restaurant, there was plenty of outdoor seating left, so the waiter put them at a wrought-iron table on the patio. The air was still warm, so neither David nor Alex objected to the arrangement.

As he held the menu in his grasp, David caught himself looking at Alex. She wore a brown graphic T-shirt and a pair of boyfriend-style denim capris. Still in love with flip-flops, she had a pair of leather ones on her feet. Her hair was pulled up off her neck, tendrils brushing her cheeks while the breeze blew gently against her face.

He noticed an amulet hanging from her slender neck. The pendant was quite unusual. He'd never seen anything like it before.

She felt him staring and touched the necklace. "What's wrong?" she asked as she looked down at herself.

"Nothing. I was just admiring the jewelry," he admitted.

Although he couldn't completely make it out, there was a blue sheen to it, and things were printed or engraved on the medallion.

"Oh, thank you."

"What is it? I can't really tell," he said, squinting.

"Come here," she said as she patted the empty chair right next to her.

David got up and then sat down beside her. She held it between her fingers while he carefully examined it. It looked like blue clouds inside the pendant and a vine of some sort etched around the edges. Inside were two half-moons opposite each other and a female figure in between them. The pendant hung on black leather.

"It's called the Triple Moon Goddess," she clarified.

"What does that mean?"

"The simplest explanation is that it represents the power of the female form, the female mind, body, and spirit. It's sort of weird, I know."

"It's not weird. It's beautiful."

"Thank you," she said as she dropped her head and looked down at it.

"Was it a gift?" he asked curiously.

"From my mom, yes," she nodded.

David couldn't take his eyes off of it, but then his eyes drifted up and met hers. It felt like time stood still. Quickly, he snapped out of it, and he worried that he might be making Alex uncomfortable, so he moved back to his chair to create some distance.

"So, how's your sister?" Alex asked, trying to lighten the mood.

"Hope? She's good," he answered as he took a drink of the water sitting on the table.

"She still seeing Will?"

David shook his head. "Does everyone know about Will and my sister? Am I that unobservant?"

Alex laughed. "She's a friend. She tells me things. I figured you knew, though. You guys were always close."

"I did not know," he bit out. "My little sister and my best friend. That will be awkward if something goes wrong there."

"It won't go wrong. This has been going on for a while, and I think they have an understanding," Alex assured him. "She's still a profiler, right? Like your sister, Olivia?"

"Yep. They have their own gig going on in Dayton."

"I think what they do is just absolutely fascinating," she remarked.

"You would think so, but try being at Christmas dinner with those two," he joked.

She laughed and smiled again.

"So, I talked to Richard today," Alex said, shifting the subject.

"And?"

"He got angry, just like I thought he would. David, you have no idea how nasty he is."

"Did he yell at you?"

"He did," she answered as she straightened her napkin. "He said that I had no business leaving. That I was making a terrible mistake. He told me I'd be broke within a month and that he should have never hired me."

"Wow. I'm really sorry he said those things to you," he said as he shook his head disapprovingly.

"I recorded the conversation on my phone because I knew he would do something like that. I told him the two-week notice was null and void. When he said he would make sure I never practiced law in this town again, I played back the recording of him ranting and raving like a lunatic. I told him I would go to my dad with the tape and then to the other commissioners. I then proceeded to tell Richard that I would be taking two weeks to relax and collect myself before I came to work for you."

"Exercising your one-party rights, I see, and maybe a little blackmail. That's sort of dangerous, but you always were gutsy. Still, there's no sense in being treated like that. He sounds terrible. I had no idea. He has always been nice to me and very respectful during court."

"That's because you're a man," she quickly replied. "Those of us with vaginas get treated differently."

He couldn't help but laugh. "Well, at least you have a couple of weeks to yourself," he added.

"I could use it. I've worked for the county for only three months, and it feels like I've been there for a lifetime. Richard just sucked the life right out of me. I knew better than to accept the job, but the money blinded me."

"Don't beat yourself up, Alex. Money tends to have that effect on people. Let's face it, we have to live."

She nodded. "I'm just glad I'm done with it. I feel so sorry for everyone left behind, but I have to do what's best for me."

"Richard must keep his rage locked down pretty tight."

"Like I said, it isn't the things he says as much as the energy he puts off. He's just mean, and there's something in his eyes, the way he looks at me. It's like he's judging me for simply being a woman. The other women have seen it and felt it, too. No one dares to cross him though. That's why I recorded everything. I knew what he'd pull."

"I just hope you don't regret leaving when you see your paychecks. I just can't pay you that much."

"I would rather have a healthy working environment than money."

"We have fun at my office," David said with a smile. "Will is a little much sometimes, but you know that."

"Oh, yes. I remember. He doesn't bother me though. He's just a man-whore," she joked. Then a grave countenance covered her face. "Oh, I'm so sorry, because I know he's, like, involved with Hope." She paused for a second and then followed up with, "Open mouth, insert foot."

David chuckled and then took a drink, thinking the conversation about Will was over.

"But, you should know, I've never slept with him," Alex added. "There's no way."

David almost spit his water out. Then they both laughed hysterically.

"Hope is my friend," she continued. "I would never do that to her," Alex clarified. "And I'd hate to see his list of successes. It's probably longer than any legal report I've ever read."

"Please tell me Hope knows about his extensive history."

Alex nodded. "She does. She doesn't care. I think they're in love with each other and just won't own it."

"I think you're right," David agreed. "I also think you're going to fit in just fine with us at the office. You have a dark sense of humor. You'll be just fine."

"Dark humor is definitely my thing. As long as you treat me with respect, I will hook the moon for you. If you don't respect me, then that's a different story," she said bluntly. She wasn't into playing games and false faces. Judging by David's expression, she knew she had either offended him or shocked him.

"You have certainly changed," he remarked.

"I'm sorry," she continued. "The little wounded girl has grown up. I just don't pull punches. What you see is what you get with me. I don't pretend to be someone I'm not. I use foul language and do all sorts of offensive things," she admitted.

"I want and respect blatant honesty. I don't like getting to know someone and then they turn out to be someone totally different. I've dated those types of girls; very scary and not fun at all."

"You don't ever have to wonder what I'm thinking, David. It will come rushing out of my mouth. It'll be written all over my face, too."

"Good. I suck at reading subtleties in my personal relationships."

After enjoying the dinner and walking back to the office, David realized he was too tired to keep going through boxes. He wanted to go home.

Peering down at his watch, he lingered as they stood between their vehicles. He wanted to stay and talk, but he just couldn't muster the willpower. "I'm heading home," he said with a defeated tone. "I don't think I can read one more file," he admitted.

"I don't blame you. It's past 8:30 anyway. You've been at it for hours, haven't you?"

"Yes, I have."

"How about I come by tomorrow and help you?" she asked.

"Oh, you don't have to do that," David replied as he shook his head and put his hands in his pockets.

"Come on. It's because of me that you're even cleaning out that room." She truly did want to help, but she also wanted to spend more time with him catching up. She felt like she owed him, too. He had gone out on a limb to hire her, and now he was knee-deep in files trying to make space for her.

"You don't mind? Really?"

"Of course not. I have two weeks off now, remember? I have to find something to do."

"I can definitely keep you busy. You could shadow me. I would pay you, of course. I have a hearing at 10 a.m. in Juvenile Court tomorrow if you'd like to shadow me. Do you want to meet me at the courthouse and sit in? It might help you understand the nature of the jungle. That's what Juvenile Court is. It's a jungle. Then we'll go to lunch, come back here, and deal with your office. You can do anything you want to it. Paint it. Decorate it. Whatever you want to do. With both of us working, we should be done with the files by Sunday."

“I think shadowing you would be really helpful. I would like that. And, David, I don’t mind working on the office over the weekend if you need me to,” Alex agreed.

“Sounds good. I will have Joan get a key made for you tomorrow morning. I will see you at court. Thanks for dinner, too.”

“Of course,” she said.

An awkward silence lingered. The connection between them made them hesitate to leave. David quickly found a solution.

“We should probably exchange numbers,” he suggested.

“You’re right,” she agreed.

They pulled out their phones.

After that, they parted ways, anticipating what would come next.

9

David set his alarm fifteen minutes early to ensure that he wouldn't be starting off the day in a frenzied fashion. The next morning, David arrived at the courthouse by 9:30.

He walked into the front office of the courthouse and checked his mailbox for any entries or orders that had been stamped. There were several. In fact, there were too many. The agency kept taking children, and the hearings kept going on and on. He'd advised the agency of the dangers of removing so many children, but it seemed to fall on deaf ears.

David had learned everything he needed to know about child welfare from his mother. The countless stories of corruption were burned into his memory. Politicians had always been behind the scenes pulling the strings. This county was no different. From where he stood, David could see the puppeteers and all of the marionettes dangling in front of the curtain. He refused to take part in it, however.

The child welfare administrator, Tamara Owens, was stubborn and arrogant, borderline narcissistic. It was impossible to reason with her. She was only twenty-five years old and had never been a director of anything. David knew her egotism would be her downfall.

As David looked down at one of the entries in his hand, he heard Judge Meyers' voice.

"I heard you stole Alexandra Ritezal from Richard," he blurted out.

Briefly looking up from the paperwork in his hand, David replied, "I didn't steal her. She made a choice."

Steven sat down behind one of the empty desks in the office and propped his feet up. He was in his late fifties. Fighting as hard as he could against the aging process, he regularly colored his hair blond and had lots of cosmetic work done. To make things worse, Steven had a horrible case of little-man syndrome. He was around five-foot-five, and he reminded David of an albino rabbit. His skin was dreadfully pale, and his eyes were almost clear blue.

He was on his fifth marriage, and he had a terrible habit of being unfaithful. The wives just kept getting younger, too. This time, he'd married Geraldine "Gerri" Hamilton. She was a beautiful thirty-year-old, twice widowed.

Everyone in town knew all about her. In college, Gerri had been in a long-term relationship with one of her female professors. The erotic behavior made small-town life a little more exciting for a short time. Gerri and the professor stayed together until the professor tragically passed away. Gerri moved back to the small town and attracted the attention of Herbert Schider, the local police chief who was almost twenty years her senior. They were married by the time she was twenty-three.

Herbert died behind the wheel of the cruiser one night as he drove to a crime scene. The coroner determined that he had died of a heart attack. When David heard that, it didn't surprise him. Herbert had been a diabetic for many years and didn't really take care of himself. He'd been in and out of the hospital for about a year before his passing.

By the time Gerri was twenty-seven, she was working for the Clerk of Courts. Steven met her while he was still married, of course. The affair ensued. He divorced his wife and married Gerri. Now, Gerri stayed at home in their brick mansion by the lake. She worked only a few days a week for the Clerk's office.

David was familiar with Gerri not only because of living in the small town but mostly because he'd met her at Christmas parties and public gatherings. He hadn't really paid much attention to her, but any male with red blood in his veins could see how perfectly attractive she was. Lean and fit, men swooned. Her long blond hair and tanned skin complemented her beautiful brown eyes. She was a specimen.

The conversation continued between David and Steven.

"Alexandra is quite a looker," Steven remarked.

The comment offended David more than it should have. He nodded. "She's always been quite beautiful."

"I think she'll do good work for you. She comes from good stock," he added.

"That's true. Her dad is one of the best commissioners we've ever elected into office. He's honest, which is rare these days," David agreed.

"You've been friends with her since you were kids, right?"

"Yep."

"Will she be helping out in Juvenile Court?" Steven inquired.

David knew Steven's motives. He didn't like it.

"Eventually, but you'd better be careful. Her dad could make sure you lose the bench," he said with a superficial chuckle. "I will have to talk to Tamara to make sure she can add her to the representation contract."

"Good luck. That woman won't listen to anyone," Steven remarked.

"She'll listen," David disagreed.

"She is one stubborn little bitch."

"Are you saying that because you don't like her, or are you saying that because she wouldn't sleep with you?" David asked frankly.

"Ahhh, ancient history!" Steven replied without missing a beat. "So, how are Will and Joan?"

"Oh, they're good."

"Joan just as feisty as ever?"

"Of course. She keeps us in line."

"Well, Will certainly needs someone to keep him in line. I think you're a different story," Steven chuckled.

Before the conversation could continue, a knock on the doorframe stopped them. David turned to see Alex standing in the hallway.

"Hey, you," David said kindly. "Come on in."

She smiled shyly and stepped into the open office area. She had chosen a taupe-colored pantsuit and brown heels. Her hair was up off her neck again, and she wore the amulet.

"Alex, you know Judge Meyers," he said.

Alex walked over as Steven stood and held out his hand. They shook as she replied, "I do. I have never gone before you in court, but I feel like I've known you all of my life."

"I've been on the bench for a long time," he said. "I hear that David grabbed you up, and you're leaving Richard."

"Well, I actually groveled to David. He had mercy on me," she answered.

"I think you'll fit in nicely at David's little firm," he remarked.

"I am really looking forward to it," she agreed. "I'm just here today as an observer," she explained.

"Well, make yourself at home. There's coffee if you need a caffeine boost, and we always have fresh pastries in the breakroom. If you have any questions, I'm happy to help," Steven concluded. He walked away and headed back to his office to prepare for the hearing.

Alex was very aware of Steven's reputation. She didn't care much for him either. Still, she had to play the game just like her father taught her to.

David and Alex walked out and made their way into the courtroom. It was still empty. Juvenile hearings were always closed anyway, so an audience wasn't anticipated.

David sat down at the plaintiff's table as Alex took an empty chair directly behind him.

"So, what's this case about?" she asked as she leaned up. His aftershave drifted to her nose, and she shifted a little in her seat.

David gave her a verbal summary. Alex nodded after the spoken synopsis, but she was a little confused and a bit overwhelmed. David could see it by the expression on her face.

"It will take some time for you to get acclimated to the juvenile system," he said. "After you shadow me for a little while, you'll be fine."

"I know," she replied. "It sounds like a damn mess to me."

"Juvenile court usually is. I promise I'll help you understand it, though," he reassured her.

The courtroom began filling up with primary parties to the case. Cain Mowery, the ongoing caseworker, and Carleigh Canter, the initial investigator, were the last to arrive.

Carleigh was oddly shaped, short with flabby extremities, and terribly obnoxious. Her skin was blotchy from acne scars, and she had frizzy, curly black hair and brown eyes. The skin oils on her face caught every ounce of light from the bulbs hanging in the lamps above. Always adversarial in her approach, her colleagues avoided her and clients despised her.

Cain, on the other hand, was funny and personable. He wasn't a tall guy, and he had a beer belly. He was going bald, so he kept his head shaved but had a goatee. His clients engaged with him well, and he got along with everyone.

Alex stood, anticipating an introduction. David got up and held out his hand to shake Cain's.

"Hey, man," Cain said. "We ready to be done with this?"

"Yes, sir," David answered with a confident nod.

"I need to talk to both of you," Carleigh insisted as her eyes darted between David and Cain.

"No, you don't," David argued. "This case is settled. You were the investigator a year and a half ago. What are you even doing here? The investigator is off the case within ninety days and only needs to attend the initial hearings in case testimony is needed. What could you possibly need to say?"

"Well, I just feel like this family...," she answered.

"Stop," David interrupted. "Just stop. Have you had any more abuse reports since they have been on unsupervised weekend visits?"

"No," she answered.

"Then this case is closing. It's the final hearing," David bit out.

He turned his attention to Alex. "This is Alexandra Ritezal. She is coming on as my partner. This is Cain and Carleigh."

"Please, call me Alex," she said as she shook Cain's hand. He smiled amiably and nodded. Carleigh glared at her. When Alex offered her hand, Carleigh reluctantly took it.

"A partner, huh?" Carleigh asked, annoyed by the situation. "Are you that overloaded, David?" she asked, dropping Alex's hand.

"I'm swamped."

"Well, you're a good attorney, David," Cain complimented.

"Thanks, Cain."

Cain turned his attention back to Alex. "This guy is awesome to work with," he said, pointing at David. "I think you will really like it at his office."

"I think so, too," Alex agreed. "We've known each other since we were kids, so that helps a lot."

"That's really awesome. So you two grew up together?"

"We spent a lot of summers in his uncle's pool," Alex answered with a smile.

Steven walked in, and everyone took their places. He started court.

It was a simple hearing, just as David predicted. It took about twenty minutes to finalize everything.

As they walked out of the courthouse and to their vehicles, Alex took the lead. David eyed her as she walked ahead of him. He took note of her confident gait and excellent posture. He would have been remiss not to acknowledge how well built she was.

Carleigh suddenly called out to David. Alex looked over her shoulder to see her desperately trying to catch up.

"What can I do for you?" he asked with obvious agitation in his voice.

"I wanted to ask about the Perlin case. Where are you on that?"

"Carleigh, do you do anything besides work? And you aren't even the worker assigned to that case anymore."

"Well, maybe if you'd ask a girl out every now and then, she could do more than just work," she hinted with a wink.

Unsure of how to respond, he just looked at her as they kept walking.

Alex's mouth dropped open at the apparent flirtation. She held back a hysterical laugh and then arrived at her car. She pushed the keyless entry and opened the door. She was relieved to leave behind the drama she had witnessed. She wasn't built for that sort of thing anymore.

With Carleigh still on David's tail, Cain swept in and saved him. "Hey, man, can I see you for a second?"

"Sure," David said, retreating from Carleigh.

Once they were beside Cain's car, David managed to breathe a sigh of relief.

"Is your sister still having her end-of-summer cookout this weekend?" Cain asked.

"You know it," David replied quietly.

"Excellent," Cain said. "You, uh, gonna ask Alex to come, too?"

"I'd certainly like to."

"What do you need me to bring?" Cain asked.

"Beer and make your chicken wings," David answered.

"Will do."

"You're bringing Suzanne, right?" David asked.

“Absolutely. She wouldn’t miss it. She’s already requested the night off from the hospital.”

10

After leaving the courthouse, David stopped to grab food for everyone at the office. He parked in the back and walked around the house to the front door. He knocked on the door with his foot. Joan peeked out and saw David struggling to open the door. She hopped up and rushed to his aid.

“Where’s your briefcase?” she asked.

“Out in the car. I have entries for you to type up and file. The juvenile case this morning closed,” he clarified.

“Okay,” she said as she walked out the door intent on grabbing his briefcase.

After dropping off the bag of food in the kitchen, David loosened his tie as he made his way back down the hallway to his office. He peeked into the room that would be Alex’s office. She was already on the floor going through boxes. She had changed into a pair of jeans and a black t-shirt. Her hair draped around her face as she leaned down, examining a file in her lap.

“Hey,” he said.

She looked up at him and tucked her hair behind her ear.

“I got Chinese food,” he continued. “Hope that’s okay.”

“Oh, I love Chinese. Did you go to Golden Garden?”

“Yes. They are the best in town. Come and eat.”

She put the file aside, put her glasses atop her head, and stood up. She followed behind David. He stopped at his office and shed the tie and suit jacket, tossing them onto the sofa. All that was left of his ensemble was his black suit pants, white Oxford, and black lace-up dress shoes.

He loosened the buttons on the shirt.

"I think I'm going to change out of this," he announced as he shed the shirt.

Alex froze, her mouth agape. He forgot she was even there. Joan and Will were used to David changing out of his court clothing and into more casual attire. However, he didn't even think about how Alex would react.

"I'm so sorry," he said as he pulled the shirt back over his shoulders.

"Oh, God, don't… don't… be sorry," she said as she stuttered a little. Her palms started to sweat as she admired the view.

He looked down at himself.

"What? What's wrong?"

"David," she said with some hesitation, "you're… like… ripped."

The blood rushed to his face. "Oh," he said shyly. "I just don't want to offend you, and I didn't even think about you being here. I just usually change when I…"

Alex interrupted him. "Please don't apologize. You don't have to be somebody you aren't."

He smiled. "Well, let me change and I'll meet you in the kitchen," he said as he walked into his office.

Alex slowly walked past his door and then peeked back in.

"Sorry," she said. "Is that sexual harassment? Me saying that you're ripped?" she laughed.

He shook his head and laughed, too. "No. Sexual harassment is an act of unwanted attention," he joked.

Hearing her laughter as she went into the kitchen brought an even brighter smile to his face. He shut the door, put on a pair of jeans and a gray V-neck t-shirt. Walking around barefoot was his signature look. He hated shoes.

Alex stood in the kitchen. She grabbed a plate and scooped out some chicken, then slowly sat down at the table.

"So, I know I'm new here," she started, "and this is probably something that you all are used to..."

"What's wrong?" Joan asked as she poured soy sauce onto the fried rice in her bowl. "Did that asshole-of-a-judge say something to you this morning?"

"Oh no. No. Nothing like that," she replied as she shook her head.

"What's the matter?" Joan pushed.

"I was walking behind David… I guess it's normal for him to change clothes after a hearing, right?"

"Yep," Will answered as he shifted in his chair. "He hates those stuffy suits."

"Well, I had no idea he was so… so… healthy."

"He took off his shirt, didn't he?" Joan whispered.

"Yes."

"And he warned me not to be inappropriate," Will stated.

"I was just surprised that he was so… well, you know. Does he work out? I mean, obviously he does. I was just…" Her thoughts were as jumbled as her words.

"Total eye candy, right?" Joan chuckled.

"Well, yeah. I mean he's not bodybuilder buff, but he is jacked as shit. Does that even make sense?"

"He has a workout room in his basement," Will explained. "He runs with me at least four days a week. He does light lifting. Says he doesn't want to get huge. He just wants to look good."

"Well, mission accomplished," Alex replied.

Alex had no idea that David was listening outside the door. His lips curled up into a delighted grin. He was flattered by the compliment.

Joan laughed. "And he isn't an arrogant ass about it either, which makes him even hotter, right?"

"What do you mean?" Alex asked.

"He doesn't have a clue how gorgeous he is," Joan clarified. "You know how some guys are all about how hot they are? Kind of like Will," Joan joked. Will glared at her disapprovingly. "Not David. He is modest, and if you compliment him, he blushes. Blushes! His sister told us he gets it from their mom. I guess if you give Robin even the slightest compliment, she turns red. Still at 68 years old, she gets embarrassed by compliments. Now how sweet is that?"

"He's a good guy," Will added. "When we go out, girls buy him drinks. He accepts, reciprocates, but then lets it go. He isn't interested."

"Why? Is he gay?" Alex asked directly.

"No. No, I think he's just selective. He's kind of a geek, too. He writes and edits all those textbooks for colleges. He's up half the night writing. The guy is a wealth of knowledge. He always struggled in school, but he was an overachiever. Everything came so easy for Hope. She is super smart and didn't have to lift a finger to study," Will continued. "She probably should have been a doctor but didn't want a thing to do with the medical field. I used to sit with David for hours studying. Things had to be perfect, and he worked so hard."

"I remember Hope in college. She had one hell of a memory," Alex agreed. "So, has David even dated?" she asked, shifting the subject, still unaware of his presence.

"Not really," Will replied. "There was this girl in college. Her name was Andrea. She tore his heart out. In high school he took girls out and stuff, went to homecomings and prom, but nothing too serious. He was really focused on school. He was valedictorian, so I guess it paid off.

"Anyway, this Andrea chick really messed him up. They started going out during his junior year of college, and they dated until he was almost done with law school. She went into a study-abroad program, and they broke things off. I think that's why he hasn't really gotten serious with anyone. They were really in love. They parted on good terms, but he was still pretty devastated by it."

"That's sad," Alex commented.

"He never got depressed or anything. He just became even more determined and focused on working. The textbook thing sort of fell into his lap, and he loves doing it, so it sort of takes center stage," Will continued. "And then there's the dogs and stuff."

"Dogs?" Alex asked curiously as she grabbed a piece of chicken with her chopsticks.

"He has two at the house," Joan added.

"And he volunteers at the local shelter sometimes," Will continued. "He loves animals. Sometimes he even goes out with the rescue teams and then helps set up adoptions; his way of giving back. At Halloween he has a fundraiser for the shelter. There's games and stuff."

"Oh my God, he's behind the Fall Fun Day Carnival at the fairgrounds?" Alex asked.

"Yes," Joan answered. "Isn't that sweet? All those games, the bouncy house for the kids. He contracts with some of the local farms to bring in animals for a petting zoo. The money that's raised is given to the shelter. All of it. Every cent. There is always enough money to pay staff to do follow-up visits with the adoption families. I have never heard of another shelter doing anything like that. He is a guardian angel for those folks."

"That is the sweetest thing I think I've ever heard," Alex said. She was impressed, to say the least.

"He has a big heart," Will agreed. "Wait until Valentine's Day. He and I go out selling candy grams and the money goes…"

"To the shelter?" Alex asked.

"Yep."

Becoming a little misty-eyed, she smiled and nodded. "I definitely made the right decision begging for a job here. I can't say I'm surprised that he is so generous. He always was."

She remembered the nightmares, the terror, and the grief she felt when she lost her brother. Her mother nearly lost her mind. David's grandparents were so supportive. She remembered David's compassion and the support he'd offered her. It was one of the most difficult times in her life, and she received unwavering care from him along with his family.

David composed himself and then walked into the kitchen. The hushed conversation ended.

"Did they do a good job with the food?" he asked curiously as he grabbed a plate out of the cabinet.

"As always," Will answered.

"You guys are coming to Hope's for the cookout, right?" David asked.

“You know I wouldn’t miss it!” Will admitted with a smirk.

David shot Will a condemning glance.

“Well, we’ll be there,” Joan said.

“You know you’re invited, Alex,” David said as he turned toward her.

“Yes. Hope texted me a few weeks ago.”

“Well, if you want, we can go together. You can come to my place and we can walk… I mean… if you want to…”

“That sounds like a good plan,” she agreed with a nod.

“So, is Carleigh coming?” Will joked.

“Uh, definitely not,” David answered.

Will laughed hysterically. “She has such a crush on you, dude.”

“Jesus,” David uttered under his breath.

“She definitely has stars in her eyes for you, David,” Alex commented.

David sat down at the table.

“She is pretty persistent,” he commented.

“Persistent is a very nice way to put it,” Joan laughed.

“She thinks that if she flirts, she will get me to do what she wants with her cases.”

“And with her underpants,” Will joked.

Instead of being offended, Alex covered her mouth to keep from spitting food all over the table in laughter. Once she swallowed, she cackled. “Oh my God, Will!” she exclaimed.

David just shook his head, amused by the banter.

After eating lunch, Alex and David attacked the office. Will followed up on some investigations. Joan typed up some of the entries.

The radio echoed classic country music as David and Alex sat on the floor going through the files. Between making trips to the attic and to the basement, they were certainly getting a workout. The papers that didn't need to be stored had to go in a "destroy" pile for Joan to take care of.

With the sun setting behind the nearby buildings, both David and Alex realized just how long they had been working on their project. David glanced up at the clock.

"Wow," he started. "It's almost six. Are you hungry?"

"I could eat," she replied. "Just look at what we've accomplished."

"I don't think we'll need to come in this weekend," David said happily.

"I think we could get by with hitting it hard again Monday," Alex agreed.

"I have court all day Monday."

"I can do the rest of this. After working on this today, I know pretty much what should stay and what should go."

"Are you sure?" he asked, not wanting to inconvenience her.

"Of course. I already told you I'm fine with helping. If I get confused, I can always ask Joan or Will to help me."

David stood and stretched. His back was sore, and his head ached. He looked down at Alex, still sitting on the floor. She diligently read another file. She wasn't giving up so easily.

As he stood admiring her determination, he started feeling things that he hadn't felt in a very long time. He kept reminding himself that they weren't kids anymore. He didn't want to be attracted to her only because of their history. He wanted to discover who she was now. Admittedly, though, he was interested in her. He wasn't certain how smart it would be to start an office romance, but he knew plenty of attorneys who had met their spouses either in law school or in a law firm partnership. Others met their husbands or wives while working opposite one another in court. They seemed to do just fine. Nonetheless, he hesitated. The prospect frightened him.

Alex looked up at him, her mouth slightly open. He was lost in thought and then met her gaze. She felt the energy in the room change.

"Where'd you go?" she asked curiously. "You were far away for a minute there."

He shook his head and decided not to answer the question. "What do you want for dinner?" he asked.

"I don't know. Certainly not leftover Chinese," she answered.

"Why don't you follow me out to my house? I'll grill something. We can hang out and catch up," he offered.

"That sounds nice," she replied.

11

The drive to his house gave both of them too much time to ponder outcomes. David wasn't the only one struggling with feelings. As the headlights passed steadily, they only offered momentary distractions. Alex wondered if it was a bad idea to accept David's invitation. She had heard around town that David was an extremely private person. She didn't want to impose or infringe on his time at home. No one even knew where he lived.

David was literally off the grid. He used solar power, and with a highly industrialized filtration system, the nearby pond supplied the cabin with water. All of his personal and business mail came to the cottage in town. He used Hope's summer cottage as his home address. When the Miller case broke, the media didn't descend on his cabin. Instead, they found themselves at an empty house that looked like it had been locked up for months.

David also managed to keep many things in his grandfather's name. All of the land and sales records referred to the trust.

Before he was even fifteen minutes out of town, David's phone rang. The screen in his car lit up. It was the emergency number for Children Services. He rolled his eyes and pulled off to the side of the road, flipping his flashers on.

Alex stopped behind him, turned on her flashers, and got out. He unlocked the doors. She opened the passenger-side door and hopped inside.

"What's wrong?" she asked.

"You may as well be in on this, too. I just got a call from the emergency on-call number for Children Services. I'm betting they want to take more kids, and they need an emergency order. If they do, I'll have to type something up at home, call Steven, fax him the paperwork, he'll have to sign it, and then I'll meet the on-call worker to hand them the pick-up order," he explained.

Alex was confused. Her expression blank, she shook her head as she realized how little she knew about juvenile law. "Will I ever get the hang of this?" she asked nervously.

"You will. I promise. It will take time, lots of observation, and plenty of practice," he said reassuringly. "But I have no doubt you will get it."

He called the number, and Carleigh picked up. Rolling his eyes, he knew without a doubt she was planning to take more kids and did, in fact, need paperwork.

Leaning across Alex, he pulled the glove compartment lid open and grabbed a small notepad with a pen neatly tucked into the spiral wire of the notebook. He caught the faint smell of Alex's perfume, and the scent of his aftershave wasn't lost on her either.

"Sorry," he said, apologizing for invading her personal space.

"It's okay," she whispered.

Carleigh gave him the necessary names and dates of birth. After writing everything down, David said, "Give me about an hour. I'll text you when I'm ready to leave. Then I'll meet you at the park-and-ride on 32."

He hung up and looked over at Alex. The light from the dash illuminated her skin.

"Now what?" she asked.

"Follow me to the house. I'll call Steven, and then we'll get the fax back. We'll meet Carleigh. After that, we can eat. I have things to munch on at the house in the meantime. I know you're starving," he said.

They arrived at the cabin. David parked in the garage, the dogs greeting him as usual. Alex parked in a gravel pull-off beside the large metal barn.

David got out and waited for her. The dogs were saying hello as they ran around her. She smiled down at them as she patted them on the head. She loved dogs, but she couldn't justify having one. She didn't spend very much time at home, and she felt it would be an injustice to have a pet.

The dusky sky didn't allow Alex to see much of the cabin's detail. She followed David through the mudroom and into the kitchen. When he flipped the light switch, the kitchen and living area lit up. Alex was awestruck. Large logs made up the walls of the kitchen and living room. Everything was custom-made to perfection. The home was truly breathtaking.

"This place is unbelievable, David," she said as she looked up at the log rafters.

"Thanks," he replied as he turned back and hung his messenger bag on a hook in the mudroom. "I need to feed the girls. We can get started after that."

"Where do you keep their food?" she asked.

"The closet in the mudroom," he replied.

"I'll feed them. Go start on everything."

She grabbed the dog dishes in the corner of the mudroom as he watched her. She opened the closet door, lifted the lid on the large blue plastic container, scooped up some food, put it in each bowl, and then set them back on the floor in the corner. She also took the liberty of picking up their water dishes and bringing them into the kitchen. The dogs waited patiently, watching closely for their command to eat. Once David gave the signal, they gladly complied.

After giving water to the dogs, Alex returned to the kitchen and washed her hands. Unsure where to find paper towels, she glanced around. David realized he had forgotten to replace the roll and fetched a clean dish towel from the drawer. As Alex's hands dripped with water, she spun around, nearly colliding with him. Using the towel, he dried her hands, their eyes locking in a moment filled with wonder and anticipation. She leaned up and kissed him, taking the initiative, which he found relieving, not wanting to make her feel awkward, especially since they were going to work together. Her boldness and confidence were incredibly attractive to him.

Her lips tasted like pure bliss to him, and he felt himself becoming aroused, his erection pressing against his jeans. Alex set the pace and pulled away, opening her eyes.

"Was that weird?" she whispered, feeling a little unsteady.

"Not weird," he answered softly as their noses touched.

"So, we should work, right?" she asked, her hands still wrapped in the towel.

David came to his senses and nodded. He took the towel away and hung it on the stainless-steel oven.

"Yes, this won't take long," he promised, still trying to calm himself. "If you're hungry, I have snacks," he said, walking to the pantry just off the kitchen. Opening the door revealed an assortment of foods—canned items, nonperishables, and snacks. Alex grabbed a pack of almonds and some crackers.

They ascended to the loft. The space was quite large and arranged quaintly. His large desk overlooked the living area, positioned opposite a wall of windows that offered a view of the front yard. Adjacent to this setup was another bedroom and a full bath.

"Grab a chair," he suggested as he nodded toward the upstairs bedroom. "I'll show you how to do this."

Alex came out with the small wooden chair and plopped down beside him. She watched him as he typed the information into the document.

After completing the paperwork, David called Steven and then faxed the document to him. The signed order returned within ten minutes. Once they received the paperwork, David sent a text to Carleigh to arrange a meeting.

The drive to the highway seemed to take an eternity. Alex broke the silence between the two of them.

"Your cabin is stunning," she complimented.

"Thanks."

"Did you have it built?" she asked.

David elaborated on the origins of the cabin but omitted the details regarding the inheritance. He described living essentially off the grid, with solar panels on his roof providing electricity and water sourced from a pond, filtered through a system in his basement, eliminating the need for public utilities. He maintained privacy by using only a P.O. Box for his address and utilized the office cottage's address for parcels and mail requiring a physical location. David emphasized his preference for privacy, expressing a desire to keep his exact living location undisclosed.

Once he'd finished with his explanation, Alex commented, "Well, it's a beautiful home. I love the rustic style."

"My sisters and my mom helped decorate it. I suck at that stuff."

"Well, they did a great job."

"Where do you live?" he asked as he turned his head toward her for a second.

"I have a little house over by the fire station in town. Nothing much, but it's only me. It's a two-bedroom brick—simplistic. Just the way I like it."

"Are you buying or renting?"

"Renting. Lyle Mathis is the landlord."

"Oh, he's a good guy."

"He is an angel. He fixes whatever I need and mows the lawn. He also comes and removes the snow from my driveway. I don't have to worry about a thing. I can take care of things on my own, but he won't have it. I don't know if that's because he is a good landlord or because he is one of my dad's friends," she laughed.

"I'm sure that being the commissioner's daughter has its perks," he said.

"And its disadvantages. Everyone thinks I'm rich or have profound influence," she said candidly. "It makes dating somewhat difficult. Most just want to get in my pants anyway," she shrugged.

David chuckled. "You just tell it like it is, don't you, Alex?"

"I warned you," she said.

"I like it," he remarked.

"Well, you can bank on my bluntness."

"It's refreshing," he admitted. "I don't have to pick your brain for answers. What made you so outspoken? You were sort of quiet when we were growing up."

"I outgrew what everyone expected of me," she replied. "I was always told to 'be a good little girl.' That meant, 'Don't be disagreeable.' My mother was a good woman, but she was bad at parenting—very heavy-handed and too taken by what everyone else thought.

"When my brother died, I changed. When I went off to college, I changed even more. When I decided I wanted to go to law school, everything changed. I knew I needed to embrace who I truly was. Being shy and quiet wasn't really me. I don't want you to think that I'm argumentative or hateful, though. I'm only adversarial when I need to be, and that's usually in court," she clarified.

"Oh, I don't think that about you at all. There's a difference between being real and being obnoxious. Carleigh is obnoxious. You're real," he reassured her.

"Well, I just don't believe in wasting time. If you want to say something, say it. If you want something, go get it."

He grinned from ear to ear. "Is that why you kissed me?" he asked.

In his peripheral vision, he saw Alex drop her head shyly and smirk. "I take risks, too, which is often a character flaw."

"I don't think it's a character flaw at all. I like that you are audacious."

"I hope I didn't make things awkward between us," she admitted.

"Not for me."

"Good. I'm not impulsive. I just wanted to kiss you," she shrugged. "So, I did. I've always wanted to kiss you, even when we were kids."

"Really?"

"Yep. I had an insane crush on you, David," she admitted with a smile.

He smirked. “I didn’t know that.”

“You were my hero. You comforted me at one of the most tragic times of my life.”

12

They pulled into the park-and-ride. Carleigh stood by her car, arms crossed, awaiting their arrival. David exited the SUV, handing her the pick-up packet. They engaged in a brief exchange, all while Carleigh glared at Alex. Afterward, David and Alex drove back to the cabin. It was quiet. At one point, David glanced over to find Alex reclined slightly in her seat, peacefully sleeping.

Upon pulling into the garage around 10:30 p.m., David felt a pang of guilt for not having eaten. The lateness of the hour and his fatigue made the idea of cooking seem daunting. He gently reached out, touching Alex's leg to rouse her from her slumber. She blinked groggily, slowly opening her eyes.

“Hey you,” he whispered.

“Hey,” she said as she stretched.

“If you want, you can bunk here. I’ll give you my bed, and I’ll take the guest room,” he said softly.

She nodded and opened the car door. Following behind him and holding his hand, David led her to the master bedroom located right off of the living room. She kicked off her shoes and crawled up onto the bed.

“I have some sweats and a t-shirt if you want to change,” he whispered.

“No thanks,” she replied as she fell back to sleep.

David gently retrieved the blanket from the nearby rocking chair and tenderly draped it over Alex. He stood there for a moment, silently observing her peaceful slumber. It bewildered him how swiftly and intensely his feelings had grown. Perhaps it was the shared history they had, but he couldn't deny the depth of emotion he felt. He hadn't realized Alex's interest in him during their upbringing, a fact that flattered him now. Witnessing her transformation into a spirited and straightforward young woman filled him with admiration, particularly considering the challenges she had faced.

The following morning, David was roused from sleep by the tantalizing aroma of sizzling bacon wafting through the cabin. The sounds of conversation emanated from the kitchen, gradually becoming more distinct as he lay in bed. It was Will and Alex, their laughter mingling in the morning air.

Sitting on the edge of the bed, David realized he hadn't even changed out of his jeans and t-shirt from the night before. While Alex had slept, he had remained awake, engrossed in his work on the textbook, eventually succumbing to sleep around 2 a.m.

Descending the stairs, David was greeted by the sound of Will cracking another joke, punctuated by Alex's infectious laughter.

“Hey sleepyhead!” Will said as David walked into the kitchen.

He waved, but didn’t say anything. Coffee was the goal.

“I hope you don’t mind, but I went to the market on Route 124 and grabbed some bacon and eggs. I figured we could both use some food since we didn’t eat last night,” Alex said.

“I’m so sorry about that, and you sure didn’t have to go buy food,” David said as he poured the coffee into a mug. “There’s a deep freezer filled with food in the basement.”

“It’s okay. You didn’t have anything in the fridge. Besides, I wanted to,” she said as she flipped a piece of bacon.

The sound of the sizzling pork in the frying pan brought a contented smile to his face. He leaned back against the sink and took a drink of the coffee.

“So, Will, what brings you over here?” David asked.

"Carleigh. When she couldn't get a hold of you, she started calling me."

"I think my phone's dead. What the hell does she want now? I gave her the paperwork she needed."

"She took another set of kids last night."

"Are you serious? Another set?" Alex asked as she loaded up David's plate. "Can she do that without a court order? Is she an officer of the court?"

"No, she isn't, and no she can't," David answered as he shook his head angrily. "Does she want to get the agency sued?"

"If you want my honest opinion, I think it was an excuse to get in touch with you," Will answered. "Did she know Alex was with you?"

"Yep."

"Then that was probably it."

"Very perceptive," Alex interrupted.

"So, she took kids just to make sure she could ruin my night? Do you know how crazy that sounds?" David asked.

"Maybe she'll get fired," Alex said spiritedly.

"That will never happen as long as Tamara is the director," David said.

"You'll have to call her, David," Will added.

"I want to eat first. I'm starving," he complained as he grabbed the plate and sat down at the bar.

Once Will finished his breakfast and left, Alex sat down on the bar stool beside David. She drank some coffee and ate some scrambled eggs.

"Thanks for making breakfast," he said as he took the last bite of bacon from his plate. "It was very good."

"You're welcome," she replied. "I'm going to need to go home and get a shower and some fresh clothing if you want me to come back to go with you to Hope's," she added.

"I need a shower, too. I also need to call Carleigh. I've got some more things I need to do with the textbook before I head to Hope's, also."

Alex rose from her seat, collected the plates, rinsed them, and neatly placed them in the dishwasher. With a wet cloth in hand, she meticulously wiped down the stove. David observed her attentively as she worked.

Standing up, he made his way to the sink to wash his hands. Drying them with the familiar cloth towel, he observed Alex bustling about, tidying up the breakfast bar and countertops.

Without hesitation, he approached her, gently grasping her wrist to halt her movements. Pulling her closer, he leaned in, tenderly brushing his lips against hers. The sound of the washcloth hitting the tile floor punctuated the moment as he felt her arms wrap around his neck. Drawing her in even closer, he rested his hands on her waist, savoring the closeness between them.

He moved his focus to her neck, brushing his lips gently against her soft skin. He felt himself quickly losing control of the situation. Fear held him back, and he pulled away.

Gazing down into her inviting eyes, he surrendered again and kissed her. Still, he didn't want to be the one to take the next step.

Feeling his hesitation, she stopped kissing him. "Tell me what you're afraid of?" she whispered into his ear.

"Everything," he admitted.

"I want this," she assured him.

"Are you sure?"

"I promise, David," she answered.

He nodded a little and kissed her again. The passion coursed through his heat-filled body as he cupped her face in his hands. Slowing the pace slightly, he knew if this was going to happen, he didn't want to rush it. He wanted to do it right.

As they began backing into the living room, a knock on the front door startled both of them.

13

"Are you expecting anyone else?" she asked breathlessly.

"No," he said as he put his forehead against hers. "I have no clue who that is."

"It's okay. It might be important," she said as she pulled away from him.

"It better be," he remarked.

As he walked toward the door, he took a few deep breaths to calm himself. He needed a few seconds to calm his body before opening the door. Finally, he pulled the door open, and much to his disappointment, Carleigh stood on his porch. Unable to keep his cool, he huffed and rolled his eyes.

"Carleigh," he began as he opened the screen door. "How the hell did you find out where I live?"

She pushed past him. When David turned, Alex was nowhere in sight.

"I bribed a sheriff's deputy to tell me where you live," she admitted.

"I'll make sure he's fired within the hour," David said angrily.

"I tried to call, but it went straight to voicemail."

"My phone is dead," he said. "This better be good. It's Saturday."

"I just had questions about a case."

"Are you serious?" he shouted.

He heard car tires on gravel, and as he glanced out the screen door, he saw Alex driving away. He wasn't sure why. Fury rose quickly throughout his body.

The anger had nothing to do with Alex. She'd walked away from the chaos, not from him.

David decided to take a strategy from Alex's playbook. He could hear her voice in his head: "If you want to say something, say it."

David always kept in mind that he had to have a positive relationship with Carleigh as well as her colleagues because of his responsibility as the agency's attorney. However, she'd crossed a major boundary. None of the other caseworkers acted like this. They respected his time and his space.

"Carleigh, I'm going to need you to leave," he said harshly as he folded his arms. His candor must have caught her off guard because she didn't move a muscle.

"What?" Carleigh asked in stunned disbelief.

"Whatever questions, legal questions, you have can wait until Monday. You shouldn't be asking me anything case-related anyway. You should be asking Tamara. She is your boss."

"But you said if any of us ever needed help…"

"This is going too far. You bribed a cop. I am a very private person, and my house, my off-time, is off limits. I don't like anyone knowing where I live, Carleigh. It isn't something I share."

"But you let Alex know where you live after meeting her once?"

"How is this any of your business, and why do you think I owe you any kind of explanation about it? Who do you think you are? Alex and I grew up together. We've known each other all of our lives. Now, I'm going to ask you again to get the hell off of my property, or I'm going to call the sheriff and have you arrested for trespassing," he concluded as he pushed the screen door back open.

The words were out before he'd fully thought them through, but his attention was already elsewhere.

Without a word, she stomped past him and out to her car. She stood beside it for a moment, a hopeful expression on her round face.

"I'm reporting you to Tamara first thing Monday morning. I was also told you took more kids last night. I truly hope you had the legal right to do that, given that you didn't have a pick-up order. One last thing, if you tell anyone where I live, Carleigh, I'll sue you," he concluded as he let the screen door shut and then slammed the front door.

With the entire afternoon stretching ahead of him and hours still to fill, David found himself consumed by worry and uncertainty. Alex's sudden departure left him bewildered, with no understanding of the reasons behind it. He felt at a loss for how to react or what steps to take next.

The realm of dating felt foreign and intimidating to him, as he realized he was out of practice and unsure of where to even begin. It wasn't regret he felt, just uncertainty. Moreover, he questioned whether he could accurately label their connection as "dating," given the complexities and uncertainties surrounding their past relationship.

His landline rang.

"Hello," he said anxiously.

"Are you alright?" Hope asked curiously.

"No, I'm not," he replied as he ran his hand through his dark brown hair. "I'm really pissed. Are you in town already?" he continued.

"Yes. I'm at my place. Do we have a headcount yet?"

"Honestly, Hope, I don't know."

"Tell me what's wrong," she encouraged.

David told her everything that happened. She was always able to offer helpful insight, and he was praying she could do that now.

"I have no idea what to do here, Hope," he admitted. "She just left without a word," he concluded.

"First of all, breathe. Your brain creates the worst kinds of scenarios when, in reality, the situation is never that bleak. Secondly, text her. It's not too personal but sends a message of concern," she advised.

"I swear I'm going to have Carleigh fired!"

"You probably should," Hope agreed. "What she did was so far out of line and wrong."

"Hope, I really like Alex. It's like we picked up right where we left off, ya know? Did you know she had a crush on me when we were growing up?"

"I absolutely did. She swore me to secrecy."

"I had no freakin' clue. None."

"I know," she said with a chuckle. "It's going to be alright. Alex probably needed to take care of some things before coming to the party. You likely didn't do anything wrong. I'm going to go and start getting things ready. Are you going to be alright?"

"Yes," he replied breathily.

"I'll see you later, okay?" she asked.

"Yes. I'll be there."

"Love you, big brother," she said sweetly.

"Love you, little sister," he concluded.

14

Despite Hope's sound guidance, David let a few more hours pass. His phone needed to charge, and he very much needed a shower. As he stood looking in the mirror, a towel wrapped around his waist, he just couldn't stand it anymore. He had to know if he'd done something wrong with Alex. He walked into his bedroom and grabbed his phone, pulling it free from the wall charger. Typing, he sent her a message:

Sorry about this morning. I hope I didn't upset you in any way. If I came on too strong, I apologize. I just want to make sure you're okay.

He waited for a reply, but nothing came.

David walked to his office upstairs and did his best to return his focus to the textbook he was editing. It was no use, though. The frustration and insecurities welled up inside of him, and he ended up right back in his bedroom.

Flopping onto the bed, he lay on his back, his eyes fixed upon the ceiling. He put his cell phone on his stomach and watched the fan blades spinning around. Before he knew it, he drifted off.

The banging on the front door and the dogs barking woke him up. He slowly came to. As he sat up, he wondered who was at his house now. The irritation started to burn inside of him, and he feared who would be standing on the other side of the front door. If it was Carleigh, he was finished with the niceties. He knew he would probably lose the contract with Children Services, but he didn't care. That place was a headache anyway.

The knocking continued along with the barking.

"Just a minute," he said as he grabbed a white cotton undershirt out of the chest of drawers.

The front door was right next to his bedroom door. When he looked out his window, he didn't see a car anywhere. Finally, he unlocked the deadbolt and pulled the door open. Alex stood on the porch.

"Oh hey! Come in," he said earnestly. He was pleasantly surprised.

"God, I'm so sorry I had to leave," she started as she stepped inside. "I needed to go to my house and shower. I couldn't stand it anymore. I didn't have a change of clothes with me. I didn't mean to just take off like that. I figured Carleigh needed to talk to you about the case, and I figured she'd be here for a while," Alex continued as David shut the door behind her.

"Oh, it's okay. I just wondered if I offended you or something. I sent a text."

"My phone was dead. I didn't get it until I got into the car to come over. I'm not upset," she said, shaking her head.

"Good. I didn't want you to think I was coming on too strong this morning. It worried me."

"David, you do not scare me or worry me or bring about any negative feelings for me. If you did, I would never have come to you for a job."

"Well, I know," he said as he walked to the sofa and sat down.

She followed him to the sofa as he continued talking. "I just… I don't want to make things awkward at work. I also don't want you to feel disrespected," he admitted. "I don't want you to feel like you have to fuck me for job security." He couldn't even believe he'd said that. The stunned expression on his face signaled to Alex that he required saving.

"Listen to me," she said as she sat down beside him. "This will take us wherever we want it to, whatever this is. I'm not worried about it. I'm not asking for anything from you. I'm not expecting anything from you. I want to get to know who you are now. I want to rediscover you, but if it doesn't feel right to either of us…" She stopped. "I'm rambling. I'm sorry."

He smiled. "It does make sense. I think what you're saying is if something's going to happen, let it happen. If it's not, don't force it."

"Exactly," she said as she slapped his knee gently and nodded.

"You crack me up," he said. "You aren't like anyone I have ever met. You're so bold, but so sexy in the way you do it." He chuckled.

She sat back. "Life changed me at a very tender age. I realized that all we have is right now. This moment. We're not promised anything beyond that. Sometimes I get carried away, but I really do try to keep my head. I'll admit, though, your kiss really distracted me," she said as a devilish grin settled on her lips. "I need more distractions in my life." She winked.

David smiled. "Do you now?"

She blushed. "I do."

"Would you like me to distract you again?" he asked, shifting his body toward her.

She nodded. "I would."

He leaned over, raised one hand to her chin, and tilted it up. He kissed her lips softly as he felt her hand on his forearm.

They stopped for a moment. "See what I mean," she whispered seductively. "You make it very difficult for me to concentrate."

"I'd apologize," he whispered, "but I'm not sorry."

He tenderly caressed her cheek with the back of his hand and stared into her eyes. He leaned in and kissed her again. He felt her hand move from his forearm to his inner thigh.

She was so tempting. With her touch, he felt himself falling. He didn't have any qualms about giving in, though. He didn't want to stop. He wanted to get lost in her.

Carefully, he laid her back on the sofa and kissed her neck. Hovering over her, he put most of his weight on his hands. She ran her fingers through his hair. All logic and rational thought left him, and all he could think about was the desire to touch her, to take her. He could feel himself being swept away by the passion and heat between them.

They kissed for a time, as their hands learned the feel of the other. David's body pressed against Alex's as they soaked in every sensation and feeling.

Alex sat up, gently pushing him away. He sat up on the edge of the couch. She grabbed the hem of his t-shirt and pulled it off, tossing it onto the coffee table. She traced an invisible line down the center of his body, stopping just above the waistline of his sweats. Alex leaned down, brushing her lips lightly across his abdomen. His fingers laced through her dark hair.

She eased back onto the couch again, and he leaned over her once more, kissing her. She rubbed her knee against his erection. It was just the encouragement he needed. David sat back. He watched as Alex unbuttoned her shirt. She didn't take it off. Instead, she left it open slightly.

She sat up, and he felt her mouth on his neck, her breath hot against his skin. She slipped her hand down the front of his sweatpants and wrapped her fingers around him. He could barely move as the sensation caused his breathing to hitch and his heart rate to intensify.

He opened his eyes to see her looking up at him. "Feel good?" she asked.

"Yes," he sighed.

He pushed her back, leaned down, and kissed his way down to the cup of her black lace bra. He pushed it aside. His lips found their target, and he flicked her erect nipple with his tongue. He nibbled and pulled it with his teeth as she arched under him, moaning with pleasure.

He ventured lower and kissed her stomach all the way to her belly button. This forced her to release him. He then kissed his way up to her lips, balancing himself on his palms once more. He wanted to taste her.

He stopped kissing her for a moment and glanced down at her jeans. "May I?" he asked.

"Yes," she replied.

He unfastened her jeans and helped her wiggle out of them, her black panties going with them. She was trimmed but not completely shaved. He liked it. David knelt on the floor. He picked up her bottom and moved her to the edge of the couch cushion. He sat up and looked up longingly at her.

"Can I kiss you?" he asked.

"Yes," she said as she smiled.

"I want to taste you… and smell you…" he whispered.

He gently spread her legs apart and kissed from her knee to her inner thigh. He nuzzled into her sex, parting her with his nose. He kissed her softly, listening for her body to tell him what to do next. He licked the inside of her as she responded with an arched back. He slowly inserted his index and middle finger, all while still licking her lightly and slowly.

She moaned softly, and he yearned to be inside of her. He wanted to bring her to climax if he could. He wondered if she might be shy with this sort of intimacy, though. He didn't know her well enough yet. There had been absolutely no discussion regarding sex and what they liked or didn't like. He was playing everything by ear.

"I want you inside of me," she whispered.

He stopped, and she sat up. He stood. Alex pulled his pants off, exposing his erection. She brought her hand back to him, stroking him as he steadied himself. The sensation of her hand around him made him yearn for her warmth, but she wasn't having that yet. She put her mouth around him, still stroking him with her hand. The feeling was inexplicable. She instinctively knew just how to touch him. Still, he wanted to feel her, be inside of her.

He pushed her away slightly, and she rested on the couch. He positioned himself between her legs, hovering over her while supporting himself on his hands again. As they looked into each other's eyes, the intensity growing, he pushed into her. They both closed their eyes as the feeling took them over.

She felt like a velvet vice wrapped around him. He felt her hand on his bicep as he moved steadily, her body tensing and then relaxing with each thrust. She pushed herself up on her elbows and kissed his neck as they became more and more intoxicated with each other. He felt her breath against his skin as their quiet sounds carried through the air.

She pulled him down to her, causing him to grind against her. He leaned down and teased her nipple again with his tongue. He felt her hands on his back, pulling him into her each time.

"You're so close. I can feel you," he whispered. "Do you want me to go harder?"

"Just don't stop what you're doing," she whispered.

"I won't stop," he promised as he kissed her neck.

She got louder with each thrust, and that drew him closer still. He loved the sounds she made. They made him harder as he plunged into her time and time again.

"Let me feel you," he said softly, kissing her forehead.

The words encouraged her to let go, and he felt her tighten around him even more. Her sounds intensified, and he felt the intense rush around him. She cried out his name as her hands squeezed around his biceps again. She pulled him into her, her spasms radiating from deep within.

Her orgasm and the sound of her voice made it difficult for him not to fall over the edge himself. Still, he resisted until he felt her body completely relax. Then he let the rush of the climax overtake him as he pressed into her. His heart sped, and his chest heaved. The familiar lightheadedness overcame him as he found oneness with her. His body numbed momentarily as the exhaustion began to set in.

David leaned over Alex as he still shuddered. She rested under him, seeming completely satisfied with the experience. He kissed her forehead and then her eyebrow. Just like an addict, he was hooked, and there was no turning back now.

He kissed her lips, her body rising to meet his. Finally, he stood up and tried to balance himself, but his head was still spinning. He sat on the couch at her feet for a moment. Tossing his head on the back of the couch, he closed his eyes, his breath slowing slightly.

"I want to hold you," he said. "Come lie with me." He opened his eyes and turned his head toward her. She smiled and nodded.

"I need to get cleaned up first," she said, accepting his invitation.

"You won't need your clothes," he assured her.

A sly smile found its way to her lips. "Is that so?"

"Yes. It is."

She stood, letting her shirt drop to the floor, and unhooked the back of her bra. He admired her curves. She was beautiful. Her skin was like silk, and her breasts were perfectly made, round and beautiful.

He also stood. He leaned in and kissed her lips. "Go get cleaned up. I'll do the same. I'll meet you in the bedroom."

Once David was finished in the master bath, he went into his bedroom and pulled the blankets down. He stood beside the bed, thinking about their brief encounter. Her scent still lingered on his nose and chin. This wasn't a dream. This was real. She was real. The connection he felt with her was somewhat overwhelming, but also exhilarating.

She walked into the room. He was already snuggling under the covers.

“Come here,” he said, his arm outstretched.

She got into bed and rested into the crook of his arm. She looked up at him, her chin on his chest. He could see in her eyes that she was unsure. He was somewhat surprised to see such vulnerability and possibly some insecurity. She seemed so confident.

Before he could offer assurance, she said, “Is this going to be a one-time thing?”

“Not if I have anything to say about it,” he answered.

“Are you okay with what just happened between us?”

“More than okay,” he answered.

“So, you don’t feel rushed or pressured?”

“Do you?”

“No,” she said tenderly.

“I don’t either. It felt like it was meant to happen,” he replied. “I’ve known you my entire life, Alexandra.”

“Are you afraid?” she asked. “Because when I asked you what you were afraid of, you said ‘everything.’ I don’t want our friendship to be ruined by this. I also don’t want things to be strained at work. You’re basically my boss.”

“I’m not your boss. We’re equals,” he refuted.

“I know it’s been years, but we depended on each other when we were younger.”

"I know. Alex, I don't do one-night stands or flings. I'm playing for keeps. I couldn't have sex with you if I didn't feel a mind-body connection. This wouldn't even be happening."

"Same here," she agreed. "It's more than physical for me."

David was serious, and his countenance reflected it. "Here's the thing you need to know about me, and I'm saying this because it's who I am. I'm not saying it to scare you or creep you out, okay?"

She nodded.

"We haven't talked about sex or relationships or expectations. I feel like I need to say a few things, though."

"Of course," she replied, propping herself up on her elbow.

"I'm loyal to a fault, Alexandra. I'm trusting. When you've earned my loyalty and my trust, you've got it forever. You earned that a long time ago. Once that bond is broken, it's highly unlikely that it will be repaired. I am monogamous, 100 percent. I always have been, and I probably always will be. I don't share, and I don't like to be shared. So many of my friends are in open relationships, and I honestly don't understand how they do it. I don't sleep around. And like I said, I have to have a connection with someone."

She nodded and observed him. Then she smiled. "First of all, I want 'loyal,'" she explained. "I've been with too many people who don't know how to be. Secondly, I'm also monogamous. I am looking for someone who wants to be with me and only me. So, none of what you've said alarms me. I think the key is to communicate."

"I agree." He paused. "I crave honesty, Alex," he continued. "When you walked back into my world, somehow deep down, I knew you were supposed to be there. And, mind you, I'm not a 'spiritual' man. In fact, I don't believe in anything, really."

"What do you mean?" she asked.

"Here and now is all that concerns me. I was raised around a very spiritual family, but you already know that."

"Well, I have a confession," she continued.

"Oh?" he asked as his fingertips danced on her bare back.

"Sex is a deeply spiritual thing for me. Just like you said, there has to be a mind-body connection. Sex or lovemaking, whichever term you want to use, for me, is an outward demonstration of an internal feeling."

"Mmm..." His jaw fixed, and concerns now rose to the surface. Alex noticed the shift immediately.

"What did I say?" she asked.

"I don't do 'spiritual,' Alex. In fact, I'll run from it."

She changed the subject quickly. "I was sort of afraid to come back here today. I knew that if I did, we would end up right here. I didn't want to seem too easy or pushy, but I am deliriously attracted to you."

His cheeks warmed. "I think you are pretty hot yourself," he said as he pulled the sheet down, exposing her breasts. He caressed her, never losing eye contact.

She smiled. "So, are you with me in seeing where this goes? Are you in, Mr. Gregory?" she asked curiously.

"I'm so in, Miss Ritezal."

She rested beside him again. Instead of sleeping, David and Alex spent the afternoon exploring their sensual nature, making love. They made up for lost time as they dove headfirst into the ocean of pure ecstasy.

15

The sun was already gone as David stood on the deck with his flashlight in his hand. They were very late for the cookout. Instead of taking the car, David wanted to take Alex on the trail through the woods.

Alex pulled the back door shut behind her.

"It's chilly," David said. "Do you have a jacket?"

"Damn it. I forgot it at my house."

"Don't worry about it. Let me go in and get a hoodie." David opened the door again and walked to the closet in the mudroom. He grabbed his navy blue hoodie and then walked back out, pulling the door shut again.

Alex took it from him and put it over her head. She pulled it up to her face and sighed.

"What's wrong?" he asked curiously.

"Not a thing. Your scent is all over this thing," she answered as she closed her eyes momentarily. "It's heaven."

David was flattered. He leaned in and kissed her forehead. "Are you okay to walk, because after today, I wondered if you would be able to…" he smirked.

"Very funny. I think I can manage," she answered with a wink.

"You do realize," he continued, "I would rather take you back inside and sink right back into you. I could totally skip this cookout."

She looked up. "That wouldn't be right."

After tracking through the woods for ten minutes, they arrived at the far end of Hope's backyard. The glow from the fire lit the area, and laughter drifted up into the cool night air.

As they approached, David saw Cain and Suzie sitting in chairs around the fire. There were several empty lawn chairs as well. On the deck, Will stood over the grill flipping burgers. Scott stood beside him, laughing hysterically about something.

Through the large glass door, David could see Hope and Joan standing in the kitchen. Cain spotted David and Alex first. He threw his hand up.

"Nice of you guys to finally make it. You're only an hour and a half late," he joked.

David smiled. "Yeah, yeah. I brought beer. Am I forgiven?"

"Absolutely!" Cain answered as he raised his half-empty beer bottle.

David stopped and introduced Alex to Suzie. Then they continued up the hill toward Hope's cottage. As they stepped onto the deck, Will turned and grinned.

"Hey! David! Alex!" he slurred. "Are you guys hungry?"

"Starving," he replied. "You okay, buddy?"

"I'm fine," he said, clearly inebriated.

"Should you be over an open flame?" David laughed.

"Ha, ha. Very funny, smart-ass."

David politely introduced Alex to Scott and then said, "Let me put the beer in the cooler."

He walked to the large red cooler and opened it. Beer and soda nearly overflowed onto the deck. David stood up straight and looked over at Will.

"So, there's no room for my beer. How are you guys even drunk?" he asked.

"Hope's got bourbon in the kitchen. That's why we're all drunk."

"Ah," David said with a nod.

He pulled the sliding door open. The mixed conversations poured out. With the case of beer still in his arms, he stepped inside.

"I don't know where you want me to put this," he said.

Hope turned to him immediately. Her dark hair was in a thick ponytail, a cascade of waves falling effortlessly. She seemed to be wearing Will's hoodie, the fabric hanging loosely over her slender frame, embodying a comfortable and laid-back vibe. Her slender legs fit into a pair of black leggings, and the sandals with socks on her feet were her signature look, a quirky touch that somehow added to her unique charm.

The contrast of the dark hair against the hoodie and leggings highlighted the casual yet effortlessly cool aura that surrounded Hope. Her fashion choices spoke of individuality, and the sandals with socks, once considered unconventional, had become a distinctive part of her personal style. As she turned toward him, her expression reflected a blend of confidence and ease, making it clear that she was comfortable in her own skin.

Smiling, she rushed to him, taking the burden from him.

Once she put the case on the counter, Hope turned back to David. She threw her arms around him, squeezing him in a bear hug. Then she turned her attention to Alex.

She walked to her and pulled her in. "It's been too long," Hope whispered.

"It has," Alex agreed.

"I'm so glad you could come," Hope followed up as she broke the embrace and held her at arm's length. "You look so good."

"You do, too," Alex said softly.

David observed Alex as she mingled with the group members. She mixed well. Her sensational humor had everyone eating from the palm of her hand. David was extremely pleased.

As he continued to watch her, he realized how easy it would be to fall in love with her. Everything just fit. He couldn't deny it. Still, the speed with which the feelings were coming alarmed him. He wasn't one to rush into anything, and he was trying very hard to keep things steady and light. However, he was a one-woman man. Once he was intimate with someone, he had trouble moving backward from that. He knew he wanted more than just friendship and sex with Alex.

David also studied the contact between Hope and Will. Although things were subtle, now that he knew what to look for, a spark became easily recognizable. Occasionally brushing against each other, leaning in to each other as they talked. These were all signs of something more than a sexual relationship between them.

He was truly happy for them. Even though he and Hope had their distinct and often intense differences, David wanted her to be happy and cared for. Most of all, he wanted her to be treated well. Deep down, he hoped that they would realize that they were better together than apart. But for now, if the situation worked for them, that was what mattered.

After hours of sitting among friends, talking and laughing, David's inebriation and exhaustion tugged at him. Alex only drank a few shots of bourbon, and although she seemed a little fuzzy, she wasn't quite as drunk as he was.

When he stood, everyone booed. They knew he was preparing to leave. He held up his hands as if to defend himself.

"I'm tired," he slurred.

"Party pooper," Hope called out.

"I am going to pass out. I have got to try to get back to my house," he admitted.

"Stay here," Hope implored. "There's the guest bedroom."

"I want to go home to my bed and to my dogs and crawl into bed with my girlfriend."

Everyone stopped. He realized it slipped out.

Alex stood unaffected by the implication. "I'll get him home," she said reassuringly.

"Good luck," Will added as he took another drink from his beer bottle.

Alex walked to David to try to steady him. She put her arm around his waist as he draped his arm around her shoulders. Cain handed the flashlight to her and smiled.

"You guys be careful," he said.

Alex nodded and then they started toward the forest.

David really didn't have much to say as they walked the path toward the cabin. He noticed Alex stopping several times, scanning the woods with the beam of the flashlight. David wondered if the woods frightened her.

When they arrived at the cabin, she helped David to bed. She took off his jacket and tossed it onto the rocking chair. She removed his shoes, socks, and jeans next. He now lay in his boxers and a t-shirt.

"You're beautiful," he said as he turned on his side. She put the blankets over him as he continued. "And you're hot. And you're smart. God, why didn't I see it when we were kids?"

"We were kids, David," she replied. "And you're drunk right now, so you're probably seeing two of me."

"I am very drunk," he admitted. "Stay with me," he said in a more serious tone as he held out his hand. "Let me touch you again."

She climbed onto the mattress, settling down facing him. He felt her soft touch as she traced along his cheek, sending a shiver down his spine. The warmth of her lips brushed against his forehead tenderly, a gesture that filled him with comfort and reassurance. With her presence beside him, he surrendered to a peaceful, dreamless sleep.

16

Alex

The path from Hope's house to David's cabin put Alex on edge. She scanned the trees and the path carefully, shining the flashlight in various directions. Sometimes she felt as if they weren't alone. Her intuition and her heightened senses kept her on her toes.

Following her discussion with David about sex and spirituality, she pondered whether he could ever embrace her spiritual journey. She worried that his inability to grasp her beliefs might hinder his understanding of her as a whole.

In college, Alex and Hope became very close. Of course, David already knew that. What he didn't know was that Alex confided in Hope about her spiritual practices. Alex was an eclectic Wiccan. The circumstances made it much easier for Hope to tell Alex about her own gifts as well as Olivia's.

Based on the many conversations with Hope, she knew David was shut down to any type of spiritual belief system. As best she could figure, David was truly an atheist. Alex hoped that one day he would be more open to possibilities. Moreover, she wanted him to be considerate of her beliefs even if he didn't agree with or understand them. Still, she was very apprehensive. She didn't want to be accused of being crazy.

Alex celebrated all of the traditional Wiccan holidays. Out of respect for her family and others, she celebrated traditional Christian holidays as well.

As far as death and the afterlife were concerned, Alex believed that every single human being had an infinite soul and that reincarnation was not only possible, but factual. She also believed in soul recognition. She felt that souls traveled together through time, which was why she felt so close to Hope and many other people in her life. She felt that she had likely already lived many lifetimes with them.

Alex was a healer. She was well versed in energy healing as well as healing power of herbs and oils. She'd also experienced prophetic dreams at different times in her life. Alex believed that everyone possessed a core gift and that other gifts opened as the branches grew from the rooted foundation. She was mastering some of those branch gifts through meditation and self-education.

The focus of Alex's practice was on positivity. She made healing salves, medicines, and soaps. She even sold them at her aunt's metaphysical shop in town. No one knew her true beliefs, though. She kept them private. Members of the community saw her as a talented young woman who practiced holistic care, and that was exactly how she wanted to keep it.

As an eclectic Wiccan, she engaged in spell work, and she prayed she would never have to use it in a malevolent fashion. The Rule of Three taught her to be very careful. For Alex, spells were no different than praying. Both methods involved intent.

Keeping secrets… that wasn't the way she wanted to start things with David. She felt that lasting bonds were created through truth and transparency. She hoped that maybe as they grew closer she would be able to share more, but she knew she had to be patient. Patience wasn't something she'd mastered yet.

David really didn't have much to say as they continued walking the path toward the cabin. He was wobbly from drinking too much, but once they got started, he was fine. She held his hand in hers as she led him back to his place.

Although she didn't see anything out of the ordinary, something was lurking in the shadows. She could feel it. She kept a close spiritual eye out for anything that seemed out of place. When they reached the cabin, the foreboding fell away.

Once inside, Alex helped David to bed. She took off his jacket and tossed it onto the rocking chair. She removed his shoes, socks, and jeans next. He lay in his boxers and a t-shirt.

"You're beautiful," he said as he turned on his side. She put the blankets over him as he continued. "And you're hot. And you're smart. God, why didn't I see it when we were kids?"

"We were kids, David," she replied. "And you're drunk right now, so you're probably seeing two of me."

"I am very drunk," he admitted. "Stay with me," he said in a more serious tone as he held out his hand. "Let me touch you again."

She crawled atop the mattress and then lay down facing him. She caressed his cheek lightly, watching him fall asleep. She kissed his forehead and then drifted off into a dreamless sleep.

17

The next morning, Alex was the first one up. David was still passed out. She put on a pair of black leggings and one of David's t-shirts. She went to the kitchen and prepared coffee.

She didn't feel much like making breakfast. Bourbon usually took a toll on her, and eating as soon as she rolled out of bed wasn't a good idea. She opted for a nice warm shower instead.

After that, she let the dogs out and walked onto the enclosed back porch with her coffee in her hand and a warm blanket wrapped around her shoulders. Before she sat down on the wooden deck chair, she saw Hope walking out of the woods and toward the cabin. Alex waved happily and made her way to the yard, meeting Hope in the middle.

"Morning," Alex said quietly.

"Good morning. Did you have a good time last night?" Hope asked with a bright smile.

"I did. Felt like old times," she admitted. "Do you want some coffee? It's fresh."

"No thanks. Will made some along with breakfast. We've been up for a while."

Alex nodded. "Hope, do you know if there's anything fishy with the woods here?" she asked, nodding toward the forest.

"Did you feel something last night?"

"It just felt off."

"It's not the woods. It can't be. My mom and I blessed the woods when we accepted the land. I bet what you're feeling is David's doubt," she smirked. "The arguments we used to have were pretty intense at times."

"You told me, which is why I can't tell him about me," Alex admitted.

"I know it's scary. It's okay," Hope replied. She paused. "So, you guys… are you together or…?"

"I don't know. It just sort of happened. And then he used the word girlfriend last night. That threw me off a bit."

"That's how it usually starts," Hope agreed. "You are going to make each other very happy."

"I don't know. He doesn't really know anything about me. I'm so different now. I'm not a kid anymore."

"Not much scares him. Everything is more of a challenge."

"As all of the years have passed, he's always found his way back into my thoughts," Alex admitted. "It usually happened at the strangest moments. Little things reminded me of him, or he would just cross my mind for no reason."

"When Claudia told me he needed help, I jumped at the chance. It wasn't just because of our past. I really did want to get away from Richard. I have a bond with David. It doesn't hurt that he's incredibly hot, too," Alex said as her lips curled up into a bright smile.

Hope dropped her gaze and then met Alex's eyes again. "I know he is handsome. Girls used to fall all over him. He was never interested. Honestly, at one point I thought he might be gay."

"I know I've told you this over and over, but I had the biggest crush on him. It sounds so minimalistic now."

"It doesn't. You've always had a connection with him. It could be a soul recognition from a past life."

"Or it could be trauma bonding, which is not good."

"Don't get flustered. It will be much more than the physical, although that's a pretty good place to start. I don't think it's a trauma bond either."

"I don't want to come on too strong either; too needy."

"Listen to me," Hope started as she took Alex's hand, "a relationship has to be built on something. If it's sex and exploration, then so be it. But for you two, I don't think it is. You knew him long before now. Will and I started out with the physical, and that worked for us."

"But you're not serious about each other," Alex protested.

"We don't really talk about it. We probably should, but I live three and a half hours away. Long-distance relationships don't work. Will loves what he does here. I would never ask him to move."

"But he could work anywhere. He's freelance and works through contracts. Realistically, so do you."

"I think if we were to start an actual relationship, Will would feel trapped. I don't want that."

"Have you asked him what he wants?" Alex challenged.

Hope shook her head. "Well, no."

"Maybe you should."

"I don't know, Alex," she said discouragingly.

"Why are you scared? You've known him your entire life. You grew up with him. You have great sex. Do you love him?" Alex asked.

She nodded, and without hesitation she said, "I do. I always have. Since we were kids," she shrugged.

"Then you have to tell him."

"What happens then?"

"You know how I roll. I go where the moment takes me. If you want to make plans, make plans. If you want to be exclusive, be exclusive. If you want to keep things the way they are, do that, but get his input too. You're not alone in this. Maybe finding out what he wants will help you figure out what you want."

Hope nodded. "So, you've closed off the option of telling David about your beliefs, and you're giving me advice about Will?"

Alex shook her head. "You know David wouldn't understand."

"Give him time to grow. He has amazing gifts, too. He just doesn't know it yet. His determination and his incredible kindness are two of his greatest gifts. My dad doesn't have any 'abilities,' per se, but as a doctor he helps people. You don't always have to be able to see the future or talk to the dead to make a difference. Some gifts are subtle, like yours. And look at my mom and dad. Total opposites, a ten-year age difference, and she was a gifted believer. He was an atheist. They made it. I've never seen two people more in love, even still."

With a nod, Alex exhaled heavily. "Now's not the time."

"You're right. It isn't. But all healthy relationships have to have honesty. Will and I have always been honest about what we've wanted. We didn't expect to fall in love. That wasn't the plan. So, I guess I need to be honest with him about my feelings, right? Because I am madly in love with him," she said with a shrug.

"You should tell him what's going on."

"One day you'll be able to tell David everything about yourself. Give it time. Be patient."

"I don't do patient," Alex bit out as she looked down at the ground.

"I know," Hope concluded as she dropped Alex's hand. "I've got to get back. We'll talk soon, okay?"

"Of course," Alex concluded.

Hope walked back into the woods, leaving Alex alone with her thoughts and uncertainties.

18

Alex packed her laptop everywhere. So, after retrieving it from her car, she spent the rest of the morning on the back porch working. The day grew older, and by 1 p.m. she heard David rooting around in the kitchen. She closed her laptop and placed it on the empty chair beside her. As she passed through the mudroom, she could already smell a fresh pot of coffee brewing.

She stood in the doorway between the kitchen and mudroom.

"You hungry?" she asked.

"I am," he nodded as he turned and smiled. "You look good in my clothes," he remarked.

"I hope you don't mind."

"Not at all," he said. He poured the coffee into his mug. "Why don't you hang out with me today? We can spend the day together, maybe watch a movie and talk?"

"I don't want to crowd you," she admitted as she walked to the counter.

He seductively walked to her. "I want you to crowd me, Miss Ritezal," he said as he leaned down and kissed her lips. "Stay with me today," he implored.

She didn't want to leave, but she was trying to exercise some kind of restraint.

He lifted her off the ground. She felt his palms under her bottom, and she wrapped her legs around his waist. He carried her into his bedroom and gently put her on the bed.

"I thought you were hungry," she said as she looked up at him.

"Oh, I am," he said, pulling her leggings off her body.

Alex rested on the bed as David crawled to her and lay on his stomach. He traced a line up her inner thigh with his nose.

"Take the shirt off," he said. "I want to see all of you."

Alex pulled the t-shirt over her head and lay completely naked before him.

Relaxation settled on her first. It was so different to be with someone who actually took their time with her. She closed her eyes as she soaked in the sensations of his hands caressing her legs, the light kisses on them, and the nuzzle of his nose opening her up.

She felt his mouth brush against her slightly as he then focused on kissing her thighs once again.

"You're teasing me," she whispered.

"I am," he said between kisses. "I want to make you cum this way."

He spread her apart with his fingers and licked her teasingly. Then it was back to her thighs, but this time he inserted his fingers into her, and with that sensation, she arched her back slightly.

As he played with her, his tongue found its way back to her.

She held tightly to the sheets, her body inching toward the edge. Then he stopped. He went back to kissing her thighs.

He put his hands on her breasts and teased her nipples, all while kissing, nuzzling, and licking her. "Tell me what I need to do to get you there," he said with anticipation.

She caught her breath. “No one has ever gotten me off with oral,” she admitted.

“Your body is sacred to me. Understanding what you like and what you want is my job as your lover,” he said. He wasn’t trying to be poetic. He was simply being honest.

She felt fire race through her body with those words and became even more aroused.

“I’m going to study you like a book,” he promised. “My body is yours to explore, too.”

He refocused and went back to her, using his fingers and tongue to pleasure her. His tongue flicked against her gently, side to side. The motion of his fingers stayed consistent. He moaned every now and then, causing a slight vibration. It felt good and intensified the overall sensation. Again, she felt the edge growing closer. She shifted her hips, gripped the sheets even harder, and opened her mouth slightly. The pleasured moans became louder as David continued.

Closer and closer, she surged toward climax. The energy radiated from her. Finally, she felt it, sweet release. She moaned loudly as she came. She called his name as she tightened around his fingers. He didn’t stop. With each motion, each lick, he prolonged her orgasm. She was locked into it, enjoying every single second. He reached up, tweaked her nipples, and intensified the flames that were already consuming her body.

She felt herself relax finally as he slowed his touches. He kissed just above her pubic hair. Her breathing calmed after a few moments. He stood and inched out of his sweats. Their eyes met, and she knew it wasn’t over. He wanted her again. She pushed up further onto the mattress as he knelt between her legs. He guided himself into her and moved slowly.

Their eyes locked as he steadied himself on his elbows and touched her face. He kissed her neck and collarbone.

"You feel so good," she whispered.

She touched his face. In his eyes, she found a part of herself that had surely been missing all of these years. She was going to fall, and it was senseless to fight against it. Nothing about it felt like surrender. It felt like decision.

He was making love to her. She knew the difference. It was slow and systematic. He raised up and steadied himself on his knees. He pulled her feet to his chest, still moving into her. He turned his head and kissed her toes, his hands resting on her outer thighs.

They were melting into one another. It was the most sensual experience she believed she had ever had. She had never been treated this way. It had never felt this good.

"I want you to cum again," he admitted as he thrust into her harder. His movements were so deliberate. She could see he needed release, too.

"I don't have to," she said softly.

"I need you to cum again," he implored.

He began moving quicker. He placed his thumb on her clit and made circles. His lips on her feet, his hands on her body, and the thrusts pushed her there. She felt the familiar bliss overtake her as she released again.

His chest muscles tightened, and she could see he was going to finish with her. His eyes closed, and he groaned, still moving with her. Both of his hands rested on her inner thighs now, and his grip strengthened. She saw it happen. The energy released from his body, and his breath became heavier. His heart chakra glowed brightly as she watched him. She didn't see it as a sign or a message, only a moment of connection.

Gradually, he calmed and rested beside her, both of them breathless and gazing up at the ceiling as the fan rained cool air down onto their overheated, bare bodies. Neither of them rushed to define what it meant.

Alex looked over at David. She shifted to her side. "My body is sacred to you?"

"Absolutely," he answered as he met her gaze.

David turned on his side as well. He caressed her arm and then touched her face. "I told you that I will study you. I'll learn your subtle movements, your sounds, the cadence of your breath. I'll learn what will get you there quickly and when I can take my time. I'll learn what it means when you shift your hips. I'll learn to give you what you want, and you won't even have to open your mouth to ask."

She smiled. The depth of his words resonated with her. She still knew some truths required time, not confession.

"Lovemaking is an art. Of course, I'll fuck you whenever you want me to, however you want me to, but the buildup to the actual act, that's where it's at. That's the best part of lovemaking."

"You know that I will reciprocate, right?"

"You will, but I want the opportunity to memorize you first. I take pleasure in getting you off. I don't feel right about getting off if you don't."

"Well, I'm a giver, too, so how are we going to work this out?"

He leaned over and kissed her softly. "I think we'll figure it out."

19

After tidying up and dressing themselves, they settled into the living room, engaging in conversation. As Alex listened to him recount the adventures he'd had in the years they'd been apart, she realized quickly that falling in love with him would be as easy as breathing.

The hours passed by quickly. Soon it was time for Alex to return home and ready herself for the work week. David walked her to her car. She leaned against it, enveloped in the moment.

He smiled as he gently touched her cheek. "This was one of the best weekends of my life," he said as he leaned in and kissed her forehead.

"You are very sentimental. I like it. You have depth."

"I'm just being honest," he assured her.

"Well, I had an incredible time with you," she said.

"You still have the entire week off if you want to take it," he reminded her.

"I thought we had to meet with the agency tomorrow about Carleigh's debacle."

"I can handle it if you want to take tomorrow to yourself. After all of the extracurricular activities this weekend, you might need to recover," he joked.

"You think you're just too much for me, don't you?" she laughed.

"Naaa. I'm just kidding."

They embraced.

"Drive safely, please," David said.

Alex pulled away. "I'll text you when I get home."

"Okay."

Alex settled into her car, the engine purring to life as she navigated down the lane, disappearing from view. With each mile that passed, she found herself enveloped in David's lingering scent, a tangible reminder of the moments they had shared together.

As the road stretched out before her, she couldn't shake the incredulity that swirled within her. She had found her way back to him after all this time. It was a beautiful twist of fate, a serendipitous journey guided by the unseen hand of destiny, or at least that's how it felt in that moment.

20

David

September passed into October, and Alex was adjusting to her new responsibilities as David's partner in the firm. She fit right in. David added Alex to the Children Services contract, and after shadowing him for a couple of weeks, she took many of the juvenile cases off of his shoulders. She also worked on wills and estates, leaving divorces and domestic cases to David.

Alex often spent time at David's place, but he hadn't yet visited hers. Uncertain whether he would appreciate her environment, she held back from extending an invitation. In her spare room, she meticulously arranged her oils, herbs, and equipment for making medicine, with her altar nearby, symbolizing her spiritual devotion.

Their shared moments were rich with laughter and profound discussions, nurturing a connection that surpassed mere physicality. As their intimacy grew and evolved, both Alex and David quickly recognized that their bond transcended surface-level attraction.

It was a Saturday morning. David got up early to meet volunteers and staff for the yearly fundraising festival for the animal shelter. He let Alex sleep. He knew she would be meeting up with him at the fairgrounds later to assist with the festival activities.

A surprise party was planned for that evening. Alex's father was turning sixty. Although she would be helping at the fairgrounds, she would be expected to spend most of the day decorating the community center for her dad's party. Luckily, friends and family would be able to help. David felt terrible that he couldn't, but the Fall Festival had been planned for months.

Adoption after adoption and game after game, the children and families of the small town gathered to enjoy the day. Joan and Will helped, of course, and Hope made sure she manned some of the games as well.

By 3 p.m., the crowd was still surprisingly large. The event was bigger than the year before. David was very pleased by the turnout. Hope sat down beside David at the registration table.

"Do you still want to have lunch tomorrow?" he asked.

"Absolutely. I've missed my big brother!"

Hope got a glazed look on her face.

"What's wrong?" David asked.

"Your girlfriend just got here."

"How do you know?" David said, looking around for her.

"Because I can feel her energy."

"Oh Christ," he whispered. "Here we go."

But there she was, walking toward them, smiling warmly with her hands tucked in the front of her blue hoodie. Her cheeks were pink from the cool, crisp fall air. Her hair was up in a neat ponytail. She wore a pair of bootcut jeans and brown hiking boots.

"Hey guys," she said as she approached.

"Hey girl," Hope said as she stood and walked around the table, offering a very friendly embrace.

"Are you and Will coming tonight?" Alex asked.

"We wouldn't miss it. Six-thirty, right?"

"Yes. Penny will bring him in at seven. She told him some story about taking him to a fancy dinner on the river."

"We will be there," Hope said as she gave her a kiss on the cheek and then walked away.

David stood up, beaming. "Hey you."

"Hi," she answered bashfully.

"You were asleep, so I…"

"I know. I felt you leave," she stated.

"You did?"

She only nodded.

"So, everything ready for your dad's party?"

"Yes. If it weren't for all of the help, I'd still be there. How are things going here?"

"Really well."

"There are a lot of people here," she observed.

"The turnout is much better than last year," he remarked. He paused for a moment and then continued. "Would you be okay with me staying at your place tonight since we'll already be in town for your dad's party?"

Seeming surprised by his boldness, she stammered for a moment and then answered, "You want to stay at my place?"

"Well, we've been staying out at the cabin a lot, and I just figured it would be easier to crash at your place since we'll already be so close by."

"That makes sense."

"Okay. Sounds like a plan. I need to run to the cabin and pick up my clothes, but I can come over dressed and ready to go."

"Okay," she said.

"I'm meeting Hope for lunch tomorrow afternoon."

"Brother and sister time," she replied.

David stood up and leaned over the table. She leaned into him.

"I love the way you look in those jeans," he whispered.

She smiled and blushed. "Why thank you, Mr. Gregory."

"You're welcome, Miss Ritezal."

David kissed her lips gently, but the moment was quickly stolen by Will.

"Hey you two, no PDA! There are kids here," he joked as he approached.

"You are insane, Will," Alex protested.

"Certifiable," he agreed as he smiled. "Hope and I are coming tonight."

"I know. She told me."

"Open bar and naked women? Anyone popping out of a cake?" he asked.

"Yes to the alcohol, and no to the naked women. My dad will be sixty. I think a stripper would give him heart failure."

"Ah, damn. Strippers are always good. I don't care how old you are."

Alex just shook her head.

"So, where do you need me?" she asked David. "How can I help?"

"We'll actually be closing things down in about an hour, so if you want to walk around and mingle, you can."

"Mingling isn't really my thing. Do you want me to sit with you and help you with paperwork?"

"Sure."

"Well, mingling is my thing," Will concluded. "I will catch up with you two later," he said as he walked away.

After shuffling through all of the applications, David knew that the workers for the shelter would be very busy doing follow-up visits. He was very pleased with how things turned out this year.

"You have a gift, David," Alex observed. "As oppositional as you are to spirituality, you possess the gift of compassion. It is a gift that can elude many of us at times."

He looked at her and wondered how long she'd been staring at him. "I just do what's right."

"That's what makes you so wonderful," she added. "Your soul is beautiful."

David felt immense joy seeing her at the festival, knowing how important it was to him, and her presence there supporting him meant the world. As the event wound down, it was time to transition to their next activity. David returned to the cabin, swapping his attire for a snug pair of jeans and a gray scoop-neck sweater that accentuated his physique. Completing his look with black chukka boots, he styled his hair with precision, trimming his goatee for a polished appearance.

Meanwhile, Alex spent some time around the house, opting to close the spare room door, avoiding a conversation she wasn't yet prepared for. Selecting a short black wool skirt and coordinating it with black tights and her favorite knee-high black boots, she settled on a red V-neck angora sweater, a departure from her usual style. Tying her hair up in a messy bun, wisps framing her face and neckline, she adorned herself with simple diamond earrings and a signature necklace, completing her ensemble effortlessly.

As David arrived and rang the doorbell, anticipation filled him as he heard footsteps approaching. Upon seeing Alex when she opened the door, he was struck by her beauty, momentarily tempted to forgo their plans and simply stay in.

"Come in," she said as she opened the screen door. As he walked into the living room, the smell of nutmeg surrounded him.

"I have a few things to finish up. If you want something to drink, grab something," she said as she retreated into what he could only assume was the bathroom.

David stood in the living area, wandering around. He took note of photographs sitting around the little cottage. He also noticed the artwork on the walls. There were landscapes on canvas.

Shortly, Alex emerged again. David looked at her, his eyes moving up and down her body. "You look really hot," he said as he walked toward her.

"Thank you. You look very handsome too, Mr. Gregory."

As he stood before her, a savage passion reflected in his eyes. "You are so very tempting," he admitted.

David was completely oblivious to the rush of insecurity Alex felt about him being in her house. He didn't realize that the wheels in her mind were spinning. She was very on edge.

21

Arriving promptly at 6:30, the room buzzed with conversation as loved ones and guests gathered. The room was bright, the fluorescents reflecting off the old cream-colored tile flooring. The table with the cake had a vegetable and meat tray along with several crock pots. Champagne glasses sat on the tables, and beautiful centerpieces made with baby blue gossamer and white roses brought an elegant feel to such a commonplace venue. Alex and her family had truly outdone themselves with the decorations.

When Alex entered, her foster brother Ben rushed to her. A tall, thin ginger-haired man with crystal blue eyes and wire-rimmed glasses, he was a nurse practitioner by trade. He worked at a local clinic, but he loved helping with research any chance he could. Besides the fact that he was openly gay and married to the love of his life, Jeremy, he was Alex's best friend.

Ben's lifestyle was certainly out of the norm in the small town. His inability to fit in nearly broke him as a young man. He beat to his own drum, and eventually didn't give a damn if anyone approved of his orientation. Thankfully, over the years, the ridicule had diminished. Now he was a well-respected physician in the community. He didn't get as much resistance or awkward glances from folks now.

After a warm embrace, Alex smiled at David. "You remember Ben?"

"Of course, I do," David said, offering his hand.

Ben obliged with a warm smile. "So good to see you, David," he said thoughtfully. "I saw Hope and Will. They're around here somewhere. I don't know what you are doing to my sister here, but my God, you've just knocked her off her pretty feet! She is damn-near glowing."

"Ben!" Alex rebuked.

David was amused by her obvious embarrassment. It was very unusual to see her turn so many shades of red. She almost matched the color of her sweater.

"Well, she certainly is a mysterious creature, but well worth the exploration," David remarked sensually.

"Oh my," Ben said as he fanned himself. "Feel that heat? You two may need a private soiree in the restroom this evening if you keep that shit up." He concluded with a smile and a wink.

"Ben, you're so scandalous," Alex said with a chuckle.

"I know," he said with attitude. "Isn't it great?" He paused and looked around. "I'm gonna go socialize. I'll catch you two kids later."

As they walked around the room, Alex introduced David to countless other family members. Knowing most of them made it easier, but it was nice to be reminded of just how wonderful they all were.

Hope and Will made sure that they were also accounted for as they offered warm hugs to both David and Alex. Joan wasn't able to make it. Her husband caught a stomach bug and wasn't up for an evening out.

Ben whistled. Everyone turned to look at him. "They're here, everyone. Places!" he said.

Everyone gathered into groups and hunkered down. A stillness fell on the room. Jeremy was standing by the lights, anticipating his part in the celebration.

Penny and Russell argued outside the large double doors. He complained about being blindfolded and wondering "where the hell" he was. She pushed open the doors, ripped the blindfold off, the lights came on, and everyone jumped up yelling, "Surprise!"

Startled but happy, he smiled. "You guys!" he shouted.

Alex left David's side and ran to her father, throwing her arms around his neck.

"Was this your idea, young lady?" he asked.

"It was mine, Penny's, and Ben's," she replied.

He shook his head. "You all and your secrets!"

David approached, smiling graciously.

Russell held out his hand. "David Gregory, how have you been, son?"

"Good, sir. Very good."

"You don't have to call me 'sir.' I've known you too long for that sort of thing," he said politely.

He nodded acceptingly. "Well, happy birthday, Russell."

"Thank you. You sure do have my Alex beaming. She just talks about you all the time."

She looked at him as if he were revealing too much and then scolded him. "Dad! Please!" she rebuked.

"I'd do anything for her," David said as he took her hand and brought it to his lips. He gave her knuckles a quick kiss and watched as she flushed scarlet again.

"I'm glad to see her so happy," Russell remarked.

Ben spoke up again. "So, everyone has an assigned table. You were given a little Post-it note with a number on it when you came in. That's your table number. The buffet is officially open, too. So serve yourself and just enjoy everybody! Happy birthday, Dad!"

The room erupted with applause. David grabbed the Post-it note from his pocket. He noted the number and took Alex's hand, leading her across the room.

22

The lights dimmed and music came over the sound system. Classic country, Frank Sinatra, Elvis, all of Russell's favorites were on the itinerary.

David and Alex were seated with Hope, Will, Ben, and Jeremy. They made conversation among themselves. Suddenly, David felt a hand on his shoulder. He looked up and saw Steven standing beside him. Courteously, he stood and offered a handshake.

"David," Steven nodded.

"Steven," he replied.

As David looked him over, there was something odd about him. He didn't look well. The pigment under his eyes was unusually dark. He was even more pale than normal, and he seemed weak, his handshake lacking strength. It had only been a few weeks since he'd seen Steven.

"You feeling okay?" David asked, releasing his hand.

"Oh yes, I'm fine. I've been fighting off some kind of bug, I think." Steven motioned for someone in the crowd and smiled. "You've met my wife, Gerri," he said.

Politely, she held out her hand to David.

"Yes, I have," he replied. "How are you, Gerri?"

"Fit as a fiddle," she answered with her heavy southern accent.

As they shook hands, Alex stood up from the table, snaking her arm around David's waist.

"And Alexandra," Gerri said, shifting her attention. "So good to see you. My, my, it's been ages."

"Hello, Gerri," Alex said, shaking her hand. Her voice was cold, and David quickly felt the tension.

Gerri's long, blonde hair lay on her shoulders, draping around her face in soft curls that framed her delicate features. Her tanned skin looked smooth and perfect, even in the dim light of the room. A bright smile played on her lips, seemingly harmless. Despite the outward warmth, David couldn't shake the feeling of an icy distance between her and Alex. The tension lingered, making the air feel noticeably colder than Gerri's sunny appearance suggested. It was a mystery to David, the subtle undercurrents and unspoken words creating a palpable chill between the two women.

Gerri wore a pair of cream-colored linen slacks, paired with a gold silk cami and a matching linen jacket. The ensemble was completed with a set of expensive pearls adorning her neck. The combination of luxurious fabrics and carefully chosen accessories made her appear very upscale, standing out noticeably from the others in attendance. However, it became increasingly apparent that she was somewhat overdressed for the occasion. While her attire exuded an air of sophistication, the casual atmosphere of the event seemed to swallow her up, creating a visual disparity that lingered.

Hope stood and interrupted. "Gerri, how are you?" she said as she held out her hand, a warm smile attempting to diffuse the tangible tension in the air. It was apparent that Hope felt the chill as well, her gesture of reaching out both literal and symbolic. She was obviously trying to rescue the situation, bridging the gap created by the unspoken tension. The room seemed to hold its breath for a moment as Gerri hesitated before accepting the handshake, the subtle exchange revealing more about the dynamics at play than words ever could.

Will stood beside Hope, seemingly salivating like a dog waiting for a pork chop. David couldn't help but observe the almost comical eagerness in Will's expression. Meanwhile, Hope, aware of the unspoken tension in the room, shot a pointed look at Will that seemed to say, you'd better put your eyes back in your head.

In response, Gerri, ever the master of social finesse, flashed a gorgeous smile at Will, giving a playful wink before redirecting her gaze to David. It was a momentary diversion, a well-executed maneuver that left a lingering impression. The subtle exchange added another layer to the intricate web of unspoken dynamics in the room.

"I'm going to get some more Champagne," Steven said. "Do you want more, dear?"

"Yes, I would. It's really quite good," she answered with a sly smile. "Your Mama certainly outdid herself with this party, Alex."

"My stepmom," she corrected.

"Oh, that's right. I forgot. Seems like Penny and your father have been together forever."

Alex didn't respond to the statement. Instead, she found David's hand and laced her fingers in his. The touch was a silent understanding, a connection that needed no words. Meanwhile, Hope had already made her way to the dance floor with Will, leaving them to navigate the subtle currents of the room on their own.

The dance floor seemed to mirror the intricate dance of emotions between Alex and David. As the music played, they were left to navigate their own private sphere, the unspoken tension and the warmth of their entwined fingers creating a unique rhythm that only they could hear.

"So, I heard you two are an item," Gerri said, still smiling at David deviously. She shifted her focus to Alex. "The most eligible bachelor in this little town and you managed to do somethin' to get his attention." David heard the sarcasm in Gerri's voice. The animosity was even clearer now, but why?

Alex nodded and spoke up. "We've been dating for a little over a month now."

"I also heard that Richard is wounded over losing you at the prosecutor's office. You must have been rather good, Alexandra."

Alex's grip tightened, and David, feeling the increasing pressure, glanced down to make sure his hand wasn't turning colors from a lack of blood flow.

"Playing the doormat to Richard wasn't my style," Alex replied, her tone sharp. "I wonder if the man has a soul," she bit out.

"Maybe you didn't get to know him as well as you should have. He's really great at his job, but sometimes people just break under the pressure," Gerri said flatly. "It happens."

The tension in the room continued to build, an atmosphere thickening like a storm forming over the ocean. David sensed the need for a break in the mounting intensity. He also wasn't going to leave Alex defenseless, although he knew she could easily defend herself.

"Alex is excellent under pressure," he interrupted, his voice calm but firm. "She has done very well thus far. I don't know what I would have done if she hadn't walked through my door." He turned to her and kissed her hair, a silent reassurance.

"Isn't that sweet?" Gerri mocked.

"And anyone who can take on that mess over at Children Services needs a medal," David added, looking down at Alex's frozen features. It was a side of her he hadn't experienced yet, serious, sullen, with a jaw set like a fortress and a body ready to attack.

The weight of the conversation hung in the air, and David couldn't help but admire the strength he saw in her, even if it came with a level of force he hadn't witnessed before. In that moment, he recognized a resilience that added a new dimension to his understanding of her character.

"So, I take it you don't like Tamara either," Gerri said.

"She's definitely a different kind of personality," Alex replied diplomatically.

"I don't care for her either. She is a vixen, thinking she has all of the assets to pursue someone like my Steven. You know she tried to break up our marriage?"

"Tamara will learn her lesson the hard way, I'm afraid," Alex remarked. "One day she will piss off the wrong family, and they will go after that agency. I dread it because then we'll have to clean up the mess."

"Maybe she needs a lesson. Might bring her down a few notches." Then Gerri sighed. "But let's not ruin this evening with more talk of that wench."

"I hear that Steven is very impressed with your abilities in the courtroom. He says nothing but nice things about you, although I think he misses the casual banter with David," she said, her eyes meeting his and then immediately shifting back to Alex.

"Alex is certainly a nose-to-the-grindstone type. She doesn't have time for meaningless chatter," David defended again. "All work when she's in the arena."

"Well, you just have to know how to deal with Steven. Alexandra, he's a teddy bear. He might put on a good show, but he melts when there's a pretty face."

Neither Alex nor David knew how to reply to such a statement. Their facial expressions mirrored the speechlessness they felt. It was as if the weight of Gerri's words had rendered them momentarily without words. In the pause that followed, the air seemed charged with unspoken thoughts and an understanding that some things were better left unsaid. Their eyes met, silently acknowledging the complexity of the situation as they navigated the uncharted waters of the conversation.

"Oh, I know he's a devil," she said. "That's why I married him. If you can tame the devil, then you may just hold all of the power in the universe, right?"

"Gold lined," Alex bit out as she took a drink of Champagne.

David looked down at her, astonished. He knew exactly what she was insinuating.

Before Gerri could come back with a crushing reply, Steven returned with the Champagne. "Darling," he said, handing her a full glass.

"Thank you," she said, giving him a quick kiss on the cheek.

"I saw Lyle. We need to go say hello," he insisted.

Gerri smiled at Alex, regarding her cautiously, and then at David. "So good to see you again, David," she concluded. "And Alexandra, you be good now. Stay out of trouble. And good luck taming your devils, darlin'."

23

Alex sat down, red-faced and brooding, her jaw still stiff. Even in the low light, David saw a notable difference in the shade of her eyes. The spark that usually danced within them seemed dimmed, replaced by a stormy intensity. The air around her crackled with unresolved energy, leaving David to wonder how deep the currents of her emotions ran. As the subdued ambiance of the room enveloped them, he couldn't shake the feeling that the atmosphere had shifted and that the repercussions of the conversation lingered in the unspoken spaces between them.

"Are you okay?" he asked as he sat down beside her.

"I'm fine," she nodded.

"You're lying," he pushed.

She shook her head. "She reminds me of a viper."

"Are you jealous?"

"Absolutely not," she said in protest.

He heard the offense in her tone. "I didn't mean to insinuate that you were less than."

"I know what you meant. I'm sorry for my reaction to all of this. She can be rather intimidating to most. She doesn't do that to me. She just pisses me off."

"Is there some bad blood or something between you?"

"My brother."

"Marvin?"

"Yes. I'd rather not discuss it right now if you don't mind."

"No, no. I don't mind. I understand."

"Simply put, she's a gold-digger, and I don't trust her as far as I could throw a bull by the ass. She makes my stomach turn."

"How about I take you out on that dance floor and get your mind back where it needs to be?"

"And where should my mind be?" she asked as she looked over at David.

"On me, of course," he replied as he stood and took her hand.

After leading her through the crowd of people, they found themselves on the dance floor, swaying and twirling to the music. Finally, a slow song played, setting a perfect rhythm for the quiet connection they shared. Alex rested her head on his shoulder, and he reveled in the warmth of her presence. Her body felt like a perfect fit against his, and the fragrance of her perfume hung in the air, a subtle yet intoxicating scent that aroused his senses.

He kissed her hair, savoring the moment and the shared dance. The music surrounded them, creating a bubble where time seemed to slow and the outside world faded away, leaving only the two of them caught in the gentle embrace of the dance.

Alex looked up at him, her eyes locking with his. "I want you," she whispered.

The words hung in the air, a declaration of desire that sent a thrilling shiver down David's spine. In that simple utterance, the world around them seemed to fade, leaving only the intensity between them.

The music played on, a perfect backdrop to the charged atmosphere, as they continued to sway in the dance, lost in the shared moment of longing and anticipation.

“You want me?” he replied quietly.

“Yes.”

She stopped dancing and took his hand, leading him into the hallway. Ben may have been onto something earlier when he mentioned the soiree in the restroom.

24

There were four restrooms in the building. Three of them were private bathrooms requiring a key for entrance. They had sofas and vanities.

Alex took a key from her cleavage, still leading David down the hallway. They stood in front of a doorway. Alex put the key in and turned the knob. She pushed open the door and pulled David inside.

As they entered the dark, tiled room, their mouths locked together in quick, passionate kisses. The air between them crackled with anticipation as David flipped on the light, the room instantly bathed in a soft glow. With a swift motion, he kicked the door shut, the click of the lock sealing them in a cocoon of desire.

Kiss after passionate kiss, the blood inside their veins ran hot. In that private space, the world outside ceased to exist, and the anticipation rose with every shared breath and tender touch.

"I've never fucked in a public place," he admitted.

"No one will bother us here," Alex assured him.

Leaving his mouth for only a moment, Alex unzipped his pants and pulled them down a little. He pulled her skirt up only to find that her tights weren't tights at all. They were thigh-high stockings with a garter belt holding them on. She wasn't wearing underwear.

"You don't have panties on, Miss Ritezal," he whispered.

"Very astute observation, Mr. Gregory," she replied with a smile in her voice.

David guided her to the sofa, their eyes never breaking contact. She lay down and spread her legs apart. His fingers traced down her thighs and then found his target. The sweet warmth made him smile.

"Ready for me so soon?"

"Fuck me," she whispered as their eyes locked.

He pushed into her, watching her head fall back as the sensation rushed through both of them. His thrusts were quick and deliberate. He knew it wouldn't take long.

This was different for them. For the last month, they had always taken their time with one another. The deliberate touches and endless study of their bodies usually consumed them for hours. This encounter would have to be enough for now.

He kissed the crook of her neck, feeling her tighten quickly around him.

"Come on, baby. That's right. Come for me," he whispered into her ear. "Let me feel you."

He felt the solid grip of her hands on his arms as he pushed into her harder and faster. She watched as her eyes closed, and she bit her lip, trying to silence herself as she squeezed around him.

Her release pushed him right over the edge of bliss as he found himself in the throes of a breathless climax. He slowed his pace, trying desperately to get his bearings.

Leaning over her, and still inside her, he kissed her lips softly. They were motionless for a moment, their foreheads touching.

He looked into her eyes, completely captivated by her. "You amaze me, Alex."

She beamed and cupped his cheek with her hand.

"I owe you a longer session later," he said.

Her eyebrows furrowed and her nose crinkled with confusion.

"Quickies are great, but the way we are with each other, the time we take with one another… I prefer that. I'm sensual, I guess," he explained as he kissed her forehead again.

"I adore the way you are," she assured him. "I thought this would be fun, something different. I'm a little adventurous, I guess."

He stood, finally calm. He pulled his pants up over his hips and zipped them.

"I like the spontaneity. Again, your boldness is showing, and that gets me every time."

Offering his hand, he helped Alex up from the couch. She stood before him, straightening her skirt. He admired her appearance as she turned to look in the mirror. Polishing her appearance, she smiled at him in the looking glass.

"I love it when you smile," he remarked. "And when your face is flushed from sex," he concluded with a wink.

"You have that power over me," she admitted.

He kissed the back of her neck.

"You sure you don't want to go home yet?" he said, insinuating he was ready for another round.

"Let's stay for a little longer, and then we can take this up where we left off," she suggested.

"Fair enough," he agreed.

25

They arrived at Alex's cottage around 9:30 p.m. They walked in through the front door, and Alex closed it behind them. She stood against the wall and unzipped her boots, tossing them to the side.

"Is it okay if I stay with you?" David asked sheepishly.

"Of course, it is," she answered, hiding the apprehension in her voice.

"Do you mind if I get a shower? I have some spare clothing in the trunk."

"Sure. I will go to the basement bathroom and shower. You can use the master bath," she replied.

"You don't have to…"

"It's okay. The basement has a really nice stand-up shower. I don't mind," she promised.

After David's shower, he put on a pair of gray sweatpants and a white V-neck T-shirt. He roamed around the cottage for a moment, observing the place closely. Alex's home was tidy. Everything was in its place. Her bedroom was rather small, but the cottage itself wasn't very large.

As he stood at the mantle looking at the array of photographs, a sound from the spare bedroom caught his attention. It was a bell. It immediately put David on alert. He worried that someone had gotten into the house. He was fully prepared to defend Alex and her home as he made his way to the closed door.

Cautiously, he turned the knob and pushed the door open. He flipped on the light. There were no intruders. Instead, he saw a very large antique-style desk. There were several cabinets with glass doors. They were filled with vials, amber bottles, small baskets with lids, and other things he couldn't quite describe.

On one side of the room was a medium-sized, waist-high table with an herb garden sitting on it under a lamp. The aroma of various plants filled the air, creating a subtle, earthy fragrance. Some plants hung gracefully from the ceiling, while others were placed in large pots and smaller containers on tables.

The sound of something falling over caught his attention. Looking toward the bedroom door, he saw hanging on the wall a canvas painting of the same symbol inside Alex's necklace. Beneath it was a small table, a purple velvet tablecloth draped over it. A statue sat in the middle. To the right of the statue was a white used candle. To the left of the statue was a bowl with what looked like herbs in it. Close to the bowl lay a small brass hand bell lying on its side. In front of the statue was an incense holder. A small wooden carving of a wolf sat next to the statue. Underneath the table was a book bound in leather, its binding adorned with different colored stones, each surely telling a story of their own.

The room held an air of mystery, with every item seeming to carry a significance known only to its creator. David found himself intrigued by the rich tapestry of elements that ornamented Alex's private space, each revealing a layer of her that he had yet to discover. However, he also felt apprehensive.

He had very strong feelings about spirituality, and most of those feelings were very negative. He knew Alex had hidden this part of herself from him, and he felt somewhat betrayed. He wondered how he could truly know her if she was holding these sorts of things back from him. He had been open and honest about everything with her. The hurt swelled within him.

He heard her feet on the basement stairs as she ascended to the ground level. Her footsteps hastened toward the hallway and then to her bedroom. Clearly, she hadn't discovered where David was. When she did, she immediately appeared in the bedroom doorway wearing her blue terrycloth bathrobe.

"What is this?" he asked, unable to hide the hurt and anger in his voice.

Alex's mouth hung open. "It's my hobby room," she replied.

"What's this?" he said, pointing at the table.

She sighed and walked to the desk chair, absently setting the bell upright as she passed by. Turning the chair around so she could face David, she sat down. "It's a Pagan altar," she answered without hesitation.

"Are you a witch?" he asked pointedly.

"I guess you could say that I am," she shrugged. He could see that she wasn't going to lie. Her eyes were set. She wasn't one to shy away from a confrontation.

The room held a charged silence as David grappled with the newfound knowledge, and Alex sat there, her honesty a stark contrast to the secrets the room had held. The revelation hung heavy in the air, and the moment called for a conversation that would unravel the intricacies of their relationship.

"Have you been a witch for a long time?" he asked as he pulled up an empty chair from the corner of the room.

"I've been practicing since I was very young. My mom and aunt taught me everything," a heavy sigh accompanying the words. "This room is my sanctuary, David. It's the one place I can be who I am. The place where I don't have to hide. I can be free here. It's a sacred space to me," she explained.

"Do you sacrifice living things?" he asked, astonishment in his tone.

"Of course not. I don't eat babies either," she said with an eye roll. "I'm a healer. I believe in the sanctity of life. I'm an eclectic Wiccan, not a savage."

He stared blankly.

"Look, I know how you feel about spirituality. I know that you used to get really angry at Hope when she was open about her gift. You closed yourself off to all of that. I knew I couldn't tell you yet."

"You lied to me. In a relationship, you share everything. You talk. You listen. You communicate. You give me the chance to form my own opinion and reach my own conclusions. You denied me that," he argued.

"Would you rather me have told you the moment you asked about my necklace? Because I don't think that would have gone very well given your history with Hope," she rebuked.

He sighed. "I want to know all of you. Even if I don't understand it."

"You used to get so angry. How was I to know you would be accepting of my beliefs, my calling? I wasn't there for any of those arguments, but Hope was one of my closest friends in college. The level of disrespect you had for her practices and her gifts was always incredibly intense. I didn't want you to hate me for who I am."

He got up and walked to her, kneeling before her. He cupped her face in his hands. "I could never hate you," he assured her. "I just know how important transparency is. We talked about that the first time we slept together."

Tears welled in her eyes. "I didn't know how to share this part of myself with you, so I just didn't. It was wrong, I know. I'm so sorry." A tear found its way down her cheek. David immediately brushed it away.

"There's a difference between you and Hope. You aren't pushy with what you practice. She totally is," he smiled.

Taking in a deep breath, he exhaled a sigh. He found that he was curious about this revelation. Maybe if he understood it, he wouldn't be so hurt. Knowledge was power, after all.

"So, as a Wiccan, what do you do? What does that mean?" he asked as he turned and pulled the chair to Alex. He sat down, intent on listening and asking questions.

"I can only speak for myself because I don't do what everyone else does. I celebrate the Pagan holidays. I honor nature and the phases of the moon."

"Alex, I was raised in a very odd family setting. You know that. I had no choice but to try to understand, but I didn't want it forced on me. That was my issue with the entire thing. I don't believe the way they believe. I don't believe there is anything out there that gives us any kind of power or abilities or that guides our life."

"You don't believe that the gifts your mom and your sisters have are real? After what you've seen Oliva do? After you have seen what Hope and your mom can do? You still don't believe? Because what's the alternative of not believing? Are they delusional? Mentally ill?"

He shrugged. "I don't know. Maybe they are. I have been honest with myself over the years. I don't believe that there is any part of me that will ever truly understand any of it, and I don't even know if I want to."

"I understand. Religious trauma is a thing. Most of the time it comes from the direction of Christian practices, but I suppose it can be brought on by other practices as well," Alex admitted.

"I guess I was traumatized. Everything was pushed on me. At every turn, everything was about Hope's abilities and her 'gifts,'" he said with air quotes. "Mom was a little less heavy with it. Oliva never talked about her gifts much. Hope drove me crazy with it."

"I don't believe it is my place to convert people. I believe that everyone has to forge their own path."

He leaned forward and placed his elbows on his knees. He took her hands into his and looked into her eyes. "You have to promise me something. No matter what, you have to be honest with me. I will always be honest with you, even if I'm afraid. Can you please do the same? Trust is so important to me. I know my history with my sister made it hard, but you have to talk to me."

She nodded. "I promise I will be open with you."

"I believe that when you love someone, you should accept all of them, not just the pieces you like. I believe in investing in the whole person," he clarified.

She smiled, tears still streaming down her face. "I've loved you since we were kids. I've dreamed of you and wanted you for as long as I can remember."

"Look," he continued with a comforting smile. "You're my best friend, Alex. We've got history, and even if we didn't, I would still honor your autonomy."

He brushed the tears from her cheeks again and kissed her forehead.

"I love you, David, more than you could possibly know."

"I love you, too," he replied, pulling her into an embrace.

26

David sat across from Hope as they drank coffee at her kitchen table. The distance in his eyes must have been obvious because Hope rescued him, as usual.

"What is it, David?" she asked curiously.

"I know about Alex," he replied blankly.

"What do you mean?" she asked.

"She is a practicing witch. I found everything in her spare room."

"Wow. How did that conversation go?"

"I felt betrayed. She basically lied to me. A lie of omission is still a lie," he said as he took a sip of coffee.

"She was afraid to tell you. She was scared you would never be able to understand, that you wouldn't accept her."

"That's basically what she told me."

"So, did you break up with her?"

He shot a disapproving glance at her. "Of course not. We talked everything through."

She smiled slyly.

"What?" he asked.

"You're changing," she observed.

"She means everything to me. I've fallen in love with her so incredibly fast. She's easy to love, though."

"She is a wonderful person. She has a beautiful light."

"I have never felt about anyone the way I feel about Alex."

"She is your twin flame, dare I say, your soulmate?"

"We are definitely compatible," he said as he remembered their encounter in the restroom during her dad's party. "When we first got together, she alluded to the fact that sex was spiritual for her."

"It is very spiritual. It has to do with chakras. Besides that, touch transfer is the most intimate way you can bond with someone."

"What the fuck is a chakra?"

"Did she tell you she is a Reiki practitioner?"

"No. I don't even know what that means."

"Well, a Reiki practitioner uses a massage table most of the time, but they can do a treatment from a distance if need be."

He thought for a moment. He did remember seeing what looked like a massage table propped up against the wall in the room.

"Everyone has chakras. Right down the middle of your body, you have energy wheels. When she does Reiki, she focuses on those points in the person to encourage healing. When she has sex with you and tells you that it's spiritual, believe her. She is connecting to your chakras, and perhaps to your very soul."

"Christ, here we go," he said angrily.

David took another drink of coffee. “And what about Will? You’re spiritual. How have you managed to avoid that kind of connection with him?”

“I have really had to shield myself. It’s been terribly difficult. I know who he is. I know how he is. I don’t want to get hurt. I don’t know if I would ever be enough for him.”

“He’s in love with you,” David said matter-of-factly.

“No, he isn’t,” she argued.

“Yeah, he is!”

“You claim to be a psychic, and you can’t even see when a man loves you. That’s bad,” David scoffed.

“Shut up!” she bit out. With a pause, she looked back up at him. “He loves me?” she asked timidly.

“Yes, he does. Are you blind?” He took a deep breath. “Does he know everything you can do… spiritually, I mean?”

“He knows everything about me. I’ve hidden nothing. He’s also known me since I was a kid, so he knew before we ever got involved with one another.” She stood, taking her cup of coffee with her. Suddenly, David observed her body stiffen.

“What’s wrong?” he asked with concern in his voice.

She shook her head. “Something’s coming.”

“Don’t, Hope. Just don’t,” he said as he threw up his hand impatiently.

“I’m not saying anything else. I just know that there’s something coming. There’s a test you’re both going to have to pass.”

"Okay, time to change the subject," he remarked sharply. "Why doesn't she like Gerri? Have you noticed the tension there?" he asked.

"Gerri is a bitch. She's not a good person."

David laughed. "She's a gold digger, but that doesn't mean she's evil."

"I think you need to ask Alex why she doesn't like her. What I can tell you is that Alex doesn't trust easily, and sometimes her radar goes off around certain people. She has a strong intuition, David. It's a branch gift. It serves her very well and has most of her life," she explained.

"I know I'm going to regret this, but what is a branch gift?"

"She is a healer above all else, so that's her foundational gift. It's the gift her soul came into this lifetime with. From that root system comes growth. We learn other things as we live our lives and delve into spiritual work. If I dropped my shield, I could easily see what's coming, but I've learned how to turn it on and off. A branch gift of mine is reading tarot. It took practice. My ability to touch people and see things comes naturally. I didn't have to work at that. Alex likely had to practice the art of intuition, and anything outside of her healing abilities."

David looked down at the liquid swirling around in the ceramic mug. "Has she ever been involved with anyone who has her same gifts, or at least believes the way she does?"

"That's something I think you need to talk to her about."

"So, she has," he assumed.

"Like I said, ask her. She will be open now that she isn't afraid."

27

David walked back to the cabin and immediately made his way to the loft. He sat down at his desk and began researching words like “Reiki” and “chakras.” He investigated shielding and read up on various abilities. He researched Paganism and witchcraft.

Based on deductive reasoning, he knew someone else had come before him. She must have had a spiritual connection with someone else. He wondered why it hadn’t lasted and how it was different from what they had. He wanted answers.

He took his phone into his hand and texted her. *Can I come over?*

Less than five minutes passed. His phone vibrated with a reply. *Of course.*

He drove to her house, parked, and got out. He walked to the front door, and she was there to greet him. He leaned down to kiss her lips gently.

“How was the visit with Hope?” she asked as she shut the door behind him.

David walked to the living room sofa and sat down. He took note of Alex’s appearance. She wore a pair of black leggings, what appeared to be a gray T-shirt, an apron, and a handkerchief on her head. The leggings hugged her figure comfortably, and the gray T-shirt hinted at an effortless, laid-back style. The apron suggested she might have been busy with some culinary pursuits, and the handkerchief added a touch of practicality, keeping her hair out of the way.

"Coffee with Hope was good." He paused momentarily. "What have you been doing?"

"I was making some soaps and some medicines for the shop. I have some products that are on backorder, so I'm finding recipes to make my own ingredients. It isn't hard. I just need to make sure I have the right supplies," she explained.

She made her way to the sofa and sat down beside him. "What's going on?" she asked.

"How many people have you been intimate with?" he asked bluntly.

"Making out or having sex with?"

"Sex. If I counted all of the people I made out with, I would be ashamed to tell you," he clarified.

"I've been with six people. How many people have you slept with?"

"Four. That's how I figured out one-night stands weren't my thing. One of those was a relationship. The others weren't." He paused for a brief second. "And out of those six people, have you ever had a spiritual connection with any of them?"

"One. Although you are the most spiritually connected I've ever felt to anyone."

"Will you tell me about that relationship?" he asked.

"If you'd like. Why is this bothering you?"

"I just want to know."

She inhaled sharply and seemed to hold her breath. "I was in college. He was my Cultural Studies professor. He was tall, broad-shouldered, had a ginger beard, light brown hair, and the strangest hazel eyes I had ever seen."

"So, he was much older?"

She nodded. "I was nineteen years old. He was in his early thirties," she replied. "Not married. No kids."

"So, no attachments."

"None." She continued. "The cultural studies class was an elective. I figured it would be interesting, especially given my spiritual preferences. He and I sat and talked for hours after class. After his grades were submitted and the semester ended, he asked me out. I gladly accepted. Nothing was holding either one of us back then. He was at least ethical, which I liked. He never crossed a line once when I was his student."

"So, then what happened?"

"We started dating. I quickly realized I'd known him from another lifetime, several in fact. I felt the bond between us, and he did too. We both received past-life readings from a spiritual counselor, someone we both trusted. We were able to trace everything back.

"That spiritual bond caused me to fall absolutely, madly in love with him. He said he was in love with me. The bond also made me blind to what was happening. He had a lot of narcissistic tendencies. He gaslit me a lot. He didn't know how to be faithful, either. There were also other girls coming out of the woodwork. Former students. Ex-girlfriends. He had a major hero complex. He had to save every damsel in distress. He also loved attention, especially female attention. I saw all of the signs, and I ignored them. I just couldn't imagine him coming into my life and not being permanent.

"Sexually, he was very rough with me. I don't think we ever made love once. He was into a lot of bondage. I had to submit to him, and he reveled in that power. I did it because I loved him. I thought that was what I was supposed to do.

"He degraded me a lot. He refused to offer oral sex to me because he said that I didn't smell good. He also told me I had gained too much weight once when he traveled out of the country for three weeks. The bedroom was often either dead or filled with his power trips. Still, I stayed.

"I gave him three years. I turned twenty-two in December, and by Christmas I had confirmation that he was cheating on me. He had been the entire time. He kept me hidden. Never introduced me to his family. Never took me around his friends. He purposely left me out of everything. A friend of his was stupid enough to post a picture of them at a Christmas party. He was lip-locked with a woman I'd never seen. She looked really young. I confronted him immediately. He gaslit me, just as he always did. I was fed up. I did a severing ritual. I cut the connection between the two of us. The moment I did it, my body got so cold, but I knew it had worked.

"He called me the second it happened. I told him I didn't want to see him anymore, never to contact me again, and that there would be no more lifetimes with him."

"He sounds like a creep."

"He was terrible. He fucked up my self-esteem and self-image for a while. I have been in therapy on and off since my brother died, but having a narcissist come into your life is a mindfuck no one can prepare you for."

David nodded. "Thank you for telling me."

She nodded. “No one has ever been the way you are with me. You are the most incredible man I’ve ever met. The way you touch me assures me that there’s nothing wrong with me.”

“That’s because there isn’t anything wrong with you. You smell good. Your body is beautiful. Your heart is open. You are kind and compassionate. We respect each other. I would never want to make you feel less. Ever,” he explained.

“I still have my insecurities. We would go to a restaurant, and his eyes would wander everywhere. I was never quite enough for him. Never quite good enough. He would outwardly flirt with waitresses, strangers, bartenders. It didn’t matter. He had absolutely no respect for me or the relationship. It was a pretty terrible three years,” she confessed.

“Well,” he said as he leaned over and put his hand on hers, “it’s over now, and we’re together. I will never treat you like that.”

“I know you won’t. You’re one of the best people I know,” she said, leaning over to kiss his lips.

28

November began on a calm note, but by the second week things started to change. Alex and David were called to Children Services for a special meeting. They sat at the large wooden table waiting.

"What's going on?" Alex whispered.

"I have no idea. They called me and asked us to come over immediately. So here we are," he answered.

The door opened, and an unfamiliar woman walked in. Neither Alex nor David had met her before. With shoulder-length black hair and porcelain skin, her eyes were dark brown. She wore a pair of navy-blue slacks, brown shoes, and a white blouse. David estimated her to be in her 50s.

They stood to greet her. She reciprocated with a handshake.

"I'm Cynthia Pastell. I'm from the State."

"I'm David Gregory, and this is my partner, Alexandra Ritezal," he replied.

"Please, have a seat," she advised.

They sat down. David watched Ms. Pastell as she too sat down. The skin on her neck turned bright red. She seemed nervous, and it appeared her blood pressure might be going up.

"Mr. Gregory. Miss Ritezal. I wanted to bring you in to tell you that Tamara Owens and Carleigh Canter have been terminated from the agency."

“Why?” Alex asked.

“Well, we’ve been watching them for some time and, to be frank, their behavior has been reckless. They don’t seem to understand the word ‘probable cause,’ and as such, a class action lawsuit has been filed against the agency. We cannot possibly win the suit, so we’re going to have to settle.”

“Have we been implicated in the suit?” David inquired.

“No. The information Carleigh provided to you was false.” She sighed and dropped her eyes. Then, making eye contact once more, she went on. “The reason I called you here today was to ask you to draw up a settlement agreement. Since you’re considered the agency’s legal counsel, we will definitely need your help with all of this.”

“And you said it was class action. That means a number of people are suing. How many people are we talking about here?” Alex asked.

“The Clifton family, the Lawrence family, Mandy Hall, the Swarez family, and the Roberts family. They are not only coming after the agency, but they are suing Mrs. Owens and Ms. Canter civilly.”

“We won’t represent Mrs. Owens or Ms. Canter,” Alex began. “It would be a conflict of interest.”

“I am aware,” Cynthia said. “All we need is a settlement proposal for the families. We’re searching through candidates to fill Mrs. Owens’s job, but until then, I will be steering the ship. So, you can come to me with things. We’ll work through cases together until I can find a suitable replacement.”

“I knew this would happen,” David said.

"You did?" Cynthia asked with surprise.

"I did. Tamara and Carleigh didn't exactly use caution when doing their job. I think the power went to their heads. They took children that didn't need to be taken. I kept warning them, but they ignored me. It was a constant battle with them."

"Their behavior worsened when I came on board," Alex added.

"Well, your contract with us is good for at least another year. We won't be terminating that contract as a result of this lawsuit."

"I'm not certain we will be interested in renewing the contract," David said.

"Oh?" Cynthia asked.

"Working with this agency has been extremely taxing. It isn't what either one of us got into law to do. We can cross that bridge when we come to it, though," David explained.

"What ballpark are we looking at with the money for the families?" Alex asked.

"I've looked at the budget. If we do not replace Ms. Canter, we'll have some wiggle room."

"Numbers, please?" David insisted.

"$50,000."

"They won't do it," Alex interjected. "Each family is going to need a chunk of that. At that number, that's only $10,000 per family. They will laugh in your face. It may even piss them off."

"Try it first. If we need to go higher, we can," Cynthia replied.

"No. $50,000 is an insult," David agreed.

"Well, then what do you suggest?" Pastell asked.

"$500,000. That gives each family $100,000. That might satisfy them."

"$500,000!" Pastell exclaimed.

"Do you want this lawsuit to go away, or would you rather go to court?" Alex asked pointedly. "Better yet, how much unwanted press do you want? That's an even better question. This is a small town, and people talk. This agency already has a black eye. After this, no one will trust this agency or want to work with them."

"I certainly don't want the agency dragged through court, and I've already had to stave off calls from newspapers and cable news. This is going to be a publicity nightmare anyway."

"Then offer them $500,000 out of the gate," David insisted.

29

At the office, Alex and David sat in the kitchen, stunned by the meeting. Both were relieved, nonetheless. Maybe this would make working for that agency bearable until the contract was up.

"Thanksgiving," David blurted out as he took a drink of coffee.

Alex turned to him, confused.

"What are you doing for Thanksgiving?" he asked.

"Well, I don't know. What are *you* doing for Thanksgiving?"

"I'm going home. I want you to go with me. I just didn't want to interfere with anything you may have with your family."

"You want me to spend Thanksgiving with you?"

He took her hand into his and kissed her knuckles. "Of course, I do. I won't ever leave you out of anything. I won't ever leave you behind."

She smiled. "My family's big holiday is Christmas. Everyone sort of just does their own thing at Thanksgiving. So, I can come with you."

"Perfect," he concluded.

30

The week progressed with its usual cases and responsibilities. Then came the weekend. A relaxed date night and cards with Will and Hope marked Friday night's activities. On Saturday, David needed some help around the cabin with some minor repairs, so Alex was happy to lend a hand. Sunday was when they migrated to Alex's house for some cuddles, conversation, and television. She ordered a pizza, and they had a blanket picnic on the floor while watching some of their favorite shows. Sunday night, David went back to his house to gear up for the week ahead.

One more full week until Thanksgiving. David decided to close the entire week this year. He had the financial cushion to do so.

David agreed to fill in for Alex in juvenile court. She scheduled a doctor's appointment for her yearly. He'd never really discussed birth control with her and always assumed she was on the pill. At least he'd hoped she was. They'd never used a condom. Surely, she wasn't going to the doctor for a pregnancy test. A knot rose in his throat as he contemplated that possibility, but then that was quickly followed by a sense of hope.

As he waited for the caseworker to arrive, his mind occasionally wandered back to the unanswered questions about Alex's doctor's appointment. The uncertainty played on his mind, and a mixture of anxiety and anticipation lingered beneath the surface. While immersed in his professional obligations, personal matters introduced a subtle tension, complicating his thoughts. Hope flickered within him, suggesting a yet-uncharted future, as he wrestled with the intricate interplay between his professional duties and personal complexities.

Renee Morris rushed through the door. She was the ongoing worker assigned to the case. She sat down beside David.

"I thought I was going to be late," she muttered.

"You're right on time," David assured her.

At the defendant's table sat Lori Gladstone, a single mom who had lost her children due to a dirty home. Beside her was her attorney, John McConnell. Of course, Carleigh had been the worker who took the children without even giving the mother a chance to clean up. Today marked thirty days from the date of the removal. Given the circumstances, David was moving to close the case.

As Steven sat on the bench taking notes, David began. "Your Honor, Ms. Gladstone has completed a thirty-day case plan and has resolved the situation that led to the removal of her children. I have filed a motion to close the case."

David observed Steven. He looked much worse than he did at Russell's party. David wasn't sure how that was even possible. His eyes were sunken in, shadows of exhaustion etched beneath them. The lines on his face seemed deeper, and his once vibrant gaze now held a weariness that spoke of something more profound than physical fatigue. His hair, once full, appeared unusually thin.

Steven's hands shook, and his eyes drifted over to Renee. "And, as the caseworker, are you in agreement with this motion, Mrs. Morris?"

"I am, Your Honor."

"And Mr. McConnell, is your client in agreement with the conditions of the termination of her case?"

"Yes, Your Honor," the defense attorney replied.

Before he said anything else, he coughed a little. Then, suddenly, he put his hand on his chest. He was instantly ashen.

"Your Honor?" David said as he stood up and rushed to him, Mr. McConnell right on his heels.

David got close to him and turned him around in his seat. "Steven," he started, "are you all right? Do you need me to call someone?"

"My chest," he whispered. "I can't breathe!"

"He's having a heart attack. Call 911!" David shouted.

Steven slumped over in his chair, gasping for air. Then he passed out, falling to the floor.

David checked his pulse and couldn't find one.

"No pulse!" he exclaimed.

David started CPR immediately, checking for a pulse intermittently. Steven was dying right in front of them, and there was nothing anyone could do.

The ambulance arrived and rushed him away.

David drove back to the cottage after the ordeal. He sat in his office, just staring blankly at the wall, the weight of the day settling heavily on his shoulders. The events in court had taken a toll, leaving him mentally drained and emotionally exhausted.

When Joan walked in to ask what happened and if he had an entry that needed to be typed up, David didn't even move. The usual rhythm of office tasks felt distant and insignificant in the face of the emotional turmoil he carried.

Joan could see that something was very wrong. The unspoken heaviness in the room lingered, creating a space where words felt inadequate, and emotions hung in the air like a silent storm.

"What's happened?" she asked.

"Steven Meyers had a massive heart attack this morning in court."

"What!" Joan asked.

"He's dead. They couldn't call it until the paramedics took him to the hospital, but I know he's dead."

"Jesus…" Joan said, clasping her hand over her mouth.

David's eyes were hollow. "He was despicable, but as long as you're alive, there's always hope, right?"

Joan sighed. "You know what this means?"

"No."

"You will be appointed as interim judge. The party will also ask you to run in the May primary."

"Seriously?"

"I'll bet you my next paycheck it happens," she said as she crossed her arms.

"I don't know."

"I do. You're a pioneer and, because of your compassion, you have this unrealistic idea that you can change the world," she argued. "This will be your chance to do that. To cut down the corruption in this town and all of the things that are wrong inside the system. You will be campaigning your heart out."

His eyes brightened at the prospect, but he tried hard to push his ambitions aside. He thought of Alex and what such a change would mean for them. She wouldn't be able to bring cases in front of him, and it would definitely mean that the contract with Children Services would be over. He wasn't sure how she would feel about any of this. He knew she hated the agency, but the money was good, and she'd already taken a huge pay cut to work for him.

As he considered the implications of a career shift, David couldn't ignore the ripple effect it might have on their professional and financial dynamics. The brightening of his eyes reflected a genuine enthusiasm for the potential change, but the shadow of concern loomed as he grappled with the impact on their shared endeavors.

He recognized the sacrifices Alex had made to work alongside him, and the potential alterations to their work dynamic brought forth a cascade of considerations.

"Is she still at the doctor?" David asked as he looked at Joan.

"Yes. She sent me a text. She's on her way here."

"Is she pregnant?"

"What?" Joan asked, rather dumbstruck.

"Is she pregnant? She told me she was going for her yearly."

"First off," Joan began, "she would tell you before she would tell me. Secondly, I don't think you have to worry about that. She's pretty cautious. She has a career to think about, too."

31

Alex walked in the door a little after 2:30 p.m. David leapt to his feet. He met her in the reception area, took her into his arms, and just held her. He didn't want to let go.

"Where the hell have you been? You text Joan at 12:30 and it's 2:30. Are you okay?"

"Of course, I am," she said. "I needed to drop off some things at Municipal. They told me about Steven. It sounds just awful. I'm so sorry."

David didn't move. He wanted to keep her against his body. He leaned in and whispered in her ear, "Are you pregnant?"

She pulled away quickly, mortified by his question. "Do you want me to be?"

"I just…"

"No, David, I'm not pregnant. I have an IUD," she answered as she stormed into her office.

He didn't understand why she was so upset by the question. He followed her into her office watching her shimmy out of her black wool coat.

"What did I say?"

"I would tell you if I even thought I was pregnant. And I'm not, so we're all clear. I needed to get my yearly. That's all."

"Okay. You don't have to get so angry."

"I'm not," she said with a heavy sigh. She pinched the bridge of her nose and shook her head.

Cautiously, he walked to her and sat down on the edge of her large wooden desk. He held out his hand to her. She took it. Pulling her to him, he saw fear in her eyes.

"Tell me what's wrong, Alexandra."

She shook her head. "I don't know if I can," she answered as the tears welled in her eyes.

"You can tell me anything. You know that. That's part of our deal."

"I don't know if you'll understand. I keep so much tucked away out of respect. Sometimes, things happen, and it's hard for me to process it."

"Talk to me. Help me understand."

Ace to the dead"David, I had a dream last night."

"Okay. Tell me what it was about."

"When I have these dreams, they're filled with symbolism and it's up to me to interpret that. What I saw was so troubling. That's also why I took my time getting back here. I stopped at my aunt's. I needed her help."

"And what did she tell you?"

She hesitated.

"Please just tell me," he pleaded.

"She confirmed what I already knew. Something significant is going to change with us, with you and me. It's going to be bad." She exhaled, still holding back.

"Alexandra, I may be skeptical, but I'm willing to hear what you have to say. You don't get upset like this… ever. You always tell me what you think. So, when you are upset, I know I need to stop and listen. That's what a boyfriend is supposed to do, especially when their girlfriend is level-headed and calm most of the time."

"David, I saw a raven."

"A raven? Like Edgar Allan Poe's raven?"

"Yes, like Edgar Allen Poe's raven."

"Okay."

"I've been doing this long enough to know that a raven is a messenger. It doesn't matter what the message is, whether it's good or bad, the bird serves as a medium between the spiritual world and the physical, earthly plane.

"Then I saw an arrow and I watched it pierce the bird's chest. It was as if someone stabbed me in the chest, too. I ran to it and scooped it up. I wanted to save it, so I took it into my arms, and I started screaming for someone to help me. No one came.

"I looked around, searching for someone. Something that might help the bird. It was foggy, so I couldn't see, but I knew someone was in the fog. I felt female energy. Whoever it was wanted to harm me. I knew she shot the arrow and killed the raven. She wanted it silenced so I wouldn't receive the message it was meant to give me. Then I heard a noise, but I couldn't quite make it out. It was coming from the fog. There were bats everywhere, hitting me, biting me. I got up and I ran through the fog. I woke up screaming."

"What did your aunt say?"

"She told me that I was right about the raven. There was a message. The fog meant that something was being hidden from me. She also told me the bats meant people were either dead or going to die. She told me that the arrow to the heart was significant because my heart was going to break. Someone or something was going to cause great pain, and I would never be the same. It would change me forever."

"And she got all of that from a dream?" he asked, puzzled by the notion.

"My aunt is basically a shaman. I trust her. I've come to her with things like this before. She's always been right. She was right about you."

"Me?"

"She saw you coming. I went to her for a reading after a dream I had. She predicted your appearance. 'Someone you shared your childhood with is going to offer you a gift. It will change your life.' And you did offer me a gift. You offered me the job here."

He had so many questions. He wondered if he'd been on the wrong side of all of this. He wondered if there could be more than the here and now. It was conversations like this that made him curious, but he was skeptical.

Hope's approach turned him off. That's exactly why he didn't want anything to do with spirituality. He watched his mother and sisters do things that seemed insane. When he walked away from all of the mysticism, he stayed away from it. However, Alex seemed to bring order to what he had come to know as chaos.

She was sharing more of herself, yet again, welcoming the vulnerability and embracing trust. He admired that. She was one of the sanest people he knew. For her to be so rattled, he knew she wasn't making anything up.

"Hey," he said as he stood and lifted her chin. "Nothing's going to happen to us."

"It already has."

The unsettledness in her eyes frightened him. Suddenly, he felt an urgency to pull her close again.

"David," she continued her head hard against his chest, "Steven died this morning."

"It doesn't mean…"

"Yes, it does. It means that the warning was clear. Steven was the first casualty. That's what the bats were about. Death."

"Look at me, Alexandra," he said as he put his hands on her shoulders. "I will not let anything happen to us. I talk to you about everything. You know me. And I love you. Nothing will change that."

"Everything changes. It has to." she said doubtfully.

"What can I say to convince you that you're wrong?"

"Nothing, because I'm not wrong. I've seen this before. It's time to buckle up, David. Change is coming."

32

As David lay beside Alex, he contemplated all that she had told him. His eyes fixed on the ceiling, he just couldn't sleep. He was a worrier when it came to the people he loved. The prospect of losing her made him very anxious. The dream was intriguing but also troubling.

The weight of Alex's revelations lingered in the quiet of the room, and David's mind became a battleground of conflicting emotions. The vulnerability of his worries surfaced, overshadowing the intriguing aspects of the dream. In the darkness, the fragility of their relationship became more pronounced, and David found himself grappling with the fear of losing her.

Maybe she's wrong, he thought.

Still, he couldn't shake the looming possibilities. Restless from thinking, he decided to head to his study. Editing the textbook currently in queue would surely take his mind off things and, even better, the monotonous task might help him get sleepy.

He sat on the side of the bed, head in his hands, frustrated and angry. Glancing over his shoulder, he watched Alex as she slept. She was teaching him so much. He had to admit that the mystical, the spiritual, and the unseen were starting to interest him.

The dichotomy of emotions played on David's features as he observed Alex's peaceful slumber. As his gaze lingered on her, a subtle transformation began to happen inside him. The allure of the mystical and the spiritual, once sources of resistance, now kindled a newfound interest.

The lines between skepticism and curiosity began to blur, and David found himself contemplating the unexplored realms that Alex seemed so intimately acquainted with. Her presence, even in sleep, carried an undeniable influence, and the silent lessons she imparted were slowly reshaping his view. He grappled with the internal shifts, acknowledging the evolving landscape of his beliefs and the profound impact of the woman beside him.

The glow of the nightlight covered her exposed skin like a warm blanket. He stood, careful not to wake her, and walked out of the bedroom. Quietly, he made his way up the stairs to his study. Before he sat down, he grabbed his mobile phone off the charging table. To his surprise, there was a text message from Hope. It was 2 a.m. The message had come through at 1:53 a.m.

There's something wrong. Alex messaged me earlier, but I knew something was wrong before she sent her text. She told me about her dream. And I'm up because I can't sleep, and I know it's because you're up. Call me or text me. We need to talk.

For once, he was thankful for Hope's intuition. Maybe she could shed some light on the situation for him. He quickly typed a message back:

I will come over. Alex is sleeping. I will leave a note so she doesn't worry just in case she wakes up while I'm gone. Be there in a few.

Almost instantly, his phone buzzed with a reply.

Just so you know, Will is here. He's asleep in the bedroom. I am going back to Dayton tomorrow night. There's a case I'm working on. I just wanted to spend a few extra days here before going to Mom and Dad's. Good thing I did.

He pulled into her driveway and hopped out of his car. The soft glow of the porch light illuminated the pathway, casting a warm invitation as David approached the open door. Hope's presence, wrapped in a blanket on the sofa, added a touch of coziness to the scene. The comforting aroma of tea filled the air, creating a tranquil ambiance in the room.

As he stepped inside, the door creaking softly behind him, David couldn't help but feel a sense of curiosity about the unexpected meeting. Hope, with her blanket-clad form and cup of tea, seemed to have orchestrated a moment of solace and revelation. The air was thick with unspoken words, and David, standing in the doorway, felt the weight of anticipation.

David stood as if his feet were glued to the floor.

"Get over here and sit down," she insisted.

He walked to the vacant recliner and sat down, taking a deep breath. "So, she told you about the dream?"

"She did."

"And may I say how proud I am of you. You didn't rip her head off or tell her she was crazy. That's a huge step for you. You must really love her."

"Stop it. I wouldn't do that to her. She confided in me, and she was really shaken up. She didn't act like you when she was explaining everything either, so that helped." Hope threw up her middle finger.

"Do you think there's any merit to her dream?" he asked as he rocked in the recliner.

"Of course I do. It was definitely a warning, or at least it was supposed to be until the raven got killed. There was a message, but it was muted by whoever was in the fog. You know I could touch you and see if I could figure anything out."

"Oh no. You aren't doing that. No thanks. I'll figure it out on my own."

"I'm not always right."

"The answer is still no."

"Joan is right, too," she added. "You are going to be appointed as the interim judge in juvenile court."

"How do you know any of this? Did Joan call you?"

"Call it an educated guess."

"That means I'll have to campaign to keep the seat."

"But being a judge is what you want. There is no way you'll walk away from an opportunity like this."

He sat quietly.

"That gift of compassion pulls you toward so much," Hope continued. "One of your branch gifts is justice. You want to see corruption cut down. It's what drives you. I'm afraid your compassion is going to get the best of you, though. Sometimes it isn't always an attribute.

"When I first started using my gift, it was horrible. My friends took advantage of me. I didn't know what I was doing. I had no training. Once I was able to start exercising control over it, things became bearable. If you don't get that compassion under control, someone will take advantage of you. People are always looking for a free ride. Alex isn't like that. She sees your compassion and doesn't abuse it. Not everyone is like her."

"You think I don't know that? And why are you saying all of this?"

"Because I think the person in the fog is dangerous. Whoever that person is will try to cause problems. I get the sense that this person understands the craft, too. Alex would need to get her cards read for clarification. I can do it, but I feel like I shouldn't. I am too close to the situation. I'm too invested. I don't know if I could be objective."

"This is exactly where I get lost. I don't understand this stuff. You all depend on these things way too much."

"And you depend on the physical world way too much."

"So, what do I do? Say no when they offer me the judge's seat?"

"The decision is up to you. I don't know if the change Alex was warned about has anything to do with the judge's seat. It could be something else, but a dream like that tells me that someone is at the root of the change. It isn't just circumstantial. There is someone pulling the strings."

"I don't want to lose Alex."

"I sense a 'but' there…"

"I've worked my entire career to do the right thing. Being a judge would give me the opportunity to apply fairness, to do what's right for folks."

"See. There it is. Compassion, ambition, and justice."

"What's wrong with that?"

"Make sure that in running after your ambition, you don't trample on the people who love you."

"Sometimes you talk in riddles, Hope."

"It's because if I put things the way I do with those who are like-minded, you would be so freaked out that you'd probably stop talking to me completely."

"Hope, how can I reassure Alex that things are going to work out?"

"You may have to face the fact that you can't. Even more, you may have to face the fact that things may not work out. No matter what, though, it sounds like this is something that has to work itself out without human intervention."

David stood angrily. "Well, I don't like that option."

"You can't control everything, David," Hope concluded.

David drove back home feeling worse than he did before he talked to Hope. He just wanted to hold Alex. He knew he would move heaven and earth to make her happy. In his heart, he knew he would never do anything to jeopardize what they had.

As soundlessly as possible, he walked into the bedroom, shed his coat, and climbed into bed. Alex was still sleeping peacefully, her back facing him. He pulled her in close, snaking his arm around her waist. She stirred a little and then quieted again.

The weight of his troubled thoughts seemed to lift slightly as he held her close. The quiet intimacy of the moment offered a sense of solace, a sanctuary where the troubles of the outside world could be momentarily set aside. Touching her gave him some level of reassurance, a silent vow of commitment that transcended the uncertainties that plagued his mind. In the stillness of the night, the warmth of their shared space provided a respite from the complexities of the day, grounding them in the simplicity of their connection.

"I won't ever let you go," he whispered. "I promise."

33

As the weekend arrived, Alex decided to stay at her house instead of spending the weekend with David. He was not pleased by this. She explained that there were orders she needed to fill, and with the Black Friday sale at her aunt's shop, she had a lot to do.

David decided to take the weekend to finish winterizing the cabin. He didn't have much to do, but he knew the snow would begin flying next month. He wanted to be completely finished with all of the preparations.

Steven's visitation was scheduled for the Monday before Thanksgiving. The funeral was scheduled for Tuesday. David felt it was only right to pay his respects. He didn't like Steven, and he certainly didn't agree with him, but after watching him die, he knew he needed to attend.

With a resolute spirit, David decided to chart his own course, unwavering in his dedication to his profession and community. The dream that cast shadows over their relationship wouldn't define the trajectory of his life. He embraced the notion of moving forward, maintaining his focus on the legal practice that had been a cornerstone of his identity.

In his commitment to service and the pursuit of justice, David found a source of strength. The decision to leave any potential relationship adjustments in Alex's hands reflected not only his confidence in their connection but also his unwillingness to let external uncertainties dictate the course of his life.

Alex agreed to accompany David to the visitation on Monday night and to the funeral service on Tuesday. It would be a very emotional, stressful week. Neither of them was looking forward to the services. They awaited their time away at Pikeview Manor.

As he sat on Alex's couch, waiting for her to emerge, his cell phone vibrated in his hand. He had been browsing social media when he was startled by an unknown number.

He answered, "This is David."

The voice was male. "David Gregory?"

"Yes, speaking."

"I'm Rowland Blevins of the Ohio State Supreme Court."

David's heart was in his throat.

"Yes, sir. How are you, Your Honor?"

"I'm well. I'm so sorry to hear about the passing of Judge Meyers. A very tragic loss."

"Yes, sir. It is," David replied. He felt a twinge of guilt, but then quickly recovered.

"Well, we needed an interim judge. We have the authority to appoint someone for that spot. With your track record, your name found its way to us. Your work made national news when the murders happened in your remote area of the world. We wondered if you would consider sitting on the bench in the interim."

David was already prepared. "Absolutely."

"Do you need to think about it?"

"I don't need time to think about it. I will need to square some things away for my practice."

"Good. Very good. You'll be receiving a packet via fax. Then there's the swearing-in. Fill out the packet, return it, and you'll be all set. We'd like you to start as of the first of January, if that's acceptable. There's a magistrate from a visiting county who has agreed to preside until you can take up the mantle. That gives you time to inform your clients and, as you said, square some things away for your practice."

"Yes, sir."

"Congratulations, Mr. Gregory. If you decide you like the position, please consider running for the primary. I know campaigning with such short notice might be a little overwhelming."

"I will certainly consider it, sir."

David hung up and stared down at his phone. The shock mixed with excitement washed over him.

"Who was that?" Alex asked as she stood in the middle of the living room, putting a small silver hoop into her earlobe.

"It was Judge Blevins from the State."

"They offered you the interim seat, didn't they?" she asked.

"They did."

Her smile was hollow. "Congratulations."

He nodded, glancing back down at his phone. "This won't change anything with us."

"It will change everything, but it's what you need to do," she said. "I'm happy that you are happy," she added.

She walked back into the bathroom, with David following her. As she finished up with her hair, her cheeks looked like they were on fire. Her eyes began to well up with tears.

David stood behind her and leaned against the wall. No matter how cross she was, she still looked beautiful. The play of shadows and light in the room accentuated the elegance of Alex's form as she twisted her hair, revealing the graceful curve of her neck. The black dress embraced her silhouette. The amulet, a constant accessory, hung delicately around her neck, a subtle touch that carried a hint of mystery.

"Alexandra, I wish you could see my heart," he said bluntly.

Her eyes met his in the mirror. "I can see your heart, David. I know how good you are, which is why I understand why you have to do this."

"I won't leave you to drown. I promise."

"I know that, too."

"Then what are you worried about? Why are you so upset about this?"

"You know what I'm worried about," she said as her lips pursed into a hard line.

"No, I really don't. It just seems like you're jealous. You've been distant since you told me about the dream. Alexandra, it's a dream. It doesn't necessarily mean anything."

"First, I'm not jealous. Not at all. You were born to be a judge. You have the fortitude for it," she started. "Another thing is Steven's death. He was perfectly healthy, and then suddenly he wasn't. That doesn't feel right to me. Something is off there.

"About the dream… it wasn't just a dream. It was a warning. I wouldn't expect you to understand, though. Let's just get through this tonight. There'll be time to argue later."

"I'm not arguing," he replied as his voice raised an octave. "We don't argue. We talk."

Alex abruptly concluded the discussion. She walked past him and into the kitchen. David followed her. He watched her as she took her coat off the wall hook and put it on.

The visitation was ordinary and drama-free. They paid their respects and then arrived back at Alex's house around 7:30. David followed behind Alex as they walked in the door.

"Can we please talk?" he asked as he watched Alex walk into her bedroom.

"Of course, we can," she replied as she began shedding her clothing.

David immediately became distracted by her. She stood in her bra and panties. Her face flushed, she looked extremely alluring. He tried to focus, letting his eyes move over her body.

"What are you doing, David?"

"Well, I'm distracted now," he admitted as he walked toward her.

"Oh," she said shyly.

"Can we please table this discussion?" he asked sincerely.

"Sexy time?" she asked in a soft tone.

"Only if you want to," he replied.

“Things feel better when we are intimate, I know,” Alex agreed.

“They really do. Take a shower with me first?” he inquired.

“I’m all yours, Mr. Gregory,” she said with a sly smile.

34

As they navigated the somber atmosphere of the funeral, David couldn't help but feel the undercurrent of tension persisting between Alex and Gerri. The drama-free event belied the palpable strain that lingered beneath the surface. Despite his curiosity, Alex hadn't provided even a glimpse of the Cliff Notes version of what had transpired between them.

David's inquisitive nature wrestled with the desire to understand the origins of the tension. The unspoken rift added a layer of complexity to the already charged atmosphere. As the day unfolded, the unanswered questions became a lingering presence, prompting him to consider the delicate balance of untold stories within the fabric of their intertwined lives.

As an observer, David found himself grappling with the palpable lack of respect, contemplating the origins of the tension. The intricate dance between stepmother and stepchildren unveiled a narrative of tense relationships, prompting David to reflect on the intricate balance required in blending families and the complexities that can arise when respect becomes a fragile thread within the familial tapestry.

On Tuesday night, he sought the solitude of the cabin. It offered a quiet space for introspection. As he grappled with the complexities of his relationship with Alex, her reluctance to support his professional endeavors and her profound trust in a dream cast a shadow, creating a chasm that he was unsure how to bridge.

The emotional toll was evident, but David resisted the urge to lose his patience. Instead, he embraced the challenge of understanding Alex's beliefs without casting judgment. The delicate balance between frustration and empathy became a tightrope he walked, attempting to preserve the integrity of their relationship while navigating the uncharted waters of differing perspectives.

On Wednesday morning, David loaded up the dogs into the back seat and tossed some of the luggage in the back. He drove into town, picked up Alex, and they made their way to Western Ohio to celebrate Thanksgiving with his family. Olivia and Danny were coming in with their children. Hope was coming, too. Will hadn't formally accepted the invitation, but it was safe to assume he would join the family festivities since his family lived so close to Pikeview Manor.

The weight of the silence in the car pressed on David's nerves, creating an atmosphere charged with unspoken tension. The car ride, initially anticipated as an opportunity for open communication, now seemed to magnify the communication gap between them. David had hoped for a chance to discuss the crucial details of his transition out of the practice, a conversation that carried significant weight for both of them. Instead, the uncomfortable silence cast a shadow over the journey.

Finally, he broke the silence. "Alexandra," he began, "I know you're still upset. I don't exactly understand why, but I need to talk to you about some business-related issues."

"Okay," she replied cordially.

"Since I will be sitting as the judge in juvenile court, you'll have to terminate your contract with Children Services. It will be a conflict of interest since we're in a relationship."

"We weren't going to renew the contract anyway, or at least that's the idea that had been tossed around," she replied.

"Right, right," he trailed off. "Well, I am signing the practice over to you," he continued. Alex quickly interrupted.

"Why would you do that? That makes no sense at all," she argued.

"Well, I think it will be necessary."

"It won't. This is your practice. You built it. There are plenty of judges who keep their private practices, especially as interim judges."

He thought for a moment. She was right. There was no reason to do anything with the practice. He could keep it while serving. He just wouldn't be there as often.

The energy in the car shifted. David took a moment and glanced over at Alex. Her face was twisted as she let the words settle into her brain. The weight of the revelation hung in the air, and David watched the subtle play of emotions on her features. It was a moment frozen in time, as her expression morphed in response to the information he had just shared.

"I know all of this is very sudden," David said. When Alex didn't reply, he breathed a heavy sigh. "I'm going to help you with whatever you might need help with. You'll have Joan and Will, too. I won't leave you hanging, Alex," David assured her.

Still, she didn't respond. The uncomfortable tension in the confined space of the car acted as a tangible acknowledgment that things had reached their zenith.

The realization dawned on him that perhaps this conversation should have been delayed, that his eagerness to share the information had inadvertently stirred a storm within the vehicle. "I know this is difficult, and it is very unexpected. I'm sorry that you came to me for a job and now you have been put in this position."

She shifted in her seat. "David, change is part of growth. It can be painful, often unwanted, but it is necessary in order for all of us to become who we are meant to become. As scary as this is, I have to believe it is meant to happen." Glancing back over at her, he recognized that her features had softened.

"As you sort of transition out of the practice, I won't let you down," she continued. "You've worked very hard to make your practice what it is. I won't do anything to harm that. I know you will still have an active role in it, but not necessarily with the day-to-day."

"I can still take on some minor cases. I just wish you weren't so angry," he said.

"I wouldn't say that I'm angry," she clarified. "I just want to enjoy this weekend with you and your family. I wonder if we could just drop this for now. I want you to know that I am very proud of you, David. I think you're a brilliant attorney. You deserve this chance. I'm a little scared, I guess."

"Really?"

"Absolutely."

"What is there to be scared of? What makes you feel so insecure about this?"

"Whether you realize it or not, David, you've quickly become my anchor. I find myself depending on you a little more than I should. I'm not used to needing someone. I don't like it."

"It makes you feel out of control?" he assumed.

"Yes, very," she replied.

"Alex, I'm not going to abandon you. Not for any reason," he assured her as he reached over and put his hand on her leg. "And any help that you need with the practice."

She nodded.

David could see that the subject did, in fact, need to be closed. There was nothing more to really say on the matter, and he didn't want to ruin their first holiday together. He knew the situation would be waiting for them when they got back home. He wasn't interested in wasting any precious time with her. He loved her. He knew she was worried, and he had hoped to offer some reassurance. He didn't know if he was successful, but he had an idea that might help. Still, that would have to wait until they returned home. He also wanted to talk to his dad about it.

They stopped for lunch before proceeding and looked around some of the local shops. David always got something for his mother every time he came to visit. She loved baskets, but she had too many of them. As they stood looking at the various trinkets, he noticed a small prism in the shape of a heart. It was simple, but definitely something his mother would like.

"What is it?" Alex asked as she observed him.

"I always get something for Mom when I come home. This fits her perfectly," he answered.

"That's sweet," Alex observed.

35

They got back on the road after a couple of hours and arrived at Pikeview just before dinnertime. As they pulled down the lane, David quickly recognized the cars lining the driveway. Everyone had already made it to the house. After parking the car, David and Alex went in through the kitchen. He reintroduced her to his parents and Olivia. Then they busied themselves with the luggage and the dogs.

The upstairs room, once David's sanctuary, had undergone transformations mirroring the shifting phases of life in the household. From a hobby room where dreams and aspirations were pursued, to a study where the weight of professional endeavors was carried, the room had absorbed the imprints of various chapters. With the joyful arrival of grandchildren, the room underwent yet another metamorphosis. Robin and Matt, in their dedication to family, had revamped it into a warm and inviting spare room.

Soon everyone was called to the dining room to eat. The aroma of the meal wafted through the air, inviting everyone to gather around the dining room table. Laughter and animated chatter filled the space, creating a vibrant symphony of family connection.

In the midst of the lively conversations, the clinking of utensils and the passing of dishes became a rhythmic accompaniment to the familial harmony. The dining room, a stage for the unfolding Thanksgiving Eve festivities, witnessed the rekindling of bonds and the celebration of togetherness, as each family member contributed to the chorus of love and laughter that echoed throughout the room.

As David cast his gaze toward his parents, a smile played on his lips. Their body language spoke volumes, a testament to the genuine delight they found in Alexandra's presence. The easy laughter that echoed between them created an aura of warmth, reaffirming the connection that had grown over the years.

His parents, having known Alex for just as long as David had, seamlessly picked up the threads of familiarity. The shared history painted a canvas of comfort, and it was evident that the bonds forged over time had not only endured but flourished. In the harmonious exchange of laughter and conversation, David found reassurance in the seamless integration of his parents and Alexandra into the shared tapestry of family.

The door in the kitchen opened and slammed, causing Robin to jump. She turned to Matt, a look of fright across her face, but then Will walked in, breathless and trembling.

"Will," Robin said, relieved by his appearance. "Come sit down. There's plenty to eat."

Hope looked up at him, her mouth slightly open and her face pink with embarrassment.

"I thought you weren't coming," she bit out angrily.

Disagreeing couples seemed to be a theme from what David could tell.

"I couldn't stay away," he began.

"What are you talking about?" Hope asked as she took the napkin from her lap and gently laid it beside her plate.

"I can't stay quiet anymore, and I can't keep pretending," he continued.

Eyes were fixed, expressions frozen, as if the dining room had transformed into a theater and the family into an audience enraptured by the unfolding spectacle. The shared moment of suspended animation created a unique energy, heightening the intrigue and suspense that hung in the air. In this collective pause, the dining room became a stage for a narrative yet to be unveiled, leaving everyone captivated by the mystery that held them in its grip.

"Hope, I love you," he admitted. "I've loved you since we were kids, but I knew you had to go your own way."

The ladies in the room all looked around at one another as they sat silently.

"Are you drunk?" Hope asked.

"I've never been clearer," Will answered. "When we talked the other night, you said that we could never work. We were too different. That the distance would break us if we had a commitment. The distance hasn't been an issue yet. We've been doing this for how long? I will go anywhere you want me to go. I will do whatever you want me to do. Hope, I want to marry you. I want to spend the rest of my life making you happy. We're a team. We always have been."

Everyone's stares shifted to Hope. Her eyes filled with tears, but she didn't offer up a sound.

"Look, I know that we've been doing our own thing. We didn't want to crowd each other, but damn it, I want you to crowd me. I want you to expect me home at a certain time, and I want you to miss me when I'm not with you. I feel totally lost when we're apart."

Will walked to Hope and knelt. He pulled a small square box from his coat pocket and opened it. The ring was beautiful. David recognized it. It was his paternal grandmother's ring. He suddenly realized that Will and Matt had this planned. It also meant that his maternal grandmother's ring was still in the care of his mother. That made him feel relieved.

"Hope Gregory, please marry me. I will screw up. I'll screw up a lot, and I may do everything wrong, but I will try my damndest to make you happy every single day of your life."

The tension in the room was suffocating as everyone waited on the edge of their seats. Tears poured from Hope's eyes. She turned and threw her arms around Will.

"You're such a stubborn fool! Of course, I'll marry you!" she shouted.

He lifted her into his arms and kissed her.

Everyone clapped. Olivia was on her feet, ready to embrace the bride-to-be. Alex, Amelia, and Robin followed as the men at the table just looked at each other blankly.

36

The creak of the porch swing echoed in the tranquil night as David and Matt found solace in the simplicity of the moment. The amber glow of bourbon in hand reflected the warmth of the silence between father and son. The crisp air carried the promise of winter, a subtle reminder of the changing seasons.

As they sat under the vast expanse of the night sky, stars glittered like diamonds, and the moon cast its gentle glow. The celestial display added a touch of magic to the night. In the stillness of the evening, the porch became a haven of reflection, where the bonds of family intertwined with the beauty of nature.

Matt broke the silence first. "Alex is pretty amazing, huh?" he asked rhetorically.

"She is. The most amazing woman I've met."

"When are you going to take the plunge? I can see how much you love her."

"I wanted to talk to you about that," David said and then took a sip of bourbon.

"Okay," Matt anticipated.

"I've only been dating her a few short months, but I know she is the one. I feel like I would be rushing into things if I proposed."

"Time means nothing when it comes to emotion. I knew I loved your mother instantly. We didn't waste any time getting married. When you know, you know," Matt encouraged.

"Does mom still have Grandma's ring?"

"Yep. In the safe. You thinking Christmas?"

He nodded. "I am. I want to make sure I talk to her dad, and I want to make sure she is on board with it, but yeah… Christmas." He paused, reflecting on the short journey he'd made with Alex. "She makes me feel things I've never felt before. She is my best friend. I've known her so long, it just feels like the fact that we finally dated just finished out the chapter, ya know? Like the best part of the book is being written."

"I know exactly what you mean," Matt agreed. "Do you want me to ask your mom about the ring?"

"No, I will. I bought her something on the way here. I need to give it to her, but I didn't want to make a big production of it."

"You always do that. Buy her something each time you come home. You've always had a special connection with your mom. It's different than the one she shares with your siblings."

"Probably because my life is so boring," he laughed.

"Why would you say that?" Matt asked.

"Well, she has dealt with Hope and Olivia and their wild gifts all of her life. Then look at me. I'm ordinary."

"Son, you are far from ordinary. You are talented and brilliant. You are a pillar in the community. You're loved and respected."

"I was offered the bench as juvenile judge. They called me on Monday. They want me to sit in the interim and consider running for the fall," he blurted out.

Matt shifted in his seat. "That's great. Why didn't you say something sooner?"

"Well, with Will coming in on his white charger, I didn't want to steal his thunder."

"Hang on. I'm going to go get your mom," Matt said.

"Dad!" David protested, but it was too late. Matt was already up on his feet and through the door.

Quickly, Matt came back out with Robin following behind. She was drying her hands with a kitchen hand towel.

"What's wrong?" she asked, her facial expression reflecting alarm.

"Tell your mom," Matt said as he sat down on the swing.

"I have been appointed interim juvenile judge."

Robin's mouth dropped open, and she smiled from her eyes. "That is wonderful! Why didn't you say anything earlier?"

"When could I have said anything? We've all been nonstop since we walked in, and then Will proposing…"

"Well, we're very proud of you," Robin said as she sat down in the rocking chair on the porch. "This is what you've been working so hard toward. I'm so proud of you."

"It's a little bittersweet," David admitted.

"Why?" Matt asked.

"Well, Alex just came on board a few months ago, and now I feel like I'm leaving her holding the bag. She didn't sign up for this. She also told me about a dream she had. She thinks it's foreshadowing this situation and not in a good way."

"Hope told me about the dream," Robin admitted. "I agree with Alex's aunt's interpretation. It feels like she might be right."

"You know how I feel about anything like this. It makes me uncomfortable."

"I know," Robin said.

"Well, you seem to be accepting it a lot better than you ever accepted anything from Hope," Matt observed.

"Alex is delicate with her delivery," David explained. "She understands that I don't believe. I think it hurts her, but I can't really help it. I just don't know how I feel about anything beyond this physical experience. She believes something different. Her beliefs align more with yours and the girls," David continued. "I don't fault her for her beliefs. I don't judge her for them. They are part of who she is, and I love her completely, which means I love that part of her, too."

Robin and Matt shot a glance at one another.

"This sounds serious," Robin stated.

"I think she is the one. I want to marry her," David admitted.

"I know. I already have your grandmother's ring out of the safe."

"I shouldn't be surprised that you knew already," David said with a quick smile.

"Have you mentioned anything to Alex?" Robin asked.

"No. She is putting up barriers. I can feel her pulling away."

"She may be afraid of what that sort of change might mean for your relationship," Matt interjected, trying to offer some sort of insight.

"That's precisely what she is afraid of," David said with conviction.

"I don't think so," Robin disagreed. "She is afraid of the message from the raven. Because she wasn't able to receive it, she is now operating in the dark," Robin explained. "She isn't afraid of how the relationship may change as a result of the position. She is afraid of the person she couldn't see in the fog."

"I asked her if she was jealous," David blurted out.

Matt dropped his head in disapproval.

"Why would you immediately jump to that?" Robin asked.

"I don't know. She is always so level-headed and then she wasn't. It seemed to align with the judicial appointment."

"Son," Robin continued, "I would highly recommend that you try to see things from her perspective. I know that will be difficult given your resistance to anything spiritual. She truly fears for the safety of your relationship not because she is uncertain about your feelings but because of the darkness surrounding the situation. She believes you love her. She doesn't think you would ever do anything to jeopardize the stability or health of the relationship. What she is afraid of is the person in the fog staying cloaked while wreaking havoc on your bond together, on your job."

"Did you have a dream, too?" David asked.

"You already know the answer to that," Robin replied.

"I want to propose at Christmas. Maybe that will help her feel more secure."

"Propose for the right reasons," Matt interjected again. "Propose because you love her."

"I don't think I can live without her. The minute we met again, I felt it. I couldn't stop the progression between us. I didn't want to," David confessed.

"You should definitely discuss things with her," Robin encouraged. "Sometimes simple reassurance can calm a lot of those irrational fears. It can calm rational ones, too," she smiled.

37

The next day, everyone enjoyed the Thanksgiving festivities. The lingering aroma of a delicious Thanksgiving feast filled the air, and laughter echoed through the house as family and friends came together in celebration. The table, adorned with the bounty of the season, was a centerpiece for shared joy and gratitude.

Amidst the delightful chaos of conversations, a genuine happiness permeated the atmosphere. Robin's radiant smile reflected the joy she felt having her children gathered once again. The familial bonds, strengthened by the shared meal and camaraderie, became the heart of the celebration.

As they reveled in the warmth of togetherness, the house echoed with the harmonious chorus of shared stories and laughter, encapsulating the essence of Thanksgiving.

After the kitchen was cleaned up and everyone sat in the living room to watch football, David wanted to take Alex on a walk through the woods. He wanted to investigate how she felt about him. He wanted to be sure she wouldn't reject him when he asked for her hand in marriage.

As David sat with his arm around her on the sectional, he leaned over, whispering in her ear.

"Will you take a walk with me?" he asked.

She turned to him, their noses almost touching. "Sure," she replied softly.

Coats would be needed, so they excused themselves and walked upstairs. David observed Alex as she walked in front of him. She moved with a quiet grace, her ensemble echoing a blend of casual comfort and rustic charm. The skinny jeans adorned with intentional rips added a touch of edginess, complemented by the warmth of wool socks. The red scoop-neck shirt and tartan flannel created a cozy yet stylish look, embodying the essence of a relaxed autumn day.

Her hair, neatly braided down her back, added a hint of simplicity. The scene unfolded like a curated snapshot of a fall day, capturing the subtle details that painted a portrait of Alex's unique style.

Seated on the bed, Alex's actions revealed a thoughtful consideration for comfort. The transition from thick to thinner socks, paired with the sturdy brown combat boots, hinted at a practical yet fashion-forward approach. The room became a pause in time for the quiet transformation, where each article of clothing contributed to the overall tapestry of Alex's individuality.

In contrast, David prepared for the outdoors with a touch of earthy elegance. He wore a pair of black bootcut jeans, a forest green thermal, and a matching flannel. From beside his old desk, he retrieved his black treaded boots, sitting down on the chair to lace them with a practiced ease.

Completing his attire, David took his black wool coat off the hanger in his closet and slipped it on, the fabric providing an extra layer of insulation against the impending cold. Despite the dropping wind chill and the prediction of snow, he opted to forgo a hat, perhaps confident in the warmth that the layers of clothing would provide.

Alex pulled her camel-colored quilted coat from the bedpost and slipped into it. She pulled out the matching toboggan from her coat pocket along with her gloves. They descended the stairs and walked through the living room.

"Where are you two off to?" Danny asked.

"We're going on a walk before the snow starts flying," David answered.

"You better hurry," Will added. "The snow is well on its way. Should be here within the hour."

"How much?" Alex asked.

"They are calling for three inches before 10 p.m. and then another four overnight," Olivia answered.

They exited the house, the dogs running outside in front of them. They played in the field as David and Alex made their way toward the back of the property.

Walking through the woods, the skeletal branches above swayed in choreography directed by the wind, their stark silhouettes against the autumn sky creating an enchanting dance. David led Alex through the familiar terrain. He'd lost count of the hours he had spent playing in the woods as a child. He and Will camped there every fall and summer. The memories flooded his mind.

David stopped at an undesignated spot, still holding onto Alex's hand. He turned to face her.

"What's wrong?" she asked, knowing something was amiss.

"Do you love me?" he asked.

"You know I do."

"Do you believe I love you?" he continued.

"Yes," she answered.

"I know that you're afraid of what you can't see, of what you can't figure out. I know the dream has really put you off balance. I get that. Our relationship will go through different phases. We'll grow. And, yes, we will both change, but the way I feel about you won't. We'll face difficult times, but we will face them together. I won't abandon you."

"What are you trying to say, David? It feels like you're trying to make a point about something," Alex inquired.

"Do you think you love me enough to stay with me for the long haul? I know it's only been a few months…"

"Stop," she said as she dropped his hand and put both of them in her pockets.

As David braced himself for a moment of vulnerability, his cheeks took on the hue of a rosy blush. The fear of potential rejection cast a shadow over his expression, leaving him momentarily exposed to the uncertainty of his emotions.

"Are you asking me about a lifetime commitment? Marriage?" she asked.

The forest bore witness to a silent dance of emotions as David, taking a few steps away, grappled with the weight of his feelings. The crunch of the leaves beneath his boots echoed the internal struggle that unfolded in the serene landscape. When he turned back to her, a subtle distance lingered, underscoring the vulnerability in his admission.

His gaze, initially directed at the ground, reflected the complexity of emotions he wrestled with. The quiet acknowledgment, accompanied by a slight nod, revealed the sincerity of his conviction.

Their eyes meeting, and with unprecedented vulnerability, David unveiled the truth. “Yes. I want to know how you feel about marrying me. You’re the one. I am supposed to be with you for the rest of my life,” he confessed, the words hanging in the stillness like a promise etched into the fabric of the forest.

“I think I’ve made it clear that I’ve loved you my entire life, David. My heart waited to belong to you. My body waited to belong to you. Are you afraid I will fall out of love with you? I don’t want you to consider marriage out of a sense of panic. I also don’t want to get married to you to further your political career.”

“Do you think I’m that shallow?”

“No, but I also don’t want to get ten years in with two kids and realize how much of a mistake a marriage was after only dating for a few months,” she argued.

“I understand how scary this is,” he said as he walked to her.

In that tender moment, David’s hands cradled her face, a gesture laden with a desire to bridge the gap between their hearts. His eyes, a window to the depths of his soul, locked with hers in an unspoken vow of transparency.

“I love you more than anything in this world, Alexandra. You are it for me. I know it. You are the one I want to be with for the rest of my life. I want to share this life with you, have a family with you. I want to be your husband, and I want you to be my wife.”

With these words, David laid bare the sentiments that had been nestled within his heart. The declaration, spoken with unwavering sincerity, wove a tapestry of love that enveloped them in a shared cocoon of vulnerability.

Tears trickled down her rosy cheeks.

"Do you feel the same way about me? Do you want to be with me like that?" he asked bluntly.

She nodded, tears spilling onto her cheeks. "Yes. I just don't want you to make a rash decision out of desperation."

"I'm not. I know what I want. It's you. It will always be you," he promised.

She nodded. "Promise?"

He pulled her into an embrace. "I promise."

As David inhaled the comforting fragrance of her skin, a rush of emotions overwhelmed him, surfacing in the form of teardrops that welled in his eyes. The scent acted as a trigger for the tears that mirrored the depth of his feelings.

"I love you," he mumbled against the bare canvas of her neck. The quiet declaration, spoken in the hallowed space where skin met skin, became a whispered vow that lingered in the air.

In this tender exchange, the tears served as silent witnesses to a love that transcended words. The moment unfolded, leaving behind a trace of tear-stained sincerity and an unspoken affirmation that love, in all its raw beauty, had found a home in their hearts.

38

In the quiet cocoon of the bedroom, the soft flicker of the electric candle created a mood of serenity. Its warm glow painted a calm picture, accentuating the contours of their faces as Alex and David lay facing each other. The dance of shadows on the walls became a silent masterpiece, mirroring the tender dance of sensations that played out between them.

Alex was only covered from the waist down, her ivory breasts exposed, and David's fingers dancing on her bare skin, teasing her from time to time. As they lay silently, the contours of their bodies mirrored the intertwined paths of their lives. David, with a hopeful heart, wished that the revelation of their commitment had infused a sense of security and assurance into Alex's being.

"I want to make love to you," David whispered.

"I thought maybe you did the way you've been touching me for the last hour or so," she replied softly.

He smiled.

"I want to please you first, though," she said. "So, you'd probably better take those clothes off."

David uncovered himself and stood beside the bed. She watched with anticipation as he untied his plaid flannel pajama bottoms and shed his white undershirt. He crawled back into the bed, not bothering to cover himself back up.

Alex leaned over to him and kissed his lips invitingly. She caressed him, teasing him and heightening his yearning for her. Feeling her breast against his skin only added to his desire.

As she kissed an invisible line down his chest, she whispered, "I love you."

He stroked her hair as she moved toward his erection. "I love you, honey."

He felt her warm breath as she took him into her mouth. He exhaled as he felt her hand tighten around him, her mouth moving up and down on him. He closed his eyes, accepting her touch, allowing himself to be vulnerable to her.

She breathed against his skin as she teased him, taking him to a place of ecstasy. The pressure of her hand as she twisted around him brought him closer to climax. In their moments of quiet intimacy, she had brought him to completion in her mouth before. He was tempted by that, but he wanted to give to her as well.

She stopped for a moment and moved, kneeling beside him on the mattress. Her mouth slid down on him again, her hand following. Her change in position was welcomed because it allowed him to touch her while she was pleasing him. He teased her nipple with his fingers. With every flick and squeeze, her moans vibrated around him, inching him closer to orgasm. Her strokes became more intense with his touch, and he pushed her panties aside so he could touch her more intimately.

He fondled her as she moved on him, twisting her palm again with the lubrication of her saliva, her groans still coming. She was quiet, but he could feel her body changing. His body began tensing, too. She was pushing him closer and closer to the edge with each stroke.

"You're gonna make me cum," he whispered.

She stopped, her mouth still on him, met his eyes, and kept going. This told him that her purpose was to please him. She wasn't looking for reciprocation.

She sped up again as David closed his eyes once more. He continued touching her, feeling her tighten around his fingers. She intensified her movements even more as he drew closer and closer to the familiar feeling of bliss. His body tensed again, tighter and tighter into a knot. He felt the knots begin to unravel, his heart speeding and his breath shallow.

She persisted as he writhed beneath her touch. Despite how good it felt, he remained as quiet as he possibly could. He could no longer focus on her and balled one hand into a fist, gripping the sheets, and the other woven into the dark locks of her hair. He pulsed uncontrollably as she drew out his release.

Finally, the lightheadedness began to subside. He felt himself start to calm. His heart slowed as she rested beside him, reveling in her success.

He looked over at her. "Do you want me to…" he began.

She shook her head, meeting his gaze. "No. I just wanted to get you there."

"I don't feel right about it, though."

She turned over to face him. "It's okay for me not to receive sometimes."

"I like when you receive, though," he argued.

"It's okay. I'm good," she assured him.

"Are you sure?"

"I'm positive. Can we just lie here in each other's arms and fall asleep? Would that be okay?"

"Come here," he said as he extended his arm. She rested her head on his chest and pulled the blankets up to cover them. Their breathing slowed as they fell into a soundless, dreamless sleep.

By Friday morning, David, Matt, Will, Brock, and Liam were hanging all of the outdoor Christmas lights. The ladies decorated inside. By late afternoon on Friday, Robin was making cookies with all of the grandkids. In the evening, Matt ordered a pizza, and the family enjoyed some board games.

On Saturday, Olivia, Danny, and the grandkids left to return home. David could see how much it pained Robin to see them leave. They didn't live too terribly far, but still, she found joy in having the entire family in one space.

Seeing how much their absence bothered Robin, Hope and David suggested that they take the Suburban into Dayton and ice skate. Both Matt and Robin were more than happy with this plan, so they piled into the large SUV and headed into the city.

Arriving at the ice-skating rink, the chilly air buzzed with anticipation. Hope and David, aware of the void left by Olivia's departure, aimed to create a new memory, a distraction wrapped in the joy of the present. The rhythmic swish of skates on ice became a cathartic melody.

The evening became a respite, a temporary escape from the ache of separation for Robin. As they glided on the ice, the joy painted a mosaic of family love against the backdrop of the night.

For David and Hope, witnessing their parents embrace the joy of the present moment became a poignant reminder of the love that anchored their family. The legacy of a strong and enduring partnership added another chapter to the cherished story they continued to write together.

On Sunday morning, Hope and Will departed. David knew he would need to speak to Will first thing Monday morning. He hadn't told anyone other than his parents and Alex about his upcoming career change.

After they left, David and Alex gathered up their belongings. They put the dogs in the car and put their bags in the back. Robin and Matt stood in the kitchen. David held out his hand. The prism he had picked up on his way to Pikeview gleamed in his palm.

"I got this for you, Mom," he said sweetly.

"Oh, thank you! It's beautiful," she said, taking the prism into her grasp. "I will put it in the window right over here," she said as she walked to the kitchen window and set it next to the window latch.

She walked back over to him, Alex now standing beside him. They embraced one another systematically. Robin lingered, holding onto David, resisting his departure.

"I love you," she said, still holding him tightly.

"I love you, too."

She stepped away and smiled, taking Matt's hand.

"It was wonderful seeing you both. Don't be strangers," she said.

"Christmas is right around the corner, so I'll get the spare room ready and the basement cleaned up. It's my turn to host this year," David said.

"That's right," Matt agreed. "It is. We'll be down the week of Christmas if that's okay."

"I thought you were staying through New Year's," David said.

"I believe we are. Two weeks?"

"That sounds right," he remarked.

"Are you sure we won't impose?" Robin asked, with concern in her voice.

"Not at all. I am looking forward to it."

"We can stay with your sister some, too," Robin added.

"I think Olivia and Danny and the kids are staying with her."

"But they will only stay a few days," Robin argued.

"True. We'll figure it out. Don't worry about it, okay?"

"I put that thing in your bag," Robin said, trying to hint about the engagement ring.

"Oh, okay," David said with a smile.

With every mile that passed, David found solace in the rhythm of the road, mirroring the steady beat of his heart. The plan he had crafted was more than a roadmap; it was a declaration of intent.

David wanted to be with Alex for the rest of his life, and he was taking the first step toward that future. The road ahead unfolded like an unwritten chapter, waiting to be filled with the stories of their shared endeavors. With each passing moment, David felt a profound sense of purpose, fueled by the unwavering commitment to a love that transcended any uncertainty now or in the future.

39

On Monday morning, David stood in the kitchen of the cottage. Joan, Will, and Alex sat at the table.

"I've been offered the position of interim juvenile judge," he blurted out.

Silence was the only reply.

"I will be here, but seldom. We will be terminating the contract with Children Services within the next month."

"It's about time. They've been terrible to work with," Joan interjected.

"When do you start?" Will asked.

"January 1st. Nothing will really change. The property is still in my name. Payroll will still work the same. I just won't be around as much."

"Well, you've finally gotten what you've always wanted," Joan said sourly.

Everyone turned their attention to her, shocked by her reaction. David could see that Alex was very interested in what she had to say.

"You've been practicing law like a superhero or something. It's almost like you were a vigilante. You think you can change the world. You think that by becoming a judge you can stamp out all of the perceived corruption. You can't. The corruption will swallow you up, and the very thing you've worked so hard to rid the world of… you'll become it," she explained.

"Is that what you really think?" David asked angrily.

"I believe that we enter situations like this with the purest intentions, and then the world has a tendency to swallow up those intentions, twisting them into darkness," she continued.

"So you think it's a mistake, too?" he asked, alluding to the fact that Joan wasn't the only one with concerns.

"I think you need to keep a very close watch on the people around you and the steps you are taking. Weigh everything. Most importantly, always remember who you are. Don't ever let anyone or anything turn you into someone you know you aren't."

David observed Alex as she listened. Her face settled with peace as well as support for Joan's words. She was in total agreement with Joan's concerns and advice. Joan had simply put it into words David could comprehend. Alex had failed in that, but it was evident that she was grateful someone had said the words out loud.

David sighed. "You all know me. You know who I am. You know how I operate. I won't betray any of you, let alone myself."

"You believe that, I know," Joan continued. "I just hope you can resist the temptations that are ahead, because they will be many."

Joan sounded like some sort of sage as she spoke in such a prophetic, cautious tone. David was desperate to change the subject.

"Does anyone have any questions about anything?" he asked.

Will shook his head but said nothing. Joan and Alex just sat quietly.

"So, if we're done here, we can all get back to work. I will contact Children Services and schedule a meeting to terminate their contract."

Will was the first to stand. He nodded and then walked out of the break area. Joan stood next, taking her coffee with her, silent in her exit. Alex sat waiting. David sat down in one of the empty chairs.

"What am I not seeing?" David asked.

Alex put her hand on his. "Everyone sees the huge risk here, and we want you to stay true to your values. Joan is right. Many people step into positions of power only to lose themselves."

"If they lose themselves, then it's safe to say they had a weak constitution anyway," he bit out.

"Just be careful. I know you don't put much stock in what I see, but something is coming; something that will test both of us. If we keep communicating, maybe we'll be okay."

"I know we will be okay," David said forcefully.

The rest of the day was quiet, though the buzz of productivity filled the shared workspace. David navigated the logistical aspects of the transition with Children Services. The phone call to them marked the beginning of the end of one chapter, and as he meticulously drafted the contract termination agreement, he felt a weight lifting off his shoulders. The commitment to their obligations would soon be fulfilled.

The next step in David's planned agenda was to prepare for the proposal. That had its own process, but he was less apprehensive about that. Asking Alex to marry him would be easy compared to what he had just experienced with Joan.

As he moved through the practicalities of their professional decisions, David couldn't help but acknowledge the contrasting nature of the challenges. The upcoming engagement, a celebration of love and commitment, seemed to hold a simplicity and clarity that provided a welcome contrast to the complexities of their professional journey.

40

The Christmas holiday season brought so much joy. The air was filled with festive spirit, and the twinkling lights adorned the town, creating a magical backdrop.

As he prepared to propose, David immersed himself in the details, each element carefully chosen to create an enchanting tapestry. The delight of the season served as a harmonious melody, infusing his actions with a warmth that transcended the winter chill. As he embarked on the journey of planning, the anticipation of the upcoming proposal added an extra layer of sparkle to the holiday festivities.

He talked to Will about his plans. Will, sworn to keep the secret, became a conspirator in crafting the perfect moment, understanding the significance it held for David.

The first order of business was speaking to Alex's father. David was nothing if not traditional. So, he went to the county offices for a surprise visit. Once he got past the secretary, he offered to take Russell out to lunch.

They drove to the Market Deli next to the courthouse. The snowflakes flurried but didn't make much of an impact as the two men made their way up onto the sidewalk and into the café. After being seated, they ordered their lunch and made small talk. Finally, David began, his intent pushing him forward in the conversation.

"So, I want to talk to you about something, Russell," he began.

"Sure. Everything okay?"

"Oh yeah. Everything is fine," he replied as he took a sip of his soda. He smiled courteously and then continued. "Russell, I'm sure you know that I've fallen in love with Alex. I want to ask her to marry me, but I want your permission."

"Oh," Russell said. "I didn't realize things were so serious, but then again, Alex keeps her personal life very personal."

"I know how sudden this must seem," David began. "I want you to know I've put a lot of thought into this. I can assure you that we aren't rushing into anything."

"Listen, Alex has always gone her own way. She has never asked for permission to do anything. I wouldn't dare speak for her. I will, however, give you my blessing. I don't know a whole lot about all of that emotional stuff, but what I do know is that Alex has loved you since she was a young girl. You really helped her out when…" he choked up for a moment and then quickly composed himself. "Well, anyway, you have my blessing to marry Alex. I think you will be very happy together."

"I think we will be, too. Things have been kind of a whirlwind with her."

"When you least expect it, that's when it happens," Russell agreed. "When are you planning on doing it?"

"Well, I'd like to do it Christmas Eve. My family is coming in for the holiday, and I wondered if you and Penny would be there. Maybe Ben and Jeremy, too. I don't want to make it a big public production. Something simple and elegant at my cabin."

"You definitely know Alex. She doesn't like public productions. We will definitely be there. You can count on that. I won't say anything to anyone other than Penny, though. Ben tends to get overly excited about these sorts of things. I was surprised he was able to keep my party a secret."

David smiled, relief settling on his countenance. "I will host Christmas Eve dinner at 4:30. I will tell her that I've invited you all, and she will be none the wiser."

"Sounds like a plan, son. I am so proud of you both! I heard that you'll be interim juvenile judge."

"Yes. I'm a little nervous."

"You'll do great. You're exactly what this town needs," he concluded.

They finished their lunch, and then David drove Russell back to the county offices. The discussion had gone better than he expected. The weight of anticipation lifted from his shoulders, replaced by a sense of relief and appreciation.

After dropping Russell off, the echoes of their conversation lingered in the air. David reflected on the significance of the day. The successful conversation marked a milestone. He felt a growing sense of gratitude for the support he had received. The prospect of making Alex his wife appeared on the horizon as a reality, and it was certainly one he was ready to fully embrace.

41

The days passed quickly. David closed the practice the week of Christmas, and he wouldn't reopen until the week after New Year's. The news had finally made its way around town about David's new career venture. The Democrat and Republican parties had already approached him about running in the November election. He was unsure about which party he agreed with, however. He was more of a Libertarian, so he put that in his back pocket for after the holiday.

Robin and Matt arrived on December 23rd. Despite the protesting, David graciously gave them his master bedroom for their stay. He and Alex took the spare room upstairs.

Sensing the buzz of the holidays and the anticipated arrival of family, the dogs were overexcited. Olivia, Danny, and the kids were going to stay at Hope's place.

Amelia would be adding a new dimension to the family gathering by bringing her boyfriend, Devon. The prospect of meeting the new addition heightened the festive atmosphere.

Christmas Eve was filled with cooking and preparing. Because David, Matt, and Ben loved to cook, they were more than happy to participate in the kitchen. Robin, Hope, Penny, and Alex manned the desserts and breads, along with some side dishes. David and Matt, on the other hand, worked on the ham and turkey, their laughter and shared camaraderie infusing the kitchen with a contagious holiday spirit.

The delightful chaos of the kitchen echoed with the clatter of pots and pans, the aroma of savory delights wafting through the air. Amidst the bustling activity, the clinking of utensils and the hum of conversation created a beautiful symphony.

Meanwhile, Danny, Russell, Jeremy, Liam, Brock, and Devon embarked on a mission to tidy the barn. Its rustic charm promised a unique setting for the Christmas meal. Under the guidance of Will, they adorned the space with festive lights, transforming it into a winter wonderland. Will's meticulous touch ensured that every detail was perfect, creating a picturesque backdrop.

During the meal, there was a lot of conversation surrounding Amelia and Devon's relationship: how they met, what he was involved in with school, his goals, his hopes, his dreams. He was very well suited for her. She was spunky, and he was fairly quiet. He seemed to bring some calm to her chaos. This made everyone very happy for her. She had experienced a lot of turbulence in her life, so finally seeing her settling down was a comfort to her family.

After the meal, everyone made their way back into the cabin for the gift exchange. The packages and paper began piling up on the floor as everyone ripped into their respective gifts. Laughter and exclamations of delight filled the room, creating a cacophony of joy.

Amidst the cheerful bedlam, David felt a growing anticipation in the pit of his stomach. Although he had carefully chosen and wrapped gifts for Alex, earbuds, a gift certificate to her favorite store, and a sweater she had been eyeing for the last few weeks, he had deliberately saved the proposal for last.

As the room purred with the excitement of gift-giving, David discreetly handed his beer to Will. Everyone was so engrossed in their own conversations that no one really noticed David walking toward the majestic ten-foot Christmas tree in the corner next to the front windows.

The glow of the Christmas lights illuminated the room, casting a warm and intimate feel. With each step toward the tree, David's heartbeat echoed in his ears.

A hush fell over the cabin as David reached the tree, and he took a deep breath. The knot in his stomach tightened, but determination gleamed in his eyes. The room, unwittingly, shifted its focus as David stood beside the tree.

He cleared his throat and put his hands into his jeans pockets. "Um, I want to thank all of you for being here," he began, looking around the room at everyone. "I am so incredibly grateful for each of you. Thank you for being here."

He paused a moment. His eyes locked with Alex's. "Honey, can you come up here with me, please?" he asked.

She smiled and handed her wine glass to Hope. She stood and walked to him.

David took a deep breath, the weight of the moment hanging in the air like a delicate snowflake. The glow of the Christmas lights danced in Alex's eyes as he looked into them.

"Alexandra," he began, his voice steady but carrying a hint of nerves, "from the moment we met so long ago, my life has been touched by your light. When you came back, you brought so much joy to my life. The time we've spent together has been incredible. You make me a better man, and I honestly don't think I could breathe without you now. Life before you, it's a faint memory."

He reached into his pocket, retrieving a small velvet box. The room seemed to hold its breath as he opened it, revealing his grandmother's ring. The jewelry sparkled like a promise. Alex's eyes widened, mirroring the vivacity of the ring.

"I can't promise that I'll get everything right, but I can promise to do my very best to make you happy every day for the rest of your life. Will you do me the tremendous honor of becoming my wife?"

The room fell silent. Time seemed to stretch, capturing the essence of the moment. The weight of David's question hung in the air, and in the hush that followed, he saw the answer he had been hoping for in the tearful yet joyful glint in Alex's eyes.

And then, breaking the silence, a heartfelt "Yes" escaped from Alex's lips.

As David slid the ring onto Alex's finger, a symbol of their newfound commitment, the room erupted with clapping and everyone was on their feet. A wave of emotion swept over them both. In that moment, time seemed to stand still, and the world faded away, leaving only the two of them.

With the ring securely in place, David gently lifted Alex into his arms, her laughter echoing in the air. Her arms wrapped tightly around his neck as they found themselves suspended between the ordinary and the extraordinary.

"I love you so much, Alex," he whispered.

"I love you, too," she said, her voice breaking as she pressed her face into his shoulder.

42

The excitement of the holidays continued through New Year's. The two engagements, Hope and Will's and David and Alex's, gave the family something to look forward to. Hope and Alex spent hours discussing options. Hope wanted something audacious. Alex wanted something simple, set against the autumn colors and out in nature. Hope, on the other hand, wanted a destination wedding to an exotic beach. Hope was planning on a June wedding next year. Alex wanted a wedding this year.

David was sworn in and began serving in juvenile court. As promised, he split his time between juvenile court and the cottage. Things felt calm, with a cadence that was comfortable for everyone.

Living arrangements had been a topic between the couples. Alex was moving out of her cottage and into the cabin. Hope decided to move into her summer cottage full time and work remotely as much as possible. She was also contracting with local law enforcement as a consultant to supplement her income. She was going to finish her graduate studies online.

David decided to step outside of the box. He ran on the Libertarian ticket. He couldn't align himself with the Democrat or Republican philosophies, so he decided to break the mold and fly solo.

To top it off, Alex decided to run for county prosecutor on the Republican ticket. She aligned with the Libertarian Party, but Richard was a Republican. She wanted his job, and her intent was to take it.

As the snow fell outside, David sat in the lavish leather chair in his office at juvenile court. He looked up from the law books for a moment. He peered out the window to admire how beautiful the flakes were as they settled on the windowsill.

The knock on the chamber door brought him swiftly back to the present. He looked up to see his administrative assistant, Laylonie, peeking around the door.

Laylonie was only twenty years old. She was working her way through college and would graduate in June with her associate's degree in legal assisting. She hoped to move forward toward a paralegal degree thereafter. She was motivated and insightful. David was happy to have her on board.

"Sir, Gerri Hamilton-Meyers is here. Do you have some time to talk to her?"

"Absolutely," he replied as he stood up. He assumed she wanted to collect some of Steven's personal belongings. No one had really seen her since Steven's funeral.

Stepping out of his chambers, David walked to the open reception area, his hand outstretched expectantly. Instead, Gerri gave him a friendly hug. David pulled away, and then led her back to his office.

"Please, come in," he said. "How are you holding up?" he asked as he shut the door behind them.

She nodded. "Oh, I'm okay. That's kind of why I'm here," she admitted.

David wandered to the front of the large desk and leaned against it as Gerri sat down in the empty chair in front of it. She crossed her legs as she shimmied out of her powder pink parka, unveiling a long, wool, cream-colored sweater that embraced her lean silhouette. The soft fabric clung to her. To complement the color of the sweater, she wore a pair of sleek black leggings, and her boots were snow-covered.

Her blonde hair, dusted with delicate snowflakes, peeked out from beneath a woolen toboggan that matched her sweater. With a carefree shake, she released the captured snow, letting the crystals fall like tiny diamonds to the floor.

David thought that Gerri looked rather well, considering she was supposed to be a grieving widow. There were no dark circles or bags under her eyes. In fact, she was completely unblemished, untouched by the grief.

"What can I help you with, Gerri?" David asked as he folded his arms.

"Steven's kids are contesting his will," she blurted out.

"Oh, I see."

"He left everything to me: the house, the cars, the accounts, all of it. His kids never really wanted anything to do with him after he married me, so he wrote them out of his will. I tried to talk him out of it, but he refused to change his mind. They broke his heart."

David nodded. He wasn't entirely certain he was getting the truth, however. He knew he was only getting one side of the story.

"I need an attorney to help me fight them. They will hold this up in probate for years if I don't get something done. I'll pay you whatever you want. I have the money. That's probably another reason the kids are throwing such a fit."

"Why not go to Alexandra? She deals specifically with wills and estates. That's one of her specialties. She's very good."

"In case you haven't noticed," she continued with a deep southern drawl, "she doesn't think very highly of me. I can't presume to understand why." She stopped momentarily to toss her hair over her shoulder. "David, I really feel like Steven's kids need a male attorney to come after them. I don't think they would take Alex seriously. You know Steven had all sons, and they don't really respect women."

"When you said that the other reason they were throwing a fit was because you already have money, what did you mean by that?"

"My first serious relationship was with Maureen Wynberg," she said as her eyes glazed over. "She was my first love, really. I never thought I would get over her death. I was so lost without her. I took one of her classes in college, and afterward, we just hit it off. We fell deeply in love with each other. Of course, we couldn't marry because of the laws then. Gay marriage wasn't legal. Still, she made sure that if anything happened, I'd be taken care of. When she died, she left me what little she'd saved, and I was the beneficiary on her life insurance policy at work.

"Then, when I married Herbert and he passed away, I was the beneficiary on his pension and his life insurance policy. His kids were upset, but they got all of his rental properties and the income that came with them, so they didn't protest too terribly hard."

"Gerri, how much money do you have exactly?"

"Well, I…" she hesitated.

"Listen to me," David said as he leaned forward, his arms still crossed. "I can't help you if you're not honest with me. Steven's kids are going to drag out skeletons if there are any. They are going to make your financial holdings public anyway. You've got to tell me what we're looking at here."

Gerri's eyes dropped, and she cast a gaze upon her perfectly manicured hands. Her wedding and engagement rings adorned her left hand, the white gold bands glistening against her sun-kissed skin.

"Between Maureen's money and Herbert's money, I already have over a million in assets and investments," Gerri admitted, her voice carrying a tone of both vulnerability and matter-of-factness. "With Steven's life insurance and his assets, I believe it all comes out to about $3.5 million. He was very smart with the way he invested his money."

She continued, a calm expression gracing her perfectly symmetrical face. "I don't know why I should be punished. I didn't ask for any of this to happen. He changed his will and his policy completely on his own. He always said he wanted me to be taken care of if something were to happen to him. He just stayed true to his word," she concluded, punctuating her words with a shrug.

"My guess is that they feel betrayed," David remarked. "Aren't you the same age as one of his sons?"

"Yes, but that doesn't mean Steven and I weren't in love," she replied defensively. "They deserted him. That's why he left everything to me."

"They want the house sold, I'm assuming, and then the profit split between them. There's, what, five children total?"

"Yes. Kyle, Lyle, Harry, Dresden, and Lorenzo. The property won't bring them much. We refinanced to do some upgrades and were still making payments. His life insurance will pay off the mortgage, though. It doesn't matter," she said. "They just walked off and left him when he married me. Why should they be entitled to anything now?" The venom in her tone wasn't easily hidden.

"I know you're angry," David said, "and I understand where you're coming from. Legally, it sounds like Steven set everything up the right way. I'm going to need a copy of his last will and testament so I can go through it with a fine-tooth comb. If there are any loopholes, then we've got some work to do. If the will is solid, then really, the kids don't have a leg to stand on. I think maybe what they are trying to do is keep everything tied up in probate. If they drain you out of money, the problem solves itself."

Gerri nodded, her doe eyes filled with innocence. "No one knows how much money I actually have. Only you, my accountant, and my investment manager know exactly how much I have in assets. I only keep about $50,000 in the local banks here. The rest is in the Caymans and the Bahamas, offshore accounts."

"Are your taxes clean?" David inquired.

"Yes. Of course," she answered. "All I want to do is honor Steven's wishes and go on with my life, try to heal from all of this. I think I'm cursed," she said as tears welled in her eyes. "Everyone I love dies. First Maureen, then Herbert, and now Steven. I don't think I'll ever marry again."

David's sympathetic nature took over, and he sat down in the empty chair beside her. He grabbed the tissue box off his desk and held it out to her. Gerri pulled a tissue from it as she cried softly.

"You're young. You'll find someone," he said kindly.

"I don't care what anyone thinks," Gerri said as she sniffled and blotted the tears under her eyes, being careful not to smudge her perfectly applied mascara. "Steven loved me. We had a wonderful marriage. Age didn't matter to either of us. We had so many things in common, and we loved each other. We didn't care what people said."

"And that's what matters," David said sympathetically. "You have that to hold onto moving forward."

"And I hope you're right about me finding someone. Alex is so lucky to have you," she said, smiling innocently. "I heard you all got engaged over the holiday."

"Yes. We will be married in the fall."

"Not waiting around then?" she said as she held tightly to the tissue.

"No. We're pretty eager to be married. She is moving in with me, which is great, but I want it legal."

"Well, I wish you two all of the best," she said. "So, you'll help me?" Gerri asked, changing the subject.

"I don't see the harm in it. I think this will be resolved very quickly. No one deserves this kind of grief. It's bad enough when someone dies, let alone people fighting over money."

"I couldn't agree more."

"Like I said, I need a copy of the will, and I need your financial records for the last decade. I also want copies of Herbert's will and Maureen's. I need copies of your taxes, too. The important thing is not to worry. Being stressed out about this is not going to help you at all. Just stay calm. Don't talk to Steven's kids either. You leave that to me. Have they retained someone yet?"

"Yes. Someone out of Dayton, I think," Gerri answered. "They already sent me a letter."

"I need the attorney's information so I can send correspondence that I'm representing you."

“Okay. Well, I can get you everything you need,” Gerri replied. “And the retainer? How much do I need to write the check for?”

“We’ll figure that out later.”

“Oh, David. Are you sure?”

“Positive.”

“I can’t thank you enough for doing this,” she said gratefully. “Like I said, Alexandra is the luckiest woman alive. You are so kind and selfless.”

“Thank you, Gerri. I’m pretty lucky to have her, too.”

Gerri rose gracefully, slipping her coat back on. David escorted her to the door before returning to his office. As the door closed behind her, he couldn’t help but ponder the intricacies of her situation. The truth remained elusive.

A few days passed, and David headed into the courthouse. Walking through the corridors, David shed his warm navy-blue pea coat and leather gloves, the familiar routine of courthouse life unfolding before him. Laylonie acknowledged him with a nod as he passed, the professional camaraderie a silent acknowledgment of shared duties in the legal realm.

Moments later, before David could even hang up his coat, Laylonie knocked on his chamber door. He motioned her in.

“Mr. Gregory,” Laylonie began as she stood just outside the door.

“Laylonie, I told you to call me David.”

“David, um, this was dropped off this morning. Mrs. Meyers told me to make sure I gave it to you.”

She handed David an envelope and a long, rectangular box. Then she excused herself as David turned his attention to the box, an item filled with mystery.

Upon opening it, a beautiful black pen lay nestled on red velveteen, a symbol of refinement and thoughtful craftsmanship. The golden cursive inscription of his name adorned the side, a personalized touch that added a layer of sentiment to the gift.

A note accompanied the pen, revealing Gerri's appreciation in graceful words.

If you aren't going to let me pay you, the least you can do is accept this pen as a gift. Thank you for helping me. —Gerri

The gesture resonated with gratitude, a silent exchange of acknowledgment between attorney and client, veering into the realm where professionalism intersected with personal connections.

A smile graced David's face as he admired the elegant pen and read Gerri's note. The gesture resonated with gratitude. However, a subtle hesitation lingered within him.

Taking his cell phone out of his suit jacket pocket, David contemplated reaching out to Gerri. Yet a realization struck him. He didn't have her mobile number. An unexpected moment of self-awareness washed over him, tinged with a hint of embarrassment. Despite the professional engagement and the generous gift before him, the simple act of securing her contact details had been overlooked.

In the midst of this realization, David considered the best course of action. Coincidentally, his office phone rang. It was Laylonie informing him that Gerri was on the line.

David picked up the receiver. Before she could say anything, he began. “Mrs. Meyers, thank you for the pen, but it isn’t necessary.”

“Oh, come now. If you won’t let me pay you, you have to accept it. It would be awfully rude to send it back to me, now wouldn’t you agree?”

“I suppose you’re right. Thank you.”

“I also dropped off all of the paperwork you asked for,” she continued. “If you have questions, you just call me.”

“Well, I would, but I don’t have your phone number.”

“Well, I can solve that problem.” She shared her number and hung up.

43

After a very long, productive day, and the end of yet another week, David just wanted to go home and relax. A fire, some pizza, and snuggling would be the primary mission for the weekend. He also intended to look over Gerri's paperwork.

The buzzing mobile phone on his desk pulled him back to the here and now. Alex's number showed up on the screen. With a grin, he picked up the phone and answered.

"Hey you."

"Hey," she started. "I've got supper in the oven. I thought we could cozy up by the fire and watch a movie tonight."

"That sounds like heaven," he said agreeably. "I'll spring for pizza tomorrow night."

"Okay. Sounds like a plan," she agreed.

"We are supposed to get several more inches of snow tonight," he said.

"We may get trapped," she teased.

"My, my. What will we do all weekend?"

"I can suggest a few things," Alex replied with a smile in her voice.

"Well, I'm leaving right now, so expect me within a half hour or so. They've been plowing the roads here in town. How are the county roads?"

"They aren't bad. Be careful, okay?"

“Always.”

“I love you,” she concluded.

“Love you, too,” he said, and then hung up.

David opted to leave the elegant pen on his desk. The envelope, harboring potentially pivotal documents, took precedence as he prepared to leave the office.

Upon arriving at the cabin, warmth enveloped him, accompanied by the enticing aroma of freshly baked bread. The comfort of home welcomed him, setting the stage for an evening of domestic tranquility. As they settled in, David and Alex shared a delightful meal of spaghetti adorned with homemade sauce and accompanied by the tempting scent of garlic bread.

“This is delicious,” he remarked as he took a bite of the food.

“It’s my aunt’s recipe.”

“It’s good. Thank you for cooking,” he said, leaning over and kissing her cheek.

“So, how was your day?” she asked curiously.

David told Alex about Gerri’s situation. He knew he would need her help. She was better at probate cases. If, after they reviewed the paperwork, he still had questions, he planned to ask Gerri to allow Alex to be signed on as co-counsel for the case.

As Alex tidied up the kitchen after the meal, David decided to run a hot bath. It was the perfect way to start off the evening and to thank her for the wonderful dinner. He had some romantic ideas for the perfect snowed-in weekend.

He lit some candles and poured some of Alex’s lavender oil into the swirling water. The flickering flames cast a soft, warm glow around the bathroom, creating an ambiance of intimacy. David undressed, savoring the anticipation of the evening ahead, and wrapped a towel around his waist. He walked to the bedroom and turned on some music, selecting a playlist that echoed the sentiments he felt for Alex.

Quietly, he walked into the kitchen and watched Alex as she put the last plate in the dishwasher. She wore one of his old t-shirts and a pair of sweats. It didn't matter how she dressed. She was the sexiest thing he'd ever seen.

In that unassuming moment, David found himself captivated by the effortless allure of Alex. The familiarity of her attire only heightened the appeal, a reminder that it was the essence of her, the way she moved, the way she smiled, that held an irresistible charm. As he stood there, bathed in the soft glow of the kitchen lights, the stage was set for an evening of intimacy.

"I've run a bath if you want to join me," he said.

She turned to see him in the towel. A devilish smile found its way to her lips.

"I thought maybe we could relax in the tub for a while," he continued, "and then see where things go after that."

"Count me in," she said as she closed the dishwasher and walked to the bathroom. She slid her sweatpants off of her hips and then peeled off the t-shirt. She stepped into the water. David dropped the towel from his waist. Alex admired the view as he stepped into the tub.

They sat in the garden-style tub talking about their week. David listened intently as Alex told him about the cases she had been working on. He missed being in the office with her every day. Once Alex finished speaking, she looked around the room.

"This is just perfect," she remarked.

"I wanted to seduce you," he said with a wink.

"Ahh, I see," she replied with a giggle.

"Is it working?"

"It might be."

"I miss you," he admitted.

A perplexed scowl **showed** on Alex's face. "What do you mean?"

"I miss being with you every day at the office. I miss everything about it. Your singing. Your coffee. Your laugh."

She moved to him. Cupping his face, she looked into his eyes. "You see me quite often."

"It still isn't the same," he admitted, sadness in his tone.

"David, this is a calling for you. It's a call you had to answer. I was afraid, and at times I still am. We're strong enough, though. We'll handle it. You convinced me of that at Thanksgiving."

As he soaked in the touch of her hand on his face, the bath water swirling around them, he didn't want to imagine his life without her in it. Being married to her was exciting and put some of his fears to rest.

"I love you," he whispered as he leaned in to steal a kiss.

"I love you, David. Nothing will change that," she assured him.

After the bath, they put a soft, cozy comforter down in front of the fireplace, scattering pillows all around. They lay naked, allowing the fire to dry their skin.

David was grateful that he had been able to put many of Alex's fears to rest. He was glad she had quieted the idea that there was some sort of impending doom lurking in the shadows. Things were better between them for now.

Wrapped in the warmth of the comforter, the crackling fire casting a dance of shadows on their entwined bodies, David marveled at the peace that enveloped them. The level of trust they shared was like nothing he'd ever felt before.

He just stared, speechless and captivated by the raw beauty that rested beside him. Every now and then, she'd reach up to the coffee table for her wine glass, take a sip, and then rest easy once more. The motion became a cadence, and David studied it like an animal in the wild.

With her next sip, he allowed her to finish and then gently took the wine glass from her and sat it back down on the coffee table. Her mouth dropped open a little, and he could see she was preparing to protest, but she didn't. Instead, she laid back, her head resting on the pillow. He moved in closer and sat on his knees. Gazing down at her perfect features, he caressed her cheek with the back of his hand.

"You set me on fire," he remarked. "You consume me with who you are, Alexandra. Every ounce of you burns away years of doubt. When I look at you, I can feel myself heat up. It's like you've struck a match, but you never let me burn without saving me. Your touch," he continued as he caressed her collarbone and then her breast, "always saves me."

Her smile was seductive, yet appreciative. “Fire is cleansing. It brings us back to where we belong. It forces us **to** grow.”

“You have shown me parts of myself that I never even knew were there. I unravel. Your touch feels like a spark against my skin every single time.”

He leaned down and kissed her, starting the sensual dance they had engaged in many times. The yearning they shared for one another called them to a place filled with desire. It invited them in for more every single time. This rush that filled them met a primal need, something deep within them, a recognition of souls.

The feel of her soft skin, her lips on his body, and **her** hands. He always wanted this. The gentle touches he had offered her over the past few months and the rushed need enveloped him once again as he made love to her. The sound of her voice and the warmth of being inside of her was something he would never take for granted. He would always want her this way. He would always honor her this way. He would always want to touch her this way. He would always want to please her this way, and he was so thankful she showed him the same earnest worship.

44

David was awakened with a jolt. He remembered holding Alex in his arms as they drifted off, resting after the much-needed session of lovemaking, warmed by the fire. He also remembered waking briefly and following her into the bedroom, making love to her once more before they fell completely into deep slumber. He was still disoriented and wasn't sure where he was. Then he realized the jolt he felt came from Alex.

He looked over at her. She was having a nightmare. Her chest heaved. Her fists were clenched, holding tightly to the sheets. She was mumbling unintelligibly, and her eyebrows furrowed. Sweat beaded on her naked skin. This was the first time David had ever witnessed her in this state.

He sat up and gently touched her with the hope that he could drag her from whatever hell she found herself in. However, she was trapped, so he shook her a little. Her eyes opened. She sat straight up, and she started crying and shouting things that didn't make sense.

He shifted toward her and pulled her into his chest. "Alexandra, I'm right here. You're safe. It's okay."

She shuddered against his chest and pulled herself tightly to him.

He stroked her damp hair. "I'm here. I won't let anything happen to you."

Finally, she calmed. "That's what you used to say to me when we were kids," she reminded him.

He kissed her cheek. “Are you okay?”

“It was horrible.”

“The dream?”

“Yes.”

“Do you want to tell me about it?”

“I don’t think you’d understand it. I don’t even think I understand it.”

“Try me.”

She hesitated.

“Please. I want to understand. Tell me.”

“I was standing outside of my body, right at the end of the bed. I saw you with someone else. She was on top of you. At first it was sexual, and then I watched her choke you. She was killing you. I couldn’t see her face. She wore a golden cloak. I tried to help, but I was frozen.

“I looked up at the ceiling, and when I looked back down, I was standing on the edge of a cliff, looking down into an abyss below. I knew someone stood behind me, and I knew it was the person in the golden cloak. I knew I was going to die. I saw the raven flying just above me, and I knew it had come to collect me. There was so much it needed to tell me, but its purpose changed. Now it would take me to the next world. Then there were bats flying up from the abyss, and they devoured the raven. I knew there was no hope of survival, but I knew you were waiting on the other side. So, I begged to go. I begged to die so I could be with you.”

David held her even tighter. “It’s just a dream, Alexandra. It’s just a dream.”

"It was a vision, David," she said as she pulled away from him. "It's another warning, just like before."

He was disappointed to hear this. He didn't want to venture back into that dark place of doubt and fear. Things were too good right now.

"I will never betray you. Never! I would never let anyone touch me. I love you and only you," he said as he tilted her chin up and then tucked a strand of hair behind her ear.

45

Saturday morning revealed a beautiful snowfall. More was expected. The cozy seclusion allowed for the perfect opportunity to comfort Alex. He wanted to make some breakfast for her after the terrible night she'd had, but before that, David stood in the mudroom, looking at the majesty of winter. The bare trees against the backdrop of a gray sky told him that more heavy snow was on its way. The snowfall wasn't usually this bad, but he remembered that the Almanac predicted a bad winter for their area.

He felt arms snaking around his waist and lips on his neck. Alex's fragrance enveloped him, and he closed his eyes, relishing her warmth against his back.

"Morning," she said in a hushed tone.

"Morning," he said as he looked over his shoulder at her. "You okay?"

"I will be," she assured him.

"That nightmare was pretty intense and quite detailed. You sure you're okay?"

"I'm okay. I just need to process it. If I can analyze it, I'll be fine. Knowledge is power. I will call my aunt Shayleen in a bit. I'll tell her about it and see if she can offer some insight."

"Are you hungry?" he asked. "I want to make you breakfast."

"I am."

"I can make pancakes. We can picnic in front of the fireplace."

"We know where that took us last night, so maybe we should eat at the breakfast bar," she laughed.

"True," he agreed.

A stack of pancakes sat on a plate in the middle of the counter. David was famished. He grabbed a few and then walked around to the bar stool. Alex was already devouring her food. They had a great excuse for needing nourishment. Their sexual exploits often had such an effect on them. They were typically ravenous afterward.

Gerri's situation crossed his mind, and he knew that he had some work to do despite his desire to spend the entire day tangled up in Alex. He also wanted to play in the snow with her. He had a side-by-side, and winter weather made for the perfect playground. Still, he needed to show Alex the paperwork Gerri dropped off at the office.

"Although I do want to take you in the side-by-side and make snow angels and then tear your clothing off to engage in carnal relations once more," he half joked, "I need you to take a look at Gerri's paperwork."

Alex took a bite of her pancake and then put the napkin to her mouth, placing it beside the plate when she was finished. "I'm not shocked that the kids are going after her," she admitted.

"Me neither, but I don't think it's right. Whether they agreed with their father or not, Gerri is who he chose."

"You do realize that you have to prove that Steven wasn't murdered in order for the money and property to be released?"

"Murdered? Why would you think he was murdered? He died right in front of me."

"Well, it is obvious he didn't commit suicide, true. And yes, he died right in front of you. However, insurance companies tend to hold up money if the death is under investigation. Is it under investigation?"

"I would assume it isn't. Why would it be?" He was astonished at the prospect.

"Think like a criminal for a second, David. Better yet, think like a grieving child. If this was your father, and he had married a significantly younger woman who had already buried two other people, wouldn't you be suspicious? And he wasn't in poor health, and then suddenly he was? Remember, two of his sons are beat cops, the other is a fire chief, and the other two are detectives. They are likely already digging into this, which might be why they want to hold things up for a bit."

David drew a blank. He hadn't even considered that.

"You think Steven was killed?" he asked as he looked over at Alex.

"I don't know. I do know that when suspicions are raised by the family, they are usually taken seriously," she continued. "I also know that when people are hurting and grieving, they try to find logic in death. As far as insurance companies are concerned, before handing out millions of dollars, they dive into every possibility, especially with a contested will. If Steven was generally healthy, the coroner should have ordered an autopsy. You need to make sure you look into that, too. There are many facets to this that Gerri has failed to fill you in on, but that isn't her job. It's your job as her attorney to investigate every possibility."

"Wow. No wonder I hired you," he said with a smile. "Either way," he continued, "can you take a look at her paperwork and make sure it's in order? It's not up to me to decide how Steven died, but it is up to me to make sure his last wishes are carried out. It sounds like his kids are trying to stand in the way of that."

"I can look at what you have. I also want to see her list of investments and past taxes. I would advise you to get a copy of the medical report, a list of medications he was taking, if any, and pull his general health records. Something isn't right here. I can feel it."

Murder? David realized Gerri was a sly little lynx, but she certainly wasn't a murderer, surely. She was sincere, and being a gold digger was no reason to impugn her grief.

As David cleaned up the breakfast mess, he couldn't help but steal glances at Alex, who sat in front of the fire, engrossed in the contents of the envelope. Her eyebrows furrowed many times as she read over the paperwork. He could see her thoughts racing, her legal mind running through scenarios. This case wasn't going to be as simple as he thought.

Alex, absorbed in the intricacies of the case, seemed to be unraveling layers of a puzzle. David, despite his initial skepticism about Gerri's involvement in something as grave as murder, found himself drawn into the unfolding mystery. The cozy mood of their home belied the storm brewing in the form of legal challenges, and David couldn't help but wonder how deeply they would be entangled in the enigma Gerri had unwittingly presented them.

46

Taking the side-by-side through the woods, ice fishing, wrestling with the dogs, and making snow angels made for an exhausting day. David and Alex felt like kids again. For so long, they had been consumed by adult responsibilities, and it took finding each other to feel that rush of youth. While it was true that they were only in their twenties, when they were together, they felt like kids once more.

As they parked the side-by-side back at the cabin, breathless laughter echoed in the crisp winter air. The snow-covered landscape bore witness to their playful escapades, a canvas of memories etched in every foot and paw print.

Inside the warm embrace of the cabin, David and Alex shed layers of snow-dusted clothes, feeling the pleasant ache of muscles used in joyful abandon. The burdens of adulthood momentarily lifted, replaced by the sheer joy of being present in the moment. In each other's company, they found a sanctuary where responsibilities faded, and the spirit of adventure danced freely.

After dinner, Alex and David sat on the sofa going over the paperwork Gerri left at the office. David watched as the crinkle in Alex's forehead deepened. She was always careful to have a poker face with clients, but when she was alone in the throes of analyzing material, she couldn't hide her true reaction.

"What is it?" David asked.

She shook her head and took off her reading glasses. "Something isn't right here."

"What do you mean?"

"Well, she's omitted things. I don't see a letter from the plaintiffs' attorney." Alex shuffled through the paperwork as she continued. "I see tax documents. I see investment documents. I see bank statements. I see everything I need to see financially, but where is the letter from the attorney contesting the will? Why was that not included? Didn't you ask for the opposing counsel's information?"

"Yes, I did."

"It doesn't make sense why she would leave it out," Alex reflected, malice in her tone.

"Okay," David said, shifting in his seat. "I have to know where all of this animosity stems from."

Alex took a deep breath. Hesitation reflected in her gaze, but then she gave in. "I believe that my brother died because of her."

"Really?" He was surprised. "Was she in the car?"

No. She and Marvin dated. She gravitates toward people who can elevate her. My brother was the commissioner's son. He was a star athlete. He was smart and gorgeous. He was driven. He wanted to make something of himself. He wanted to be someone. She saw his potential, just like the rest of us did. She was always so cruel to him, though. The things she used to say to him made my blood run cold.

"So, how did she have anything to do with his death?"

"Gerri didn't have a clue how to be faithful to someone, even then. She never has understood that concept. Marvin found out that she was sleeping with someone else. Turns out it was the professor. He walked right in on them."

"How do you know all of this?"

"Because he called me on his way back. He was older than me, but we told each other everything. We confided in each other.

"He was irate. He had always had a horrible temper. He said he was stopping at his best friend's house on the way home. Allen was his voice of reason. If I couldn't calm him, Allen could." Alex paused, choking back tears. "It was really snowy. I told him he should just go back to the dorm and then leave in the morning when the roads were cleared off, but he wouldn't listen. He was seeing red. He hung up with me. I guess he crashed soon after that."

The emotion was too great as Alex recounted the events, and tears streamed down her cheeks. "He took a curve too quickly and slid on black ice. The car rolled down an embankment. They didn't find him until the next day. I kept calling and calling and calling, but he wouldn't pick up. I knew something was wrong. I didn't know what part of the road he was on, and I had no way of going and finding him. When I called Allen, he wasn't even in town. He was way up north at a basketball game. I told my dad that Marvin was in trouble, that we should go look for him, but no one listened to me.

"Of all things, he died of hypothermia. The coroner said he had head trauma, too. The head trauma wasn't severe, though. He could have easily been saved. The crash didn't kill him. The cold did."

"I am so sorry," David said as he pulled her close to him. "I never knew. You never talked about it. When we were kids, you just cried. All the newspaper would say is that he died in a car accident."

Alex came to herself and took a deep breath, brushing the tears from her face. "My dad and mom wanted to downplay what happened. Of course, they didn't know what Gerri had done. Only I knew."

"That was quite a burden for a fourteen-year-old, Alex."

She nodded. "It was, but he was my brother. And it wasn't my secret to tell."

"Now I can see why you don't like her." David sighed. "If you want me to refuse the case, I will. I won't even ask for your help. I think it would be categorized as a conflict of interest anyway."

She calmed. "No, I can do this. I'm a professional," she insisted as she pulled away and looked up at him.

"I don't know," he said, shaking his head.

"Please, let me help you. I can do this."

David sighed. "I'm not too sure this will work."

"You know me. Do you think that I would jeopardize a case for personal reasons? If I didn't think I could handle it, I wouldn't do it. There are vital pieces of documentation missing from this file. It doesn't matter who the parties to the case are, there are things that should be in this packet that aren't."

"What are we missing besides the letter and the will?" he asked.

"As I said, we need medical reports, Steven's medical records to determine whether or not he was healthy, but most of all, we need to understand why the kids are contesting. What are the grounds?"

David looked down at the paperwork. "Look at how much this policy is for," he said, handing a piece of paper to Alex.

"Wow," she said, reading over the paper. "She is going to be a very rich woman."

"She already is a rich woman."

"I am betting the kids are contesting, citing undue influence."

"You're probably right."

"These figures, this policy," Alex continued, "would make her the richest woman in the county."

"Not quite the richest," David disagreed. "Hope is pretty wealthy," he answered, gauging Alex's expression.

"Yeah, I know."

"You know?"

"Of course, I know. I know that all of you are sitting pretty well. I don't give a shit about your money or hers. I'm not exactly destitute."

"Oh?"

"David, my mom left me with a significant amount of money when she died. Sure, Dad got most of it, but she certainly didn't leave me wanting. My grandparents were very well off. They were almost as well off as yours.

"I can trace my ancestry back to the roots," she continued. "My mom's family lived in the South. They invested very wisely before the Civil War. The steel plants and industry in the North made them rich. My great-grandfather also invested in the railroad. Thanks to their foresight, our family has been wealthy for a very long time."

David felt foolish. He hadn't discussed finances with Alex. It wasn't because he didn't trust her, but he didn't feel like it was important.

"So," Alex continued, "are you going to let me help you with Gerri's case or not?"

Pursing his lips, he exhaled. "I suppose."

She nodded. Determination in her gaze. "Good. I have a feeling there is more to this situation than meets the eye," she concluded.

47

On Monday morning, plans were made to meet with Gerri at 2 p.m. David had three things he needed. The first was the document from the attorney representing Steven's children. He needed to understand why they were contesting the will. Second, he needed a copy of the will. Lastly, he needed to get Gerri's approval to add Alex to the case. He knew that was a long shot, but Alex had insight that would be both beneficial and necessary.

As the hour approached, David began to feel very uneasy. He had been signing orders all day. He was weary, and his hand was beginning to ache. Gently, he laid the pen on the desk, then rubbed his temples. His head pounded. *Great. I'm getting sick,* he thought.

Laylonie buzzed David on the intercom and alerted him to Gerri's arrival. He stood and instantly felt dizzy. Quickly, he steadied himself against the desk, shutting his eyes and trying to find his balance. A deep breath helped him recover a little. As he collected himself, he managed to make it across the room to the door.

David waved Gerri into the office. Today she wore a pair of skinny jeans with brown treaded snow boots. Her parka was ivory, and she had a golden scarf wrapped around her neck. The toboggan on her head matched it, along with her golden gloves. Rosy-cheeked and smiling, she waltzed through the door and took a seat in front of David's desk.

Her facial expression changed the moment she noticed his grave countenance. "My goodness, you're pale," she remarked.

He nodded as he moved back to his desk chair. "I think I might be coming down with something. I'd keep your distance."

"Well, let's hope not," she continued. "Did you have questions, David?"

Nodding again, his head still felt fuzzy. "Yes," he admitted. "Gerri, where is the letter from the kids' attorney? I need a copy of the will, too."

"Oh my," she began. "I can't believe I forgot to put that in there. I mean, if it makes a difference, the letter doesn't really give much of an explanation, though. It just says that they are contesting."

"Well, I need the information so I can contact the attorney representing them. Most of all, I need a copy of the will."

"I have everything with me. It's right here in my purse," she said. Pulling her gloves off and placing them neatly in the vacant chair, she dug into her purse. "I am so sorry."

"It's no problem. I just need it."

She took out a legal mailing envelope. It was thick with what looked like several papers. She reached over the desk and handed it to David.

"Let me make copies of these," he said as he stood and excused himself.

He walked out of his office to the copier. The disorientation lifted slightly. Still, his head ached.

He walked back in and handed the envelope back to Gerri. He examined the letter from the attorney.

"This is perfect. I will contact the attorney today. Columbus, huh?"

"Yes. The kids went out of town to retain someone. Probably a lawyer out of some high-end firm who doesn't really care what they do to someone like me," she said pitifully.

"I have one final question," he continued cautiously. "I was wondering if you would agree to Alexandra being a cocounsel for the case. Truly, this is Alexandra's realm. Probate is what she does. I am pretty well read on it, but she is definitely the expert. Her assistance would be very helpful."

"I'm sorry, but no. I don't want Alexandra as cocounsel. She hates me, and I don't think she could be objective or fair."

"She is very professional and would never do anything unethical. Why would you say she couldn't be objective?" he asked, already knowing the answer.

"Oh, it's something silly, and it was a long time ago."

"So, if it was a long time ago, why would it be a problem now?" he inquired.

"I won't budge on this, David," Gerri insisted.

"Okay," he said with a nod. "I do wish you would reconsider."

"I won't. I really don't think she is right for this case. That's why I came to you."

"Well, here's the thing, Gerri," he continued as he leaned forward. "I am well within my rights to ask her to consult. I need her knowledge. So, whether you agree or not, she will be assisting me in some capacity. If you are uncomfortable with that, then perhaps I'm not the right person to help you out with this."

The atmosphere in the room shifted as displeasure covered Gerri's expression. David, perceptive as ever, noted the subtle signs of indignation etched across her features.

She sighed. "I just think you doubt yourself. You do not need her to help you with this. This is a simple, cut-and-dried case."

"If it were truly simple, you wouldn't even be here," he remarked bluntly.

She smiled at him sheepishly. "Well, I suppose it would be fine if she consulted. I just don't want her named as cocounsel. That's all. We just didn't get along growing up. Too much bad blood there."

"If at any time I feel her judgment is clouded, I will stop consulting her."

"I trust you," Gerri replied. "If I didn't, I wouldn't be here." She sighed heavily. "I hate doing this, but I'll be damned if I let those kids just disregard their father's wishes. I won't stand for it. I had to be quiet when we were married for the sake of his relationship with them. Not anymore."

Gerri paused and then said, "So, I take it you had the chance to go through the documents over the weekend?"

"I did. I have some consent forms for you to sign," he said, handing Gerri a clipboard with papers securely attached. "I need access to Steven's medical records, autopsy report, anything that will strengthen our case," he continued. "My guess is that his children are contesting because they feel that you unduly influenced Steven to change his will. Either way, we need to prove that he died of natural causes and that he was of sound mind. I'll need all supporting documentation for the life insurance policy as well. You gave me most of what I needed, but I'm afraid there's still more."

She reluctantly took the clipboard and looked down at it. Gerri's eyes glazed over. "And do you like the pen?" she said, quickly changing the subject.

David's face twisted in confusion. "I do. I will keep it here so it doesn't get lost."

"Now that's not why I gave it to you. You should carry it with you for good luck. That's what Steven always did when I bought him things like that. Every year we were married, I gave him an engraved pen with the year on it."

"That's a sweet sentiment."

"I miss him," she admitted as she looked out the window.

"I'm sure you do."

David brought the focus back to the consent forms. "Can you please sign those for me? I'd like to get those to the parties as quickly as possible."

"Oh, yes, of course," she said as she took a pen from her purse and scribbled her name on the forms. She handed the clipboard back. "Is there anything else? I don't want to keep you."

"Nothing for now."

"I have to admit, I don't quite understand why medical records have to be obtained. Won't a death certificate suffice?"

"It's standard procedure in a case like this," David replied.

"Oh." She rose from the chair. "Well, I'll leave you to it."

She turned and started toward the door, but abruptly turned around. “You and Alex doing okay?”

“Yep.”

David stood and walked around the desk. The weight in his head got worse, and he steadied himself against the desk again.

“Oh my, David,” Gerri said as she rushed to his side. “You look like you might pass out.”

“I think I’m coming down with something,” he answered, squinting and pinching the bridge of his nose. “I probably need to eat, too.”

“Well, why don’t you let me take you somewhere? You’re in no shape to drive.”

“It’s fine,” he replied as he desperately tried to recover.

“At least let me get you something to eat and bring it back,” she insisted.

Defiantly, he shook his head. “It’s fine. I’m sure Alex will be by with food.”

Gerri touched his arm and met David’s gaze. She lingered, and they stared at one another. As beautiful as she was, there was something behind her eyes that David couldn’t quite put a finger on.

“I hope you feel better,” she stated in a hushed voice.

“Me, too,” he concluded.

After Gerri left, David went to work with phone calls. Still feeling under the weather, he fought through it, knowing that he had responsibilities.

He grabbed the letter from the opposing counsel and looked at it again. Picking up the receiver, he dialed the number. The administrative assistant answered. She told David that the attorney he needed to speak to was out, so he left a message with his cell and office number.

With little accomplished and feeling very ill, David decided to go home early. It wasn't like him to cut out before five, but he felt physically drained. All he could think about was sleeping. Perhaps that was precisely what he needed. He knew the extra rest would help him fight off whatever it was he was coming down with.

Driving out of town, he suddenly felt better. His focus returned. The light-headed, fuzzy sensation fell away. He knew an evening of rest would do him good.

48

David stood in the woods, enveloped by a dense, impenetrable fog. His vision blurred, and his ears felt as if stuffed with cotton, muting the world around him. He wasn't scared, just profoundly disoriented and acutely aware of an unseen menace lurking beyond the mist.

From somewhere above, the caw of a raven pierced the silence, only to be abruptly swallowed by stillness once more. A dull thud drew his gaze downward, where he saw the raven's lifeless body, an arrow embedded in its chest. Sorrow welled up inside him as he knelt to touch the fallen bird, its feathers cold and stiff.

As he knelt, a gentle hand rested on his shoulder, radiating calm and reassurance. He turned slowly, his heart pounding, to see who was behind him. A figure stood a few paces away, shrouded in a long black hooded cloak, strands of gray and black hair spilling from the hood. At her side sat a large black dog, its eyes gleaming with quiet intelligence. In her hand was a lantern, illuminating with a warm light. From the light came peace and tranquility. In her other hand were the scales of justice. David couldn't see her face, but he knew he was safe with her.

"You are chosen," her voice resonated in his mind, though her lips remained still. "You are destined to defend the light."

Quickly, he shot up out of bed, sweat pouring and his body shaking. Alex lay sleeping peacefully. He was thankful that he hadn't waken her.

The dream disturbed him. He had never experienced anything like it. So vivid and puzzling. He knew he was too alarmed to even begin to go back to sleep.

He glanced over at the clock on his nightstand. It was 4:30 a.m. He decided to get up and go to the study. He could pass the time editing a textbook.

As he sat hunched over his desk, the weight of exhaustion pressing down on his shoulders. With a weary sigh, he reached for a steaming cup of coffee, the warmth seeping through his fingers like a lifeline.

The bitter aroma filled his senses. Lifting the mug to his lips, the hot liquid scalded his tongue in its haste to revive him from the lethargy that gripped his weary frame. He drank deeply, willing the caffeine to infuse his veins with renewed vitality.

Even as he sought refuge in his quest for a caffeine fix, his mind remained stubbornly fixated on the fragments of the dream. It was a rare occurrence for him to remember his dreams with such clarity, and yet this one seemed to cling to him with an unsettling persistence, its meaning elusive yet tantalizingly close.

He knew it held significance, that it was more than just a random jumble of images and sensations. With each passing moment, his curiosity grew, a gnawing hunger for understanding driving him to seek answers where none seemed readily available.

Turning his thoughts to Alex, he wondered if she might hold the key to unlocking the meaning of the dream. Despite their recent struggle surrounding her own dream-state, he respected her intuitive nature and deep connection to the spiritual realm. He didn’t understand it, and he admitted to himself that he was a little afraid of it.

His long-lived skepticism was in jeopardy. In fact, he felt an openness to the possibility that there were forces at play beyond the confines of rational explanation. Perhaps, he considered, it was time to embrace the unknown, to explore the hidden truths that lay dormant within the recesses of his soul.

49

David heard Alex's alarm go off at 7:30 a.m. She had a hearing at 9:00 a.m. He knew she would be concerned when she woke up alone, so he made his way down the stairs.

He walked into the bedroom to see her still lying under the blankets, her arm outstretched, searching for him in the bed. Her eyes opened and met his.

"Where were you?" she asked groggily.

"I was upstairs."

"Couldn't sleep?"

"Yeah. I had a rough night," he admitted.

"Are you still feeling under the weather?" she asked as she flung the covers off and sat up on the side of the bed.

"I don't feel as bad today. Now I'm just tired."

"Is there anything I can do?" Alex asked sweetly as she stood and stretched.

"No," he said, walking to her. He put his hands on her waist and kissed her forehead. "I'm going to get back upstairs. I don't have any hearings this morning, so I'm going to take my time getting into work," he explained.

"Okay," she replied as she walked to the closet to choose her attire for the day.

David walked back upstairs to the study. He sat down and began reading emails. He listened to Alex bustling around downstairs.

A text message alert chimed on his phone. He took the device into his hand and looked down at the screen. The message was from Hope.

The dream you had means that a message is trying to come through, but someone keeps killing it. The woman in the black cloak isn't someone you should fear.

The crease between his eyebrows told a story of confusion and wonder. He typed out a reply:

How did you know?

He waited for a moment. A reply quickly came through.

I just know. Are you going to tell Alex?

He quickly punched in a reply:

Yes. I need her help.

Instead of continuing with the text, David abandoned the conversation. He refocused on preparing for his day. He stood from the desk, stretched, and walked down the stairs. Alex stood behind the kitchen counter, drinking coffee.

As he rounded the corner and stepped into the room, his gaze was immediately drawn to her. She stood out effortlessly, her choice of clothing reflecting a casual elegance that captivated him. She wore a long blue plaid skirt that fell gracefully over a pair of well-worn brown boots. An ivory scoop-neck sweater clung to her figure, highlighting her natural curves and adding a touch of softness to her look. Her hair was swept up in a twist, tendrils of dark locks cascading around her face.

The morning light coming through the wall of windows in the living area cast a warm glow on her ivory skin. She looked tired but composed, already halfway into the day ahead. David stood still, watching as she leaned against the sink and took a drink from her coffee mug, her attention drifting between the moment and the clock on her wrist.

"You look beautiful," he commented as he finally moved to the coffee pot.

"Thank you," she smiled, her cheeks warming with the compliment.

She looked down at her watch. "I need to get going," she said as she put the coffee cup in the sink. "See you tonight, love," she said as she walked to him, pressed herself against his back, and kissed his neck.

He heard the back door close and sighed. He looked over into the living room to see both of the dogs lounging on the couch. They snoozed contentedly. He found solace in the silent companionship of his loyal canine friends.

By moving into the living room and starting to tidy up the space, he roused their curiosity. Both of them raised their heads to see what David might be doing. Cocking their heads as he returned to the kitchen, he smiled at them.

"What?" he said humorously. Their heads dropped back onto the cushion of the couch, and they drifted back to sleep.

With meticulous care, he dressed for the day, opting for a sleek slate gray suit. A subtle touch of flair came in the form of a black-and-gray patterned tie, adding a dash of personality to his ensemble.

Running a hand through his tousled hair, he met his reflection in the mirror. His gaze lingered on the familiar contours of his face. He trimmed his goatee and then dabbed some cologne on his neck.

Moving back into the living area and then to the kitchen, he once again caught the attention of the dogs. They both stretched as they got off the couch and trotted into the kitchen.

"I know you've both eaten," he said as they sat on the tile floor, their tails wagging and tongues hanging out. "Do you girls need to go out one last time?"

Immediately, they darted through the mudroom to the back door. He followed, opening it and stepping into the chill of the screened-in porch. He unlocked the door and pushed it open, allowing the dogs to race into the snow. The door slammed shut behind them, and David returned to his morning preparations.

As he stared out the front windows, he watched them frolicking in the snow, playing carefree in the beautiful white blanket covering the yard. He smiled, remembering how they had come into his life.

50

David had always harbored a deep affection for animals in general. He'd grown up with dogs, so he naturally gravitated toward them. His love for them brought him to volunteer at the local animal shelter, especially when he first moved to the area.

On a crisp autumn morning, David arrived at the shelter, eager to lend a helping hand. A small, tattered box sat near the door. It had been placed in front of the door. He knelt down to investigate, hearing faint whining coming from inside. With gentle hands, he lifted the lid, revealing a pair of brown eyes peering back at him. There, nestled within the box, was a puppy no more than eight weeks old. The pup's eyes held a mixture of curiosity and hope. In that moment, Cycily found her way into his life.

David's commitment to animal welfare extended beyond the confines of the local shelter. One day, he found himself drawn into a heartbreaking situation that demanded his intervention. Some concerned citizens had come to the shelter to report a puppy mill. The stories of maltreatment made David's heart sick.

He contacted the dog warden and urged him to intervene. Upon investigating, the mill was shut down. Most of the dogs were adopted out. Some were placed in foster homes. One caught his eye immediately. The little pup, a mere ball of fur with sad eyes, had spent her early days in those deplorable conditions, devoid of love and proper care. And so, Artemis came to live with David.

Taking legal action against the breeder, David filed a lawsuit for animal neglect. It was an uphill battle. Fueled by his passion for animal rights, he persisted, determined to hold the breeder accountable for his actions. Eventually, the breeder faced the consequences of his neglectful practices.

51

David finished up his morning at home, secured the dogs inside, and made his way into town. He arrived in the parking lot just before noon. He got out of his car, put on his wool peacoat, and grabbed his messenger bag from the back seat. Once he shut the door, he ran across the street and onto the freshly salted sidewalk. The deputy met him at the door with a cheery, "Good afternoon, David." He nodded in acknowledgement.

Pushing the glass door open, David walked into the atrium and to the Juvenile Court office. He heard Laylonie on the phone and then heard the phone fall back into the cradle as he walked in the door.

"Who was that?" he asked.

"Mr. Blanchard from the law firm in Columbus. You called him yesterday," she answered.

"Shit. I missed him. I really need to talk to him."

"He said he was going to call your cell," she continued.

Before she could say anything further, his phone vibrated in his coat pocket. Pulling it out, he put it to his ear and greeted Mr. Blanchard. For privacy, David walked into his chambers and shut the door, placing his messenger bag on one of the empty chair.

"Mr. Gregory," Mr. Blanchard began, "I'm returning your call."

"Yes, thank you so much. I was calling on behalf of Geraldine Meyers."

“You’re representing her I take it,” Mr. Blanchard bit out.

“I am. Is it possible for you to fax me the information as to why your clients are contesting the Will?”

“I can, but I can also tell you over the phone.”

“That would be great,” he said wedging the phone between his ear and shoulder. He sat down and picked up Gerri’s pen.

A rush of lightheadedness hit him. Still, he steadied himself so he could take notes. However, it was no use. His head started to spin.

“I’m sorry, Mr. Blanchard,” he interrupted, “can I call you back.”

“Of course. I’m heading into court in about an hour.”

“It won’t be that long. I just need to get settled in here.”

“In the meantime, I’ll fax you what I have.”

“Perfect.”

He hung up and tried to find focus. It was pointless. He stood, and was overtaken by complete darkness.

52

Loud beeping and unfamiliar voices dragged him back to consciousness. Groggily, David struggled to open his eyes. Squinting from the bright light, he was disoriented and confused. Gradually, the light blue walls and the hospital curtain hanging from the ceiling came into focus. As his awareness slowly returned, he looked over and saw Alex sitting beside the bed. She held tightly to his hand, her eyes filled with worry.

"Hey," she said softly, stroking his thick, dark hair with her other hand.

"Hey you," he replied. His mouth felt unusually dry. He assumed it was from dehydration.

"You passed out at work. Laylonie called me after she called the squad. You're in the emergency room at Mercy."

"I don't know what happened. I was fine one minute, and the next minute I was down for the count. I don't even remember passing out."

A twinge of pain made him squint again. His head throbbed. Raising his hand to his forehead, he winced in pain.

"You hit your head on the desk when you dropped," Alex explained. "Just a superficial cut. They are going to do a head-CT, but they think you're fine. They have already taken blood, too. They are making sure you don't have some kind of infection," she explained. Forging further into reality, David realized he felt much better already. He wasn't sure if it was due to the IV fluids or just being near Alex.

"I'll go to your office to grab your things," Alex continued. "They want me to keep an eye on you through the night because of the head injury. So, we're definitely not going to work tomorrow. We can work remotely." She paused for a moment taking account of his coloring and looking him over carefully. "Is there anything else you want me to get while I'm at the office?" she asked.

"Gerri's attorney should have faxed information to me. Please grab it off the fax machine."

"I will, but I'm not leaving until they run all of their tests. I called Hope and Will. They should be here shortly. I am going to let Will help you get settled in at home while Hope and I go to grab your belongings. We'll also get you something to eat, or Hope and I will cook. Did you eat this morning?"

"Yeah, I did. I took my time today. Took things slow so I wasn't even in any kind of rush," he replied.

"I don't know what I'm going to do with you," she said smiling at him.

"You're always good at figuring something out," he joked.

Hours passed. The tests didn't show anything alarming. So, David was diagnosed with extreme dehydration and exhaustion. He was ordered to rest and not return to the office until next week. Because of the head injury, Alex was told to check on him every two hours during the night.

53

Alex arranged for Will to take David home while she and Hope went to the courthouse. As they walked into the building, the deputy stopped them.

"How's Judge Gregory?" he asked kindly.

"He's headed home," Alex answered.

"He gave us all quite a scare. Some kinda bad juju or something. First Judge Steven and then David?"

Alex smiled. "He's fine now. He's been feeling a little under the weather lately."

"Well, I'm glad he's okay," the deputy concluded.

Alex looked up at the clock in the atrium. It was nearly five. As they walked into the Juvenile office, Laylonie smiled at them as they entered.

"How is he?" she asked standing up behind her desk. Genuine concern covered her face like a shroud. Alex also felt her energy. Laylonie had a sweet disposition and a deep kindness.

"He's okay. He won't be back until next week," Alex replied. "I'm just going to gather some of his things so he can work remotely. If he has anything on the docket, it'll need rescheduled."

"Not a problem," she replied. "I will take care of it first thing tomorrow morning."

"Thank you," Alex concluded as she walked into David's chambers. Hope followed behind her.

When she stepped into the room, it was as if she walked right into a brick wall. The negative energy in the room was nauseating. She immediately felt weak. Alarmed by the physical drain, she looked over at Hope.

"I feel it, too," Hope assured her.

"What the hell is that?" Alex asked inquisitively.

Hope closed her eyes. She concentrated intensely. When she opened her eyes, she walked to the leather chair behind the desk and sat down. Carefully, she picked up the pen from Gerri.

"It's the pen. You can feel the nastiness dripping off this thing," she remarked.

"What is it?" Alex asked.

Hope closed her eyes again and held out her hand. "Take my hand. I will show you what I see."

Alex did as she was told. The visions rushed her. She saw Gerri seated in front of an altar, the pen in her hand. A spell book lay before her. With her eyes closed, Gerri began casting a spell on the pen.

"It wasn't meant to make him sick," Hope clarified.

"It was meant to make *me* sick," Alex stated. "She cast the spell on the pen hoping he would bring it home. Then the energy would transfer to me. When he didn't, it made *him* sick."

"Exactly," Hope encouraged.

"Hope," Alex said with a panicked gaze, "my dream. The raven. The presence in the fog. The golden cloak. It's her. It's always been her. The raven has a message, but she keeps silencing it."

"She is doing the same thing with David."

"What do you mean? He hasn't said anything to me."

"I was shaken awake last night," Hope continued. "My guides showed me what he saw. He had a dream similar to yours. The fog, the raven. I sent a text this morning. He was going to talk to you about it."

"Gerri is dangerous," Alex remarked.

"Alex, she is practicing dark magic. In fact, that is where she feels the most comfortable. I believe David is her next victim. She plans to seduce him; take him from you," Hope proclaimed. "I've seen it."

"I need to talk to my Aunt Shayleen," Alex observed. She took her hand back and pulled her mobile phone out of her purse. Frantically she dialed Shayleen's number, summoning her to the office. Since the shop was on the same block as the courthouse, it only took her ten minutes to arrive.

Shayleen walked into David's office, a burst of vitality accompanying her every step. Despite her petite stature, her energy radiated power. Her physical appearance, unassuming at first glance, belied the force of personality she possessed.

Graying brown hair, cropped in a chic pixie style, brought out the features of her beautiful face. Her skin, reminiscent of Alex's porcelain complexion, was flawlessly smooth, giving her an ageless allure. Shayleen's eyes, a mesmerizing deep-sea green, held a warmth and kindness that seemed to invite trust effortlessly.

Dressed in a practical yet stylish ensemble, Shayleen sported black leggings that showcased her active lifestyle. Her fur-lined snow boots added a touch of rugged charm. A red fur-lined toboggan perched atop her head, framing her face. The matching red parka draped over her shoulders shielded her from the winter chill.

Shayleen was one of the most powerful practitioners Alex and Hope had ever met. She had many gifts, but one in particular would be helpful for this situation. She was able to physically see spells and draw interpretations and intent from them. All she needed was the object that the spell was cast upon or the person that the spell was meant for.

Shayleen looked at the pen lying on the desk. Alex and Hope hadn't told her anything. Immediately, Shayleen picked up on the energy radiating from the object. She moved to the desk and looked down at it, her finger tips touching the smooth desktop but being careful not to touch the pen.

"The spell on the pen can be broken with fire," Shayleen said. She concentrated for a few more moments. Turning her attention to Alex, she continued. "Take the pen to his cabin. Burn it in the fireplace. As you do that, put your intent into cleansing the atmosphere. Add sage to the fire. This will allow for the entire space to be cleansed along with the spell cancellation. It will dispel the negative energy attached to the object, and it will seal your intent to destroy the power of the spell bound to the object. You will also be blocking Gerri's influence. David's illness should cure fairly quickly."

"Hope saw more," Alex added.

"What do you mean?" Shayleen asked.

"Gerri is going to try to physically seduce my brother," Hope explained. "He is her next target. This pen was the first step in doing that."

"But how?" Alex asked with a perplexed tone.

“Biological agents, like hair, blood, urine, and um, other bodily fluids, give unprecedented power to a spell. Shayleen continue, “The elements—air, water, earth, fire—provide a catalyst for every part of our practice, so it stands to reason that this also applies to spell work. You both know that.”

She took a deep breath and continued. “Biology acts as a much stronger connector between two or more people. Biological agents operate as a physical representation of the person so that the spell takes hold reliably. For example, if I want to cast a dark spell on someone and raise the chances that it will take hold, I can use a strand of the person’s hair. I would make a doll, wrap the hair around it, and cast the spell. The likelihood of it taking hold goes up. The use of the hair strengthens the spell, creating a physical bond between caster and recipient. You both know that this can be done to cast both blessings and curses.

“Spell work is complex, and doing it without a full understanding can be extremely dangerous. Neither of you are very educated in spell work. Yes, you have a basic understanding, but mentorship would be beneficial. You’re dealing with Gerri, who has been practicing since she was very, very young. She functions at a very high level.” The room fell silent, but Hope and Shayleen’s eyes were locked.

“There’s more. Tell me what you know,” Alex said to both of them, obviously losing patience.

“From what I can see,” Shayleen continued, “Gerri intends to seduce David and use a biological agent to cast a much more powerful spell. Her hope is that there will be a sexual exchange. She will use hair if she must, but she prefers something much more potent. Her primary objective is to blind him with this first spell, but really, she accomplishes two goals by having sex with him. The first is taking him for herself. His wealth is alluring, and it’s about winning for her--taking something forbidden. She is addicted to the thrill of taking what doesn't belong to her both monetarily and physically. The addiction has become so strong that she can hardly contain it. When a victim falls, she feels relief and accomplishment for a brief period of time, but then the ache begins to rise again, requiring her attention."

"Sounds like a serial killer to me," Alex interjected.

"Secondly, she can hide who she really is if she is successful in blinding David," Shayleen continued. "The current case, the contesting of the Will, is something she didn't account for. She has never had to fight for what she has taken. This is uncharted territory. She needs David to believe her completely, and she can feel that he is skeptical. She blames you for that, Alex. She wants you gagged, so to speak, unable to seek or find the truth. Your guides and spirit animals are giving her a run for her money though. So that's something you've got going for you."

"Will he fall for it?" Hope asked.

"This situation still has the foundation of freewill. He has the choice to resist. As lightworkers, we don't mess with free will. However, those ethics don't apply to practitioners like Gerri. In fact, dark magic is steeped in the ability to manipulate freewill."

Alex walked to an empty chair in front of David's desk. Suddenly, defeat washed over her. She felt like she might not be able to take a full, deep breath. Everything felt bleak and very frightening. Her eyes filled with tears.

Hope pulled another chair closer and sat down. She put her hand on Alex's knee. "What is it?" she asked.

"I always knew," she started. "Ever since Marvin died, I've suspected what she was, who she was. I can't help but be afraid she is going to take someone else I love. She is very powerful."

"Your love… your light is more powerful," Hope encouraged her. "Good is always more powerful, even if takes time to gain traction over all of the negativity that exists around us. You can't give up. David needs you more than ever now."

Shayleen walked around the desk and leaned against it. She looked down at Alex.

"You have more power than you even know, little one," Shayleen began. "You are a healer. You abolish pain. You also have well-developed intuition. Honey, you've cast spells your entire life not even knowing what you were doing. You never needed a book or a guide to practice the craft. You just knew. You were born this way. So, what does your heart tell you to do to protect David?"

She sighed. "I need to cast a shielding spell around him. I need to make sure the shield is strong enough to protect his mind, especially since she intends to blind him. I also need to cast a protection spell around myself. If she is coming after me, then I need to be well armed."

"See? You already know what to do," Shayleen said with a smile.

"What ingredients will she need?" Hope asked.

"She already knows the answer to that, too," Shayleen beamed.

Alex nodded.

"Do you realize that you and Gerri have battled like this in other lives?" Shayleen asked.

"I figured," Alex answered.

"This isn't your first rodeo with her."

Hope held tightly to Alex's hand, her conviction almost tangible as she began to speak. "Listen to me," her tone filled with reassurance. "My brother is smart, and he loves you. You can tell him to exercise caution with her, and he'll believe you. He'll stay on-guard. He'll listen to you. He is opening up to the possibilities surrounding him. *You've* done that. Just speak openly with him about what you are doing and why."

"He will just think I'm a jealous girlfriend or that I'm overreacting. He'll blame my insecurities or say it's a personal vendetta."

"Not if you tell him the reasons behind your actions,'" Shayleen added.

"He trusts you even if he doesn't understand the things you practice. If you try to show him the 'why' in logical terms, he will listen. I can feel it. Now that he has had this dream, he may even be more open to understanding what's happening."

"Hope's right," Shayleen added. "He trusts you. He believes you. Talk to him.

Alex nodded. The task before her was unnerving. Anger and anxiety started to overwhelm her, but she quickly realized that she had to maintain a positive outlook. Knowledge served as power in this situation. She could stay on-guard and protect David with her knowledge of magic.

Her eyes drifted for a moment. A fax lay on David's desk. The words on the cover page grabbed her attention. *Contesting Meyers' Will: Undue influence and possible criminal investigation.* She grabbed the paper from the desk and flipped to the first page.

"I was right," Alex mumbled.

"What's wrong?" Shayleen asked.

"I--I can't. It's attorney-client privilege."

"Understood," Shayleen nodded.

"You've got this," Hope said as she released her hand and stood.

"I need to run to the shop to pick up the things I'll need," Alex said.

"Okay," Hope agreed.

"I'll have everything ready for you. I already know what to prepare," Shayleen said.

Before Shayleen left, she cast a hedging spell around Alex so she could carry the pen with her and avoid being physically sick. Once Alex had gathered up all of David's work from his office, including the fax and the pen, she and Hope ventured to the shop. By the time they arrived, Shayleen had a small shopping bag ready.

Alex looked down into the bag and then up at Shayleen as she stood behind the counter.

"So, snowflake obsidian is for deflection and protection from dark, negative energy," Shayleen explained. "The sage is to cleanse. The dragon's blood is to bind the spell and amplify it. The amethyst stone is also for amplification and protection. The new white candle represents the positive power in the universe. Make sure you carve David's name in it. The black candle represents the darkness Gerri hopes to pull into this little scheme. Carve her name into it. Use frankincense oil to anoint your doorways and windows, keeping any negativity out once you've cast the protection spell. These two small pieces of the black tourmaline are for you two to carry with you. It is a force field protector."

"How in the hell am I going to explain all of this to David?" Alex asked herself quietly.

Hope took her hand. "You'll help him understand," she said with a confident smile.

54

After the visit to the shop, Hope and Alex proceeded to the cabin. It was around 7 p.m. when they arrived to see Will's car still in the driveway. The lights from the living room and kitchen windows cast a warm glow against the freshly falling snow.

The dogs ran into the garage to meet Alex and Hope. Alex got out of the car, tending to the excitement of the dogs first. Then she turned her attention to the box filled with David's work from David's office, and the shopping bag from Shayleen's.

"We won't stay long," Hope said. "You have some work to do."

Alex nodded. She was very nervous about the entire task ahead. She worried that it would have a significant impact on their relationship.

They walked into the mudroom, the dogs following close behind. Alex set the box on the floor and then took off her coat, scarf, hat, and gloves, placing everything on the hanger in the mudroom. She bent down to take off her boots.

The smell of pizza lingered. "We're here," Alex called.

"We're in the living room," Will answered. Once they entered the kitchen, Will stood from the recliner.

"Come on," Hope began. "We need to go," she said forcefully.

"But you just got here!" Will insisted.

"We're going," she commanded. The surprise on his face was also mixed with fear.

"Thank you both for your help today," Alex said graciously.

"There's pizza. Veggie lovers, too," Will called to Hope as she dragged him out the door.

David relaxed on the sofa covered in a warm fleece, tartan-patterned blanket. Lying on his side, he seemed focused on the television screen. The fire blazed, warming the room to perfection.

Quietly, Alex moved across the room and knelt on the floor beside David. She smiled lightheartedly.

"Hey you," he said in a low, fatigued tenor.

"Hi," she replied, playing with the stray strands of his hair. "Feeling any better?"

"Yes. I do. Just very tired."

"Do you want me to run a bath for you?"

Smiling warmly, he turned onto his back and stretched. "That sounds great." She stood and walked toward the master bedroom.

"Can you put lavender and vanilla in the water?" he called to her, sounding a bit like a child begging for a new toy.

"Absolutely," she answered back.

Once she ran the bath, she assisted David from the couch to the master bathroom. She helped him out of his sweats and hoodie and into the tub.

"I'm not helpless, you know?" he said with faux anger in his tone.

"I will be your nurse for the next few days, so my help comes along with that," she replied.

"My nurse, huh?"

"Don't," she smirked.

"Yes, ma'am," he said in a defeated yet playful tone.

"Sex will be off the table until you start to completely recover," she explained. He shot her a disapproving look and sighed.

After settling him into the hot water of the bath, she retreated to the mudroom for the pen and the essentials for her spell work. She stood in front of the fireplace as she looked down at the pen. She closed her eyes and whispered, "May the Goddess bless my efforts and dispel all negativity. The intent of this spell is to cancel any spell upon this object that may be designed to cause harm and illness. I bind any spell attached to this object and cast it out with the element of fire. So mote it be."

She tossed the pen into the fireplace. Then she poured a little dragon's blood oil into the fire and added a few pieces of sage.

When Alex began moving in, David had offered a spare room in the basement for Alex to set up her hobby room. So, she ventured downstairs with the rest of the supplies, intent on completing the spell.

She opened the door to the room and shut it behind her. She took out the two candles, amethyst, snowflake obsidian, and black tourmaline. She knelt in front of the altar, got out her knife from her supply tray, and carved the names into the candles. She tore off some more sage and placed it in an incense bowl. She poured the dragon's blood into a small chalice. She lit the candles with the lighter that lay atop the altar. She then picked up the amethyst and held it tightly in her hand.

"Great Goddess," she whispered, "bless these stones and offer your protection through them. Shield us so that any arrow that may fly will not touch us. So mote it be."

She took in a deep breath and exhaled slowly. She couldn't feel anything change. Her faith was all she had right now.

She allowed the candles to burn for a few more moments. She took a small velvet pouch from the shopping bag and placed the snowflake obsidian and black tourmaline in it and tied it closed. She put the candle flames out with her fingers, took both candles in her hands, and made her way back upstairs. She stood in front of the fireplace again, listening carefully for David in case he needed her.

She tossed the candles into the fire. "Bless our union. Protect us. Honor our faith. So mote it be," she whispered.

55

Alex walked into the bathroom to check on David. The aroma of lavender and vanilla was delicious. It was inviting and calming.

David's head rested on a rolled-up towel. He looked **at ease** as he relaxed in the steaming water. His perfectly sculpted body always caused the butterflies to take flight in Alex's tummy.

"How are you feeling?" she asked as she sat on the side of the tub.

"Much better," he said.

He studied her. "Hey, are you okay?" he asked.

"Yeah. You had me worried," she admitted.

"I'm fine. I promise."

"I know." She paused for a moment. "I do need to talk to you, but I think it can wait. You've had a trying day."

"I don't like waiting," he snickered. "I asked Gerri about you being named as co-counsel, and she wouldn't have it."

"That's not surprising," she replied.

"I told her explicitly that you would act as a consultant, and if she couldn't handle that she needed to retain someone else." He paused for a moment. "I saw you brought a box from work. Did Mr. Blanchard send a fax for me to review?"

"That's sort of what I want to talk to you about. Well part of what I want to talk to you about."

"Okay," he said straightening up and leaning forward.

"The fax from Mr. Blanchard was on your desk. The reason why Steven's kids are holding everything up is because they feel that Steven was influenced. They are pushing for a criminal investigation. From what I gathered, the kids are questioning the circumstances surrounding his death because they believe Steven was murdered."

"Wow," he said, his mouth agape.

"You can't continue to represent her, David. With a criminal investigation upcoming, you know what that means. It means jury trial."

Alex helped David out of the tub. He dried off as she got a fresh pair of flannel pajama bottoms and a clean hoodie out of his dresser drawers. She grabbed a pair of warm socks, too.

After he dressed, they made their way back into the living room. David sat down on the couch. Alex stood in the kitchen pouring a short glass of wine.

"Can I get you anything while I'm up?" she asked kindly.

"No. I'm good," he replied. "Can you come and sit with me though?"

"Of course," she answered. With the wine in her hand, she sat down beside David, the television noise in the background filling the room with a low hum.

Alex smiled. "I have a gift for you," she said as she pulled the tiny velvet pouch from her pocket. The tiny stones fell into her hand.

"What's that?"

"Snowflake obsidian is a rock that repels negative energy. That's the little black and white rock. The black rock is black tourmaline, and it is a force field rock. What that means is that by having the rock in your possession, a protective field should form around you. I know you don't understand any of this, but if you could just trust me, keep the pouch and put it in your pocket every day, I'd appreciate it."

"Why are you giving this to me?" he asked.

"Well, for a few reasons. I've figured out some things about my dreams. And what I'm about to tell you, I really, really need you to keep an open mind. I know how you feel about all of this."

"Alex, just tell me. You don't have to be afraid," David assured her.

"David, I believe Gerri practices dark magic. I think she is who has been in the fog in my dreams. She is causing the messages not to come through."

"What makes you think this? How do you know?"

Alex stood and paced in front of the fireplace. Her anxiety kicked into high gear. Her shoulders tensed and her head started pounding as her heart rate rose. She worried that he wouldn't want to hear anything she had to say, that he would be offended.

Still, she plunged ahead, unraveling the layers of the situation. She explained how Shayleen helped interpret the dreams. Alex painted vivid pictures with her words, describing the symbolism and hidden messages that had unfolded in the canvas of her subconscious mind.

Transitioning seamlessly, Alex delved into the realm of spell work. She expected rejection from David, but instead, he just listened attentively. Alex spoke of her endeavors with a quiet intensity, emphasizing her intention to safeguard those she cared about.

With each word, Alex wove a narrative around the theories she had developed, the threads of her explanations intertwining with the complexities of the mystical. She didn't just present facts. She painted a portrait of possibility and the potential consequences that hung in the balance.

The air in the room seemed charged with a unique energy, a blend of intellectual curiosity and the mystique of the unknown as Alex concluded her narrative. She waited, anticipating an argument.

"So, she has likely murdered her other partners?" David asked.

"More than likely."

"And I'm her next target?"

"I believe so, yes."

"And the pen had a curse on it?" he asked seeking clarification.

"Yes. That's what made you sick." She sighed. "I know this sounds completely crazy," she said as she fidgeted.

"Honey, come sit down with me," he said.

She walked over and sat on the opposite end of the couch.

He shook his head. "Closer," he demanded.

She scooted closer still.

"I had a dream last night. I didn't want to tell you because I didn't want to put much credence behind it, but now I honestly wonder," he admitted.

He described the surreal landscapes that unfolded within the recesses of his subconscious mind, the colors vivid and the textures almost tangible in his retelling. Every emotion, whether fleeting or profound, found its expression in his words. David's commitment to not leaving anything out mirrored Alex's earlier approach, creating a seamless continuation of the narrative that seemed to bridge the gap between their shared experiences.

As David navigated the intricacies of his dream, Alex's keen intuition picked up on the gradations of his emotions. The room became a sanctuary of shared confidences. With each passing moment, the bond between them deepened, and the exchange of dreams and interpretations became a conduit for something more profound, an unspoken acknowledgment that their individual stories were interwoven with a cosmic thread, and that their collective understanding was greater than the sum of its parts.

Silence fell.

"I won't continue with the case," David resolved. "I will tell her that with an active criminal investigation looming, I won't represent her. I don't want to be centerstage with another nationally televised trial."

Alex nodded. "The thought of her touching you," she said as sadness rose in her throat.

"Baby, no," he said as he touched her hand. "I will never let her touch me. You are my person."

"So, you believe me?" Alex asked.

"I believe that something is amiss. Alex, I don't have dreams like that. I might be a skeptic, but I'm not dumb. I know my own mind. I also know my own body. I don't get ill very often. To suddenly get sick like that, it doesn't make sense."

"I figured you would be angry with me. Or think I'm crazy."

"I don't understand it, but you've explained things very thoroughly. You aren't an irrational person, Alexandra. The courage that it took for you to even tell me any of this, you deserve respect for that, especially knowing how I feel about all of it. Still, you did it. Do you know how much I admire that?"

"Well, I think we can prove that Gerri murdered Steven. I think we can help the prosecution. I also think it's possible to prove she murdered the others. She is basically a serial killer, David. I know she didn't technically murder my brother, but if it wasn't for her, I know he would still be alive. I can't help but blame her.

"We will have to get a court order for all of the medical records, tox screens, autopsy reports, and even exhumations," Alex continued. "I'm sure Judge Shanks will be happy to accommodate us. Surely Dr. Hydleburg took samples. At least I hope he did. As for Chief Schider, we'll have to hope that samples were taken at the time of his death. We'll need those, too. For the professor, we'll have to contact the Franklin County Coroner. Then we will likely have to petition a judge in Montana for the exhumation."

"Are we sure we know what we're getting into?" David asked.

"I think what's important right now is for you to rest."

"What about my dream? What do you think it means?"

"The messages keep being silenced," Alex said. "As for who you saw with the black and gray hair, I believe that is a Goddess named Hecate. Hecate is the Goddess of Witches, the Gatekeeper of the Dead, and so much more. She is very powerful, and she is known in the Greek and Roman pantheons. She is the keeper of the crossroads as well. To have her reveal herself to you is fascinating. She is courting you."

"Courting me?"

"When a deity reveals him or herself to you, they are likely wanting to teach you something, so they court you. They show you things. They are there so that you can build a relationship with them much how Christians build a relationship with their God."

David paused contemplating Alex's explanation. He smiled. "What would I do without you, Alex?" he mused, his eyes reflecting genuine appreciation.

Alex's smile deepened, and a warmth radiated from her as she responded, "Well, I'd say we make a pretty good team, wouldn't you?"

The air in the room seemed to lighten as their solidarity filled the space. David's expression conveyed a sense of gratitude. They found comfort in each other's presence, recognizing the value of their collaboration in navigating the complexities of dreams and the uncertainties of life.

56

David didn't feel like working remotely, although it was nice to be able to set his own schedule. He also enjoyed Alex being home with him. Although she hadn't moved in completely, she was there enough to be a permanent fixture in his world.

He knew he had important matters to attend to, namely the situation with Gerri. It made him extremely anxious. There were so many bases to cover. Although he knew Alex was more than capable of requesting all of the documents they had discussed the night before, he felt responsible.

The mystic world of the paranormal was a place he had fought against for a very long time. Despite the fact that his mother and sisters were very gifted, David had always struggled to believe in the legitimacy of the intangible and unexplained. He never thought that he would come to a place of openness. Alex had changed all of that resistance. He already knew that there were things in this world he couldn't put a label on. Living with his mother and sisters had already shown him that. Still, Alex made him feel safe in the space of the unknown.

Throughout his entire time convalescing, David had been communicating with Laylonie via email. He requested that she set up a meeting for Gerri for Monday at 3:00 p.m.

Alex left very early on Monday. It was apparent she was on a mission. David anticipated that there would be many early mornings and late nights while working on Steven Meyers' case.

As David readied himself for the day, he took a deep breath gazing at his reflection in the mirror. He pondered everything that had happened in the last week. He appreciated the trust Alex demonstrated. It meant the world to him.

He looked down at the velvet pouch in his hand. He stuffed it into his right suit pocket. Once he gathered up his other belongings, he made his way out to the car. He got in and drove down the lane, the snow crunching under the tires. The sun cast a blinding light upon the freshly fallen snow. As he turned onto the highway, he grabbed his aviator sunglasses.

He glanced over at the envelope in the passenger seat. He intended to make copies as soon as he arrived at the office. He would also get Mr. Blanchard on the phone. Sealing the deal with him would be essential for bringing Gerri to justice.

He arrived at the courthouse and parked the car. The bite of the cold winter air nipped at David's face as he crossed the street. Carrying his messenger bag on his shoulder and the file in his hand, he made his way up the steps of the courthouse.

Once he had dispensed with the pleasantries with the deputy, he walked into the atrium. The clock struck 11:00 a.m. He rounded the corner and pushed open the door.

Laylonie stood when he walked into the office.

"Mr. Gregory, how are you feeling?"

"Better," he said.

"Miss Ritezal is waiting in your office."

"She is?"

"Yes. She's been working in there since before I came in at 9."

David furrowed his brows, but it wasn't because he was displeased. He was merely surprised. He walked into his chambers to see Alex with the telephone to her ear. He watched as she busily wrote notes on a legal pad.

David placed his bag in an empty chair in front of his desk. He then shimmied out of his winter coat. He walked over to his coat tree in the corner and hung it up. Finally, he walked to the other empty chair in front of his desk and sat down.

He observed Alex intensely. She gracefully navigated the conversation. Her confidence in her work shone through.

Her attire, a red satin low-cut button-up top, accentuated her curves, while the necklace adorning her neck held that mysterious power that he still didn't quite understand. The delicate gold hoop earrings swayed gently with her movements, framing her face with a subtle elegance.

His gaze lingered on the engagement ring ornamenting her finger, a symbol of their impending union. The thought of calling her his wife brought a surge of warmth and longing to his heart.

When her eyes met his, a mischievous spark ignited between them, and she winked at him playfully. Despite the lingering fatigue from the spell and the injury that followed, which had temporarily robbed them of their physical intimacy, his desire for her burned fiercely, a primal need that pulsed beneath the surface.

The absence of their usual passionate encounters during his convalescence felt like a void in his life. Even amidst the pressing demands of Gerri's case, his thoughts invariably drifted back to Alex, consumed by an insatiable hunger for her touch.

"Thank you so much Mr. Blanchard," Alex said. "Yes, I will tell him... good-bye." David snapped back into the moment with the sound of her voice.

"You called Mr. Blanchard, huh?" David asked as she hung up the phone.

"Yes. I contacted him for you this morning, but he was in court so I left a message. When he called back, I told him you wouldn't be moving forward with Gerri's case. He told me that they are working with the Franklin County Prosecutor to bring criminal charges against Gerri. I told him we would help."

"So, what are our next steps, Miss Ritezal?" David asked.

"We work closely with Mr. Blanchard."

"I'm meeting with Gerri today to tell her I won't be representing her. That should be super fun," he said sarcastically.

"Do you want me to be here with you?" she asked considerately.

"No. I can handle it," he replied rubbing his temple.

"Still dealing with the headaches?" Alex asked with concern in her tenor.

"I'm just tired. That's all," David replied.

"Well, I need to get back to the cottage," she said standing up.

Alex walked to David and smiled. "I love you," she said sweetly.

"I love you, too honey," he replied.

They kissed good-bye, and David got on with his day.

57

As Gerri sat across from him, David couldn't help but feel a wave of conflicting emotions wash over him. Her disarming smile didn't have the effect she might have hoped for, especially given the weight of the situation at hand. While he couldn't deny her charm, he also couldn't ignore the gravity of the circumstances.

Recalling his conversation with Alex, David finally understood the complexities of their history. His loyalty and love for Alex and his commitment to protecting both their reputations remained steadfast. With this clarity of purpose, he resolved to approach the conversation with Gerri tactfully and cautiously.

As he contemplated his next move, David reminded himself of the importance of not revealing too much, especially considering the likelihood of a criminal investigation. He knew he needed to tread carefully, guarding his words and actions to protect himself and those he cared about.

As David observed Gerri's appearance. Her attention to detail was telling. Everything always appeared to be perfectly in place. Today, she wore a pair of skinny jeans paired with fur-lined boots. The tightly fitted pink angora sweater accentuated her figure, while her ivory-colored parka added a touch of elegance to her ensemble. Her blonde hair framed her delicate features flawlessly. Still, he was immune to her charms. He knew what he had to do.

David took a deep breath. "Gerri," he began, "I don't quite know how to say this, but I can't represent you."

Her smile disappeared. "What? Why?" she asked, the tension rising in her voice.

"I spoke to Mr. Blanchard and read over the letter. The fear is that you unduly influenced Steven to take out a life insurance policy. There are also concerns that there was foul play."

"Are you serious?" she said as shock covered her face.

"I'm afraid so."

"They think I killed him?"

"I'm not entirely sure, but from what I understand, a criminal investigation is pending. Someone from Franklin County will be getting in touch."

"He died in front of you. You saw him take his last breath. I wasn't even there. How could there be foul play?"

"I'm just relaying the information, Gerri."

"So, what do I do?"

"Well, I would suggest you retain a criminal defense attorney."

"You're an attorney. You've defended criminal cases. I would like to retain you."

"I'm not taking on anymore criminal cases while I'm a sitting judge. Alex is qualified to represent you, but there's a conflict of interest there."

"So she told you? About her brother? Her mindless theories?" The anger was palpable now.

"That isn't the point, Gerri. The point is that I won't be working on your case." He handed the envelop back to her.

"You know me," she said as her face softened. "I wouldn't do anything to hurt anyone. Please, I'm begging you to reconsider. I don't know who else to turn to. I need you. You're the best attorney in this town," she pleaded.

"I can't possibly represent you. I'm a judge now."

"Well, couldn't *you* just have easily killed Steven to take his job?" she bit out.

"I understand your frustration, but you're not thinking clearly. And you can't go around making accusations like that. Realistically Gerri, you stand to gain millions from his death. If anyone has motive here, it's you."

"You stood to gain his seat," she replied hastily.

"Look, I'm not interested in arguing with you. The best I can do is advise you to retain a criminal defense attorney. I can even reach out to some and make a referral. There are a lot of really good ones in Columbus, Dayton, Cleveland, and even Kentucky."

"I can't believe this is happening to me," she said quietly, a far-away countenance on her face.

"I'm sorry," he said sincerely. He held out the envelop of documents.

She stood and took the envelop from his hand. "Please, David, I'm begging you to reconsider," she said.

"I can't, Gerri. I just can't."

She angrily snatched the envelop from him, turned on her heel, and walked out.

David walked to the window and looked out at the falling snow. So many revelations had come to light in the last few months. He contemplated the road ahead. He knew it would be rough and fraught with challenges. He played out his next move. He and Alex would need to have a conference call with the Franklin County Prosecutor and Mr. Blanchard. Better yet, they probably needed to pay them a visit.

58

David and Alex lay entwined in bed, cocooned within the embrace of each other's arms. The relentless longing for her had surged through him, compelling him to convince her that he was sufficiently recovered to make love.

He cradled her against his chest, her head nestled in the curve of his shoulder. The hunger he felt for her seemed insatiable, a craving that consumed him entirely. In her, he found completeness, unable to fathom desiring anyone else with the same fervor he felt for her.

“I missed this,” he admitted as he kissed her forehead.

“It hasn’t been that long,” she laughed.

“Honey, we have sex at least three to four times a week. We didn’t do that last week because of what happened. You treated me like I was a porcelain doll,” he laughed.

“I wasn’t going to take a chance on hurting you,” she explained.

“You can’t hurt me,” he said.

He paused, and he found his mind wandering in the direction of work-related responsibilities. “I think we should make an appointment with Mr. Blanchard and the prosecuting attorney in Franklin County. I want to see what information they already have before we begin running things down. Once we do that, we should then talk to Hugh at the Sheriff’s Office.”

“That makes sense.”

“I’m going to call first thing tomorrow morning. I would like to book an overnight stay at the Double Tree so we can go talk to the Franklin County Medical Examiner,” David explained.

“I’ll follow your lead,” she said.

“You are going to need to take the lead on some of this. It was your brilliance that led us here.”

She smiled. “So, you think I’m brilliant?” she teased.

“Oh, I do,” David said seductively as he kissed her forehead again. “And sexy.” He kissed her neck. “And gorgeous.” He moved the sheet out of his way and teased her breast.

“Mr. Gregory, you are insatiable,” Alex said with a giggle.

59

David got in touch with the Franklin County Prosecutor as well as Mr. Blanchard. A lunch meeting was scheduled for Friday. So, he booked a hotel room for Thursday, Friday, and Saturday night. Arrangements were made for Hope and Will to care for the dogs while David and Alex were out of town.

There was an agenda for the prolonged stay in Columbus. He wanted to orchestrate a memorable weekend for Alex. Aware of her profound affinity for plants, he knew she would appreciate a visit to the conservatory.

After ordering pizza for dinner, David began packing a small suitcase. Alex sat on the bed watching him move around the room. He put a couple of suits in a garment bag as he made brief eye contact with her.

“When you pack your things,” he began, “you’ll want to pack for Saturday night, too. We’ll be coming home Sunday morning.”

“Oh?”

“Yes. We’ll do room service tomorrow night, but then we’ll go to dinner Friday and Saturday. I have something special planned for Saturday afternoon,” he explained.

“Really?”

He smiled.

“Do I even get a hint?” she asked curiously.

“Not a chance.”

After work Wednesday, Alex and David drove to Columbus. They checked into the DoubleTree and settled in for the evening. David chose a suite. He wanted their time away to feel as much like home as possible.

They ordered room service for dinner and busied themselves preparing for the meeting the next day. Admittedly, they both felt a little nervous. Their anxiety kept them from sleeping well, so when the alarm went off at 9 a.m., they were a little slow to wake.

Room service delivered their breakfast. They sat at the small table in the kitchen area. Both of them reviewed their notes and quietly ate. They were engrossed in the preparations for the meeting.

As the noon sun cast a warm glow over the bustling streets, David and Alex arrived at the upscale restaurant where their meeting was to take place. The elegant facade of the establishment exuded an air of sophistication.

They walked inside. The hostess smiled as she checked their reservation. David observed the general atmosphere. The restaurant wasn't one he was familiar with. It was a bit dark with soft lighting and elegant accents.

The hostess located the information she needed, grabbed two menus, and led Alex and David down several corridors toward a private seating area.

David looked down at himself once more as he walked behind the hostess. He was nervous, which wasn't like him at all. He had chosen to wear a navy blue suit exquisitely tailored to accentuate his frame. The crisp lines of his attire spoke of meticulous attention to detail, while the burgundy tie added a touch of subtle sophistication. With each step, his polished brown dress shoes echoed against the tiled floor as they continued making their way through the restaurant.

They entered a room where there were only a few tables, and only one of those tables was occupied. Two gentlemen sat at the table, then rose when they saw David and Alex enter the room.

David looked at Alex, who took the first step toward the men. She radiated elegance in her choice of attire. Her black two piece double breasted suit projected timeless sophistication. Paired with black heels that elongated her legs and emphasized her poise, she moved with confidence.

The man on the left offered his hand first.

"I'm John Blanchard," he said.

David estimated him to be in his mid forties based on the receding hairline. He was slender, possibly a runner from what David could tell. He had deep blue eyes and a serene smile.

Alex nodded as she shook hands. Then the man on the right offered his hand to David. "I'm Sean Lykins, the County Prosecutor," he began.

He was quite young, possibly in his early thirties. He had a thick head of black hair, deep brown eyes, and olive skin. He was smaller in frame, likely of Middle Eastern descent.

Once everyone was seated and drink orders were taken, David began.

"Thank you for agreeing to meet with us," he said.

"It's no problem," Mr. Blanchard began. "We're happy to help in any way we can, and we hope you'll do the same."

"Absolutely," David agreed.

"So, what do you already have?" Alex asked pointedly.

"Well," Mr. Lykins began, "we have already gotten a warrant for Judge Meyers' autopsy and all of his medical records. Blood and tissue samples have been sent to our crime lab, but they have a three to six month backlog. We are also obtaining information on Maureen Fitzpatrick's death. The professor was a resident of Franklin County, and the death took place here, so we will have to take jurisdiction on that one as well. I fear that we may strike out with that one though."

"Why is that?" David asked.

"Well, I don't know if an autopsy was done when she died. I'm also not sure if blood and tissue samples were obtained either."

"It sounds like an exhumation might have to happen," Alex suggested.

"We would have to petition the county in Minnesota. That's where Professor Fitzpatrick was laid to rest. She was a transplant when she took the job at Ohio State. We can try to obtain a court order if we have enough evidence," Mr. Lykins explained.

"Gentlemen," David started, "another thing we need to look at is the logistics. The chief's nephew is currently our county prosecutor. That's going to be an issue."

"Oh," Mr. Lykins said.

"I am currently running for his seat," Alex pointed out, "but, of course, until the November election, we're sort of in limbo. We will need a visiting prosecutor."

"I am happy to fill that role, especially since most of this has landed in our jurisdiction," Mr. Lykins agreed.

“That would be great,” David interjected.

“We believe that it is possible that Gerri murdered the professor, the chief, and the judge. If we can prove that, she won’t be able to hurt anyone again,” Alex said with conviction.

“So, what are the action steps here?” Mr. Blanchard asked, “Because the civil case will come after the criminal case.”

“First, we wait on the results from the judge’s blood and tissue samples,” Mr. Lykins said as he paused and took a drink from his water glass. He continued. “Once we have that, we will know how to move forward. We request autopsy results, blood, and tissue samples from the chief’s death. We also put in a request to see if an autopsy was completed when the professor died, as well as any blood and tissue samples that might have been taken.”

“Let’s plan on a teleconference in a month,” David suggested. “If you get information sooner than that, reach out to us. In the meantime, we will meet with our sheriff and loop him in.”

“Sounds like a plan,” Mr. Blanchard said. “As I said, I have to hit the pause button. Based on the criminal findings, I’ll know whether or not we can pursue a civil case,” he explained. “That means that the will can be held up in Probate until the criminal case is resolved, whether it’s a trial or a plea deal.”

Alex smiled.

“Does that please you?” Mr. Blanchard asked.

“Mrs. Meyers is very money-conscious. The wait will not be pleasant for her,” Alex answered.

Mr. Lykins reached down and pulled out a thick file. He handed it to David.

"This is everything we have so far. Take a look at it. If you have any questions before our meeting next month, let me know."

"Thank you," David said with a nod.

The rest of the lunch was filled with small talk and pleasantries. The game plan was clear. Now the mission was to move forward with purpose.

60

As Alex stood amidst the winding stone path of the conservatory, she found herself enveloped in a tranquil oasis of greenery. Towering ferns arched overhead, their delicate fronds swaying gently in the breeze that wafted between the glass walls. Vibrant blooms adorned every corner, splashes of color against the backdrop of verdant foliage.

The warmth seeping through the glass panes bathed her skin in a comforting embrace. The faint scent of earth and flowers mingled in the air. It felt like a pause she hadn't realized she needed.

"I'm so glad you brought me here," she said as she glanced over at David.

As she turned to him with a smile, David's heart skipped a beat at the sight of her rosy cheeks, flushed from the embrace of the greenhouse's balmy air. Her hair, the blend of chestnut and dark brown, cascaded in soft curls around her face. In the gentle glow of the sunlight, each strand seemed to come alive, catching the light in a dance of hues that captivated his gaze.

"As much as you love nature, I felt like it would be a great experience for you. I knew you'd appreciate it," he admitted.

"So beautiful," she said, gazing up at the foliage.

"I know the feeling," he remarked with a smile.

"You flatter me, Mr. Gregory," she said wryly.

"I tell the truth, Ms. Ritzel."

They walked on and finished their adventure among the flowers and the trees of the conservatory. Making their way to the car, David revealed the next part of his plan for the day.

"I'm taking you to a really nice restaurant for dinner. Those more formal outfits I asked you to pack… you'll certainly need one."

"Oh, okay," she agreed as she pulled the vehicle door open and slipped onto the seat.

Back at the hotel, Alex decided to lie down for a nap. David spent the time looking over some of the contents of the packet that Mr. Lykins had offered. There wasn't much to look at yet. Copies of court orders and items of discovery were all they had so far.

As he contemplated all of the facts and the information shared, he realized what a long road lay ahead. This was not going to be a simple, quick situation. He hoped Alex realized that. Because he knew the background between Gerri and Alex, it was easy for David to sometimes catch a glimpse of the fierceness in Alex's eyes. She truly believed that Gerri was a threat. He wondered if he understood all of the ways that Alex saw her as such.

He couldn't possibly fathom the grief Alex felt when her brother died. He saw it, though. He watched her nearly tear herself apart. They were young, but seeing her in such despair was something he wouldn't soon forget. He knew it must be a terribly heavy burden to carry, something she woke up with and went to bed with every day. He hoped that he could at least provide some comfort to her as he had done when they were kids.

Compelled by his empathy, he stood and walked into the bedroom where Alex lay under the covers. The heat from the unit in the wall made the air comfortable, and he could see why she had gotten so sleepy.

He undressed and crawled in beside her. Stirring a little, she moved to rest in his arms. All he wanted to do was protect her and take care of her. He loved her, and he couldn't imagine being without her now that they had found each other.

He kissed her hair and pulled her as close as he could into the crook of his arm. Her head rested on his chest.

"It isn't time to wake up yet," he whispered.

She murmured just a little and then quickly fell back to sleep. He followed her into a dreamless slumber, woken only by his phone buzzing. He peered over at it on the nightstand. It was time to dress for dinner.

He kissed Alex on the forehead. "We need to get ready for dinner. Our reservation is at 6:30," he whispered.

She roused a little and turned over on her side, her bare back facing him now. Beneath the covers, she lay only in her panties, and the sight of this aroused him. Still, he had to maintain some self-control. Missing the reservation wasn't what he wanted to do.

He leaned over and kissed her back. "We have to get dressed," he implored, his hand resting on her hip now.

Finally, he convinced her to wake up. She slid out of bed and stood, standing nearly naked before him. He felt his erection press hard against his boxer shorts.

"You are making it very difficult for me to keep this dinner reservation," he admitted.

She smiled, turned on her heels, and walked to the closet. "Later, Mr. Gregory. Later," she assured him.

About an hour after waking up, Alex emerged from the bathroom wearing a sleek black cocktail dress. The halter neckline accentuated her shoulders and collarbones, while the knee-length hemline lent a touch of elegance to her ensemble.

With a silver wrap draped delicately over her shoulders, Alex exuded an aura of refinement, her every movement exquisitely poised. The sleeveless design of her dress allowed her to showcase her arms, perfectly complemented by the shimmering fabric of her wrap.

As she glided across the room in her black stiletto heels, David watched her closely. Her French twist hairstyle, meticulously arranged, accentuated her long neck and drew attention to the teardrop earrings adorning her lobes.

"Wow," he said as he observed her and stood from the loveseat. Her attire caused his blood to run hot, and he relished the anticipation of slipping the dress off her later.

David chose a single-breasted black suit. It hugged his form with tailored precision. The slim fit accentuated his physique. He was sure to turn heads. Every stitch of the suit was meticulously crafted to fit him like a glove, enhancing his stature. His broad shoulders filled the jacket with a commanding presence.

The shiny gray patterned tie, elegantly paired with a crisp white oxford shirt, was the signature of the entire look. The subtle yet refined pattern of the tie added a touch of personality to his attire, while the pristine shirt spoke of timeless sophistication. Completing the look were his black lace-up shoes, polished to perfection, adding a final flourish of refinement to his outfit.

And then there was his hair, tousled just so, adding a hint of rebellious charm to his otherwise impeccable appearance. It gave him an undeniable sex appeal, a magnetic quality that made it difficult for anyone to resist his charm and charisma.

Alex's mouth dropped open. "You look good enough to eat," she admitted.

"Later…" he hinted with a wink.

"Promise?" she asked.

He walked to her, put his hands on her waist, and looked intently into her eyes. "It will be my pleasure to get you out of this dress and onto your back."

She blushed, her cheeks warming pink. Speechless, she only smiled.

"Did I embarrass you a bit, love?" he asked sweetly.

"Not at all. I just love when you talk to me like that," she admitted.

He leaned down and kissed her neck, catching a faint whiff of her perfume. "You smell like heaven," he whispered.

She closed her eyes and tried her best to contain herself.

"We should probably get to dinner," she suggested reluctantly.

He pulled away and nodded. "You're right," he admitted.

61

"Are you enjoying yourself?" he asked.

"Of course. Always," she said with a smile.

"Have you given any thought to how you want to do things with the wedding? I know you settled on the fall, but I didn't know if you had gone much further with it," he asked curiously.

She put the napkin to her lips briefly and then reached for her wine glass. Taking a quick drink, she nodded. "Well, I was thinking late September, early October. The leaves will be beautiful then, and it shouldn't be too terribly cold. I wondered if you would be okay with the wedding being held at the cabin or on Hope's property. Something small, with close friends and family?"

"You don't want something big?" he asked.

"I want something intimate. In nature. A handfasting ceremony."

"What's that?" he asked as he took a swig of his beer.

"Once upon a time, it was the way people were legally married. A cloth or rope was used to wrap around the couple's hands. It symbolized love and commitment between the two, their lives merging into one. It originated in Scotland and became part of Celtic tradition."

"I see you've done your research," he smiled.

"You know me." She took another drink of wine and continued. "Is there anything you'd like to do? Anything that means something to your heritage or your family?"

"Well, my parents were married at a courthouse," he laughed. "As far as our ancestry, I haven't done much research. I don't know if Olivia or Hope have either. When Olivia and Danny got married, it was a small ceremony at Mom and Dad's house. I guess my family doesn't really do big weddings."

"There's nothing wrong with that. I think smaller ceremonies have a certain romance to them. There's just a closeness to them, I guess. Not a big production for the benefit of everyone else."

"I get it. I just want to be your husband. I don't care much how it happens. Just that it does." He paused and reached across the table. He took her hand into his and looked down at the engagement ring. "Have you given any thought to a honeymoon?"

"Not really."

"Is there anywhere you'd like to go?"

"Surprise me," she said as the low light reflected in her eyes.

"Would you prefer a beach or something else?"

"Well, I've always wanted to visit Egypt. I know that is a huge ask, though. It is expensive, and everything is always in such upheaval there. I feel like Egypt speaks to me, though; like there's something there I'm supposed to find. I've felt the same way about Ireland. Don't get me wrong, I worship the beach, but those two places… my soul came from there. It's where I feel like I was truly born."

"I didn't know that," he admitted.

"I just felt like you might not completely understand," she said shyly. "That's why I haven't shared."

"Honey," he continued, "I might not completely understand everything about the way you believe, but as I've said, I'll always respect it. There are places that I want to go, places I feel like hold something special for me. Australia is one of those places. There are also places in the States where Mom and Dad have taken me, and there's some sort of familiarity to it for me. The Carolinas, Virginia, Louisiana. I can't quite explain it. It's just something I know."

"I've never heard you open up like that before," she said pleasingly. "It means a lot to me."

"I never really gave any of it much thought. You've been subtle about it. You've never tried to force any of it on me. I appreciate that. And I've watched you work in your hobby room. I've seen the things you do. You truly do have a gift, Alex. You know exactly what to do instinctively. You don't need a book or a recipe. It's something that comes from your soul. There's no other explanation," he said with admiration in his voice.

She blushed again, and tears filled her eyes. "David, that means so much," she said. "I was so afraid that you'd never be able to accept my beliefs and my gifts. I was so worried that you would disapprove so much that you may decide not to be with me."

"That will never happen, Alex. Let me make the decision as to whether or not I believe, ya know?"

"I do," she nodded.

"Hope was always really bad about just shoving things down my throat. Mom was a little subtler, but most of all, she let me find my own way."

"Well, I appreciate the respect you have given me when it comes to how I feel and what I believe," she praised. "You've allowed me to be who I am."

"That's all I ever want you to be. Don't hide who you are because who you are is so incredibly beautiful. Even as a kid, you had a way about you. You were always genuine. You never tried to be someone you weren't."

"But I did hide who I was," she said. "I had to. I didn't know how to hold it together, and you saw that. My parents were too wrapped up in their own pain to help me experience mine. I don't know what I would have done without you and your grandparents," she said as the tears began to well in her eyes again.

David could feel the heaviness of the conversation and knew it was time to lighten things up a bit. "Dance with me," he said as he put his napkin on the table and stood.

She nodded and stood. He offered his hand. She gladly took it. Leading them to the dance floor, he pulled her close to him. As they moved with the music, everything else seemed to fall away. Being there with her felt easy and right. The dance floor was crowded, but they still felt as if they were the only couple in the room. The music enveloped them as they moved slowly, carefully taking each step together, David leading the dance.

Alex looked up at David, her eyes narrowing and the crinkle above her nose more pronounced.

"What's wrong?" he asked.

"I feel like someone is watching us. It's sort of giving me the creeps," she admitted.

“Well, I’m sure that there are people watching us. I mean, look at you. You’re kind of hard to miss,” he said flatteringly.

“I mean it,” she said seriously. “I feel really uncomfortable all of a sudden, and I don’t know why.”

“Well, I’ve already paid the check. Do you want to go?” he asked with concern.

“I would. I’m so sorry,” she said guiltily.

“Don’t be. We can go,” he assured her as he kissed her forehead.

David released Alex and watched her walk back to the table. She grabbed her wrap and clutch and then met David at the exit. He saw Alex as she glanced around. Her expression told him that she didn’t see anything out of the ordinary.

“What is it?” he asked curiously.

“I feel a pit in my stomach. I just don’t know why,” she admitted.

Neither David nor Alex realized that Gerri had been watching them for the last hour. She had arrived at the restaurant wearing a brown wig to cloak her appearance. She had been seated at the bar. She had known exactly how to find them.

62

The sheriff's office was busy with deputies coming in and out with the shift change. David and Alex had no choice but to meet with Hugh at 4 p.m. He couldn't see them any sooner than that.

Hugh Jenson was a young and ambitious sheriff. He'd been a popular athlete in high school, and that popularity followed him into adulthood. He had been elected at the tender age of 22 and re-elected every year since. Now, at the age of 30, he had served the community well.

Hugh was taller than most, and he was extremely fit. His athleticism stayed with him. He was a redhead with deep blue eyes and boxy features. His wide-set eyes were filled with sincerity, and despite his rough exterior, his voice always held kindness. Still, when he needed to be assertive, he was able to do it with ease.

He sat at his desk reading over the packet that David and Alex had provided. They had already debriefed him about the meeting that took place in Columbus. When they spoke, he listened intently, but it was apparent he was a little taken aback.

"So, you all are going after her with both barrels then?" he asked.

"That's the intent," Alex answered. "She has likely murdered three people. She is a black widow, Hugh."

"I'm happy to assign a detective to the case. Keith is the best. Is Will going to help with this at all?"

David shook his head. "We had considered getting him involved, but I think it's best that we keep him out of this for now. This could get very messy. We need the backing of your department, as well as offering any help we can to Franklin County in order to make a case."

"I get that," Hugh agreed. "You all gonna exhume the professor's body? The chief's?"

"We may have to, but right now we're waiting on the blood and tissue that already might be available at the medical examiner's office," Alex replied.

"I'm going to make copies of this packet and hand it over to Keith, if that's okay," he said, looking at both of them.

"Absolutely," David agreed.

Hugh excused himself, left the room, and then came back to make small talk. After about ten minutes, the secretary walked in with the original packet and the copies. Following behind was Keith Garrison.

Keith was older and a veteran of the sheriff's office. He'd served in the military. When he finished his tour, he'd settled in the small town thanks to his sister. He found a wife and married. They'd had a couple of kids and lived a quiet life. He had started as a street deputy and worked his way up to lead detective. He was smart, with unprecedented instincts.

Tall and broad-shouldered, he had a full head of salt-and-pepper gray hair. His eyes were deep brown, and the wrinkles on his face didn't diminish his attractiveness. Both Alex and David had heard about his reputation with women, but neither of them really cared. They just wanted to be sure he'd do his job and help them solve what seemed to be an impossible case.

Keith smiled as David stood. They shook hands.

"Good to see you, David," he said.

He nodded at Alex, and she returned his gesture with a smile.

"I hear congratulations are in order," he said with a kind smile.

"Where the hell have you been, Keith?" Hugh asked jokingly.

"Well, this is the first I've had the chance to see these two," he said, turning his attention to David again and then to Alex. "I wish you the best. You kids deserve some happiness."

Keith was one of the deputies who had been called to Marvin's accident. He remembered very well the scene and delivering the news to Alex and her family. Serving overseas had desensitized him to a lot, but it still pained him to deliver news like that to anyone.

"Thank you," Alex said softly. The sting of the memory also nudged at her, and she tried not to choke up.

Keith backed up and then leaned against the door facing. Hugh motioned for him to close the door, so he did. Hugh then explained the situation with Gerri and Franklin County. He dove into the suspicions and the process of waiting on the evidence.

"I knew she was a snake in the grass," Keith said. "She's always been one to bat those pretty eyes and get whatever she wants. When Chief married her, I knew something wasn't right."

"Well, we need as many allies as we can get on this," Alex interjected. "Right now we're just waiting, but when we get what we need, we'll need cooperation to execute warrants."

"I'll help however I can," he agreed.

"We'll all be working closely with the prosecutor in Franklin County," David explained. "With Alex running for office and Richard related to the former chief, we can't have him involved."

“I understand,” Keith said with a confident nod.

“You’ve got the resources of this office at your disposal,” Hugh said.

After some more pleasantries and small talk, Alex and David took their leave and proceeded home to make dinner and settle in for the night.

63

Alex found herself enveloped by the ethereal silence of the forest, the kind of quiet that presses in on the ears and makes the world feel distant. A tall, feminine figure emerged from the fog.

"I'm Maureen," she said without moving her lips.

Cloaked in blue, she gestured for her to follow. The path they traversed was carpeted with moss and framed by towering, gnarled trees that seemed to whisper secrets in the wind. The mist wove through the trunks like spectral tendrils, tugging at the edges of her perception.

As they walked, the forest seemed to pulsate with ancient rhythm, and the air was thick with the scent of damp earth and decaying leaves. The sudden flutter of wings heralded the raven's arrival, its black eyes gleaming with an intelligence that was unsettling. As it landed on Maureen's outstretched finger, the whisper of "poison" felt like a chilly breeze cutting through the fog. Alex's heart skipped a beat, the word echoing in her mind.

Maureen spoke again. "A tattoo. A mark, hidden between the toes."

Alex understood what she meant. The notion that Gerri marked her victims in such a personal, permanent way was horrifying. Still, even in her dream state, she wasn't surprised. She looked down. Purple vines wrapped around the bottom of a tall tree. It looked like foxglove, beautiful and dangerous. The image aligned too closely with the suspicions she'd already been carrying.

Emerging at a crossroads, the sudden clarity as the fog dissipated felt almost jarring. A wooden sign, stark against the now visible sky, bore no names, only directions worn by time. The raven's choice of path, a silent command to follow, led them through a landscape that gradually morphed from forest to an old graveyard.

A noise caught Alex's attention, and she could feel an arrow poised to hit the raven. Catching the arrow was instinctual, a moment where dream and reality blurred, her body reacting before her mind could catch up. The appearance of the figure in the golden cloak added a vivid contrast to the muted colors around her. This enemy was no mere shadow but a defined threat, marked by the brilliance of her attire against the dark backdrop of the woods.

"Not this time," Alex whispered.

A gray wolf suddenly appeared at Alex's side, a protector manifested from her subconscious. Its presence was comforting despite its fierce demeanor. The wolf's growl was a low rumble of thunder, ready to defend against unseen forces at a moment's notice.

She woke as the wolf propelled itself forward in the direction of the figure in the golden cloak. Alex was disoriented, the remnants of the forest and fog still clinging to her.

She looked over to find David was awake.

"I'm sorry," she muttered.

"You were flailing. I knew you were having a nightmare, but I didn't want to wake you," he said with concern in his voice. His presence was the lifeline back to reality, grounding her.

"I need to write this in my dream journal," she said as she sat up and threw off the covers. The dogs perked up momentarily. When her feet hit the floor, Artemis got up and followed Alex to the study.

Her resolve to document everything, to capture every detail before it slipped away, was driven by an urgent need to decipher the meanings hidden within the dream's symbols, poison, the tattoo, the wolf, the figure in the golden cloak. Each element was a piece of a larger puzzle that Alex felt compelled to solve. She knew the pieces were starting to align.

64

The next morning, Alex sat at her desk in the cottage. Feeling a bit sleep deprived, she rose to pour some more coffee into her mug. Joan had opened the windows. The March air was warmer than usual, and the fresh air coming into the small office house was exactly what Alex needed.

Will's office was empty. He was freelancing somewhere in Cincinnati, from what Hope had said. That meant the atmosphere was relatively quiet, aside from the radio playing in the reception area.

She walked down the hallway and into the kitchen. She grabbed the coffee pot and poured the rich, dark liquid into her mug. The smell awakened her just slightly, and she glanced down at her wristwatch. It was only 10:30 a.m. Luckily, she didn't have any hearings today. She only had briefs and some entries to compose.

As she entered her office, Joan called to her. "Hope is out front. She just pulled in."

Alex walked back into the hallway and out to the reception area. Sure enough, Hope was getting out of her vehicle. Relief washed over her. She was more than pleased to see her future sister-in-law.

Hope opened the door and smiled. Wearing a pair of yellow straight-legged capris, a cream-colored scoop-neck T-shirt, white canvas sneakers, and a light jacket, she was the picture of spring.

"Good morning, beauties," she said melodically.

Joan smiled. "Good morning."

"Hey," Alex said in a pleasant voice.

Hope nodded toward Alex's office, and Alex walked down the short hallway to the open door. They walked in. Hope shut the door behind her and then took off her jacket, laying it on an empty chair in front of Alex's large wooden desk. She then sat down on the small loveseat against the left wall.

"Tell me about the dream," Hope blurted out.

Alex stopped wondering how Hope always knew when she was needed and simply explained the elements of the dream. Hope listened to every single word intently, nodding her head in places and offering an unintelligible verbalization at other times. Finally, once the dream was explained, they both sat in silence for a moment.

"Do you understand what it means?" Hope asked.

"I do. I understand all of it. I know the visitation from Maureen was real. She clearly wanted to help. And the raven, its message finally came through. The bird took me to the graveyard because that is where I'm supposed to find the evidence we need. When I caught the arrow, it was like a reflex. I knew it was coming. The woman in the golden cloak is undoubtedly Gerri. I know that for certain now. She knows what she's done and wants to silence the messages. The appearance of the wolf was a bit unexpected."

"She's your protector. You officially have a spirit animal who is willing to stand between you and anything that might harm you." Hope paused for a moment. "I think you should start taking Artemis with you wherever you go. Bring her here to the office. She is well trained. All she needs is a vest. I believe she is your protector on this earth. I think the gray wolf is somewhat symbolic, but you need a protector here on this Earth, too."

"Why Artemis?"

"I can't explain it. I think Artemis will be able to help you when the time comes."

Alex nodded. She wouldn't question it. She trusted Hope's gift enough to have faith in the suggestion and to do it.

Before they could say another word to each other, Joan knocked on the door. She cracked it open slightly and said, "Ben is on the phone for you."

A little startled, Alex said, "Put him through."

As the phone rang, Hope stood. "I'm going to go grab some coffee," she said, excusing herself from the room.

Alex picked up the phone. Her stomach sank. He never called her at work, so she worried something was wrong.

"Hey, Sissy," he said melodically.

"Hey, Ben," she answered.

"Do you have lunch plans today? I have an early day, and you've really been on my mind. I figured we could do a little wedding planning," he suggested.

"I think that sounds great!" she answered in relief.

"Meet you at Sam's around noon?"

"I will be there," she said sweetly.

They hung up, and Hope walked back into the office. She grabbed her jacket and smiled.

"I don't want to keep you. I just wanted to check on you. I felt the disturbance in the middle of the night. I also saw flashes of the dream, so I wanted to make sure you understood everything. You've figured it out all on your own. Your gifts are growing. If nothing else comes of this, at least you are learning to stand in your own power."

"I would have had to have help from you or my aunt before. I immediately knew what it all meant," Alex said proudly.

"Well, if you need me, you know where to find me. I'm heading to Dayton tomorrow to work on some things for BCI, but I'll be back in a few days," Hope announced.

They parted ways, and Alex went on with her morning. She busied herself with her necessary tasks. At 11:45, she readied herself to meet Ben. She grabbed her debit card from her wallet and put it in the back pocket of her navy blue capri pants. She grabbed her matching jacket from the back of her chair and slipped it over her shoulders. The yellow blouse underneath gave the ensemble a pop of color.

She looked down at her feet. She'd chosen a pair of navy ballet-style flats today. Because it was so beautiful outside, she wanted to walk and grab some of that fresh air. She opted out of putting on her clunky white tennis shoes, though. The flats would do just fine.

She picked up her cell phone and slipped it into her back pocket. Walking out of her office and into the reception area, she smiled at Joan, who was busy typing something up on the computer.

"I'm going to lunch with Ben. If you need me, just call. I have my phone on me."

"Sure thing," Joan said with a nod.

“Do you want me to bring you anything back? We’re going to the diner on 5th.”

“No. I brought my lunch today,” she replied.

“Okay. I’ll see you in a bit,” Alex concluded as she pulled open the heavy wooden door and stepped outside.

The walk to the heart of downtown was very pleasant indeed. The temperature was perfect. The sky was blue with only a few passing clouds. The warmth of the sun kissed Alex’s exposed skin as the slight breeze blew her long hair around her face. Every now and then, she tucked the strands behind her ears.

Finally, she reached her destination. The lunch crowd was dense. Ben stood outside, cell phone in hand, waiting patiently. When he saw Alex, his face lit up and he walked to her briskly, arms outstretched.

They embraced. His energy was invigorating, and Alex needed to be in his presence.

“Hey, Sissy,” he whispered.

“Hey,” she replied softly.

“I already grabbed a table. I just wanted some of this spring air. You ready to go in?” he asked politely.

She nodded.

Ben led them to a table for two in the far corner of the establishment. It offered some privacy, but because everyone in the restaurant was familiar to her, she wasn’t sure that there was any privacy to be had. Still, she was spending some much-needed time with her brother, and that’s what mattered to her right now.

After ordering their drinks, Ben smiled, sunlight bathing his features through the glass.

"So, how are you doing? You seem a little tired," he observed.

"I am. I've got a lot going on," she admitted.

The drink order came quickly, so Alex wasn't able to say much more before ordering lunch. When the waitress finally left, she continued.

"I've got a case that's driving me insane. We're waiting for blood and tissue analysis, but the crime lab and the ME's office are backlogged," she confessed.

"Oh, honey, I got you. The Franklin County ME runs in the same circles with me and Jeremy. He's gay, Sissy. I can get in touch with him and see if I can pull some strings. His husband works in the crime lab, too. Supervisor, even. I think he was recently promoted. Used to focus strictly on DNA and trace, maybe? I can't really remember. I do remember that they are both terrific people."

"Would you do that for me?" she asked, unable to hide her relief.

"Of course! I know you can't tell me anything, but whose name will all of this be under?"

"I think the Franklin County Prosecutor. Lykins is his name. It's a situation in which Franklin County is taking primary jurisdiction, and we're lending a hand," she said as she picked up her glass of water.

The condensation on the glass chilled her fingers as she sipped from the straw. "So, how are you and Jeremy?" she asked as she put the glass back on the table.

"Oh, no," Ben objected. "We're talking about you. Your wedding is in six months. Maybe even five if you choose September. Have you all decided on a definite date yet?"

"I think we're shooting for the second Saturday in October. The leaves will be beautiful then. September would be too early."

"Well, Jeremy and I would like to pay for the reception," he said.

"Ben, no. That's too much!" she quietly objected as she leaned forward.

"We insist. We have talked, and we're going to rent one of those big tents. If it's cold, we'll have heaters brought in. If it's warmer, the tent will be perfect. Please, we want to do this for you. It's our wedding gift to the two of you. We're just so happy to see you happy, doll," he said, reaching across the table to take her hands. "I've watched you my whole life. You carried so much hurt and pain, but you always did it with such grace. Now that you've found your yellow brick road, I want to make sure it's celebrated."

Tears welled in her eyes. The warmth of Ben's hands on hers made her miss Marvin. She quickly realized his absence would be painfully evident at her wedding. Her eyes gave her away.

"I know you miss him," Ben said. "He will be there. He's always been there. He's always watching over you. He's always with you," he assured her. "I know it."

"He's my angel," she said.

Ben pulled away and took a drink of his soda. "So, the dress. Have you thought about that yet? The maid of honor? The bridesmaids?"

"Honestly, we haven't really talked about it. The case we are working on is just consuming both of us."

"Damn. Must be a serious one," Ben stated.

"It is."

"I'll tell you what. Let me hire a wedding planner. You tell me what you want, and we will make it happen," he said as he snapped his fingers auspiciously.

"Ben, you don't have to do that! They are so expensive."

"Do you want quaint, or over-the-moon audacious?"

"I want quaint. A small cake. Hope as my maid of honor, of course. I don't want any bridesmaids. Honestly, I want a small gathering with just family."

"Well, then we can go smaller on the tent," he joked.

"Hope and David are both very private, so I don't want people to know where they live," she explained.

"Now it makes sense," Ben said with a sigh. "Well, how about this? Let me rent out the Rain Room. It's a little ways out of town, but not too far for people to travel to. It's elegant and stylish. You could have your small ceremony early in the day with just family and then the reception later in the evening."

Alex thought for a moment. She liked the idea. It would allow for an intimate ceremony and then a celebration with family and friends. "I think that works," she agreed.

"Perfect! So, a wedding planner for the ceremony? Is that allowed? Will you agree to that? I know you have the backdrop of autumn, but honey, there's so much to think about there."

"I honestly don't think a wedding planner will be necessary. Only my family and his will be at the actual wedding."

"I know, but the reception has to be planned, darling," Ben said with conviction. "There's the cake and the pictures. I mean, you want pictures taken at Hope's, right?"

"Yes."

"So, you are going to need a photographer."

She sighed, knowing he was making sense.

"Let me help you with this," he continued. "Let the gay man do what the gay man does! I know exactly what to do. I will run everything by you. I will pay for the reception, no issues there. I will also get the invitations for the reception, but you have to get me the guest list. Dad has already said he is paying for the ceremony."

"When did he tell you that? He hasn't said anything to me."

Ben smiled. "You are his only biological daughter. You think he will let you pay for your own wedding? I talk to the man almost daily, too. We have this covered."

"Was he ever going to say anything to me about it?" she asked.

"Probably, but he knows how busy you are with campaigning and life," Ben said.

So, there it was. Alex was getting married in October. Ben and Jeremy were planning and paying for the reception. Her father was paying for the wedding. Ben was also pulling strings at the ME's office, along with the crime lab. She was trying to keep her head from spinning. Nonetheless, the excitement welled up within her.

She couldn't wait to tell David about her day. She wanted to make sure he was okay with the plans. It was his wedding, too. She wanted to ensure he didn't feel left out or slighted in any way.

65

After lunch, Alex finished her day and drove to the cabin. She knew David was going to be late. He had a meeting with his campaign committee.

She parked the car and got out. The dogs greeted her as they always did. They followed her through the mudroom, where Alex put her belongings on the bench just inside the door.

Once the dogs were fed, she started on dinner. She turned on a podcast that echoed through the house on the surround-sound speaker. She decided on a meatloaf with some fried potatoes and green beans.

The familiar sound of tires on gravel alerted her to David's arrival. The dogs immediately responded and ran quickly to the mudroom. She opened the back door and walked onto the covered porch. She pushed open the screen door, and the two dogs shot outside toward the garage.

As she walked back into the kitchen, she muted her podcast and continued frying the potatoes in the skillet. Within a few minutes, she heard the creaking boards of the covered porch as four paws and two feet walked across the surface. The creak of the mudroom door made her smile, and she heard David set his things on the bench in the mudroom.

Promptly, he entered the kitchen, the dogs following close behind. He walked to Alex and offered a chaste kiss.

"Hey you," he said sweetly.

"How was your day?" she asked as she watched David loosen his tie.

"Productive. Really productive," he said as he shimmied out of his suit jacket and headed into the bedroom. "How close is dinner?"

"Only about 20 more minutes," she answered.

"I'm going to get a quick shower," he said.

When he returned to the great room, Alex was putting plates down on the bar. She grabbed a wine glass for herself and a bottle of beer for David. The meal was placed on the stovetop.

"Get what you want," she said. "It's ready."

They settled in for their meal together. Talking about their day, Alex told David about the lunch with Ben, the possible wedding plans, and the fact that Ben was going to see if he could speed up the case with Franklin County.

"Wow. You've had an industrious day," he said as he took a quick swig of the beer.

"I wanted to get your take on the wedding planning, especially. I don't want to make any decisions without you," she said sweetly.

"Listen," he said as he turned slightly on the bar stool. "I am okay with whatever you would like. I agree that Hope's is the perfect venue for the actual ceremony. The land is beautiful. The trees will be gorgeous. It's just going to be my family and yours. And if Ben wants to throw a big reception, I'm cool with it. If you want me to help choose a cake, I'm totally game. I will be involved as much or as little as you want me to be."

"It's your day, too," she said.

"That's true, so I'm here for it. Will is going to be my best man, no doubt there. It's easy enough to rent a couple of tuxedos if you want to go formal, or I can wear a pair of khaki shorts and a button-up. We can go as formal or as casual as you would like."

"I also want to talk to you about Artemis," she continued.

"Okay," he said expectantly.

"I'd like to take her with me to work and possibly other places."

"Well, she's fully trained. She's protective. Her vest is in the basement. I'll have to dig it out. I will also have to teach you her commands." He paused for a moment. "Is something wrong? Is that why you need her?"

"Hope recommended it. I'm not exactly sure why, but I tend not to question your sister when it comes to her instincts."

"Well, Artemis is just as much your dog as she is mine, so she can go with you wherever you need her to."

"It's settled then," Alex said with accomplishment in her tone. "I will text Ben and set him loose with the reception. I'll give Dad a call, too. I guess I need to formally ask Hope to be my Maid of Honor and ask if we can use her property for the ceremony."

"And I should ask Will to stand up with me as well," David remarked.

"I guess I've taken for granted that we are getting married in six months. I hadn't given it much thought with everything else going on," Alex admitted.

"We've both been pretty preoccupied. Campaigns. The case. Work. I agree, though. I don't want to wait to marry you. Most folks stay engaged for years. I want to be your husband sooner rather than later."

Alex smiled and blushed. "Husband," she repeated. "Sounds so odd."

He stood and took the plates to the sink. "It'll be second nature before we know it," David said.

66

Instead of convening a conference call, Mr. Lykins opted for a face-to-face format to present the results from the crime lab. It was a decision that brought him to the quaint cottage, surrounded by unfamiliar faces. Keith and Hugh were both in attendance, their anticipation palpable.

Adding to the gravity of the occasion, the Franklin County Medical Examiner, Dr. Randall Highland, joined them. Despite his small in stature, Dr. Highland commanded attention with his impeccable appearance. A Japanese-American gentleman, he seemed quite refined. He was meticulously groomed, wearing a designer suit.

Joan offered coffee to everyone, and when no one took her up on it, she left the room so that the meeting could proceed. Alex stood speaking to Dr. Highland while David, Keith, and Hugh spoke to Mr. Lykins.

“I had no idea that Ben was your brother,” Dr. Highland said.

“Isn’t he something?” Alex asked.

“We have been friends for a very, very long time. I met him when he was a nurse at Grant,” he continued. “When I got the phone call from him, I was more than happy to try to speed this process along. He never asks for favors, so I had no doubt that this was of extreme importance, not that other cases aren’t… well… you know what I mean.”

“I do, and I sincerely appreciate the expedited process,” Alex said with a genuine smile.

Dr. Highland shifted his focus and then spoke up, drawing everyone's attention. "So, when the crime lab ran the tissue and blood, they found digoxin in the judge's system. The readings were unusually high. When I did the autopsy, it was obvious that the judge's heart had been compromised over time. Clogged and hardened arteries. The medical records I received from his family physician pointed me in the direction of his cardiologist. He was prescribed medication for his heart, which would explain digoxin in his system, but not at that level."

"So, Judge Stevens did, in fact, die under suspicious circumstances?" Mr. Lykins asked.

"It is my professional opinion that he did," Dr. Highland answered.

"What do the elevated amounts in his blood mean?" David asked pointedly.

"It means that someone supplemented the judge's meds," Alex answered. "Foxglove can show up as digoxin in the blood. Based on the findings with the judge, we now have probable cause for a warrant to have the Chief's tissue and blood run, to obtain his medical records, and to exhume his body if necessary. The same applies to the professor."

"So you believe all three were poisoned?" Dr. Highland asked.

"I do," Alex answered confidently.

"We'll present all of this to our judge," Mr. Lykins added. "We should be able to obtain warrants fairly quickly. Once we get those results, we'll share everything with all of you. I am really hoping that they kept blood and tissue for the professor so we don't have to exhume her. I really don't want to do that with the Chief either if we have everything we need."

"We appreciate all of your help," David said as he looked around the room.

"Absolutely," Mr. Lykins said with a nod.

Keith sighed. "It seems to me that Gerri is the most likely suspect here. She had opportunity and motive."

"I just can't believe it," Hugh said. "She has always been so kind and accommodating. She seemed to love the Chief so much."

"You've been in law enforcement long enough to know that people aren't always what they seem," Keith reminded him. Hugh nodded in defeat.

Gerri's charm was a force to be reckoned with, a potent blend of charisma and calculated manipulation that seemed almost effortless. Her keen intuition for understanding people's emotions and motivations seemed to give her an advantage. Everything was a game to her. Whether it was a casual conversation or a high-stakes negotiation, Gerri knew just how to twist the situation to her advantage, leaving others spellbound in her wake.

For Alex, Gerri's ability to always emerge victorious was a constant source of frustration. No matter how hard Alex tried to outmaneuver her, Gerri seemed to effortlessly stay one step ahead, leaving Alex feeling outplayed at every turn. It was a bitter pill to swallow, but Alex had to believe that was all about to change.

Since meeting Alex and learning about her shared history with Gerri, David had gained a newfound insight into the depths of Gerri's manipulative prowess. It was quite something how she could navigate the complexities of human relationships with such finesse. He was cautious enough now to be a bit uneasy.

After some more discussion, everyone parted ways, anticipating the next set of results. Until then, they were in a holding pattern, but light was beginning to glimmer. Alex and David finally had some hope that they were making headway with their mission to hold Gerri accountable and bring peace to the dead.

67

Hope sat patiently in the elegant dress shop, anticipation bubbling within her as she awaited Alex's emergence from the dressing room. Being chosen as Maid of Honor was a role she embraced wholeheartedly.

Seated beside her on the loveseat were Robin, Penny, and Ben, their glasses of champagne adding a touch of celebratory flair to the occasion. Penny, with her unique charm and kind demeanor, was a welcome presence in the group. Despite being a tad eccentric, her genuine efforts to support Alex were evident, especially given her understanding of Alex's past struggles.

Close in age to Robin, Penny possessed an enduring cleverness, her once fiery red hair now softened to gray and styled in a bob. Behind her turtle shell glasses, her face carried warmth and wisdom, the kind earned through living.

The decision to embark on their dress shopping adventure on a Thursday afternoon instead of a typical bustling Saturday was a stroke of brilliance by Alex. Recognizing the need for a well-deserved break from the hustle and bustle of daily life, she seized the opportunity to carve out some precious time for herself and other members of the group.

Robin's spacious car proved to be the perfect mode of transportation for their adventure. With ample room for everyone to pile in, they could easily commence their day's journey.

As Alex appeared from the dressing room in yet another frilly dress, she couldn't help but feel a twinge of disappointment. None of the dresses seemed to align with her own personal style or vision for her special day. However, she was determined not to let her guests' choices go unappreciated, understanding that they were offering their opinions and suggestions out of love and support.

"Tell me what it is that you're seeing? What is your vision of this day?" she asked.

"I want vintage; something from another time. I want ivory, not white."

"Your happiness is what matters most," Hope said gently. "We'll find it."

Alex nodded.

"Try on the last two dresses that Ben picked out. While you're doing that, I'll go talk to the owner. And if we can't find what we're looking for here, we'll go somewhere else," Hope said confidently.

Alex smiled and put her hand on Hope's. "Thank you," she said with a warm smile.

"Always got you, girl," she whispered.

Alex slipped out of the wedding gown and into the next. It was too formal as well. Still, she made her way out of the dressing room to model for the audience.

Everyone excitedly clapped. Alex smiled courteously, knowing that she would be perfectly fine walking down the aisle dressed like a hippie.

She turned and walked back into the dressing room, put on the next dress, and made her way back out to the storefront. Again, she modeled as the others clapped and commented.

Finally, she took one last trip down the hallway to the dressing room. Standing in the mirror, she looked herself over. Then Hope appeared behind her with a dress draped over her arm. She held it up.

Hope hung it on an empty hook and assisted Alex out of the puffy, overdone white wedding gown she currently wore.

As Alex stepped into the ivory gown, Hope fell silent. Alex turned to face the mirror, her eyes widening in awe at the sight before her. The dress draped gracefully over her figure, accentuating her natural beauty with its empire cap sleeves and conservative v-neckline. The fine tulle lace whispered against her skin, a testament to the craftsmanship of the gown.

The designs in the lace were exquisite. The shoulders to mid-back were see-through, leaving the bodice solid with the lace fabric against it. The zipper in the back was disguised by a long line of intricate buttons. A keyhole of material was set between the shoulders and then topped off with two more small buttons.

As Alex admired her reflection, Hope couldn't help but feel a surge of pride wash over her. This was it—the dress they had been searching for, the embodiment of Alex's carefree and natural spirit captured in delicate lace and flowing lines.

"It's perfect," Hope whispered, her voice filled with emotion as she gazed at Alex with admiration. "You look absolutely breathtaking."

With a sense of certainty settling over them, Hope helped Alex adjust the length of the dress, ensuring that it grazed the floor just so, without dragging or catching.

“You shouldn’t have to have anything done to it,” Hope observed. “It fits perfectly.”

“It’s like it was meant to be,” she said as she admired her reflection. This truly was a joyful occasion.

"Here," Hope encouraged, "let's go show the others."

Hope took her hand and led her to the others. The warm rush of color to Alex's cheeks told the story.

Penny, Robin, and Ben sprang to their feet.

"Oh my god," Ben said as he set the glass down.

Penny nodded. "This… this is you," she commented.

"It is lovely, Alexandra. Just lovely. It suits you, truly," Robin added.

"Put some flowers in her hair, and this is perfect. Hell, you could even go barefoot if you wanted to," Ben added.

"You like it?" she asked all of them.

"Absolutely," Penny answered first.

"It doesn't even look like alterations will have to be done," Robin observed. "That's either luck or divine intervention."

The proprietor walked over with a smile. "You look lovely," she remarked. "Would you like to go ahead and pick out your Maid of Honor's dress today? Perhaps the 'Mother of the Bride' and 'Mother of the Groom' dresses today as well? I can discount it if you go that route."

Alex looked at the others, trying to gauge whether or not they wanted to commit to that yet. They were all smiling in anticipation.

"Well," Ben began, "she isn't paying for her dress. We are."

Alex shook her head in protest.

"No, Sissy. We are covering your wedding gown. If you wanna pay for the Maid of Honor's dress…" he said but was quickly interrupted.

"I am paying for my own dress," Hope said.

"And I will cover my dress as well," Robin added.

"Same," Penny agreed.

"But, I'm asking you to be a part of this. I should cover your dresses," Alex argued.

"Well, you're not," Penny insisted.

"Then let's get to it, shall we?" Hope asked sweetly.

Hope found an A-line V-neck dress with cap sleeves and illusion lace. It was a perfect match to Alex's wedding gown. The dress was made in the color of gold, and it came just above the knees.

Robin chose a pencil, scoop-neck, long-sleeve, knee-length, lace-chiffon dress in the color of burgundy. It was conservative, but the lace sleeves matched the general theme.

Penny picked out a pants-suit with sleeves that matched the tulle lace of the gown, the Maid of Honor dress, and Robin's ensemble. It was a lighter burgundy, but matched well with the general theme.

Shoes were also chosen, as well as accessories. And there it was. One of the most difficult, yet exciting, parts of the wedding planning was settled. Their trip to Cincinnati was a success.

On the drive back, Ben mentioned the flowers and the cake and reassured Alex that the wedding planner would handle most of the remaining details. When he asked what she planned to wear for her wedding night, she felt her cheeks warm and admitted she hadn't given it much thought. It was something she would think about later, so she shifted the conversation back to the colors and the overall theme of the wedding.

68

Warrants had successfully been executed to collect blood and tissue for analysis for the Chief. By the middle of May, the results reached Alex and David. It was just as Alex suspected. The Chief had high levels of Digoxin in his system. However, the medical records indicated that he had no known heart issues, and he wasn't seeing a cardiologist. No medications had been prescribed that would cause Digoxin to be present in his blood. The professor's results were still pending.

The findings related to the Chief provided enough probable cause for an exhumation. Mr. Lykins, Alex, David, Keith, and Dr. Highland all met on a teleconference call.

"I'd like to bring in a forensic pathologist," Dr. Highland suggested. "Dr. Lisa Wright is the only person I'd trust with this."

Alex's ears perked up. "Dr. Wright assisted with the Phantom serial case with Dr. Harris-Bennette. Is that correct?"

"Yes, it is," Dr. Highland answered. "That's impressive. You know about that case?"

"Yes, I do," she answered. "Both of my future sisters-in-law work very closely with Dr. Harris-Bennette. She is a colleague and friend of Dr. Wright's. I've never had the pleasure of meeting her, but I've read many of her articles. I have spoken to her from time to time about her work. She is somewhat of a pioneer."

"That she is," Dr. Highland added.

"What an incredibly small world," Mr. Lykins said.

"A warrant will tip off Gerri," David said plainly.

"True. Next of kin has to be notified," Keith remarked. "We don't have a choice. If we want to determine whether or not the Chief had a heart attack, we have to have him exhumed."

"What if we don't exhume him right away?" Alex asked, flipping through the records. "We know that the blood and tissue results are telling a story, that he has too much Digoxin in his system. He wasn't prescribed any medication, had no known heart issues, and according to his medical records, wasn't in poor health. He was a little overweight, but nothing that would indicate that he was at risk for a cardiac event.

"As I've said before, foxglove is a poison that mimics heart medication. Too much of it is fatal, causing tachycardia. The Chief wasn't prescribed heart medications of any sort, so the only logical conclusion is that he was poisoned with the herb.

"Also, according to the records here," she continued, "his death certificate says 'cardiac arrest' as the cause of death. What if we make the professor's tissues, blood, and autopsy the baseline for the case? She was the first alleged victim, after all, and we wouldn't have to involve Gerri just yet."

"I like it," Mr. Lykins agreed.

"That is a very solid game plan, Alex," Keith agreed.

David just smiled with pride.

"I'll work on the warrant for the professor's blood and tissue to be analyzed. Once we get those results, we'll go from there. Dr. Wright can travel to Minnesota for the exhumation, I'm sure," Mr. Lykins said confidently.

69

As David sat at his desk, the weight of the recently concluded phone call hung in the air. The conversation had been fruitful, yielding progress far quicker than he had initially expected. A sense of satisfaction washed over him as he reflected on the efficiency of the exchange.

Despite the challenges that lay ahead, David couldn't help but feel a surge of optimism. The hurdles were daunting, but with each small victory, he grew more confident in their ability to overcome them.

A knock on his door caused him to look up. Laylonie opened the door slightly. He motioned her inside.

She walked in and closed the door behind her. “Gerri Meyers is here,” she whispered.

David was completely caught off guard.

“Gerri?” he mouthed.

Laylonie only nodded.

He shrugged. “Well, send her in.”

Laylonie nodded, opened the door, and motioned for Gerri to come in.

Gerri was effortlessly confident as usual. Her attire was obviously chosen carefully, and she commanded attention without appearing overtly provocative. The tight denim capris hugged her in all of the right places, accentuating her slender legs and hinting at the tantalizing curves hidden beneath. Paired with the golden V-neck sweater, the ensemble struck a perfect balance between casual style and modest appeal.

The neckline of the sweater drew the eye downward, subtly emphasizing the graceful curve of Gerri's neck and the delicate slope of her collarbones. The soft fabric draped over her with understated grace. Gerri's hair cascaded in soft curls down her back, adding a touch of whimsy to her otherwise polished appearance. Her tan skin glowed with a healthy vitality.

David stood and greeted her with a nod. They smiled cordially and then sat down in their respective places.

"What can I do for you, Gerri?" he asked calmly.

"I wondered if you would reconsider representing me," she said bluntly. "Like you said, I am going to need a criminal defense attorney. You're the best. I want nothing but the best."

"With respect," he sighed, "I've told you that I can't represent you."

"Is there anyone you would suggest I contact? Anyone you trust?"

He took a pen from his desk drawer and a Post-it note. He began writing names and phone numbers on the small pad of paper.

"These are good friends of mine. All of them are excellent attorneys. They are seasoned and very good at what they do. If it were me, I'd trust them with my life," he said, ripping the Post-it off and handing it over the desk.

She reached across the desk, stretching purposely to give him a bird's-eye view down the front of her shirt. Once she had the paper in her hands, she leaned over and reached for her purse. She pulled out her wallet and put the little piece of paper inside the zipper, and then put the wallet back into the bag. She then pulled up a glittery gift bag.

"I wanted you to know," she started, "that no matter what the outcome was today, I have absolutely no hard feelings. I really appreciate everything you've tried to do, and I appreciate your honesty." She stood up, walked around the desk, and handed the bag to David.

He stood to face her. "This is unnecessary," he said kindly.

"I know. I know. Consider it an engagement gift. It's for your house. I don't think Alexandra is quite right for you, but people also thought I wasn't right for Steven. So who am I to judge?"

David peered into the bag and pulled out a golden mantel clock. The intricate details of the clock's design caught his eye, from the ornate engravings that adorned its surface to the delicate hands that marked the passage of time.

His gaze lingered on the inscription "Mr. & Mrs. David Gregory," a subtle reminder of the future he envisioned with Alex. Still, David felt uneasy about Gerri's motives.

Gerri's smile, though enigmatic, conveyed a sense of genuine appreciation as she watched David examine the gift. It was clear that she had put thought and effort into selecting it.

"This is entirely too much," he protested.

"No, it isn't. You never know when time will run out," Gerri explained.

He put the clock on the desk and then turned to Gerri once again. She was closer to him than before. The scent of her perfume filled his senses. Gradually, David felt his guard lower.

She looked up at him, pure seduction in her eyes. "But you're not married yet, Mr. Gregory, and until then, all bets are off," she whispered sensually.

He was caught completely off guard and speechless. His mouth opened slightly. She closed the gap between them as she pressed herself against him. Their eyes were locked, anticipation gripping both of them. She reached up on her toes and kissed David's lips softly.

The slow kiss inflamed into something much more passionate as Gerri grabbed a fistful of David's hair, lacing it through her fingers. She pushed against him hard as his erection grew.

"I want you to touch me," she whispered as she took his hand and moved it to her breast. She leaned in and kissed his neck, her tongue flicking teasingly against his skin.

Almost robotically, David touched Gerri's breast atop her shirt. He felt her hard nipple through the sweater. She wasn't wearing a bra, and she guided his hand beneath her shirt until his fingers brushed bare skin.

She moved back to his mouth as his fingers teased her. "Do you want me?" she asked breathlessly.

Suddenly, the stones in his pocket burned against his skin. The heat dragged him back to himself, and he quickly took his hand back. Recoiling, he stepped backward and tried desperately to catch his breath. Frustrated, he ran his fingers through his hair.

"Oh my God, I can't believe I just did that," he panicked.

Gerri stood before him, an alluring smile across her full lips. She lifted the golden shirt to expose her breasts. They were perfectly round and indicative of breast implants. David didn't deny that she was beautiful. His body roused to her touch, and that sickened him. The stones burned even hotter in his pants pocket.

"You can take me right here and right now," she said. "I can be quiet," she continued, stepping toward him and taking both of his hands, placing them on her breasts.

David quickly stepped back and walked to the other side of the desk. "Gerri, this is completely inappropriate," he said with conviction. "You're beautiful, but I am engaged, and I love Alexandra. I would never hurt her like that."

"You aren't married yet. The fun stops only then," she said as she moved toward him. "Until that time, you're free."

He held up his hand in resistance as she moved toward him again. "No. I won't do this."

The stones still burned hot as a flame, and he knew there was something going on here that he didn't quite understand. He felt it best to trust the protection of the stones and the knowledge he did have.

He didn't want Gerri. While she was attractive, he didn't have a connection with her. He wasn't in love with her. In that moment, she felt like the villain in his story. The encounter felt forced, as if he weren't even in control of his own body.

David caught his breath and put his hands on the desk. He felt lightheaded again and nauseated.

"I need you to go," he insisted as he steadied his breathing.

"If you say so," Gerri said reluctantly with a casual shrug.

Lowering her shirt, she turned and walked to her purse, grabbing the handle gently. As she made her way out, she looked down at her hand, the strands of David's hair still hanging on her skin. With a devious smile, she exited the room and made her way out to her car.

David's internal turmoil weighed heavily on him as he sat down at his desk. He grappled with the aftermath of the events that had just transpired. The realization that he had compromised his own moral code and that his expectation of loyalty lay in waste in the interaction with Gerri made his head spin.

He was sickened by what had just taken place. He had allowed himself to cross a line with another woman. And not just any woman, but Gerri, the person who had caused Alex so much pain already.

The internal battle raged within him as he contemplated telling Alex what happened. He wondered if his honesty would be met with praise or rage. As much as he tried to be optimistic, his bet was on rage.

Looking down at his calendar, he realized he had the rest of the day to himself. There were no hearings and nothing else on his schedule. So, he decided to leave and make his way to the park. He wanted to be alone, and someplace quiet. He needed sound guidance, and the only person who could ever offer that to him in such dire circumstances was his mother.

70

David drove to the park across town and pulled into a vacant spot. He got out and stood beside the car. The park was deserted, with only a few people scattered on the grass and walking the trail. It was early afternoon, so none of the usual classes were going on, and none of the sporting events or practices would even begin until around 4 or 5 p.m.

He picked up the phone and dialed Robin's cell. She answered after the third ring. Her voice was comforting as she greeted David. Nevertheless, the tenor in his voice quickly told her something was very wrong.

"David," she began, "what is it? Are you alright?" she asked with concern.

"Mom, I've done something pretty terrible," he admitted.

He told his mother everything that had happened up to the present. He told her about the pen and how Alex blessed some stones for him to carry. He elaborated on the spell work that Alex had discussed with him. Then he confided in her about Gerri, being careful to omit information that would breach attorney-client privilege. He then told her about the situation that occurred that day.

"Mom, what should I do? I don't think I can keep this from Alex," he confessed. Tears stung his eyes as the feelings of guilt and shame gripped him.

"You have to be honest with her. Every relationship has its challenges; it's just a lot harder when those challenges are supernatural," she said comfortingly. "I have faith in Alex. She will be hurt, but when the dust settles, she will see clearly what's happened."

"I could stop it," he said. "I didn't. I shouldn't have let it go on as long as it did."

"Did you really have the ability to stop it, though? You said that you felt almost as if you were on autopilot," Robin reminded him.

"It was so strange. It was the closest I've ever come to an out-of-body experience. I had no control over my own actions."

"There has to be some spell work going on here, especially if what you've told me has any merit to it. If Gerri is a practicing witch, she can manipulate the world around her." Robin paused. "Did she take anything from your office? Anything of personal value?" she asked curiously.

"No. Not a thing. At least, not that I know of."

Robin sighed. "I know that you love Alex. She loves you. I know you will get through this. Just be truthful. You have the gift of compassion. I pray she does, too. You also have an eye for justice. This is going to stir things up within her; I can't lie to you there. Let her feel what she needs to feel. Allow her the space she needs if she asks for it. Respect her enough to tell her and to accept the consequences, David. That's really all you can do."

"I hate this, Mom," he bit out, the tears rolling down his cheeks now. "How could I do this to her? I love her so very much. I have never had this with anyone else in my entire life. I knew the moment she came back to me that I would never want to let her go… and then this?"

"I know. I'm so sorry this happened, but there's a reason. There's a lesson here, and not just for you. Every single situation we encounter, no matter how bleak, presents us with boundless growth opportunities. It could be that this situation was placed before the two of you so you could grow as a couple, taking what was meant to destroy you and building an even sturdier foundation with it."

The voice of his mother offered the reassurance and confidence he needed to face Alex. So, after ending the call, he drove home to confess the events of the day.

When he arrived home, it was a little before 4 p.m. Alex hadn't arrived home yet. David occupied his time with the dogs, throwing their ball in the large yard.

He took a walk up to the pond for some fresh air. As he stood among the tall grass and budding trees, he marveled at the beauty of the land left to him by his grandparents. He took a moment to collect his thoughts and sincerely contemplate what his mother had said. Perhaps she was right. Perhaps this situation would provide strength instead of destruction. After all, he didn't sleep with Gerri. He didn't want to.

When he got back to the cabin, he decided to grab a beer. Then he walked back out to the covered porch. His mind was still a flurry of mangled thoughts.

He left the clock Gerri had given him in the car. He was sure there was some sort of juju attached to it. He didn't want it anywhere near their home.

The familiar crackle of gravel under tires alerted David to Alex's arrival. His stomach dropped, and the knot in his throat nearly stole his breath. He stood on the porch watching as she pulled her SUV into the garage. The dogs excitedly ran toward the enclosure. David heard Alex's melodic voice greeting the girls.

She walked under the awning to the porch where David stood. He was statuesque, his shoulders unmoving and his breath shallow.

"Hey," she said with a smile. "You okay?" She could easily see something was wrong.

"I need to talk to you," David began as he pursed his lips. He turned and opened the screen door of the enclosed porch, Alex following behind. The door slammed behind them, and she bent down, placing her briefcase on the floor. Making her way to a vacant wooden chair, she sat on its edge.

"What's wrong, David?" she asked, turning toward him.

He sat beside her in the matching chair. His insides shook with anxiety and fear. He decided that instead of sugarcoating anything, he'd come straight out with it.

He detailed the events of the day, being careful not to leave any part out. When Alex asked questions, he answered. He made direct eye contact with every single word. He wanted her to know how difficult this was, but he also wanted her to understand that he knew she deserved nothing less than honesty, no matter what the cost.

After the full confession and the brief questions she had posed, Alex sat quietly, her eyes filling with tears, some streaming down her cheeks.

An uncomfortable silence fell between them. It was like a brick wall coming up. This made David very concerned and even more uncomfortable. The distance was nearly tangible, and he could feel her slipping away from him. It left an even deeper pit in his center.

Alex wiped her cheeks with the back of her hand and stared at the floorboards.

"Did you want her?" Alex asked as she sniffled.

"No. Not at all. You are the only one I want."

"So, the stones stopped you? You couldn't stop yourself?"

"Honey, it was like someone else was inside my body. I had absolutely no control. I've never felt so helpless in my entire life. When the stones began to burn my leg, it was like they pulled me back into this reality. I finally knew exactly what was happening, and I put a stop to it."

She had already asked once but decided to seek confirmation. "So, you didn't have sex with her?" The tears were now pooling on her thin ivory blouse.

"No, Alexandra. I did not have sex with her. I would never ever do that to you. Ever."

"But you weren't yourself," she said, a hint of anger in her tone.

"Honey," he said, moving to the space in front of her. He knelt before her, taking her hands into his. Looking up at her, he said, "I would never be unfaithful to you. Never. I take full responsibility for what happened today. I don't understand it. I don't know how it got that far. I won't blame anyone but myself. The moment I realized what was happening, I stopped her. She wanted me to fuck her. She even asked me to, but I told her I wouldn't."

Alex took back her hands and covered her face with them as she wept softly. David's heart broke. He dropped his head, unsure what to say or do. He placed his hands on her knees as she cried. He did his best to offer comfort and reassurance.

"I'm so sorry," he said sincerely. "I would never do anything to hurt you."

Alex wiped her wet cheeks; her mascara stained a little under her eyes. Her face was red as she tried to catch her breath.

"I appreciate that you told me the truth, David. You were honest with me, and you remained loyal," she said, praising him. "This still hurts a lot. It's a lot to take in."

"I know. I know," he said. "Tell me what to do."

"I need some space. I need to think," she acknowledged.

"Whatever you need. Do you want me to leave and stay with Will? Or even at your old place?" he asked graciously.

"No," she said with a heavy sigh. "I think it's best if I leave," she said as her hands shook.

"Are you breaking up with me?" he asked.

"No, David… I don't know," she said angrily. "I need some time to process everything you have just told me. And the clock. Where the fuck is the clock?" she asked angrily.

"It's in my car," he replied.

"I want you to give it to me," Alex insisted.

"Okay. Whatever you say," he agreed congenially.

The silence grew between them. It was as if a great gulf yawned before them.

"That fucking bitch," Alex said under her breath. "Why can't she just stay away from you? Why can't she just give up?"

"I'm so sorry. I don't know how to make this better. I knew telling you was the right thing. I didn't want there to be any secrets between us."

"Like I said, I appreciate the fact that you were transparent with me. I still need time. You've had your hands on her tits, your tongue down her throat, and her energy right up against yours." She paused a moment between sobs. "I need to process what that means for us; what it means to me," she remarked bluntly.

She stood abruptly. "I need to get out of here. I'm going to go stay at my place in town."

"Please don't punish me. I know what happened is terrible, but I didn't want to hide it from you."

"You're right. It is terrible. We're getting married, David. In only a few months. Married. What happens when you have another out-of-body experience on a business trip or something else?"

"That isn't fair," he argued. "You're the one who tells me all of the time that there are forces at play that we don't understand and can't see. I'm telling you, I didn't even feel like I was there. I can't even begin to explain it. It's not an excuse. I'm just telling you how my body felt."

"Do you realize how lame that sounds?" Alex asked.

"Alexandra, stop," he said gruffly.

"I can't be here right now," she said, throwing up her hands. Tersely, she got up, turned around, and stormed into the house.

David stood and then sat down on the chair again. He felt like a hole had been torn right through his chest. He knew Alex had to work through her emotions in her time. He could not deny that. He knew Alex had the right to take time to process the situation. Still, it hurt him knowing that he had caused this kind of hurt. He worried that they had reached a point in their relationship that they could not walk back from. He was concerned that healing between them might not be possible.

About fifteen minutes later, Alex walked out with a large overnight bag, a garment bag, and her laptop.

"Do you want to take Artemis with you?" he asked thoughtfully.

"I would," she answered.

David stood, walked to the mudroom, and grabbed the service vest from the hanger. He knelt and secured it to the dog. He grabbed the lead and attached it. They followed Alex as she made her way back to her car.

She threw the bag into the passenger-side seat and hung the garment bag in the back. David opened the back driver's side door. Artemis jumped inside, and he secured her with the lead attached to the seatbelt buckle. He shut the door gently and stood beside the car.

"Where's the goddamn clock?" Alex asked.

David walked over to the SUV and grabbed the gift bag. He handed it to Alex. She tossed it onto the floorboard of the passenger-side seat.

She turned her attention back to David. "I will text you later," she said, storms in her eyes and heat still rising in her voice.

"I love you, Alexandra," David said, standing helplessly before her.

"I know you do," she admitted. "I just can't be around you right now."

"I get it," he replied sadly.

Alex got in the car, started the engine, backed out, and drove down the lane, the dust from the gravel rising high into the air. David stood helplessly watching her pull out onto the main road.

Suddenly, he felt cold. He rubbed his arms vigorously, trying to warm himself. The heaviness mounted on his shoulders. He needed to talk to someone. So, he pulled out his phone and sent a text to Hope.

71

As Alex poured out her heart to Shayleen, the weight of her emotions hung heavy in the air. With each word that spilled from her lips, the depth of her pain and betrayal became more palpable. She confided everything. Most of it, Alex cried through. At other times, she bit out words filled with spite and even hatred. She understood David's intent to be transparent, but the pain was still impossible to ignore.

Sitting beside Alex on the swing, Shayleen listened intently, her presence a comforting anchor amidst the storm of emotions swirling around them.

As Artemis snoozed peacefully at their feet, oblivious to the turmoil unfolding, Alex found solace in the rhythmic creak of the swing. With each passing moment, the weight of her burden seemed to lighten ever so slightly, as if the act of sharing it had somehow made it more bearable.

The moon was a half crescent, and the stars were nearly canceled out by the light pollution of the small town. The wind blew a storm in. The feeling of foreboding hung heavy in the May air.

Shayleen continued listening, still offering no words. She simply allowed Alex to unload, hoping that once there was considerable catharsis, a clearer picture would emerge, perhaps even the opportunity for healing and forgiveness.

"How could he fucking touch her?" Alex asked angrily. "He had his mouth on her and his hands on her tits. How does a man not know the consequences of that? Any man knows what will fucking happen!"

The sobbing started again. Shayleen pulled her close. “To be angry is to be human, and as much as we’d like to elevate to a higher level of understanding, we’re still mortal. Emotions bring pain. Love brings disappointment. It’s the ability and willingness to work through things that matters.”

Alex bawled into Shayleen’s chest. “I know he was trying to do the right thing by telling me,” she admitted between sobs.

“Yes, he was,” Shayleen agreed. “He told you what happened as opposed to hiding it. That’s respect. He loves you enough to be straight with you.”

“Then why does this hurt so much?” Alex said as she calmed down a little and lay on her side in the fetal position, her head on Shayleen’s lap.

Stroking her dark hair, Shayleen sighed. “Because you never want to think of your man touching another woman. It’s just how we’re made. We’re territorial, just like any other animal.

“Gary was wild as hell when we met. We both were. When we got together, those crazy days were over. He told me about most of his exploits, and I told him about mine. Still, him touching another woman or another woman touching him made my blood run hot. I promise you, after a while, that insecurity goes away. It just takes time.”

“Well, David did touch someone else… today,” she said quietly.

“But he says he had no idea what he was doing.”

Alex sat up and reached over for the glass of whisky sitting on the outdoor end table. She took a drink and shook her head in disgust.

"A clock… what the hell was she trying to accomplish with a clock?" Alex asked rhetorically.

"Where is the clock?"

"In my car," Alex answered.

Shayleen excused herself and went into the house. She walked outside and grabbed the gift bag out of the floorboard. Walking back through the house, she sat down beside Alex. Pulling the clock from the bag, Shayleen's eyes glazed over. The faraway look on her face immediately placed Alex on alert.

"I can see everything that happened today," Shayleen said as she held the clock in her hand. "And everything before."

"What do you mean?" Alex asked curiously.

"A seduction spell is attached to this object," Shayleen said. "So, when David tells you he felt like he was on autopilot, he was. With this spell, he couldn't have known what he was doing. It's very dark and very powerful." Shayleen closed her eyes as she continued. "This spell is sealed in blood. That means that Gerri had to use her blood to set the spell. The spell's purpose was to blind his mind and eyes." She opened her eyes and looked at Alex.

"It renders its target helpless. It's almost like giving someone a roofie. The only thing that saved David today was the stones you blessed and gave to him. They absorbed the negative energy from the spell. They became his voice of reason, his conscience, because he was not himself enough to resist.

"Gerri had every intention of having sex with David because she needed to for her next spell. She was going to use his semen to raise the bar. She had enough foresight to realize he might resist her, so she had a contingency plan. The spell will allow for a substitution of hair or urine. Gerri now has strands of David's hair in her possession.

"His rejection still hasn't deterred her. She is still intent on sleeping with him. She thinks that with sex, she can charm him just like she has all of the others. She thinks that once their bodies are joined, she can gain control of him. She is pulling your energy through the strands of his hair. She is trying to move you out of the way. You are the one obstacle that frustrates her the most. Simply put, she wants you gone, and it doesn't matter in what way you leave. You need to be careful."

Alex shook her head. "Bitch."

"She hates you, no doubt about that. You know what she is. You've managed to finally protect the raven in your dreams. You've figured out her game. You know how to beat her at it.

"The reason she wants David so badly is because he is seemingly unattainable. It's a game to her. She knows he is wealthy. She knows he has significant influence. She sees where his future might lead, and his virility is something she's never experienced with her other partners. She is drawn to him through so much more than simple attraction. But she also thinks he is very inexperienced and green." Shayleen took a deep breath. "I'm concerned for your safety, Alexandra. She is out for blood."

With a steely glint in her eyes, Alex's gaze hardened as she resolved to see things through to their conclusion, no matter the cost. Gerri's betrayal, coupled with her brazen actions toward David, had ignited a firestorm of rage within Alex, a righteous fury that demanded justice be served.

In that moment, Alex made a silent vow. She would not rest until Gerri was held accountable for her crimes, until she was stripped of her power and brought to justice for the pain and suffering she had inflicted upon others.

"Light the fire," Shayleen said as she looked down at the clock in her grasp. "We have to burn it."

Alex walked into the yard, Artemis stirring briefly. The dog didn't move from the porch as Shayleen followed Alex to the fire pit. Alex lit the wood already in the circle. The flames rose to the starlit sky. Shayleen handed the clock to her.

"You don't need dragon's blood or anything else," she explained to Alex. "All you need is the power of your intent. When you throw it in, rebuke the spell attached to it. Recast protections for you and for David," she advised.

Alex looked down at the object in her hand. She felt the curse in her spirit, and her stomach began to turn. Angrily, she slammed the clock into the fire as hard as she could, shattering it into pieces. Closing her eyes, she focused on severing the spell that was attached to it. She recast the protection over her and David.

Tears ran down her face as she prayed to her gods, determined to shield the man she loved. She fell to her knees, looking up into the night sky. She felt a close, comforting presence. The energy hummed as she realized that they weren't alone.

In the flames, an apparition appeared. It seemed to be cloaked. It was difficult to make out features, but there was certainly a being in the fire. Shayleen and Alex heard a voice coming from the fire.

"You are my chosen," the voice said clearly and calmly. "I will always protect you and yours. No harm will come to you or your beloved. I am Hecate, Goddess of Witches and Keeper of the

Crossroads. I deliver justice and protect those who suffer injustice."

Neither Shayleen nor Alex knew what to say or do as they stood stiffly, hardly believing what they saw or heard.

"These things committed toward you will not go unpunished," she continued.

The woman disappeared and was replaced by the scales of justice. Then, as quickly as the images appeared, they vanished, leaving only the warmth of the fire and the astonishment of the two women who witnessed the unbelievable phenomenon.

72

The next day, Alex arrived at the office around 11 a.m. She was overly tired from the high emotion of the day and the night before. She would have taken the entire day off if she could have gotten by with it, but something compelled her to go into work.

Alex muddled through the day, still hurting from the incident between Gerri and David. She felt like she was adrift on an ocean of emotion, being tossed around between resolution and uncertainty. In her heart, she knew the truth. She knew that David wasn't completely responsible for what had happened. The key part was that she understood it. She had been lied to before. She'd been cheated on. She'd heard the usual excuses. This was different. Still, it didn't diminish the pain she felt and the lingering sense of betrayal. It felt like a festering sore that, if not dealt with, would spread like a cancer, destroying her relationship with David.

An email popped through with the subject line "Update G.M. Case." Alex knew now why she felt that she had to come to work today. She eagerly opened the message. It was an invitation to a video conference that day at 3 p.m. Eagerly, she accepted.

At five minutes to 3, she logged onto the conference and waited for others to join. She saw a square pop up with Mr. Blanchard's headshot and then Dr. Highland's. Next to log on were Mr. Lykins and Keith. Lastly, there was Dr. Wright and then David.

Dr. Highland started first.

"We're sorry about such short notice, but we wanted to share information with you as soon as we got it. We received results from the crime lab regarding the professor. There were high levels of digoxin in her system. I'm sending the packet of medical records to each of you via FedEx. Everyone will have them by tomorrow morning. You'll see that Professor Wynberg had no history of illness or cardiac issues. She was perfectly healthy."

"This means," Mr. Lykins added, "that we can ask for an exhumation of her body. We have enough probable cause."

"I will be conducting the autopsy once the warrant is secured," Dr. Wright said. "I'm already making arrangements with the medical examiner in Minnesota. He is aware of our investigation, and he has agreed to allow me to use his space to conduct the autopsy."

"The prosecuting attorney in that county has already spoken to Professor Wynberg's family. They have agreed to the exhumation; otherwise, we wouldn't be moving forward. The attorney will be obtaining the warrant within the week."

"Excellent," David said. "This is very good news."

"Indeed, it is," Keith agreed.

"What are the action steps hereafter?" Alex asked.

"Dr. Wright will be flying out to conduct the autopsy and will document her findings. We want to confirm a heart attack. With the professor being healthy, it wouldn't make sense for the heart to fail."

"She was poisoned," Alex blurted out.

"Once we have results of the autopsy, then we can ask for the Chief to be exhumed," Mr. Lykins added.

"I'd like to attend the autopsy," Alex said.

There was a moment of silence.

"That's quite irregular," Dr. Highland said.

"I don't care. I have reason to believe that the killer leaves a signature. If this is true, we can look at both the Chief and the Judge for similar signatures," Alex explained.

"And what makes you think this, Miss Ritezal?" Dr. Highland asked.

"Call it a hunch," Alex said smartly. She wasn't in the mood to be trifled with.

"Miss Ritezal," Dr. Wright began, "I can take pictures of every part of the professor's body. You don't need to go to Minnesota. Where do you believe the signature will be?"

"Check between her toes. You'll know it when you see it," Alex answered.

"Alright. I'll check. Again, I will photograph the entire body in case something was missed. I'm just thankful they took blood and tissue samples at the time of her death. The family wouldn't consent to an autopsy at that time due to religious reasons," Dr. Wright explained.

"Since we've opened this investigation, the family is all too happy to allow us to do whatever needs to be done," Mr. Lykins said.

A few final points concluded the call. Relief washed over Alex. The more progress made on the case, the sooner the nightmare would be over. Her brother would finally be avenged, and Gerri would be in an orange jumpsuit in Marysville.

73

After the call, Alex worked on some filings. She looked over at the dog crate in the corner. Artemis lay inside on her comfortable, fluffy dog bed. The company of the dog seemed to dispel some of Alex's sadness.

The bell atop the door alerted Alex to someone's presence, startling her a little. Artemis perked up. Joan had already gone for the day, and Will was at the police station working on some investigation reports.

Alex stood and walked into the reception area. Hope stood shaking off her umbrella. She made eye contact with Alex.

"Hey," she said softly.

"Hi," Alex replied as she turned and walked back into her office.

Hope followed her, shedding her raincoat and hanging it on the coat tree. The squeak of her galoshes filled the room as she made her way to the loveseat and sat down.

"David told me what happened," she blurted out.

Alex didn't say anything, but instead walked back to her desk and sat down in the chair.

"He is sick with guilt," Hope added. "I stayed with him last night. He's in pretty bad shape."

Alex still remained silent.

"Alexandra, you know it was the clock, right?" Hope asked. "There was a spell attached to it."

She nodded. "I do." Then she sighed. "All of it just hurts. It makes me sick."

"I know," Hope said empathetically. "Do you believe that he knew what he was doing?"

"No. I don't believe he had a clue what was happening. I believe he is blameless here."

"Then why are you punishing him?" Hope asked aggressively.

Losing the battle to contain her emotions, Alex began to cry. "I don't know," she said, shaking her head.

"This is exactly what Gerri wants," Hope added. "She wants to break the bond that you two have, and if she has to use magic to do it, she will."

Alex nodded. "I know that, too."

"Listen to me," Hope continued, moving to the edge of her seat. "David loves you very much. He is faithful. He doesn't know how to be anything else. Disloyalty and fuckery… that just isn't in his nature. What happened with Gerri was beyond this world, Alexandra. She used dark magic to make this happen. You know this."

"I cannot get the image out of my head, is all," Alex admitted. "It just keeps replaying," she added. "No matter what I tell myself."

"I know." Hope paused contemplatively for a moment and then continued. "You think Will's history doesn't get to me sometimes? We all have a past—baggage that we drag into every single relationship."

"Hope, this isn't the past. This is the present. This happened fucking yesterday," she bit out angrily.

"I know. The image may be in your mind for a little while. It could take a while to blot that out of your head."

The tears came faster. "I just want this to be over," she confessed. "I need this to be over."

"I think it'll be over soon," Hope said optimistically.

"It'd be nice if that were true."

"Try to look at this a different way," Hope suggested.

"What do you mean?"

"Gerri is a witch. She avidly practices black magic. Black magic is terribly powerful. It can bend will. Those of us who practice Light Magic don't interfere with free will. We honor it. She dabbles in pure evil, Alex. Witches who work with seduction spells and such… they lack a moral compass. They don't care who is hurt as long as what they desire is brought to fruition."

Alex shook her head, pressing her fingers to her temples. "I know that," she said quietly. "I just can't make it stop hurting."

"Gerri doesn't want David for who he is. She wants him for what he can give her; how he can serve her. She miscalculated, though. She didn't understand just how deeply he loves you, and she didn't know that you had him protected with your own spells. She has gravely misjudged everything here from start to finish."

Hope paused. "That doesn't mean she won't keep trying. And at the risk of sounding crude, she thinks that her pussy is magical enough to steal and keep any man or woman. She was wrong. Not only did David reject her advances, but he told you about the entire incident."

"You are who David wants. You are who he has fallen in love with. You are who he intends to spend the rest of his life with. He's chosen you. He told you about what happened not only because he believes in honesty, but because he wanted to spare you the pain of Gerri getting to you first. He knows that if she had her way, Gerri would tear you apart both figuratively and literally. Part of his gesture was to spare you some heartache. He chose the lesser of the two evils."

Alex calmed for a moment, catching her breath and brushing the tears from her face. She knew Hope was right and nodded in agreement as she inhaled deeply.

"He would never consciously do anything to hurt you. Can you imagine how hard it was for him to look you in the face and tell you what happened? To tell you that he touched her and kissed her? To admit his loss of control?" Hope said compassionately.

Alex realized the wisdom in Hope's words. Although the pain of knowing what had happened was certainly still fresh, the knowledge of David's own pain was a perspective Alex hadn't considered. She understood that he had fallen on his own sword. He had also taken a terrible risk in telling Alex the truth. He had to have known that by being transparent, he risked losing Alex forever.

Seeing that she had made a dent in Alex's perspective, Hope rose from the loveseat.

"You are going to take vows in just a few months. Practicing for those vows begins right now… for both of you. Cherish, love, and honor. Love doesn't keep a record of wrongs. It isn't boastful.

It sees the good in everything. It isn't jealous or malicious. It's kind and peaceful. It sees the best in all things."

"Corinthians 13," Alex said with a smirk.

"I might be a practicing Pagan, but Paul had that part right," Hope said lightly. "Love never fails."

Alex nodded. "I think I need to get home," she said as she stood.

She gave the command for Artemis to come out of her crate. After putting the lead on the vest, Alex gathered up her things and walked with Hope out the door. She locked up, and they made their way to their respective vehicles. Alex opened the back door, allowing Artemis to jump inside. She shut the door and looked at Hope from the short distance.

"Thank you," Alex called to her.

"Anytime, sister. That's what I'm here for," she replied as she pulled open the door and got into the driver's side seat.

74

As quickly and as safely as possible, Alex made her way through town and onto the highway that would lead her to the cabin. Her thoughts finally calmed. She realized how much courage and humility it took for David to confess such a transgression, especially since he didn't understand exactly what had happened. That put the entire situation in an entirely new light.

As she turned up the lane, the lights in the living room were on. She could also see clearly into the loft. David sat at his desk, looking at his computer. He must have seen her pulling in because he got up quickly and bolted down the stairs.

She pulled into the garage and let Artemis out first. Cyc greeted both of them and then ran to the covered porch. David pushed open the wooden door and let the dogs in. He ran down the short set of wooden stairs, meeting Alex halfway between the garage and the cabin.

They embraced, and Alex began crying.

"Oh, honey," he whispered. "I didn't mean to hurt you. I'm so sorry," he said, holding back emotion.

He broke the embrace and firmly cupped Alex's face in his hands. He looked down at her, tears welling in his eyes. "I would never, ever betray you, Alexandra. I would just as soon not breathe as to hurt you like that. That's why I told you everything. I didn't want there to be any lies between us. I promise, I had no idea what was happening."

The tears streamed down their faces as Alex nodded, their foreheads met, and their eyes closed. A silent understanding now existed between them.

They pulled away from each other for a moment. Alex then wrapped her arms around David's waist and put her face in his chest, sobbing uncontrollably. The feelings poured out of her, and she was powerless to stop it.

"Shhh… It's okay, baby. I'm right here. I'm not going anywhere. Ever," he assured her as he stroked her hair. He kissed the top of her head and, with his body, encouraged her to come inside.

"Let me run a bath for you," he suggested. "You'll feel better."

She shook her head. "I just want a shower. Then I just want to lie down. Will you just hold me?" she asked.

"Of course, I will," he said kindly as he put his arm around her and kissed her forehead.

Once Alex had taken a quick shower, she put on a pair of cotton shorts and a T-shirt. She crawled into their bed, where David was already waiting. He stretched out his arm, inviting her to rest beside him. He pulled her close as she draped her leg over his. She felt the light cotton material of his pajama pants against her thigh. She rested her head on his bare chest, her arm extended across his torso.

He caressed her back gently, her eyes closing. Her body was exhausted. Her head was heavy, and her spirit was weary. She inhaled deeply and exhaled slowly. She felt David's lips on her forehead.

"I love you," he whispered.

"I love you," she replied softly.

"I will do whatever you need me to do to make this right," he added.

"There's nothing for you to do. This wasn't something you did," Alex began. "Dark magic is powerful, David. It controls. It's meant to hurt others. The intent is vicious, and the damage is far-reaching. Light workers are responsible for combating its effects and shielding themselves as well as those they love. I did my best by giving you the stones," she explained.

"And the stones worked," he interrupted. "They protected me."

"I wish they had stopped you sooner," she admitted, with a hint of sadness in her voice.

"I know. I'm sorry."

"It's done now," Alex said bluntly. "The only thing to do now is just move forward. We know what we're up against and just how ruthless Gerri is. I've known it my entire life. She has already taken one important person from me. I'll be damned if I let her take you."

"She can't have me. I am spoken for," he said, kissing her again. Alex looked up into David's beautiful eyes, the glow of the nightlight shining off his skin.

"Will you make love to me?" she whispered.

He leaned down and kissed her lips softly. "Always," he replied.

They began their elegant dance, bodies intertwined, moving together in perfect rhythm. The fervent and blissful touches offered reassurance, and they gained strength from their connected souls.

The kisses and fingertips on skin served as a vivid reminder that they belonged to each other.

They found strength in their physical bond, their oneness still strong after such an unsettling event. They reveled in each other's physical company and found solace in the act of lovemaking, a balm for the recent injuries felt by both of them.

75

As David gazed at Alex, he felt a familiar pull of concern mixed with quiet anticipation. The events of the past week weighed heavily on his mind, but the light spilling through the curtains gave the room a muted calm.

He lay quietly, looking up at the ceiling, thinking about the incident with Gerri. It made for a very long and strenuous week. Waiting for the results of the Professor's autopsy was nerve-wracking, too. The delay meant more waiting, more unanswered questions. This pushed back their case even further. It was disheartening, to say the least, but David was hopeful that answers would be forthcoming sooner rather than later. More patience would be required, but only for just a little while longer.

David heard the groan of one of the dogs, obviously stretching after a satisfying slumber. He rose on his elbows to see Cyc and Artemis nestled comfortably on the oversized braided rug that protruded from under the bed. David's thoughts turned back to Alex as she stirred slightly.

He turned to his side, a tender longing coursing through him. He reached out, his fingers brushing lightly against Alex's cheek. He marveled at her peaceful expression, her features softened by the embrace of sleep.

She lay on her back with the blankets covering her, her arms resting beside her. She wore a t-shirt, but David could still make out the shape of her breasts. As he admired the form of the woman beside him, he became aroused. He wanted to wake her slowly, but also pleasure her. He wasn't concerned with his own release. He wanted to focus entirely on her, to give her comfort after the week they'd had.

Gently, he pulled down the covers and positioned himself further down on the bed. She still didn't stir. Her boxer shorts presented a barrier. Carefully, he slipped them from her hips, causing her to move a little and groan rebelliously. He put one of her legs over his shoulder as he heard Alex take in a breath. He felt her stretch and heard a soft sigh. He kissed her inner thigh, nuzzling it teasingly with his lips as he made his way to her. He parted her with his nose, taking in her scent and becoming completely drunk with it.

He heard her hushed moans drift through the room and felt her hand in his hair. His tongue traced around her and his fingers teased her. The sweet taste on his lips pulled him further toward his goal.

"Mmm…" he murmured as he continued pleasuring her, listening closely as her breathing changed. She constricted around his fingers and swelled in his mouth, his tongue gently moving back and forth against its intended target.

Her sighs turned to something different, more animalistic, as her hand stiffened around a section of his hair. He knew she was very close, and as much as he wanted to be inside of her, he wouldn't leave her wanting. He wanted to make sure she finished, and only then would he offer himself to her.

Finally, the undeniable feeling of climax gripped tightly around his fingers, and he tasted her, sweet and satisfying. He stayed with her through it, aware only of her breathing and the way her body responded beneath him.

Her chest heaved as she closed her eyes, clearly enjoying her release. She opened her eyes and peered down at David, who was now kissing her inner thigh once again. Taking back her hand, she raised it above her head.

David stood and pulled down his boxers. They fell to the floor lightly. The dogs were already gone from the room, but he hadn't noticed when they'd left.

The blankets were now in a mangled mess beside Alex. She moved toward the middle of the bed, knowing what would happen next. She pulled her t-shirt off and tossed it aside.

The wildness reflecting in David's eyes was undeniable, and Alex knew he was going to go at her strongly. She welcomed it with a sly smile and her arms outstretched toward him.

"Come to me," she said sweetly.

David moved onto the mattress and between Alex's thighs, her hands brushing against his arms. He stroked himself a few times while she watched.

"I want you," she said. "Please…"

He met her request and pushed into her, causing both of them to moan with delight. He plunged hard against her, steadying himself on his knees and bringing her feet up to his chest. He held her ankles and kissed her toes. She tightened around him again.

He watched as her breasts moved with each thrust. Still concentrating on her toes, he looked down at her, taking all of her in. He loved watching her this way. The way she loved the act of sex with him. How her hair rested on the pillow. Her skin was blooming with a rosy flush in the heat of desire.

Both of them wild with longing, David moved faster, still stabilizing his body against her raised legs. Her hands fisted in the sheets, her head fell back hard onto the pillow, a loud moan replaced by a loud, enthusiastic exclamation, nearly a scream as she called his name.

Watching her, hearing her, and feeling her wrapped firmly around him pulled him into orgasm, and he stopped momentarily to soak in every single sensation. Letting out a loud groan, he pressed hard into her once more. He pulsed with his release, vibrating with ecstasy. Feeling unsteady, he depended on her legs still propped against him to provide stability.

Coming to himself, he moved from between her legs to the space beside her. Catching his breath, he stared up at the ceiling, his body still shaking. She turned on her side to face him, a hand on his forearm.

“Well, good morning,” she said quietly with a sly smile.

He turned his head toward her. “Good morning,” he answered as he concentrated on catching his breath.

“That was pleasant,” she remarked, and she moved her hand to his chest.

He nodded. “Mmm… yes, it was,” he agreed heartily as he closed his eyes.

David turned over to face Alex. “I felt like we both needed a little TLC,” he admitted with a smile. “And I want you to understand just how much I love being with you.”

Alex didn’t say anything, but simply smiled.

“So, what do you want to do today, love?” David asked.

“I don’t really know,” she replied as she turned onto her back.

“I mean, I could easily stay here in bed all day with you,” he said as he reached over and fondled her breast, rolling her nipple gently between his fingers.

"I think we need to be a little more productive than that," Alex argued playfully.

Before they were able to continue making plans, David's phone rang. He turned over, sat up, and unplugged it from the wall charger. It was Hope.

He answered and put the phone on speaker. "Hello," he said courteously.

"Hey," she began. "Will and I were wondering if you might want to go to Columbus with us today. We are going to go to German Village and then maybe hit up a rooftop restaurant in the Short North."

David looked over at Alex to gauge her expression. She nodded in agreement.

"I think that sounds great. What time are you leaving?"

"Well, we've been lazing around this morning, and we're not quite motivated just yet. Would you want to leave around 1 or 1:30 p.m.?"

"Sounds good," David agreed with a smile in his voice.

"Okay. We will come over and pick you guys up," Hope said.

As Alex and David wrapped up their call with Hope, they embarked on the familiar routine of tending to their home and furry companions. The aroma of breakfast wafted through the air, mingling with the morning light filtering through the windows. David's mind drifted to the tasks awaiting him outside. With the next day's weather in mind, he mentally mapped out his plan to tackle the overgrown vegetation by the tranquil pond and tame the unruly grass blanketing the lawn.

Amidst the mundane rhythm of chores and plans, a subtle unease crept into David's consciousness. A nagging sensation penetrated his gut. He was unsettled and couldn't quite explain why, but he knew it involved the dogs.

David took his cell phone from his jeans pocket. He dialed Joan's number and asked if she would be willing to check on the dogs while they were out of town for the day and evening. She gladly agreed to help, and his fears were suddenly put to rest.

He wasn't sure why he felt so uneasy about leaving the dogs out. The trepidation he felt was completely uncharacteristic. Still, he knew he had to be cautious.

He walked into the kitchen where Alex stood cleaning up the breakfast dishes. He explained his feelings of unease and that he had reached out to Joan. She was more than willing to look after the dogs in their short absence. He went on to explain that he couldn't explain the strange feeling that had caused him to make such an uncharacteristic decision.

"That's not like you at all," Alex observed as she wrung out the washrag in the sink.

"I don't know how to explain it. I don't know what I'd do if something were to happen to the dogs. They're like my kids," he said as he choked back emotion.

"I understand," Alex said as she walked to the empty seat beside David. "I will always encourage you to trust your gut. If something is telling you to keep them inside, then you should."

"I'm going to set the alarm system before we leave, too," he added.

Alex nodded. "Whatever you say."

"Something just feels off," he observed.

"Well," she said as she stood and put a hand on his shoulder, "best to take precautions." She concluded with a kiss to his cheek, and then exited the room to prepare for the rest of the day.

As promised, Will and Hope arrived punctually, eager to embark on their planned adventure. With smiles lighting up their faces, they ventured toward Columbus.

The tranquility felt just by spending the day away with Hope and Will allowed for a reset of sorts. They discussed wedding plans and possible color schemes. Light-hearted banter and laughter were exactly what David and Alex needed.

The couples finished with their shopping and finally made their way to the vibrant Short North. Shops and eateries lined the busy street.

As the golden hues of the setting sun painted the sky, the couples made their way up the elevator to one of the rooftop restaurants. Over the next few hours, they luxuriated in the pleasures of fine dining and savoring delectable dishes. Indulging in some wine and whiskey, they found themselves immersed in conversation once again.

Eventually, the evening drew to a close, and they embarked on the journey homeward, the car filled with the comforting hum of continued conversation.

As David and Will discussed some various sporting events, Hope and Alex conversed about the flowers for Alex's wedding. Alex envisioned an enchanting mix of lilies and daisies. Hope eagerly offered suggestions for florists who could bring Alex's floral vision to life. As they exchanged ideas and brainstormed, the excitement of planning mingled with a hint of anticipation for the celebrations to come.

Hope shared her own wedding aspirations, revealing the allure of exotic locales like the Bahamas or Jamaica for their destination wedding. Despite the allure of these tropical paradises, the practicalities of accommodating loved ones weighed heavily on her mind, leaving Hope deliberating over the feasibility of it all.

As the clock neared 9:45, Will skillfully navigated the lane leading to the cabin. The soft glow of outdoor landscaping lights illuminated the lush shrubbery and delicate flowers carefully tended to by Alex, casting an ethereal aura over the surroundings. Inside, the warm illumination from the side-table lamp spilled out through the windows, while the inviting radiance of the loft lights beckoned from within the cabin's interior.

Pulling up in front of the garage, Will brought the car to a halt, allowing Alex and David to disembark. As they stepped out, their eyes were drawn to a curious sight on the landing of the enclosed porch.

"What is that?" Alex's voice broke the silence, her gaze shifting to David for answers.

With the engine silenced, Will and Hope joined them outside of the car, their curiosity piqued as they approached the back entrance. As they drew nearer, a sense of foreboding crept over David, a chill running down his spine as the truth slowly dawned on him.

There, on the porch, lay a lifeless cat, its form peaceful yet stark against the wooden decking. It was a sight that stirred a mixture of surprise, disgust, and sorrow among the group.

Alex's shock was evident as her mouth fell open in disbelief, her expression mirroring a blend of sadness and repulsion. Sensing her distress, Hope reached out, offering a comforting gesture.

Will's reaction was one of incredulity, his head shaking in disbelief at the grim discovery. "That's messed up," he muttered, unable to comprehend the significance of the macabre scene before them.

"It's a message," Alex asserted, her voice tinged with a hint of determination.

"A message?" David echoed, his brow furrowing in confusion.

Hope spoke up, her tone shaded with knowledge and insight. "Some people believe a dead cat can be a sign of misfortune," she said quietly.

With a heavy heart, Alex voiced her thoughts, her words laced with a mixture of resignation and defiance. "I have no doubt that this is not how this was supposed to play out," she concluded, her resolve unwavering in the face of adversity.

"What do you mean?" David asked.

"You told me earlier that you had a feeling that you should keep the dogs in the house. You never do that. They are always free to roam while we're gone because they have shelter in the barn or in the garage. The only time I've seen you bring them in and make them stay in is when the temperatures were bitterly cold. Otherwise, you let them go," Alex explained.

"Yeah," he agreed with a solemn nod, his thoughts aligning with Alex's assessment of the situation.

"This cat is possibly a diversion, a substitute for the real target, which was probably one or both of the dogs," Alex speculated, her voice marked with concern.

"So, you think Gerri did this?" David inquired, curiosity lacing his tone as he sought to unravel the mystery unfolding before them.

"I do," Alex affirmed with a hint of bitterness. "She's sick, David. What she's done this past week has only confirmed it for me, not that I ever really doubted it. I've known how twisted she is for a very long time."

Hope nodded in agreement, her expression somber. "The best way to get to someone is to hurt something or someone they love. If she could have reached the dogs, she would have likely harmed them."

David's voice trembled slightly as he grappled with the gravity of the situation. "Jesus Christ… this is turning into some kind of nightmare," he murmured, his disbelief palpable.

"I think you should install cameras," Will suggested, his practicality shining through. "I'm honestly surprised you haven't done that already."

David sighed. His frustration was evident. "No one knows I'm out here. I've been pretty secluded. In all the years I've lived here, I've never had anyone besides that idiot from Children Services show up unannounced. I never saw the need for cameras. I only installed the security system because my mom insisted."

"Times have changed," Alex conceded reluctantly, her gaze darting toward the window as if expecting Gerri's presence to materialize outside. "And I'm starting to wonder if Gerri is escalating into full-blown stalker mode."

David's expression morphed into one of concern. "Surely not."

"If she was willing to do what she did this week, what's to stop her from going further?" Hope interjected, her words hanging heavily in the air, a grim reminder of the escalating danger they faced.

After Hope and Will left, David and Alex grudgingly cleaned up the remains of the cat, disposing of it in the woods. They watched over the dogs with newfound vigilance, the once tranquil solitude of the cabin shattered by the looming threat.

76

Anger simmered within David as he locked up the house for the night, the sense of safety he once cherished now replaced by a pervasive unease. Drawing the curtains closed, he couldn't shake the feeling of vulnerability that lingered in every shadow, casting a pall over his once serene home.

As David settled into bed beside Alex, a wave of concern washed over him. Despite his desire to offer her solace and reassurance, he couldn't shake the nagging sense that she was withdrawing, building walls to shield herself out of fear that there would be a repeat of his unconscious indiscretion.

The situation with Gerri had certainly cast a shadow over their once tranquil existence, leaving David acutely aware of the subtle shifts in Alex's demeanor. He longed for the open vulnerability they had shared, the unspoken bond that had sustained them. He hoped that, in time, her heart would heal.

David reached out to brush a stray lock of hair from her forehead. She met his gaze.

"What is it?" she asked as she put the tablet on her lap.

"I just feel like you're pulling away from me," he confessed.

Alex sighed, her shoulders slumping slightly as she acknowledged his concerns. "I'm trying not to," she admitted, her voice laced with weariness. "But it's going to take time. Sometimes I still see you with her in my mind. And now, with what Gerri's done… she's raising the stakes. I know she would've hurt Cyc or Artemis if she could have. She's evil, David. The sooner this ordeal ends, the safer we'll be. It's not just about what happened. She's becoming even more unhinged."

David nodded in understanding, his heart heavy with empathy for the turmoil Alex was feeling. "I just want you to know that you can trust me, that we'll make it through this," he reassured her, his voice filled with determination.

"I believe we can, but I am afraid," Alex admitted, tears glistening in her eyes. "After my brother died, I didn't think anything could shake me. He was my protector, David. I didn't think there was another person in this world who would ever have the ability to tear my soul from my body." Listening intently, David realized there was more to their bond than he had understood.

She went on. "When I was around the age of eight, he saved me. We'd all gone camping one summer. My parents loved the Carolinas, so we usually went every single year.

"I was playing near a lake. I fell in. It was much deeper than I expected, and I couldn't swim very well yet. I don't remember anything other than sheer panic once I hit the water. I kicked and thrashed, trying to find the surface, but I just couldn't."

Tears streamed down her face. "I remember waking up, my lungs burning as I coughed. My brother was hovering over me. He had pulled me from the water and given me CPR." Her voice shook with emotion. "Marvin saved my life. I should have died on the shore of that lake, but he was quick, and he pulled me from the water.

"When he died, I felt a part of myself die with him. My brother had protected me in more than this lifetime, David. I know you don't understand the way I believe, but Marvin had been my protector many, many times before. He had bled for me and laid his life down in so many other lifetimes, and there was no way I could ever repay him. When he died so suddenly, I thought I would stop breathing without him."

David listened intently, trying to keep an open mind.

"Then there was you," she continued, her voice trembling. "You offered me comfort and protection. Being with your grandparents and you the summer he died meant so much to me. I grew up so quickly that summer. Being near you filled the hole he'd left behind. The bond I have with you is just as meaningful as the bond I had with my brother because I've also been entwined with your soul for lifetimes before. The same soul connection I had with my brother… I have that with you, but in a different way. You have the same ability to tear my heart out, and that frightens me. I can take heartbreak, but if I lost you…" She trailed off. She could no longer hold back her tears, and her sorrow and fear burst through. She sobbed into her hands, her chest heaving.

"Shhh…" he murmured soothingly, enveloping her in a tender embrace as she sought solace in his arms. "I'm not going anywhere, Mi Amor. Ever," he whispered, his words a promise of unwavering devotion.

"I don't understand your beliefs," he said as he lifted her chin with one finger. "But I understand you. I have had my doubts about my sister's beliefs, but after what's happened with Gerri, my comprehension is shifting. I am at least willing to try to learn." Her eyes met his, and he saw relief looking back at him.

"Really?"

He nodded. "The stones stopped me. There is no other explanation for anything that happened. They even left marks on my skin," he admitted.

Alex pulled away as David moved the covers. He pulled up the left leg of his boxer just far enough to reveal small marks on his skin. They were red, but nothing nefarious—just simple dots of inflamed skin indicative of a first-degree burn or even an abrasion.

Her mouth fell open in shock. "Why didn't you tell me?"

"Because I didn't quite believe it myself," he said with a smile.

He turned and cupped her face in his hands. "Just because I don't understand it doesn't make it untrue. Will you teach me?" he asked.

"Of course, I will," she said with a smile. He sank onto the mattress, pulling her to him. She rested her head on his chest as he stroked her hair gently.

He'd hoped that his openness would be one more step toward their overall healing. He truly did want to understand the inner workings of her spirituality because her knowledge protected him. Her spell work with the stones had pulled him back from the brink of making a horrible decision. There was no way he could possibly pretend that wasn't a reality. As he moved forward, he would educate himself as well as lend himself to her teachings.

77

June arrived. David and Alex waited for word from Dr. Highland about the Professor's autopsy results. Their patience wore thin, but they tried to understand as best they could.

David sat on the loveseat in Alex's office. They'd planned on a late dinner in town. Alex had been working all day on briefs, and it was easy to see she was in no mood to cook.

"You expecting anyone?" David asked as they heard the cottage door open. She shook her head.

They heard heavy footsteps and then Keith's voice. "We've got her!" he exclaimed.

They both stood and walked into the reception area. Keith stood with a thick envelope in his hand. "These are autopsy results from Dr. Wright," he explained. "I wanted to hand-deliver them."

Alex walked over to Keith and grabbed the envelope. She unsealed it and began reading.

"The Professor died of a heart attack, and the digoxin caused it," he continued. "There are photographs in there, too. I don't know how you knew there'd be a signature, Alex, but there was. Between the big toe and second toe."

Keith walked to Alex and took the bundle. He flipped through to find the photographs. "See? An infinity symbol tattooed between the Professor's toes. If we exhume the chief and find this, we have her."

Alex smiled. "I'll call Mr. Lykins," she said.

Keith nodded. “I already have copies of the findings. As soon as you say ‘go,’ we’ll make this happen,” he explained.

Alex looked at David. “I think I’m going to have to postpone our date,” she said with a hopeful smile. “I need to talk to Mr. Lykins so we can secure the warrant and this nightmare can be over.”

“We still need her permission,” David said, stating the obvious.

“I know. I can at least get a game plan together, though, about how we want to approach this,” she added.

78

After the men left, Alex juggled the weighty conversation with Mr. Lykins. Every now and then, she glanced at Artemis's empty crate. She'd opted to leave her at the cabin ever since the incident with the cat.

As the conversation continued, Alex's focus fractured momentarily as the sound of the front door opening and closing pierced the air.

"Mr. Lykins," Alex interjected, her voice hushed yet firm, "can you please hold on a moment?"

She swiftly muted the call, her senses on high alert as she ventured toward the reception area. Standing in the middle of the room was Gerri. Alex's jaw clenched with apprehension as she braced herself for the confrontation that was sure to follow.

"What are you doing here?" Alex asked through gritted teeth.

Gerri's response was calm as she locked eyes with Alex, her gaze tinged with a chilling sense of determination.

"I know what you're doing," Gerri stated matter-of-factly, her words hanging heavy in the air like a sinister omen.

Alex's stomach churned with a potent mix of fear and anger. She wondered what twisted agenda Gerri had concocted. Still, she refused to let her emotions get the best of her.

"Me? You've been the puppet master your entire life, and you're throwing accusations at me?"

"Your brother was weak," Gerri said sardonically. "A weak little man."

As Gerri's taunting words pierced through the air, igniting a fierce inferno of anger, Alex felt her chest muscles tighten with tension. She balled her fists and felt the flames of rage surging through her veins. Her frame vibrated with the words and energy surrounding her. She wanted payment from Gerri. She wanted retribution for the loss of her brother's life. She wanted her pound of flesh, but she knew she must be better than that. She must tame the rage inside.

Finally, coming to herself and finding her voice, she said, "He couldn't have been weak to put up with a bitch like you."

Alex heard the phone click, and she knew Mr. Lykins had hung up. She was alone. She was uncertain as to whether that was a good thing or a bad thing. Alex felt like she was cornered by a poisonous snake.

Gerri closed the gap between them. She looked deeply into Alex's eyes and smirked. "Did David tell you about our little encounter? How he touched me? How he kissed me? He wanted me, Alexandra. I could see it. I could feel it when I pressed up against him."

The rush of adrenaline made Alex feel dizzy for a moment, but then she quickly stabilized. Still, her porcelain skin flushed scarlet as the anger boiled under the surface.

"I can't believe he's going to marry you," Gerri continued. "You're just like your brother, weak and soft. Are you sure you're who David sees when he's inside of you? Or do you think he feels my breasts under his touch?"

"You fucking bitch," Alex said in a measured tone.

"You know I'll always be one step ahead of you, don't you? I will never agree to having Herbert exhumed. And then you'll have nothing," she said confidently.

"We don't need your permission when we have probable cause for murder. You killed them all," Alex said.

"You can't prove a fucking thing."

"That's where you're wrong. You'll go before the grand jury. They'll see what a black widow you are. They'll hand down an indictment. And you did all of this for what? Money?" Alex asked.

"You stupid fool. Of course not," she replied. "Power," she said with a shrug.

Alex looked at her dubiously as Gerri turned on her heel and began walking around the room as if speaking to a great audience. "They were all mice," she continued. "A cat tortures its prey before killing it. It toys with it. Why do you think I left you the present on your back porch? I've always been the cat." As she wandered around the room, Alex listened, knowing that what was to come would be of great interest.

"It takes time to gain the necessary influence to ask someone to give over not just themselves, but everything they hold dear, but when they do, the rush it brings. Knowing that you have them, that you can move them in whatever direction you want. Watching them as they dance to the rhythm you set for them. There's nothing like it, really. It's quite exhilarating."

Gerri walked back toward Alex as she continued. "David is different, and frankly, you're in my way. He is young and strong. He isn't like anyone else I've ever set my sights on. I underestimated your influence, abilities, and talents, though. A witch. A lightworker. I knew it the moment I went into your aunt's shop and saw your medicines and lotions. Your energy is undeniable.

"There is no other way David could have ever resisted me. I knew your influence had to be involved somehow. I tried the pen first. The sickness that landed on him was meant for you.

"I managed to keep the raven quiet for a while, but then I didn't factor in Maureen's desire for justice along with your mongrel spirit animal. When she appeared in your dream, I knew it was a matter of time.

"I stepped things up with the clock. I was sure the seduction spell would be too powerful for anything you'd done to cancel it out. I was almost positive he would fuck me right there on the desk. Things would have been over for the two of you. I honestly didn't realize you could possibly be more powerful working in the light, but I misjudged. I also misjudged David's love for you, his desire for you. You must have your claws in deep with him."

"Love doesn't need power to influence, but you wouldn't know that, you superficial bitch," Alex bit out. "Dark magic is always the same. You toy with free will thinking no one will rise to meet the challenge, that people will go unprotected. That isn't how I operate, Gerri. I protect the people I love."

Gerri smiled. "Well, David will need someone to comfort him when you're gone."

Alex's blood ran cold. "What are you talking about?" confusion permeating her tone.

"Well, I'm obviously not above murder. You've just forced me to choose a different method."

"What?" Alex said as she stepped back.

"Can you not smell the smoke?" Gerri asked nonchalantly.

"Smoke?" Alex took in a deep breath. She instantly smelled something burning in the back of the cottage.

Her eyes widened. "What have you done?"

"I'm solving a problem. Once you're gone, David will be free of you in every way." She paused for a moment, a brazen smile finding its way to her lips. "I will always win, Alexandra. Always."

As Alex rushed toward the kitchen, a sickening realization washed over her as she beheld the roaring flames engulfing the room. The acrid scent of smoke filled her nostrils, causing her to cough and choke uncontrollably. Panic surged through her veins as she realized the gravity of the situation. The gas line had been opened, and the inferno threatened to consume everything in its path.

Before she could even comprehend her next move, a sudden, crushing blow to the back of her head sent shockwaves of pain radiating through her skull. Darkness descended swiftly, enveloping her in its suffocating embrace as consciousness slipped away.

The world faded into oblivion as Alex succumbed to the blackness, her thoughts swirling in a chaotic whirlwind before dissipating into nothingness. The flames continued to rage unchecked, their voracious hunger devouring everything in their path as the cottage became engulfed in a fiery inferno.

79

As David hurried through the swinging doors of the emergency room, his heart pounded in his chest like a relentless drumbeat, each step echoing the frantic rhythm of his thoughts. Panic surged through him, an overwhelming tide threatening to engulf him in a sea of fear and uncertainty.

His breath came in shallow gasps, each inhalation fraught with dread as he braced himself for the sight that awaited him beyond the threshold. He had been summoned to the hospital with little explanation. Keith had only said that there was a fire at the cottage and that Alex was trapped inside.

As he stepped into the bustling chaos of the emergency room, David's eyes darted frantically around the room. The fact that she was in their local hospital was a good sign. It meant she wasn't too badly hurt. Otherwise, she would have been well on her way to Grant's Level One Trauma Center, Columbus.

As David continued glancing around the room, the nurse, a familiar face in town, waved at him.

"David," she said, "come with me. She's in bay five."

He was led down a hallway past what felt like a dozen rooms. Rounding a corner, he saw Keith standing in the hallway, leaning against the wall. With a calming gesture, he walked toward David.

"She's fine," he said before David could speak. "The firefighter said they got there just after the fire started. Someone in the apartments across the street saw the smoke and called it in."

"Is she hurt?"

"No. Not a scratch. Minimal smoke inhalation. I was hanging around hoping to get some kind of statement from her, but she's already been taken to CT."

"That doesn't sound promising," David said.

"I've already called her dad. They are driving back home right now. He took Penny out of town for their anniversary. Ben and Jeremy are on their way. They should be here anytime."

Pinching the bridge of his nose, David struggled to make sense of the chaos unfolding around him. The uncertainty of Alex's fate weighed heavily on his mind, gnawing at his conscience with relentless persistence.

"Keith, how the hell did this happen?" David's voice was marked by a mixture of anger and self-blame. Before Keith could answer, David went on. "I shouldn't have left her this evening," he muttered, his voice thick with regret. "I had a really bad feeling. I've been getting those a lot lately. I should have insisted she come home with me and work from there."

Keith's reassurances did little to assuage David's guilt, his mind consumed with thoughts of what could have been done differently to protect Alex from harm.

"Was anything at the cottage salvageable?" David's curiosity broke through the haze of his self-recrimination, his brow furrowing with concern as he awaited Keith's response.

"No, buddy. I'm afraid not," Keith replied solemnly. "It's a total loss. The fire marshal has to do his investigation to determine the cause, but you already know that."

David nodded grimly, his heart heavy with the weight of the loss. "I know. I'm not worried about it. I'll call the insurance company at some point, but Alex is my priority right now. I just need to know she's okay. This damn case," David mumbled under his breath, his irritation rising to the surface once more. "I will be glad when it's over. Alex is just consumed with it, but I can't really blame her."

Keith sighed. "Well, once we find Gerri, we can get the Chief exhumed."

"What do you mean, find her?" David's voice was laced with concern, his mind running with thoughts of what Gerri might be planning next.

A sigh rose up in Keith's throat, and he exhaled heavily. "I have had Gerri under pretty tight surveillance. The boys assigned to her this evening lost her. She managed to slip out, and they have no idea where she went. She hasn't come home either." As the reality of Gerri's escape sank in, David knew that they were facing a race against time.

The heavy hospital doors swung open at the end of the hall, drawing David and Keith's attention. There, sitting up in a wheeled gurney, was Alex. Her smile was a beacon of reassurance amidst the chaos that had engulfed them.

Without hesitation, David rushed to her side, his heart pounding in his chest as he took her hand in his, pressing a gentle kiss to her knuckles. Despite the superficial cuts on her face and the soot that marred her cheeks, she looked unharmed.

As they wheeled Alex into her room, David walked alongside her, his gaze fixed on her and her hand still in his. Once the gurney was secured in place, the nurse smiled.

"The doctor will be reading the results shortly," she explained. "He'll be in soon. If you need anything in the meantime, just press the button or send someone to the nurse's station to get me."

"Thank you, Danielle," Alex said sweetly, her voice a soft melody that soothed David's troubled soul. David returned to Alex's side, his concern etched deeply into his features as he tenderly kissed her forehead, careful not to cause her any further discomfort.

A sudden knock at the door interrupted their moment, and Keith's head popped into the room. At Alex's invitation, he entered, his expression a mixture of concern and determination.

"How are you feeling?" he asked, his voice filled with genuine compassion.

"I'm not quite sure, to be honest," Alex admitted, her voice a whisper carried on the wings of exhaustion.

"I know this just happened, but can you give me a statement? I need to file a report," Keith requested, his tone professional yet tinged with urgency.

In a rush of words, Alex recounted the events of the evening, her voice steady despite the lingering fear. She told Keith and David about Gerri's confession and the other important nuances of the exchange.

David's face turned ashen as he listened to Alex's account, the weight of her words settling heavily upon him like a suffocating blanket. Keith listened intently, still recording the statement on his phone.

"Well, we certainly have enough probable cause now for an arrest. Arson. Attempted murder," Keith said satisfactorily.

"But you don't know where she is," David pointed out angrily.

"What?" Alex said, the shock in her voice permeating through the room.

"They have had her under surveillance for some time. I guess she's disappeared," David explained.

"You have to find her!" Alex said frantically in Keith's direction.

"We're going to find her, Alex. Don't worry. You're safe now," Keith explained. "There are officers at your cabin right now. We've even got them posted at your dad and stepmom's, your house in town, and the village offices. Officers are posted on every floor of this hospital, too. We've got this well covered, Alex. She can't get to you," he assured her.

Alex nodded.

"Right now, your job is to get some rest. I'm going to get hold of the judge, relay your statement, and then get in touch with the fire marshal. We'll take it from here. You have both done well. We couldn't have done this without you," Keith said.

The doctor opted to keep Alex overnight for observation. A uniformed officer was posted outside of her door throughout the night and into the next day. Alex's family came and went. Hope, Will, and Joan took shifts to ensure that Alex wouldn't be alone. David never left her side. Everyone was on high alert given what had happened.

While Alex was recovering, Keith took proactive steps in securing a warrant. Law enforcement raided Gerri's residence, combing through every inch for evidence that could potentially tie her to the crimes. He met with the fire marshal, meticulously briefing him on the sequence of events according to Alex.

Keith's efforts didn't stop there. Recognizing the pivotal role of forensic evidence, he ensured a warrant was obtained for the exhumation of the Chief's body. When Dr. Wright conducted the examination a week later, her findings only reinforced the mounting suspicion. The discovery of the same infinity symbol tattooed between the Chief's toes served as a damning link to the other victims. While the cause of death was confirmed as cardiac arrest, the earlier blood and tissue results provided the missing pieces of the puzzle.

With each revelation, the case against Gerri solidified. It became increasingly clear that she was the mastermind behind the deaths of Maureen, Herbert, and Steven. With meticulous attention to detail, Mr. Lykins pieced together the evidence, preparing to present a compelling case to the grand jury.

Meanwhile, Gerri's fate was sealed. With the warrant for her arrest for arson and attempted murder looming over her, there was no escape from the impending justice she would face. Whether through the arson charges or the mounting evidence tying her to the murders, Gerri's days of evading accountability were numbered. In the end, she would have to answer for her crimes before the law. Still, she was nowhere to be found.

80

Summer transitioned into fall. The fervor of political campaigning gradually waned, giving way to a different kind of anticipation, the impending celebration of Alex and David's wedding. With careful planning and unwavering dedication, they poured their hearts into ensuring every detail was perfect for their special day.

As October dawned, the culmination of months of preparation finally arrived. The last-minute arrangements were meticulously finalized for the reception. From the elegant venue adorned with flowers to the carefully curated menu that would delight their guests, the celebration would be remembered fondly by everyone in attendance.

Against the backdrop of the changing leaves and the crisp autumn air, Alex and David exchanged vows, pledging their unwavering commitment to each other in front of the small gathering of family. It was a moment of pure joy and profound significance, a testament to their resilience and unwavering bond amidst the trials they had faced.

The reception at the Rain Room was perfectly blissful. The venue was elegant and upscale. Ben had outdone himself. Friends and family gathered to celebrate Alex and David's marriage.

As Alex and David sat together at their table, they exchanged eager whispers. The dance floor was busy with their friends and family enjoying the festivities. Alex took a drink of the champagne, smiling at the thought of life now.

"So, the honeymoon," David said, skillfully drawing her attention back to him.

"I didn't think we were going to have one with the election coming up," she said.

"Well, I booked it for the beginning of December so that we can focus on concluding our campaigns, but you knew I would take you on a honeymoon. We'd talked about it," he said.

"I know. I know. We've had a lot happen since then though."

"True, but I still want to celebrate our marriage with a proper honeymoon," he replied.

"Okay," Alex said expectantly.

David smiled through pursed lips, looking as if he might burst. "Egypt," he said softly, almost in a whisper.

It took a moment for Alex to process the information. Once she did, her eyes widened with excitement, and her mouth dropped open in pure astonishment.

"What?" she asked excitedly.

"We're going to be in Egypt by early December. We will be gone for two weeks. Hope and Will are caring for the dogs while we're gone, and they're going to keep an eye on the cabin."

Alex threw her arms around David. "Oh my God!" she exclaimed. "You didn't have to…" she trailed off.

"It's your dream. I would never deny you that," he continued.

"It's too much," she said as she pulled away.

"It isn't too much. Nothing is too much. I would move heaven and earth for you. You should know that by now," he said with a smile.

Their conversation was cut short by Penny and Robin. They encouraged the couple to open their gifts. So, David and Alex got up and walked to the table of packages in the far corner of the room.

They tore open the gifts, thoughtful sentiments from their friends and family. They had more than what they needed, but still, the packages revealed items that would be useful to a couple starting out.

Alex picked up a small gift and looked for a tag. There wasn't one. She shot a concerned glance at David.

He took the package from her and tore it open. Inside was a small doll made of twigs. Strands of long and short dark hair were wrapped around it. There were fabrics that both David and Alex recognized. It was cuttings of their clothing.

Under it was a note in the most beautiful handwriting.

Wishing you the best...

--Gerri

Horror covered Alex's face.

"What is this?" David asked.

"It's something called a poppet. It's used to represent its intended target. Spells can be cast on it as a representation of its subject," she explained.

Hope arrived within moments. She looked down in the box.

"Let me have it," she said, her face red with anger. "Shayleen and I will handle this," she explained.

David gladly handed her the box. “You’ll want to give that to Keith more than likely,” he explained. “That’s evidence.”

“I will as soon as we neutralize what’s attached to it,” Hope promised.

The remainder of the evening unfolded without further incident. The earlier excitement over their honeymoon plans cast a radiant glow over the festivities. Laughter and music filled the air as friends and family gathered to celebrate the newlyweds, their spirits buoyed by the promise of love and new beginnings.

By the end of October, the annual Fall Fun Day Carnival was underway. As Alex and David worked the festivities, they were both reminded of where they were a year before. They had just met, their romantic adventure just beginning.

In November, the ballots were cast and the results tallied. David emerged victorious as the newly elected Juvenile Judge, and Alex achieved a hard-fought victory, unseating Richard to claim the title of County Prosecutor. It was a triumph born of dedication and perseverance.

Their honeymoon in Egypt surpassed all expectations, each moment more magical than the last. From the breathtaking vistas of the hot air balloon ride to the tranquil serenity of the Nile River cruise, every experience was etched into their memories, a testament to the boundless adventure that awaited them as husband and wife.

Not knowing where Gerri was weighed on David and Alex; however, they believed that her dark shadow had finally lifted from their lives. They embraced the dawn of a new chapter with open hearts and steadfast resolve. United in their shared journey of love and resilience, they faced the future with unwavering optimism, knowing that together, they could overcome any obstacle.

As they looked towards the horizon, hand in hand, Alex and David found solace in the depth of their love, a love that would weather any storm and light their path towards a brighter tomorrow. And though challenges may lie ahead, they took comfort in the knowledge that together, they were invincible.

Epilogue

Hope stood on the sidewalk in front of the hotel, hands shoved into the pockets of her jeans, waiting for the all-clear. The night air felt heavy, thick with the promise of something grim beyond that door. Beside her, Dr. Wright, Lauren, and Olivia waited in tense silence, their expressions unreadable. In the parking lot, the forensics team stood by, murmuring among themselves.

“I shouldn’t even be here,” Hope muttered under her breath.

“Well, we are here, so let’s just do our jobs and make the most of it,” Olivia bit out.

The sound of the door opening pulled Hope’s attention. Owen Grayson emerged first, leading a few uniformed officers out of the room. His face was tight, his posture rigid. He had been the one to call them home, pulling them from a much-needed vacation.

“All clear,” Owen announced.

The forensics team moved in, ready to process the scene. The rest of them followed behind, but Owen remained outside, watching, waiting.

The moment Hope stepped into the room, the stench hit her like a punch to the gut. Her eyes watered. She swallowed hard against the bile rising in her throat. The smell of decomposition was nothing new, but after being away from this world for so long, it hit differently. More brutal. More real.

The hotel room was the definition of low end, cheap furnishings, peeling wallpaper, a television blaring at full volume. On the table sat several empty pizza boxes, but no luggage. No personal belongings. No sign that anyone had actually lived here.

Lauren handed Hope a pair of black latex gloves. With a heavy sigh, she reluctantly took them. She stared at the body as she slipped them on. There was no doubt about the identity of the victim. The blonde hair and facial features were unmistakable. It was Geraldine Meyers.

"Jesus Christ," Hope murmured. "You know who this is, right?"

Dr. Wright stepped in, assessing the body with an expert eye. Gerri lay sprawled on the bed, wrists and ankles handcuffed to the posts, deep gashes marring her skin where she had fought against the restraints. Her abdomen was sliced open, entrails bulging from the wound. Her hair clung to her face, matted with sweat and blood. Her vacant eyes were an unnatural milky white.

"I'll be damned," Dr. Wright said grimly. "It's Gerri Meyers."

Hope turned to Owen, who stood in the doorway. "We need Keith down here."

Before he could respond, a forensic technician approached, holding a clear evidence bag. Inside was a typed note.

"This was in the bathroom," the technician said. "It's addressed to you."

Hope took the bag, scanning the words:

Hope & Team,

I've done your job for you. Gerri was a leech on society. A disease. A whore. So, she was selected for termination. The world is a much better place without her in it.

Consider this a gift. You're welcome.

Case closed. Problem solved.

More to come.

—The Executioner

Hope exhaled through her nose, rubbing her forehead.

“Well,” she muttered, “he isn’t entirely wrong. He solved the case. What’s more concerning is that he had knowledge of it to begin with.”

“That’s very concerning,” Lauren said, reading over her shoulder.

“Which means,” Olivia added, “it’s someone in law enforcement.”

Dr. Wright stepped closer to the body, gently parting Gerri’s toes. Something caught the light, a tattoo. An infinity symbol inked between them.

Hope’s stomach sank. “I really need Keith down here.”

She stepped outside, yanking off the latex gloves and tossing them in a nearby trash can. Owen followed her out.

“I told you that you needed to be here,” he said.

Hope shot him a disapproving glance. “I need Keith at the Sheriff’s Office on this now. Can you get him down here?”

Owen nodded, already turning on his heel. “Absolutely.”

Less than thirty minutes later, Keith’s black SUV rolled to a stop in front of the hotel. Hope met him on the sidewalk as the others continued working the scene.

Inside, Dr. Wright was still at work, piercing the skin with a thermometer. “She’s been dead at least forty-eight hours,” she noted. "I won't know the exact cause of death until I get her on the table, but I'd bet on strangulation." She pointed to the bruising wrapped around Gerri's neck like a sinister necklace.

Keith cursed under his breath. "Fuck… It's really her."

Hope nodded. He grabbed a pair of gloves, stepping toward the body. When he spread Gerri's toes apart and found the unmistakable infinity symbol, something flickered across his face.

Doubt.

Had she really been guilty of all the things she was accused of? The arson? The attempted murder? The deaths of her former lovers? Had he been wrong about her?

"Don't go there, Keith," Hope said sharply. She had seen that look before. "Don't start questioning your instincts. We know she's guilty. We have Alex's statement."

Keith exhaled heavily, shoving the thoughts away. He had no time for doubts. Not now. "Where the hell has Gerri been all this time?"

Pulling off the gloves, he stepped out of the room, Hope following close behind. He turned to her, searching for answers, but she had none.

"I'm not even supposed to be here," Hope muttered. "I'm a therapist now. I left this world behind."

Keith scoffed. "You're a damn good profiler. Your talents are needed here. Might as well embrace it, kiddo."

Hope shook her head, resentment simmering beneath her skin.

As the first light of dawn broke over the horizon, new questions circled her mind like vultures. She was exhausted, but sleep wasn't an option. Not yet.

Why had the note been addressed to her?

Why had the killer specifically targeted her team?

The instincts she had spent years honing, instincts she had tried to bury, came roaring back, whether she wanted them to or not.

She was free of this world.

Or at least, she thought she was.

ABOUT THE AUTHOR

Tracee Ford, known as the "Smart Mouth Writer," has been telling stories her whole life. She is an award-winning novelist whose work explores the intersection of love, belief, and the unseen forces that shape human lives.

Her debut novel, *The Fine Line*, received a Five Star Reader's Favorite Award. Her second novel, *Idolum*, was also honored by Reader's Favorite and nominated by the Paranormal Romance Guild for Best Romantic Suspense. *Through Glass Darkly* later earned first place for Best Paranormal Romance (General), and the *Between Worlds* series received additional recognition from the Paranormal Romance Guild.

Beyond fiction, Tracee has walked many creative paths as a playwright, director, and puppeteer. Her lifelong interest in the paranormal, paired with lived experience, informs her exploration of trauma, belief, and the quiet moments where ordinary life brushes up against something more.

www.ingramcontent.com/pod-product-compliance
Lightning Source LLC
LaVergne TN
LVHW010555100826
845148LV00014B/2724

* 9 7 9 8 2 1 8 9 3 3 4 2 5 *